The Wisdom of Billy Graham

Choosing Your Mate: "God selects an ideal mate for true worshipers. If you get impatient and refuse to wait for that choice, you wind up with His second- or third-best."

Marriage: "'Thou shalt not murder,' we're told. You claim that surely doesn't apply to you. Well, I have news. There are thousands of husbands and wives who are killing their marriage partners by neglect."

Partners: "I discovered long ago how important it is to let your mate know the bad as well as the good. I learned that confiding helps the marriage considerably. Keeps it honest."

Spreading the Good Word: "We employed every modern means to catch the attention of the unconverted. And then we punched them right between the eyes with the Gospel."

MARRIAGE MADE IN HEAVEN

THE STORY OF BILLY & RUTH GRAHAM

By JHAN ROBBINS

A JOVE BOOK

The author gratefully acknowledges permission from the following
sources to quote material in the text:
Sojourners for material from "A Change of Heart," an interview
conducted by Jim Wallis and Wes Michaelson (August 1979), in
Sojourners magazine, P.O. Box 29272, Washington, D.C. 20017.
Word Books, Waco, Texas, for two poems from
Sitting by My Laughing Fire, by Ruth Bell Graham,
copyright © 1977 by Ruth Bell Graham.

This Jove book contains the complete
text of the original hardcover edition.

MARRIAGE MADE IN HEAVEN

A Jove Book / published by arrangement with
G. P. Putnam's Sons

PRINTING HISTORY
G. P. Putnam's Sons edition published 1983
Jove edition / February 1985

ISBN: 0-515-08179-5

To Steve Stout
Pastor
Goldsboro Friends Meeting
Goldsboro, N.C.

"Thee are loving to all."

CONTENTS

FOREWORD

Regardless of the views you now hold on Billy Graham, your marriage can be strengthened through closer acquaintance with the controversial evangelist and by getting to know his remarkable wife, Ruth Bell Graham, and their extraordinary marital relationship. It is likely you will go away from this book able to build a better marriage of your own.

Billy and Ruth Graham share a tender, productive, intimate alliance. It is of deep fire and great strength, built on patience, respect and prayer. President Lyndon Johnson called them, "Envied possessors of a near-flawless marriage." He said, "Balance is one word that describes that marriage. As helpmeets they are even-steven. They never seem to get out of kilter even when one surprises and dismays the other. Once, when they were our houseguests at the White House, I asked during dinner if Billy would give me the name of a good vice-presidential candidate. Instead of answering my question he shot out of his chair and yelled, 'Ruth, why did you just kick me under the table?'

9

"She winced in embarrassment. Then she took a deep breath and said quietly, 'Bill, shouldn't you limit your advice to spiritual matters?'

"The average husband," Johnson continued, "would have been annoyed by his wife's interference. Billy reached across the table and squeezed her hand. Then he looked at her lovingly. Later, Lady Bird said, 'I would have liked to have had a snapshot showing Ruth's reaction and Billy's—two beautiful smiles derived from *really* living together.' "

Dr. Karl Barth, the noted Swiss theologian, shared President Johnson's opinion about the Graham union. Dr. Barth said, "I've observed first-hand their bonds of marriage—a true mixture of God, love and respect."

Almost any wife would be ecstatic to discover that influential people were offering her husband huge financial support to run for the presidency of the United States. She would display a sudden passion for Rolls-Royces on learning that a prominent Hollywood director wanted to star him in an epic extravaganza. She might well plunk down a deposit on a lavish country estate when told that the chairman of a major television network was urging him to sign a million-dollar-per-year contract to host a talk show.

Ruth Graham's husband, Billy, turned down all three proposals. "Your bounded duty to the Lord is elsewhere," she reminded him.

Over the years I have written numerous newspaper stories and magazine articles about Billy Graham. I have talked to critics, associates and friends of the evangelist and his wife. Some of the things they divulged sounded too good to be true. When I told Graham that as an investigating Quaker journalist I was going to search for blemishes, he smiled. "I'm certain they exist," he said. "I won't get to heaven without bearing any scars. No human can!"

The list of the people who were helpful is so numerous that it is difficult to acknowledge them all. I'll simply say, "Many thanks to everybody." However, a special note of appreciation goes to my wife, Sallie Prugh, for her dedicated encouragement; to Robert Shuster and Frances Brocker, of the Billy Graham Center at Wheaton College, for their valuable aid that was often beyond normal assistance; to the Reverend Dr. Glenn Henricksen for reading the manuscript and offering useful suggestions; to June Reno, for judicious editing; and to Anne Angelo for typing the final version.

JHAN ROBBINS

Shortly after I completed this book, Harry Prugh, my father-in-law, died. He was the finest Christian I ever knew. Before I undertook this project I told him that I had some reservations about Billy Graham—there were areas of disagreement. Harry said, "If Billy Graham has the ability to help people live more satisfactory lives, perhaps you should do it." I'm glad I took his advice.

J. R.

MARRIAGE
MADE IN HEAVEN

1
THE WAYWARD BOY
AND THE CHINA GIRL

Billy

"BILLY FRANK'S EARLY hero was not Jesus Christ," said Morrow Graham, the evangelist's mother. "It was Babe Ruth! How much he wanted to become a famous baseball player! His long legs made the idea dimly promising. He was always practicing with the ball. He lived on the sandlot. In his dreams, he'd mutter, 'Strike two!' In those days that was all he was keen on—unless you include girls. He often said to me, 'There are three things I don't want to be when I get older: a milkman, an undertaker, or a preacher!' "

Graham did, briefly, play a few $10-a-game semiprofessional baseball games for a local team. It's been said that he was scouted by several major-league teams. That, to his everlasting regret, is not so. He was never a strong enough batter to be taken seriously. However, one of his evangelistic crusades took him to Yankee Stadium, the baseball park that is often called "the House that Babe Ruth built." When Billy was introduced, the audience of 100,000 greeted him with thunderous applause. Despite the temperature hovering at 105 degrees, the excited crowd cheered for more than ten minutes.

Yankee manager Casey Stengel attended the service. Stengel, whose mixed metaphors are as famous as his management, told reporters, "I saw more yelling and hand clapping than the Babe ever got for belting a homer. That Billy-boy sure is twenty-four-carat classy in a league that really counts like milk is healthy for a baby."

Graham's association with clamor started at birth. A neighbor who observed the new baby said, "I've brought dozens of babies into this world, but I've never heard a newborn squall so loud. You could practically hear this one all the way to the center of town!"

The noisy infant was born at home on November 7, 1918, four days before the end of World War I. At the time, his father, William Franklin Graham, Sr., exulted to a friend, "This baby is sure to bring luck. Soon we'll see a finish to all the fighting in Europe."

Home was a 300-acre dairy farm in Charlotte, North Carolina, which the elder Graham had inherited from his parents. The large tract of rolling hills and pastureland is now a shopping center, bordered by multistoried office buildings. The only reminder of its rural past is a memorial plaque:

Birthplace of Dr. Billy Graham
Born November 7, 1918
World Renowned Evangelist, Author and Educator
Preacher of the Gospel of Christ
to more people than any other man in history

Following a brief honeymoon, William Senior brought his bride, Morrow Coffey, to the farm, which then was five miles beyond the town line. She was also "country bred," and had always lived in that agricultural district. Like her husband she was descended from Scottish farmers who had settled in the Carolinas 250 years ago when the lands were still colonies of the English Crown. One of her ancestors was a signer of the Declaration of Independence. Another, James Knox Polk, was the eleventh President of the United States.

Ben Coffey, Morrow's father, was a Confederate Army veteran, who lost an eye and a leg at Gettysburg. He was a cavalryman in General Pickett's famed, gallant charge. The badly wounded Coffey, nonanesthetized, was about to be removed from the operating table when he noticed his severed right leg resting in a corner—still wearing a boot.

"He accepted the loss as God's will," said Morrow. "He was a very reverent person. My mother was that way, too. We regularly read the Bible in our house and had daily prayers together as a family. We were looking for the Lord's return. It was instilled in us—faith that Jesus was coming back. We went to church each Sabbath."

Billy's paternal grandfather was different. Crook Graham, also a Civil War veteran, believed that Sunday had been invented solely for whiskey. "He drank and swore and had little time for the Lord," said the evangelist. "Fortunately, his wife was a God-fearing woman. She read her Bible every day and taught the Word of God to her eight daughters and three sons. Through her influence, all her children became Christians."

"It has been carried on," said Morrow. "Billy Frank and his

brother and sisters were reared in a house where we put our faith in the Bible. We felt that what the Bible said was the only right way to live. I can still hear my husband telling Billy Frank, 'Every word of God is pure: *A wise son heareth his father's instruction.*' "

A hired man who helped tend the Graham's handsome herd of Jersey and Holstein cows said, "For a long while religion and Billy Frank didn't mix. The boy did pretty much what other kids do—only maybe more because he was bigger. He'd always run instead of walk—like he had to get somewhere in a special hurry. He'd rush into you like the way a bull charges a pair of red bloomers. One time he piled his father into some fresh cement. Was Mr. Graham mad! Took off his belt. When it was all over Billy Frank was sweet as pie. But the very next day he was up to his old tricks. Only this time I was the aggravated party—he made me fall into a pile of manure."

When the youngster wasn't knocking over everything in his way, he engaged in other forms of mischief. The family attended a very straitlaced Presbyterian church. "When I was a kid," the evangelist said, "I used to think that preachers all wore dark suits and long faces."

One Sunday, in the midst of the sermon, Billy made use of a large rubber band and a pocketful of paper pellets. His special targets were the heads of bald worshipers. On Sunday afternoons following church, Billy was forbidden to read newspaper comics or play games.

Often, he defied these orders. Neighbors remember that when he was certain his parents weren't looking, he'd pretend he was Tarzan of the Apes. He'd jump off the back porch and race for the trees. Then he'd climb one, let out a piercing yell and swing from branch to branch. Discovered, he would obediently vault down, pause a moment, then become one of Theodore Roosevelt's Rough Riders, storming up San Juan Hill. His imagination was wild, with himself always the dramatic hero.

At age six he had so much excess energy that his worried mother hauled him to a local doctor. "My boy never runs down," she complained. After a careful examination the report was: "Premature growing pains."

Morrow felt that schooling might help calm the youngster down. She had spent a year in college and greatly respected academics. Billy was enrolled in the Sharon Grammar School. Promptly at 7 A.M., on the first morning of the new term, she took him to the bus stop. He was uncomfortably dressed in a starched white shirt, blue tie and gray checked knickers. Morrow handed him a lunchbox that she had packed. "Eat it during the noon recess," she called as the yellow bus pulled out.

When Billy entered his classroom he took a back-row seat. The bell rang, indicating the start of the school day. He thought it signaled the lunch recess. As the teacher called the roll, he quietly ate the peanut butter sandwich and apple his mother had given him. During the proper noon recess, four hours later, a very hungry Billy looked enviously at his classmates as they devoured their food.

Going to school presented new problems. He was the tallest boy in class but he was also the thinnest. One of the other students called him "A skinny marink!" and challenged him to a fistfight. Billy was the clear loser, with a black eye

19

and scraped chin. "I got the worst beating of my life," he recalls. After several more such defeats, Billy found his expertise—he could outrun anybody in the school.

He also discovered that he liked girls. His first sweetheart was the freckled, pigtailed lass who sat next to him in class: "She was brilliant as well as athletic," he recalled. "She was a real tomboy. Puppy love is laughed at by adults, but it is very real to a puppy."

Because of his height, Graham was given the role of Uncle Sam in a seventh grade school play. Barbara Linker, one of his classmates, remembers that first public appearance: "Most of us whooped it up when Billy came on stage. The white whiskers he was wearing kept falling down. He looked more like a worried, overgrown Jackie Cooper than Uncle Sam."

The evangelist's recollection of that performance was a pair of knocking knees and perspiring hands. "I vowed," he said, "that I would never again appear in public."

One Christmas he was given a bicycle. After hours of tumbling, he learned to stay right side up, and high speed became paramount. "He caused several of the farm animals to feel that way too," his brother Melvin recalled. "I'd watch him peddling furiously down the road, followed by an out-of-breath goat, a panting collie and a flock of exhausted chickens." (Billy has three very attractive younger siblings— Melvin, Catherine and Jean.)

The evangelist has made good use of memories of his bicycle technique, and often includes them in his sermons: "I found there was one thing to do on that bike if I wanted to stay on it. I had to keep moving forward. If I stopped moving forward, I would fall off and hurt myself. A Christian must learn that. He must keep moving forward in his faith."

Returning from one of the bicycle cavalcades, he was observed and admired by a hired hand. "Anybody who can do that," the man said, "deserves a reward." He reached in his breast pocket and took out a plug of chewing tobacco and handed it to the delighted and flattered youngster. William, Sr., discovered Billy chewing away. He promptly ordered him to spit, unbuckled his belt and fired the offending employee.

"I guess," said Billy, "that until I was about fourteen I was on the receiving end of quite a few thrashings. My father used his belt. Mother preferred a long hickory switch. If I broke a rule, they never hesitated. But as I look back I realize that the rules were fair. Sometimes I'm sure the things I did— or didn't do—must have been exasperating to them, but they never spanked me without good reason. And believe me, I gave them plenty of reasons."

A teacher once told Morrow Graham, "Your son isn't a very good student. I'll ask him to recite something and he won't even answer. I've had to chase him around my desk and whack him with a ruler to settle him down. The boy lacks drive. He needs to learn to apply himself."

When Billy's mother urged him to study harder, he would shuffle his feet and protest, "Why do I need to be educated? My father is a farmer, and so was his father. That's what I'll be. A farmer don't need any book learning!" As if to prove his point, he was already handy around the barn. Each morning he rose at 3 A.M. to help tend the cows and deliver the milk. Then he ate breakfast and headed for school.

Secretly, he hoped to become a big-league baseball player.

He has said that the reason so many star athletes have come from North Carolina was because "making it in baseball" was one of the few ways they could hope to beat the state's hard times.

He was very excited when he learned that Babe Ruth was coming to Charlotte to exhibit his slugging skill with a baseball bat. He pleaded with his father to take him to see the famous hitter. The Reverend Dr. Grady Wilson, a boyhood friend and currently a close associate, recalls, "Mr. Graham bought tickets for Billy and a number of his pals. He arranged for Billy to shake hands with the great King of Swat. Billy didn't wash his hand for three days."

The opposite sex was as impressed with the tall, handsome youngster as he was with baseball. The romance with his pigtailed classmate was succeeded by naive love affairs with many other girlfriends. "The list was long," his mother said. "He'd sit down at the supper table and sigh. That was a sure sign of what would follow: he'd smile shyly and tell us, 'I've just met the cutest girl ever!' "

One of them was Pauline Presson, the pretty daughter of the town's leading contractor. "She was my first *real* romance," Billy said. "I was fifteen when I met her. She was more sophisticated than any other girl I had ever dated. She was lovely and knew how to make herself even lovelier. But never in a flashy way. It was fun to be with her—we laughed a great deal."

Pauline remembers him as a tall, blond, extremely good-looking boy with a wonderful grin: "He was so handsome. He could have been in the movies, I thought. Nice to be with. Didn't cuss or act rough the way some of the other boys behaved. He'd never call for me in blue jeans. In the summertime he wore dark blue trousers, a white jacket and white shoes. Never without a tie. Although I must say that some of those ties were pretty wild. He always liked fancy clothes."

The young couple went to church socials in his father's Plymouth. "Afterwards," said Billy, "we'd drive to some secluded spot and park. We held hands and kissed while listening to the radio music of Tommy Dorsey and Glenn Miller."

In those days North Carolina had no age requirements for driving. Billy's idea of fun was to borrow the family automobile and joyride on the sidewalk. He drove around curves on two wheels. He drove across pastures. Once he got his father's car mired in deep mud, and the elder Graham had to use mules to pull it out. Billy's friends drove with the same abandon. He remembers standing up in the rear seat of a fast-moving convertible, one hand around his date and the other madly ringing a cowbell.

"I'm not trying to justify my actions," said Billy, "but remember this was during the great depression of the thirties. Hundreds of thousands of people walked the streets looking for work. Heads of families sold apples on street corners. Hitler was on the march across Europe. Ethiopia had fallen to Mussolini. Manchuria had been invaded. A few 'ridiculous' men were predicting a second world war. I understood little, and like young people today resented my parents, my teachers, my humdrum life as a farmhand and high school student."

"He was always getting into hot water," recalled a high

school bus driver. "A couple of times a week, when Billy and his friends got off the bus, he'd reach underneath and turn off the shutoff valve of the gas tank. I'd drive about a hundred yards and the engine would sputter out. I'd get out and shake my fist at him, but he'd only give me the laughing yanh-yanhs. He was a hero to his schoolmates!"

"By today's standards," the evangelist says, "this sort of misbehavior would be dismissed as 'youthful friskiness.' But try to remember, at that time, my community considered them extremely wild. I'm afraid everyone agreed we teenagers were doomed, especially 'that Billy Graham.' My parents were plenty worried. I gave them a hard time."

In the spring of 1934, concerned local farmers, Graham Senior included, and local businessmen, decided that a powerful stimulant was needed to combat wantonness and spiritual apathy. They erected a temporary tabernacle and invited fundamentalist preacher Mordeci Ham to conduct prayer meetings. The Reverend Ham specialized in the spiritual rescue of the decadent populations of southern cities. He assured the anxious town fathers that the entire community could soon look forward to purification and salvation. For eleven weeks the tempestuous revivalist thundered about eternity and redemption. He fastened in his talk on the devil's big three temptations: dancing, card playing and whiskey.

Ham indicted all of the Charlotte high school students. He claimed they would surely be damned to hell if they didn't instantly mend their deceitful ways. "Fornication on campus is rampant!" he raged. "You are all sinners!"

The accusations brought out an angry mob of teenagers—

Graham included—intent on forcing the evangelist to retract his charges. Instead, the provoked students meekly took seats in the makeshift tabernacle and listened respectfully.

Billy was spellbound. The following evening he returned; soon he became a steady visitor. Although he was not guilty of any of the vices Ham spoke of, he felt he had to promise to give them up. One night while the choir was singing "Almost Persuaded," the sixteen-year-old Billy stepped forward asking to be saved: "The grip of an old-fashioned revival is hard to explain. People are seized by a unity of consecration far more intense than occurs during any regular service. Each listener becomes deeply involved with the evangelist, who describes your sins—somehow he knows—and shortcomings and demands on pain of Divine Judgment that you mend your ways. As I listened, I began to have thoughts I had never known before. Something began to speak to my heart."

One of the first things Billy did when he returned home was to throw his arms around his mother. "I am a changed boy!" he told her. The next day, when he attended class, one of his teachers said, "Preacher Graham, will you explain the lesson? I hear you got religion last night!"

He was quieter in school and his grades improved somewhat, although he still ranked near the bottom of his class. He managed to graduate "by the skin of my teeth," he recalled. "I suspect I squeezed through because my father was a member of the school board."

Billy worried: he still liked girls. He had no intention of becoming a minister, despite his mother's urging, yet he found himself berating friends who he felt were leaning toward the devil. When one of them said, "Goddamn," he became enraged. "Don't ever blaspheme in my presence!" he shouted. "You know that I am a Christian!" At a high school class party he observed his current girlfriend dancing, waltzing with the host's father. "Stop immediately!" Billy ordered. "Dancing leads toward sin!"

The friends he saw often were, like himself, newly converted. The group became known as the "Preacher Boys." Several of them planned to attend Bob Jones College, an uncredited, ultra-fundamentalist Bible school, then located in Cleveland, Tennessee. Billy decided that he would also go there. To help pay expenses he got a temporary job as a Fuller Brush salesman. His assignment took him to South Carolina where he prayed before ringing doorbells. "The results," said John Davidson, a fellow salesman, "were amazing. He'd put his big foot in the door and not take no for an answer. His spiel worked so well that the company wanted to keep him on permanently."

"You may not think so," Graham said, "but I'm naturally sort of a shy fellow. Introverted. Selling brushes got me over some of that. It allowed me to talk with people and to sell people. My technique was to offer a free brush—in those days that was a big thing. I would have to empty my whole case of brushes to get to the free one. The woman would invariably inquire, 'By the way, what's this?' or 'How much is that?' Well, I knew I had a fish on a string. I don't want to sound too commercial. The truth is that I felt I was doing her a favor. I had become convinced that Fuller brushes were the best in the world and no family should be without them."

Billy often earned more than $50 a week—an excellent income in the mid-thirties. When he felt that he had accumulated enough money, he enrolled as a freshman in Bob Jones College. Dressed in red and white sport jacket, wide, light-gray trousers, a pepper-and-salt bow tie and maroon suede shoes, he arrived on campus.

He was disappointed at what he found there. The school was an ultimate in strictness and rigidity. Male and female students were so segregated that it was against the rules even to speak to the opposite sex. They had to keep their bodies at least six inches apart, demerits were given for loitering in the hall, and a sign was posted in each dormitory room: GRIPING NOT TOLERATED!

Once Billy told the head of the college, Dr. Bob Jones, that he was unhappy. Jones' reply was, "If you're a misfit here, you'll be a misfit anywhere . . . chances are you'll never amount to much."

When the semester ended, a demoralized Billy Graham returned home. His appearance was frail. His mother was dismayed: "He was always thin, but this was frightening. In addition, he had a bad cough." She took her son to a doctor, who advised lots of sunshine.

Billy's former roommate, Wendell Phillips, had transferred to the Florida Bible Institute near Tampa, Florida. It was decided that Billy Frank should also go there. The new school was a complete change. Also uncredited, it was less rigid. "Ninety students and our teachers lived together," the evangelist recalled. "A big happy family. We all worked together. We washed dishes, raked leaves, shined shoes. Everybody liked and respected everybody else."

One student Billy especially liked was a pretty, slender, brunette sophomore. He was in love again. This time the object of his affection was Emily Regina Cavanaugh, described by classmates as "beautiful, talented and spiritual." She and her two sisters had formed a gospel singing trio and performed at churches and local radio stations.

Together, Emily and Billy attended religious meetings and lectures. Each evening, before dinner, they would meet in the student lounge to discuss religion and prayer. "I was very, very impressed with the way he prayed," said Emily. "Such heart!"

"She was always so reassuring," Billy said. "She was a wonderful person to be with. Sometimes we would go for picnics along the beach. Every once in a while I'd steal a kiss."

He brought Emily to Charlotte to meet his family and to help him tell them that he had finally discovered his true calling: He was no longer in a quandary about his life's work. It was to be preaching. He felt they might find it amusing to learn that the decision had been made on the eighteenth hole of a golf course.

He described how it happened: "One autumn night, after a great deal of indecision, I walked out on the golf course that surrounds our school. I had practiced preaching, but believed my attempts were very feeble. I was in despair. On that night the trees were loaded with Spanish moss. In the moonlight it was a fairyland. As I stepped onto the fringe of the eighteenth green, I remember feeling that despite all appearances to the contrary, God did want me to preach. A soft breeze was sweeping from the south. I remember getting on my knees saying, 'Oh God, if you want me to preach, I will do it.' Tears ran down my cheeks. I made the surrender to become an ambassador for Jesus Christ."

Billy told his parents that he planned to ask Emily to be his wife and that jointly they would spread the Word. He was now convinced that he had an inspired purpose in life. The couple returned to school and continued to date regularly. Emily accompanied him as he preached the gospel at street corner meetings. Some Sundays he would hold seven or eight outdoor services from noon to dusk, often only to a handful of people. "No matter," he said. "All I ask is to stir one sinner."

Emily, however, began to have second thoughts about sharing Billy's life: "I had serious doubts. I attempted to tell him several times, but he would always put me off."

One evening at a school party she finally blurted it out—she had reconsidered his proposal of marriage. He tried to persuade her to change her mind. "At the time I couldn't believe it," Billy says. "I felt the world had ended for me. My confidence in myself was shattered. It took me a long while to make me realize that it was the best thing that's ever happened to me. I know now that God was preparing a girl for me in China!"

Ruth

Ruth's father, Dr. Nelson Bell, came from a fifth-generation Scottish-Irish Virginia family. For twenty-five years he served as a surgeon in a Presbyterian mission in China that was built by the father of author Pearl S. Buck. Once as the guest of honor at a White House dinner honoring "eminent humanitarians," Buck told the guests, "Of all the missionaries who ever went to China, Nelson Bell is the most hardworking and the most human."

A retired professor from the medical school that Bell

attended also spoke at the reception: "Nelson Bell was the most dedicated and gifted student I ever taught. From day one, he announced that he was going to be a medical missionary. He let nothing stand in his way. Eventually, he knew more than most of the instructors—myself included. When he got his medical degree in 1916 he had just turned twenty-one. I complimented him on his rapid achievement. 'That's to the good,' he replied. 'I'll have more time to be a medical missionary.' Four weeks later he and Virginia Leftwich, also from Virginia, were married."

Ruth's mother was equally committed. She took special nursing courses to assist her physician-husband. Shortly after their marriage they volunteered to serve in an impoverished West Virginia coal town. Fred Majewski, a retired miner who is now in his late seventies, remembers them well: "My father took me to see Dr. Bell after I had fallen out of a second-story window. Although everyone was sure that I was dying, the only damage was a broken arm. Mrs. Bell washed the blood off and Dr. Bell set the bone. Then he handed me a cherry-flavored lollypop. Candy was a real treat to poor kids in those days.

"Those two were darn good people—never demanded a single penny. Days later, my ma sent me over to their house with a blueberry pie she'd just baked. The door was open and I walked in. There were both of them kneeling on the floor, praying."

The Bells next journeyed overseas to a Presbyterian mission hospital in Tsingkiangpu, China, 300 miles north of Shanghai. It was usually well-stocked with supplies American church members shipped, but occasionally Nelson had to resort to assembling his own medical equipment. Even with the makeshifts, the lanky, erect doctor operated successfully on critically ill patients, many of whom had been given up for lost.

Nelson succeeded in treating a professional Mah-Jongg gambler who was suffering from a severe heart condition. Dr. Hsi Ch'ien, a Chinese doctor who was Bell's assistant, thought the man had only a few hours to live: "I've never seen a patient closer to death." It was in the thirties, long before pacemakers. Nelson constructed a pacemaker of his own, a contraption that kept the gambler alive for nearly a month.

Dr. Hsi said that in addition to prolonging the man's life, Bell also saved his soul. While patients were in recovery, the physician would talk to them in their regional dialects—he spoke five plus Mandarin—about the glories of Christ. His linguistic fluency was astonishing. Once during a meeting with Chiang Kai-shek, the Generalissimo told him, "Not only are you a doctor of miracles, but you speak Mandarin better than I do!"

Nelson refused credit for his deeds. "The work is solely His."

"He wasn't being coy," said Dr. Lorimer Davis, who had known Bell in China. "Nothing could shake his conviction that the Lord had given him the skill to help the unfortunates of Tsingkiangpu. He taught his children to think that way, too."

Billy Graham's future wife was born in Tsingkiangpu on June 20, 1920. It was a typical day: gunfire was heard in the distance, rats played around the town pump, bandits looted several shops, heavy rains flooded a nearby canal, and starving peasants envied the prosperous opium dealers.

The infant's mother believed that one's children came first, but she could often be found in the overcrowded wards or outpatient clinic. "We were always short-staffed," Virginia said. "I was needed to help out. It was difficult explaining it to my two very young children." (Rosa, an older daughter, had been born two years earlier.)

"Even as tiny youngsters," recalled Virginia, "they seemed to understand what I was saying. One minute they'd be crying. I'd tell them it was essential that I leave, and they'd stop their crying. Wang Nai Nai, our Chinese nurse-amah, used to say, 'Your children were kissed by the angels.' "

Ruth remembers her amah as one of the kindest people she's ever known. Wang Nai Nai had formerly been a procuress, who secured young girls for old men's pleasures. Her occupation changed radically when she heard a missionary speak about Jesus. "She really believed in the Master," said Bell. "Wang Nai Nai had truly been converted. It was such a joy to witness how each day she learned more and more about His love and mercy. I never saw anybody more deserving of admittance to the Church."

Rosa and Ruth were rarely out of their amah's sight. From early morning to late at night, the devoted Wang Nai Nai watched closely over them. The day always began with prayers and the singing of hymns, and it was a house rule that whoever came down to breakfast after the first verse of the hymn forfeited sugar on the porridge.

Nelson Bell felt the need for child-rearing directives. "Mrs. Bell and I strongly believe that structured family measures are necessary," he told John Hansberry, an American who worked in the office of the Consul-General in Shanghai. "Though children may grumble, we find they welcome guidelines. Without them, there would be total confusion."

For the two youngsters, the morning was school time. Virginia Bell tutored Rosa and Ruth because she feared they might be kidnapped if they attended a conventional grammar school. She instructed her daughters in the basic three Rs, gave them music lessons, taught them art appreciation and showed them how to knit and sew.

"Mother was a superb seamstress," Ruth said. "We never looked like refugees from a missionary barrel. She handmade most of our clothes. She believed that looking drab was a reflection on the Lord. She tried to pass her skill on to us, but we could never match her craftsmanship."

Virginia carefully studied the dresses in copies of *Harper's Bazaar* that were sent to her regularly by her sister-in-law, who lived in Waynesboro, Virginia. Then she copied them, adding her fine-needled embellishments. Although most of the garments were very plain, she had done such an outstanding job that it was rumored the Bells purchased Paris originals.

Shortly after the classes ended, Dr. Bell would join his family for lunch. Seated around the table, he would talk enthusiastically about his morning's surgery, becoming very graphic and giving vivid demonstrations.

After the noonday meal, Virginia and her husband would leave for the hospital, where in addition to her other chores, Virginia was in charge of the women's clinic. The girls, accompanied by Wang Nai Nai, would often discuss the future. Ruth, who has always had a serene faith in God, insisted that she, too, was going to be a devoted missionary. "She used to pray regularly that the Lord would allow her to become a martyr," Rosa recalled. "She so wanted to be captured by bandits and beheaded for Jesus' sake. Whenever she asked that, I would pray, 'Lord, please don't listen to her!' "

Each evening when Nelson and Virginia returned from the hospital, the family bathed and put on fresh clothes. "The clothing was not elaborate," said Ruth, "but we welcomed the change." After dinner, the Bell family gathered around the fireplace and played word games or read aloud. Ruth's favorite books of the Bells' large library were *Little Lord Fauntleroy, A Tale of Two Cities* and *David Copperfield*. Sometimes Nelson would entertain them with his guitar, followed by prayers and bedtime.

Ruth had a menagerie of beloved pets: pigeons, magpies, canaries, a baby turtle and a mongrel puppy named Tar Baby. She took excellent care of all the creatures but was especially partial to Tar Baby. She usually referred to the dog as T.B. "T.B. was a very odd-looking mixed breed," she said, "but to me she was the most beautiful dog in the world. I so loved her, but when she got older she started biting. Father had to put her down. T.B.'s death was my first real heartache. I don't think anything can be more intense than a child's grief."

Despite all the games and pets, life in Tsingkiangpu was very different from a conventional childhood in the United States. Although Ruth spoke Chinese before she learned English, in her environment she was inescapably an American, and thereby considered an oddity.

Her Chinese friends called her *yang kuei-tse*—foreign devil—and made frequent references to what they considered her big nose and huge feet. "I so wanted to be petite and look Chinese," Ruth recalled. "I would look in the mirror when washing and hope that my nose would shrink."

In the Bell home a daily battle was waged against dirt and germs. Virginia knew she had to keep the girls scrupulously clean to ward off vermin. Boiled water, yellow soap and baking soda were kept as handy as the family Bible. Mice were a constant nuisance; rats an ever-present terror. One night Virginia was awakened by screams coming from the girls' room. She dashed in and found rats crawling over their bodies. Ruth's right hand was covered with blood—a rat had bitten off a tiny corner of a finger.

Once while Ruth was playing in the mission garden, she noticed a small round metal object half buried in the soil and thought it was some kind of Christmas decoration. She picked it up, hung it on a nearby tree and admired it. Then, pleased with her fabulous find, she started to carry it into the house. Fortunately, a Chinese hospital worker who had recently been a soldier passed by. He recognized the "Christmas ornament" as a live grenade on its way to explode. Quickly he snatched the small bomb and tossed it into a bucket of water.

The routine on Sunday differed greatly from that of the rest of the week. Nelson and his wife believed that the sacred day belonged to the Lord. They didn't allow their children to engage in nonreligious activities—play outdoor games, read poetry or fiction or listen to secular music. "But don't get the idea," said Ruth, defending the practice, "that Sunday was dull or boring. Far from it. I was never forbidden to do one thing without mother or father providing a happy substitute. They made Sunday a special time, a day of refreshment, a gathering of strength. It was never dreary."

When Ruth was ready for secondary school, the Bells decided to send her to a Presbyterian-run academy in Pyongyang, North Korea. "It was a wrenching experience for me. The journey was a long one—it took a week to get there. I didn't want to go—adored my home. The idea of a classroom and competitive students terrified me. Night after night I cried myself to sleep."

Mary Edmondson, a classmate, said, "Homesick or not, she was an outstanding student; a bit lighthearted, but never without her well-thumbed Bible. She really knew its contents backwards and forwards—and fully believed. Yet she would express herself in a buoyant and easy manner. She had a crackerjack sense of humor. It kept getting her into trouble. I remember one time she was in the infirmary for the flu or some such. She was required to take her temperature several times a day and I guess she got bored. She put the thermometer under a light bulb that hung above her bed. When the nurse came to read the result she let out a shriek—it was 110 degrees!

"Another time Ruth was to be awarded some prize—it seemed like she was always winning something. Anyway, that morning we had room inspection. Just as the examining teacher was to give her stamp of approval, she heard a strange noise coming from under Ruth's bed. Upon closer inspection she discovered the noise was due to three tiny kittens. Ruth had placed them there when she found their mother had deserted them. I don't remember if, as punishment, the prize was withheld. But the next week she got into another fracas for which she was almost expelled. She crawled out of a window to make her exit. She was caught. What did she do? Reached for her Bible and prayed for guidance!"

Helen Torrey Renich also attended the Korean high school. "You knew instantly," she said, "that Ruth was a highly spiritual person. She was the first student I asked to join me in prayer. Later, four other girls joined our worship group. Every evening we would meet in my room to pray. I was so impressed by the way Ruth looked at the world. If it weren't for her devotion to God, I don't believe that Billy would be the evangelist he is today. I feel, looking at it from a woman's standpoint, that her walk with God was such that Billy always knew that his family was well cared for when he was away on his crusades. It gave him the strength he needed."

Ruth graduated near the top of her class. Again, in finding a college, the decision was to select a distant school. This time the choice was the United States, a place she had seen twice on family furloughs. The Bells picked Wheaton College, an interdenominational religious school twenty-five miles west of Chicago that their elder daughter was attending. It had an excellent academic reputation.

It was a tearful departure as the Bells saw their younger daughter off to America. Ruth, who has always enjoyed writing poetry, composed these lines during that lengthy ocean voyage:

> Test me, Lord, and give me strength
> to meet each test
>   unflinching, unafraid;

not striving nervously to do my best
not self-assured, or careless as in jest
    but with Your aid.
Purge me, Lord, and give me grace
to bear the heat
    of cleansing flame;
not bitter at my lowly lot, but meet
to bear my share of suffering and keep sweet
    in Jesus' Name.

"Wheaton sounded as alien to me as Peking University would seem to you," she said. "The little time I'd spent in America, my whole family was with me. It was going to be quite different now. Although my sister Rosa had preceded me to Wheaton, I was still mighty apprehensive. I wondered what lay in store for me."

Little did she realize that a tall, handsome, blond, wavy-haired student would soon cause her to pray, "Oh, Lord, if you wish to give me the privilege of sharing my life with this man, I would have no greater joy."

Nor could she know that, years later, this same man who so early caught her fancy would give thanks not only for his wife, but, uniquely perhaps, for his father-in-law. "I'm convinced," he said, "that one of the reasons in God's provisions why she became my wife was so Dr. Nelson Bell would become my father-in-law. He was by far the most unforgettable Christian I have ever known. . . . He and Ruth together did more to get my ministry church-oriented than any single factor and single influence."

2
MADE FOR
EACH OTHER

"GOD SELECTS AN ideal made for true worshipers," Billy said. "Of that I'm absolutely convinced. If you get impatient and refuse to wait for that choice, you wind up with His second- or third-best."

Whenever the evangelist makes this affirmation, he is asked, "How does one recognize God's choice?"

"It's difficult to explain to unbelievers or skeptics," he replies. "But the practicing Christian who really turns his life over to God's will recognizes the match at once. Everything else may be against it, but down deep inside you there is a difference. There is peace in your heart. You know this is the one; the one God wants you to have. It happened that way to me."

Billy became aware of God's selection almost from the first moment he saw Ruth Bell. "You can meet your life partner in a thousand different ways," he said. "In my case it was due to a rickety, yellow pickup truck."

Following graduation from the Florida Bible Institute, he enrolled in Wheaton College to study anthropology. At twenty-one years of age he was already an ordained minister. "But I strongly felt that I should have additional schooling," he said. "At Wheaton I needed money for expenses. I got a fifty-cents-an-hour job as a helper on a small moving truck. The owner, Johnny Streater, was a classmate of mine. He was always talking about an extraordinary coed named Ruth Bell. 'She's the prettiest girl on campus,' he would tell me, 'and also the most devout.' Naturally I was interested."

One afternoon, as Billy was about to unload an overstuffed living room chair, Johnny tapped him on the shoulder. "There's Ruth Bell I was telling you about," he whispered.

The future evangelist whirled around and saw an extremely attractive hazel-eyed girl who appeared to be in her late teens. "She was wearing a white dress," he said. "She looked like a vision. Immediately, I was in love again. But this time it was different from anything I had ever felt before. I was so flustered that I didn't make any sense in my greeting. I was told I uttered something that sounded like flub-glub."

The father of one of Ruth's girlfriends had told her about the slender young southerner who had recently enrolled in Wheaton. "He's quite different from all the other boys," he said. "Only twenty-one and already ordained. He's very intense in his love of God."

A few days later Ruth heard Billy pray. "I realized then that the description was accurate," she recalled. "It was in Wheaton's Williston Hall. A group of students held prayer meeting there before going out to teach Sunday school. I had never before heard anyone worship so devotedly. I immediately sensed that here was a young man who knew God in a very unusual way."

However, she wasn't fully aware of God's selection for her until after the first date with Billy. "Then it happened. When I got back to my room I remember thanking the Lord for allowing me to go out with Bill, who was unlike any other man I'd ever met. I always call him Bill. How could I possibly call a six-foot two-and-a-half-inch man Billy? He's never impressed me as being the 'Billy' type.

"There was a certain seriousness about him. There was a depth. Yet, for all his drive there was a winsomeness about him and a consideration for other people which I found very endearing."

That initial date came about a month after Streater's introduction. "I desperately wanted to see her again," Billy said, "but I guess I was too shy." He reasoned that he couldn't possibly impress this popular campus queen whose beauty and innocence had made her a school legend. Billy's friends realized how smitten he was and urged him to ask her out. Finally, after much coaxing, he timidly agreed to try. "It was in the school library," recalled Mary Blake, who was a Wheaton freshman at the time. "I was sitting next to Ruth. She was copying something out of a book. He started to walk over to our table. I remember being amused as I watched him make a half dozen stops and starts. He'd almost reach our table, then back off. Finally he seemed to stiffen up and stomped over.

"He opened his mouth, but nothing came out—it was as if he had suddenly lost his voice. But then he blurted, stringing the words together, 'Hey-Ruth-I'd-like-to-take-you-to-a-con-

cert-next-Sunday-afternoon-how-about-it?' His face red-
dened right after he said it. I felt he was surely going to
apologize for the interruption, but she looked up and smiled.
'Yes,' she answered. All he replied was, 'Thanks. Thanks a
whole lot!' Then he waltzed out, as they say, on air."

Billy remembers that he found it very difficult to wait for
Sunday! "I was never more impatient. Yet it was a combination of wanting the day to come immediately and hoping it
would never roll around. I was so afraid I'd say or do the
wrong thing."

Sunday did arrive, and Billy took Ruth to the concert. It
consisted of sacred music. He did not disgrace himself.
"Quite the contrary," Ruth said. "I found him very stimulat-
ing company. There was a decided purpose to his life which I
thought admirable. That evening I was already wondering if I
should share it with him."

On the walk back to her residence, the couple talked about
what they hoped to contribute to the Lord. Billy thirsted to
spread the Word in North Carolina; Ruth yearned to be a
missionary in Tibet. Her wish to follow in her parents'
footsteps presented a major obstacle to her growing feelings
for Billy: "I had mixed emotions. On one hand I wanted to
spend my life with Bill. But for years I had resolved to serve
the Lord in Tibet. I reasoned that God got me here to
Wheaton; He provided the money and helped me through my
courses; weren't those certain signs that He was leading me
straight back to the mission field?"

Billy knew that he was in love with Ruth, but he was
terrified of saying so. He feared rejection—again. His declaration took place about two weeks after the concert. She

remembers the incident: "We were out driving. Suddenly, right in the middle of a sentence, he jammed on the brakes. He did it so fast that we rammed right into the rear of a truck that had stopped for a red light. Luckily, no damage was done."

They continued to date. They would walk along the tree-shaded Wheaton streets, holding hands, sometimes in complete silence or heatedly engaged in discussions about Tibet.

"Why don't you go there with me?" she would ask.

"Because God wants me to preach right here," he would reply and quote biblical passages to aid his cause. "The Bible tells us 'It is not good that man should be alone; I will make him an helpmeet for him.' " He paused and then added, "If God caused me to fall in love with you, isn't it a clear sign that you're the helpmeet He has in mind?"

She'd look at him quizzically. "I'm praying hard for His guidance," she'd say.

Billy was certain that if Ruth did decide to marry, she'd choose him to be her husband. "Still," he said, "the reluctance to commit herself gave me a great deal of concern. Throughout the next year she tried to support her position by telling me stories of dedicated female missionaries. One of them was Mildred Cable, who rejected the man she loved in order to serve the Lord in China. Ruth also told me about Amy Carmichael, who cast aside her suitor so that she could dedicate herself to Indian children.

"I decided to let God do my courting. I wasn't above a little nudge. I'd ask her, 'Are you still praying about us?' Her reply was always the same: 'Yes. I'll tell you the moment He gives me an answer.' "

Mary Blake, the Wheaton classmate, recalls, "It seemed as if the entire school was aware of her confusion. We were all rooting for Billy. It was pretty obvious how they felt about each other. I don't know if real passion had yet struck. I'm told it came after they were married. But even then, those two had so much going for them—God and mutual respect. Maybe they're the most important ingredients for a successful marriage.

"However," she added, "there were some sharp differences. Mostly about religious doctrine. She was a Presbyterian—still is. Billy had joined the Southern Baptist Church. He gave as his reason that studying the Bible had convinced him immersion was the only proper form of baptism—and that Presbyterians didn't do it. He once said that Ruth's father couldn't possibly know the will of God because he was a Presbyterian. She was furious. He quickly apologized. I'm sure he never said that again.

"I'm told that Billy's theology has remained the same, but over the years his interpretation appears to be far more broadminded. He has clearly stated his views on differing denominations: 'All Christians hold essential convictions in common.' But during their courting there were some fireworks!"

Billy, who now was referred to as "the boy preacher," was often asked to deliver sermons at the Wheaton chapel. Ruth would sit in the front row, smiling, listening attentively. She admits that she was sometimes a little embarrassed by his frenzied bellowing and thrashing about of his long arms. (Billy speaks of his youthful zeal: "I listen to old tapes of myself and don't even know it's me. I bellowed and roamed all over the platform.")

News of his intense preaching fame spread to distant communities. During the summer vacation of his junior year he was invited to conduct a series of Gospel meetings in Tampa, Florida. Ruth was in Virginia with her missionary parents, who had been forced to leave China because of the Japanese invasion.

"I was still in a quandary regarding my future," she said. "I continued to ask the Lord for direction. Late one afternoon it became clear what His will was." She quickly posted a letter to Billy, who received it just as he was about to begin a Tampa revival meeting. He recalls that he fell to his knees in gratitude after reading: *"I'd be honored to become your wife."*

His father had given him a secondhand automobile, and in August 1941, he drove to see his bride-to-be. "Naturally," he said, "I was delighted to visit her. But I guess you couldn't tell it from my actions. I didn't kiss her on the lips. Instead, I merely pecked her on the forehead. I suppose I was self-conscious in the presence of her parents. Ruth has never forgotten that—she still kids me about it."

The first authentic betrothal kiss occurred a few evenings later. They were alone in the moonlight on a high mountain ridge. "It was a wonderful moment," Billy recalled. "But I was not as happy as I might have been: I didn't have enough money to buy her an engagement ring."

The opportunity arrived in early fall when the deacons of a church in his hometown asked him to lead them in a revival service. They were so pleased with the results that on the final evening they presented him with a special love offering of $165. The next morning he rushed to a jewelry store to purchase a small diamond ring.

In the fall Billy returned to Wheaton alone. Ruth had

decided to forgo a semester to tend her sister Rosa, who was convalescing from tuberculosis in a sanitarium in New Mexico. The affianced couple had to settle for carrying on their engagement via the post office, exchanging letters regularly. She told him in detail everything that was happening. He wrote to her about experiences at school. As the end of 1941 approached, he described the plight of the male students who were apprehensive about the impending war and how it would affect them.

When Pearl Harbor was bombed, Billy wanted to enlist immediately and be commissioned a chaplain. Army authorities told him that since Florida Bible Institute wasn't considered a seminary, he had to get a divinity degree from a recognized school or spend a year in a church pastorate.

Ruth and Billy's professors persuaded him to remain in college and graduate. Dr. V. Raymond Edman, the president of Wheaton, told him, "With more wisdom you can do your part in a much more meaningful fashion."

Billy's years at school were busy ones. After the doctors pronounced Rosa cured, Ruth returned to Wheaton. "It was good to see the change in Billy when she came back," Dr. Edman said. "He'd been moping about and was so absentminded." The engaged couple spent hours talking about how they planned to serve God together. They knew they would have to struggle not only with the physical destruction of World War II but with its heritage of bitterness and disillusionment.

Billy was now the regular pastor of the Wheaton Tabernacle Church, which served the students and faculty. Every Sunday he would preach twice to enthusiastic worshipers who crowded into the 300-seat auditorium. Ruth suggested topics for his sermons, and Billy sought her guidance in performing his duties as president of the Student Christian Council.

They graduated in June of 1943. Clutching his diploma, Billy whispered to his future wife, "Grow old along with me, the best is yet to be!"

3
THE PREACHER
TAKES A WIFE

BILLY AND RUTH were married two months later. They chose
Friday the thirteenth for their wedding day. To a superstitious
friend who expressed alarm over the supposedly unlucky
selection, the about-to-be Mrs. Graham said, "I'm afraid I
don't agree with your premonition of doom. To me it shall be
the most wonderful day of my life."

Her happiness was very apparent on the ride to the church.
"In order not to get her white satin bridal gown wrinkled,"
recalled her father, "Ruth stood up, bent over, on the back
seat of the car all the way to the chapel, but she arrived
flawlessly ironed. She kept repeating, 'It's a perfect wedding
day, just as I dreamed and prayed it might be.' "

The ceremony was performed in the Southern Presbyterian
Conference Center of Montreat, North Carolina, where the
Bells now lived. The twenty-four-year-old bridegroom was
uneasy about the guests' appraisal of him: "I was only known

as the boy Ruth was about to marry. I remember their stares. I felt that they regarded me as a somewhat erratic person because I had switched my religious denomination. I stuck closely to my own clique."

Minutes after the "I pronounce you," the couple was engulfed in a shower of rice and headed for a brief honeymoon at Blowing Rock, North Carolina, an attractive village high in the Blue Ridge Mountains. Billy had selected an inexpensive boarding inn: He had $65 to spend.

"I could always recognize couples who had just had the knot tied," said Daniel Haywood, who worked as a part-time porter in a Blowing Rock hotel. "And it wasn't only because their shades were pulled all the way down—the Grahams' sure were! But from the shy, pleased smiles they had. A kind of rapture settled on the place when the Grahams were here."

When their money ran out after five days, the couple drove to Western Springs, Illinois, an upper middle-class suburb of Chicago. Billy, anxious to fulfill the Army's chaplain requirements, had accepted a position as the pastor of a small Baptist church that was badly in debt. "I had failed to inform Ruth about it before giving my consent," he said. "It was a big mistake. She was very hurt. Not that she objected to the church or the locale, but that I had failed to take her into my confidence. She felt strongly that a husband and wife should have the opportunity to discuss their responsibilities together. She ultimately forgave me, but I learned a valuable lesson. I believe that I have never since failed to consult her in an important decision."

The church building in Western Springs had never been

completed, compelling the thirty-five-member congregation to worship in the only room that was partly finished—the basement. It didn't have a proper ceiling, and a temporary tarpaper roof had been attached to the cement foundation; a sloping tunnel served as an entrance hall.

A parsonage—a place to live—didn't go along with the moldy, makeshift sanctuary, and Billy's $45-a-week salary wasn't sufficient to rent living quarters in affluent Western Springs. The couple had to settle for a tiny furnished apartment that was four miles from the pastorate.

"We got accustomed to bumping into each other," the evangelist said, "but we never really got used to the noise of the freight trains that thundered past our windows every hour."

To make the place appear more cozy-looking, Ruth attached a sheet of red cellophane to the living room wall. "We pretended it was a fireplace," she recalled. "Bill and I used to read in front of it. It was a blessing on cold Illinois nights."

Billy tried to help his wife. "But when it came to being handy," he says, "I don't think I succeeded too well. Ruth claims I can't drive a nail in straight. As a result she has had to learn to cope with most of the fixing. That's a real stumbling block in many marriages—the husband feels he has to prove his masculinity by doing all the home repairs although he knows his wife is far better at them."

A familiar sight in Western Springs was the young clergyman trotting to work. "Nowadays," he says, "people would think I was doing it for exercise, but at that time, I'm afraid that everyone in town knew it was because I didn't have enough money to spend on gasoline."

His path always took him past a high railway embankment. One day as he was brushing a falling cinder out of his eye he got an idea for a church-connected men's club. When he told the deacons about it, they tried to discourage him. They said that it couldn't possibly be successful because there were too few members. Ruth, however, felt it was a very worthy project. "It needs expanding," she said. "Start large." Together, she and Billy sent letters to politicians, physicians and scientists who lived within a fifty-mile radius of the church. They were invited to address the new men's club—which did not yet exist. Several accepted, and the Western Suburban Professional Men's Club was created. Soon, more than a hundred local men were attending the meetings.

Before long the church was too crowded, and meetings were held in a nearby restaurant. "Billy Graham knew how to fill the place," said Larry MacEwen, one of the waiters. "You better believe it. He had a dramatic kind of entrance. Guests would look for him in the front, but he'd enter at the back, take off his coat while he was still in the aisle. Once, he accidentally knocked a pitcher of water I was carrying. It spilled right onto the head of a big, fat Rotarian. Billy treated it just like a baptism. He said, 'God bless you!' and embraced the man. Instead of being sore, the guy just grinned. He was the loudest cheerer after Billy made a speech about the sacredness of holy matrimony. No marriage can survive, he claimed, if the partners live in completely different worlds."

Billy often tells a story to illustrate this point of view:

One day a hardworking North Carolina farmer asked his equally industrious wife to help him seed the corn. She agreed.

However, he soon bawled her out for flinging out the kernels too carelessly.

"Woman!" he yelled. "Don't waste my corn that way!"

"Your corn?" she replied. "It belongs to both of us."

"No!" he thundered. "This is my territory!"

Several hours later, when they returned to their frame farmhouse, the wife asked sweetly, "Fred, did you wipe your feet before going into the kitchen?"

"No, I didn't," he said.

"Well, you better do it right away! For this is *my* territory."

The Grahams' frugal budget was clearly the territory of both Ruth and Billy. They watched over it carefully. To help widen their outlook and purse, Billy accepted out-of-town preaching assignments. One Sunday morning as the evangelist was about to deliver his sermon in the First Baptist Church of Elyria, Ohio, an usher came up to the pulpit with his collection plate. This was a practice that Graham was unaccustomed to, and in his confusion he dropped in a $20 bill, thinking it was a single. At the end of the service he was about to admit his error, make a joke about it and grab his twenty back, which he badly needed for rent. But he overheard the ushers discussing the wealthy young minister's generosity. Reluctantly, he kept his silence.

Ruth, who was ill, had remained at home. Later, as he told her about the incident, she noted that her husband was very abashed. "Without you," he said to her, "I don't know how to manage unexpected things."

She laughed and replied, "In the eyes of the Lord, you'll not get credit for twenty dollars. One dollar was all you planned to give!" She saw his expression turn from guilt to merriment.

Shortly after the $20 drop, their scrimped budget was helped by dinner invitations from members of the congregation. "They seemed to realize how badly we needed their kindness," Billy recalled. "I welcomed their hospitality. I have to admit I was slightly weary of the only cooking it seemed my bride knew how to prepare—Chinese! Chinese! All the time rice!"

4
EVEN
DEVOTED MATES
DISAGREE

LATE IN 1943, something special occurred in Billy's ministry: He was asked to take over a forty-five-minute Chicago evangelical radio program called "Songs in the Night." Dr. Torrey Johnson, a well-known midwestern Baptist pastor, had conducted the show, but had undertaken another church project and wanted Graham to become the new host. It required the signing of a thirteen-week contract and an outlay of several hundred dollars. Billy was assured that he could anticipate getting the money back through listeners' contributions.

His board of deacons thought the responsibility was much too great, but after a great deal of persuasion, they reluctantly agreed to let him give it a try. Ruth felt it was a splendid idea: "Bill accepted the challenge. There was lots of work involved, but its success let him reach multitudes outside the church. I knew that God had called him to minister to them and had given him the gift of communicating the Gospel to the unconverted."

She wrote the first script. Billy secured the services of George Beverly Shea, a popular baritone who has remained part of his evangelical team. The program, aired each Sunday evening, was an instant triumph. It continued to flourish long after Billy left it, the format the same. Listeners were still told that the show originated from "the friendly church in the pleasant community of Western Springs, Illinois."

"I've been a fan of it most of my adult life," said Reena Lowry, a native of Chicago. "I can still hear Bev Shea singing: 'And Can It Be That I Should Gain.' Billy called it one of his favorite hymns and said it represented his beliefs. He would urge listeners to make a decision for Christ. He'd do it in such a simple and compelling way that you immediately felt the Lord's presence. Billy often mentioned his wife on the air. One time, kidding, he said that she was a much better theologian than he was, even if she was a Presbyterian. He offered a reward to the person who could proselytize her for the Baptist church so that she could be baptized by immersion."

"Songs in the Night" was so successful that the young evangelist was invited to preach in Chicago's 3000-seat Orchestra Hall. The occasion was the initial meeting of a new group called Youth for Christ that had been founded by Dr. Torrey Johnson. Its purpose was to try to reach disillusioned young people who felt the future held no hope.

"That audience was the biggest I had ever seen," Billy

recalled. "I was gripped by the worst fit of stage fright of my life." Despite his fear, the sermon was well received. Johnson was so pleased that he asked Billy to make a series of addresses in Detroit, Philadelphia and Providence.

By now Billy had served a year as the Western Springs' pastor and had fulfilled the Army's requirements. He was accepted as a first lieutenant and told to await entry to the Harvard Divinity School for special training.

Returning from a Providence, Rhode Island, meeting of Youth for Christ, he seemed very flushed. A concerned Ruth took his temperature: 104 degrees. She summoned a doctor, who said that her husband had a severe case of mumps. "In a child it's usually not very serious," he told her. "But for a grown man it's far from a laughing matter."

For six weeks an extremely sick Graham was confined to bed. His fever fluctuated wildly and at one point Ruth feared that he was going to die. When he was permitted to walk around, he attempted to go back to work, but his voice was so weak that an anonymous listener of his radio program sent him $100 so he could "recuperate in sunny Florida."

Due to the ailment a very heavyhearted Billy was discharged from the Army. "How strange and mysterious are God's ways in our lives," he now says. "I felt miserable about being drummed out. It was Ruth who convinced me that I could reach many more servicemen and accomplish my ministry a great deal more effectively than if I went into the chaplaincy. But at the time I did a great deal of bitter disagreeing and wasn't the easiest husband in the world to live with."

"He wasn't," Ruth agreed. "But I have never expected or

wanted married life to be free of arguments. Just before I became a bride, a very wise woman told me that when couples have exactly the same thoughts on everything, one of them is unnecessary."

In the early days of their marriage, the Grahams held many opposite viewpoints. Some of the dissent was of a major nature, such as Billy's taking a church and departing from full-time evangelism. Others were insignificant, but also gave cause for pain and agitation. Ruth had to endure her husband's half of the closet always being in a mess and his constantly using the top of the bathroom door as a towel rack. They differed on what constituted desk-neatness and on Billy's fancy of wearing gaudy, hand-painted ties.

"Granted," he says, "most of them were small things. But, then, minor-appearing disagreements can cause some of the biggest arguments. Just think for a moment about the issues that you find disturbing.

"I had yet," he added, "to learn that young husbands and wives have a difficult time adjusting to their new life and to each other. I admit that occasionally I felt sorry for myself and wondered if habitual debating was what the future would hold. Fortunately, that feeling didn't last very long. However, judging from the mail I receive, for some couples it seems to go on for years and years."

Ruth has met wives who believe that a Christian marriage means submission in all things, regardless of the wife's better judgment. She has observed that in cases where this has been tried, both partners are badly hurt. "It makes the husband believe that wrong is right," she says. "He begins bragging how wise he is and starts feeling superior to his wife. She in turn becomes increasingly resentful. Although she may try not to show her displeasure, it becomes apparent in dozens of ways, from domestic lapses—burned stew, unmatched socks—to sexual coldness.

"However," Ruth adds, "it is a good thing to know when and how to disagree. It's possible to disagree without being disagreeable." She offers a few valuable suggestions adopted from her own experience:

1. Be sure you know what the issue is, then ask yourself if it's worth disagreeing about.
2. When arguing, carefully examine the tone of your voice—make sure it isn't too loud and you aren't talking out of turn, or interrupting.
3. Don't inject snide personal remarks.
4. Don't suddenly go off on a tangent and start introducing unrelated subjects.
5. Stick to the facts—don't embroider or exaggerate. If the facts won't carry you, you ought not to be arguing at all.
6. If you win or lose—do it graciously.
7. If you can't come to a friendly agreement—win, lose or compromise—lay it down for a while. Let it rest. Have faith that things will change, for they surely will. Postpone arguing if you're still sizzling with anger. Don't use tears to make your husband knuckle under.

Ruth remembers the first quarrel she had with Billy: "Just after we were married, he and some of his bachelor friends decided to drive to Chicago. I asked if I might go along to do some window-shopping. In those days that was all we could afford. 'No!' Bill snapped. 'This trip is for men only!' As I saw the car draw away I kneeled down in front of our living room couch and prayed, 'Lord, if you'll forgive me for marrying him, I promise I'll never do it again.'

"Later, when Bill returned, he apologized for being so thoughtless. I told him about my fatuous prayer. We chuckled as we held hands—a sense of humor sure helps those who disagree."

Billy felt it was far from a laughing matter when he told his wife about a job offer he had received to be a paid representative of Youth for Christ.

"I don't think I should accept it," he said. "The plan is to organize in every city—it would mean being away from you for weeks at a time."

"A wife has to know how her husband really feels," Ruth said. "I realized how strongly he felt about evangelism." She took his hand, and together they knelt and prayed for guidance. He gave up the Western Springs pastorate and took the Youth for Christ position.

Because Ruth was expecting their first child, it was decided that she would temporarily move in with her parents in Montreat. The interim arrangement became permanent. For three years the Graham home was in a Bell second-floor bedroom. Between crisscrossing the United States and Canada, Billy managed to spend brief moments with his wife and new daughter, Virginia, who was born on September 21, 1945, as he rushed home from Mobile, Alabama.

"Billy drove himself pitilessly," said Torrey Johnson, the Youth for Christ founder. "He always seemed to be in a hurry to serve the Lord. Yet he worried that he couldn't find more time to spend with his family. I remember several months after Virginia was born he appeared conscience-stricken as he showed me a photograph of her. 'Wouldn't it be ironic,' he said, 'if she desperately needs her father while he's out saving other children?' Then he put the picture away and returned to the case at hand: How best to attract youth to Christ? He sure had some bright ideas."

Magicians, ventriloquists and cheerleaders were used. In Minneapolis, Billy once borrowed one hundred pianos for a gala revival concert. He explained his florid methods: "We employed every modern means to catch the attention of the unconverted. And then we punched them right between the eyes with the Gospel."

Munroe Erbsen, who now drives a taxi in a Minneapolis suburb, was a fifteen-year-old dropout when he attended the rally. "I went because the advertisement of all those pianos sounded positively bananas. They sure made a lot of noise, but they were whispers compared to Graham. I had never seen him before and expected some little white pipsqueak. Here was this tall, good-looking guy—tough-looking, too, especially when he talked about Jesus.

"I was there with a couple of the fellows. I thought we'd be the only blacks, but there were a few others. That was surprising because I had heard 'Youth for Christ' was definitely anti-black. Some of them started to razz Graham. Me, too. But I soon stopped. He really got to me when he started speaking about racial tension. He said that one of the most urgent tasks of a Christian was to overcome personal prejudice and hate. He sounded like he really meant it. I found myself believing him when he told us that following Christ was the only answer. When it came time to march down the aisle and declare yourself for the Lord, I did.

"Billy took a good position on integration long before the Supreme Court decision. I was told that once in Dallas he went to a lily-white hotel elevator accompanied by a black friend. The operator refused to take the black man up and ordered him to use the rear stairs. This made Billy real mad and he yelled for the manager. 'Either he rides with me or we both use the rear stairs!' The manager was afraid of offending the famous preacher. He gave in quickly. Billy and his black friend rode up. I heard that Billy got a lot of cursing letters from the Ku Klux Klan because of his racial ideas. If you ask me, he's a very decent sort." (Names of many of the people Billy helped convert have been changed.)

The lavish compliments became somewhat subdued as twenty-eight-year-old Graham temporarily left the limelight to head three religious institutions in Minnesota called the Northwestern Schools. They consisted of an interdenominational Bible Training Institute, a seminary, and a college of liberal arts. At first Billy refused the switch to academia. Ruth strongly counseled against his making the move. However, eighty-six-year-old Dr. William Riley, the founder of Northwestern Schools, was persistent. A former evangelist himself, he had heard Billy preach and was convinced he would be the ideal successor.

"I was summoned to Dr. Riley's bedside during a heavy rainstorm," Billy recalled. "I'll never forget the darkness of his room, broken only by the flashing of lightning and a bony finger pointing at me. 'For years I've run this place,' Dr. Riley gasped. 'Now it's your turn. God has willed it so. I'm leaving it to you as Elijah gave his mantle to Elisha. As Saul appointed David, King of Israel. You'll be disobeying God if you refuse.' "

Billy continued to protest, but now admits feeling exhilarated by the idea of being hand-picked as heir to a minister whom William Jennings Bryan once called "The greatest Christian statesman in the American pulpit."

He told Dr. Riley that he would accept the presidency of the schools on an interim basis.

Ruth, who was expecting their second child, remained in Montreat. According to Dr. Bell, "At the time, my son-in-law seemed to be the busiest person in the world. Not only was he now responsible for an 850-member student body, but he was still the vice-president of Youth for Christ. He tried to get home as often as possible, but it wasn't easy. With an expanding family, he and Ruth secured a $4000 mortgage and bought a small house across the road from us."

Dr. Bell recalled that early in May of 1948 he phoned the evangelist to come immediately, for Ruth was in labor. "He managed to board a plane right after my call. He took a taxi from the airport and rushed to the hospital, carrying a bouquet of flowers. As he marked time in the waiting room, he fell asleep. I had to shake him awake to announce, 'You're the father of a baby girl. Your wife is doing fine.' "

It was about this time that Billy became solemnly bothered by doubt: "Not about the deity of Jesus Christ, not about the Gospel of His preaching, but concerning the authenticity, authority and inspiration of some of the Scriptures. I wondered if the Bible could be trusted completely. A close friend of mine had experienced a change of heart and mind toward the Scriptures. He was a successful minister of my age. We had many long discussions. He was forever pointing out contradictions. He was one miserable man. Now, so was I."

After a six-months struggle, Graham did something he advises for all 'doubting Thomases': "I had forgotten that when you have a serious problem, there is a wonderful, certain way to solve it. I fell on my knees and asked the Lord for guidance. I prayed a long time. I asked Him if I was wrong. If His Word was true.

"Suddenly I sensed the presence and the power of God as I had not felt Him for a long time. I was confirmed in my total faith and trust. Doubt left me. And I knew that I had passed an important crisis in my ministry."

5
MY CUP
RUNNETH OVER

AN OLD FRONTIER tale concerns Hector Baylor Jenkins, M.D., who practiced his healing art in the Texas panhandle during the late 1800s. Not only was Dr. Jenkins a very industrious physician, but he also served as the hardworking town marshal, mayor, school principal and undertaker. For miles around his grateful constituency exclaimed: "That Hector sure is dedicated!"

Mrs. Sadie Jenkins, Hector's uncomplaining wife of thirty years, agreed. "My cup runneth over," she said. Then added stoically, "And over and over."

"Occasionally," Ruth Graham recalled, "I felt exactly the same way. I suppose at times every wife does. Some complain of their husband's devotion to his job, or of being a golf widow. Husbands frequently gripe about the children and the housecleaning having first priority. In my marriage it was sharing Bill with his call to the Lord. From the outset I was committed to it, but his being a college president wasn't exactly the direction I'd had in mind."

Billy soon realized that his wife was right in urging him to spread the word of God. He found himself devoting fewer and fewer hours to the Northwestern Schools as he delegated academic responsibilities to assistants. Gradually he resumed the hectic life of the full-time evangelist.

"We could plainly see it happening," said Dr. O. E. Sandsen, dean of the liberal arts college. "It became pretty obvious that Billy Graham's heart and soul belonged to making people accept the Lord Jesus Christ. He frantically wanted to bring the Gospel to as many as possible."

In the 1948-49 season, Billy accepted crusade invitations to a half dozen small-and medium-sized cities. Repeatedly, he told audiences that marriage was sacred. "But you'd never know it from what you read in the newspapers!" he thundered. "When a Hollywood movie star weds for the third or fourth time, column after column glorifies the new union. You're made to think that a single marriage is old-fashioned and that modern living calls for a wide variety of mates. . . . What can you do? Right now you can turn to Jesus!"

Graham's first major crusade was in Los Angeles. He told Ruth he was worried about reaching so many people. She tried to convince him that he'd do just fine. Still, he expressed doubts. Her usual practice had been not to accompany him to out-of-town campaigns. They had agreed that her role was to stay at home and care for the children. This time, however, he seemed so disconsolate that she decided to join him.

"Her having faith in me helped tremendously," he said. "Over the years I've discovered how vital it is to have your marriage partner believe in you; not to keep saying, 'You're sure to fail!' Too often, a spouse down plays you so much that you begin thinking, 'That's what really caused my defeat!' The result is two estranged mates."

Spot radio announcements heralded the sensational young evangelist and his dazzling array of Gospel talent. Billboards showed a clergyman spreading butter on a slice of bread. The caption read: IT'S A SIN TO SPREAD IT SO THIN. COME TO THE BILLY GRAHAM RALLY AT THE LARGEST TENT IN THE WORLD! Posters advertising the TWENTY-TWO TREMENDOUS NIGHTS IN THE CANVAS CATHEDRAL were plastered throughout Los Angeles.

William Randolph Hearst heard about Billy's mission and issued strict orders to his editors: "Puff Graham!" They did, and dozens of stories glamorizing the "amazing young evangelist who is saving us from the devil" started appearing.

Billy says that he had never talked to or communicated with Hearst. "But I've always believed," he told reporters, "that if anybody wants to extol Jesus Christ, it would be sinful to object."

Henry Luce, founder of Time-Life, also impressed by Billy Graham, followed Hearst's lead. Both of Luce's magazines carried stories about the crusade. After being introduced to Billy by Bernard Baruch, he told the financier, "He is indeed the Pied Piper of revivalism. I predict that very soon his converts will sharply multiply. They'll number in the thousands."

The Los Angeles crusade had been scheduled to last a month. The sponsors were so pleased they decided to extend it. For eight weeks, the tall, handsome evangelist clipped a tiny microphone to his necktie and rapidly strode to the pulpit of the gigantic tent, which had been enlarged to accommodate 9000 people. Despite the additional seats, there was nearly always standing room only. He'd pause, stare straight ahead, open the top button of his shirt, raise his long arms and start preaching with a desperate urgency.

He never spared his audience from what he thought the truth to be. "Christianity isn't easy," he'd say as his fists clutched the air. They listened anxiously as he told them, "All of you, at one time or another, have violated the Ten Commandments. 'Slightly,' you say. But in the sight of God, there is no such thing as a slight sin." He'd suddenly close his eyes and bow his head; then he'd jerk up straight as he lashed out. " 'Thou shalt not murder,' we're told. You claim that surely doesn't apply to you. 'Why, I even go to church on Sunday!' you protest. Well, I have news. There are thousands of husbands and wives in this city—some sitting right here—who are killing their marriage partners by neglect. Yes, you are guilty of murder!"

A smaller tent—500 seats—was used for prayer and counseling sessions. It was staffed by volunteers and open twenty-four hours a day. Ruth Graham was one of the advisers who talked daily to prostitutes, pimps and alcoholics. One streetwalker remembers her as being an excellent listener. "For maybe twenty minutes or longer she just let me do all the talking. She seemed to sense how badly I wanted to spill my guts."

Jim Vaus was one of the 350,000 who visited Billy's tent. Vaus, the son of a Baptist minister, had tossed religion aside and drifted into crime. He had been jailed twice. Currently, he was in the employ of Mickey Cohen, who was known as the czar of the Los Angeles underworld. Vaus' speciality was wiretapping racetracks and bordellos.

"One day my wife, Alice, and I were just driving around," Vaus recalled. " 'Why don't we pay a call on this Graham fellow who's been getting all this publicity,' I said to her. 'It ought to be good for a lot of laughs.' "

They found seats near the back of the tent just as Billy boomed, "There's a man in this audience who has heard this story many times before, and who knows this is the decision he should make. . . . This may be his last opportunity!"

"It startled me," Vaus said. "I was convinced he had singled me out. I pretended not to hear. But a few minutes later he repeated, 'This may be your last opportunity—your moment of decision!' I couldn't keep still any longer. I shouted, 'I'll go! I'll go!' "

John Pollock, Billy Graham's official biographer, said, "Vaus was one of the more sensational converts. Much has been written about the gangster turning to God. However, Billy feels that the writers have overlooked one of the most moving and wonderful results of the transformation—the rebirth of the Vaus marriage. He says that it quickly turned from hopelessness to jubilation. One of the things that pleased Billy best about the Los Angeles crusade was that many divorced couples, or near divorced, came to hear him preach. There, right in the tent, they decided to reunite."

Another convert was a former American medal winner at the 1936 Berlin Olympics. Louis Zamperini was not only a champion long-distance runner, but had electrified spectators by pulling down a Nazi swastika flag. During World War II he survived forty-seven days on a liferaft and thirty months in a

Japanese prison camp. Back home, the authentic athlete-soldier hero was toasted by some of the country's leading citizens, including the President of the United States. He was given a ticker-tape parade. However, Zamperini's fame quickly vanished and he turned to alcohol.

"I hit rock bottom," he said. "I was lower than low. That's when I attended the Graham revival meetings in Los Angeles. I was pretty hostile at first, but I kept coming back. I will be forever thankful that I did. It changed my life. For the first time I felt peace in my heart."

6
"MAY THE LORD BLESS YOU REAL GOOD"

IN THE FALL of 1950, Billy was asked to lead a weekly radio revival service to be known as "The Billy Graham Hour." At first he rejected the suggestion, saying it would be too time consuming.

Ruth, who has always believed that true evangelism practiced on radio or television would attract many converts, liked the idea and offered to help. However, she felt the name might be considered in poor taste. Instead, she proposed calling it "Hour of Decision."

By now, Billy had learned the value of his wife's advice and agreed to try her suggestion for thirteen weeks. The program, with Ruth's title, made its debut several months later on fifty-two ABC outlets. He wound up the initial session with a signature that became his trademark: "May the Lord bless you real good."

Soon, 800 ABC stations, coast to coast, carried the show.

A Gallup poll revealed that it had become the most popular religious program ever to be aired. It was estimated that more than 15 million listeners heard it regularly. Billy's radio sermons often included his favorite Bible verses:

Luke 12:15
And he said unto them, Take heed, and beware of covetousness: for a man's life consisteth not in the abundance of the things which he possesseth.

"This verse indicates," Billy said, "that our lives are far more than materialism. That's why so many people in the affluent western world are disillusioned. Our obsession with materialistic things has brought about a great sense of emptiness and boredom. I often quote this passage and similar ones to myself so that I do not get absorbed with the materialism of our age. There are other deeper spiritual and moral things that are much more important to building character and preparing one for eternity."

I Corinthians 10:13
There hath no temptation taken you but such as is common to man: but God is faithful, who will not suffer you to be tempted above that ye are able; but will with the temptation also make a way to escape, that ye may be able to bear it.

"Often when I have faced trial and temptation, I have quoted this verse to myself. It has been a great encouragement and comfort to me. It indicates that when temptation comes, God always provides a way to escape. The Scriptures indicate that we are tempted daily, thus a verse like this memorized can provide great comfort and might to the Christian."

Philippians 4:13
I can do all things through Christ which strengthenth me.

"When the challenge is too great or I become bone weary in the midst of a long crusade or I become discouraged, I find solace in this passage. Concerning the great prophet Elijah, the Scripture says he was 'a man of like passions.' So am I. I need the encouragement of God's word daily."

Matthew 25:35-36
For I was an hungred, and ye gave me meat: I was thirsty, and ye gave me drink: I was a stranger, and ye took me in: Naked, and ye clothed me: I was sick, and ye visited me: I was in prison, and ye came unto me.

"This verse makes me remember that I have a responsibility to the poor and friendless. Nothing expresses that responsibility better than this passage."

John 3:16
For God so loved the world, that He gave His only begotten Son, that whosoever believeth in Him should not perish, but have everlasting life.

"These twenty-five words actually compose the entire Gospel. John 3:16 is a Bible in miniature. It is the very essence and heart of what I believe and preach."

Proverbs 3:11
My son, despise not the chastening of the Lord; neither be weary of his correction.

"It has been my experience that when I get off track, God has a way of spanking me and putting me back on the straight and narrow. He has had to chastise me many times in my life. His discipline has hurt, but it has been good for me. I know He has always done it from a heart of love."

Proverbs 3:5
Trust in the Lord with all thine heart; and lean not unto thine own understanding.

"I suppose over the years I have quoted this passage several thousand times. And each time I feel it intensifies in rightness."

Proverbs 3:6
In all thy ways acknowledge Him, and He shall direct thy paths.

"My mother gave me this verse as a Christmas present when I was nine years old. She insisted that I memorize these words so they could live in my mind forever. That verse has been a staff and strength in my life. What little I may be, I am because of them."

In addition to conducting the radio program, Billy began writing a widely read newspaper column called "My Answer," which was syndicated in seventy-five newspapers. Many of those surveyed in the Gallup poll reported they read it daily and had also purchased the evangelist's book, *Peace with God,* which appeared on best-seller lists, sold more than a million English copies and several million more in foreign translation.

"I wrote it because of my conviction that a book was badly needed that would present the Gospel in utter simplicity," Graham explained.

Myrna and Bradley Henderson, II, are two of his most enthusiastic advocates, won by that plain matter-of-factness. "We belie the notion that all Billy Graham converts are hard-hats or go around in undershirts," Bradley Henderson said. "I was a Rhodes Scholar and have a doctorate in jurisprudence," he adds proudly. "Myrna majored in sociology and anthropology. We met at a chamber music get-together. I play the violin. She, the cello. We both like French wine, bird watching and Quiche Lorraine. We even rang doorbells for Adlai Stevenson when he ran for President. So I don't think we can be dismissed as a pair of Bible Belt followers.

"It was at a chamber music rehearsal at Jeff Miller's house that Billy Graham's name was first brought up. Midway through Bach's Sinfonia Number 3 in D, I tossed my bow down and started yelling at Myrna. 'Can't you read music? It's supposed to be cheerful. You're playing it like a dirge. You're at least five beats behind! Cooperate, you nincompoop!'

" 'You're the nincompoop!' she yelled back. 'You're sick! Sick! Sick!' Then she stamped out, not even bothering to take her cello.

"We were always fighting—not just about music. It seemed that the squabbling went on from the moment we opened our eyes until we wearily dropped off to sleep. Even that wasn't immune from fighting. Sometimes Myrna would wake me to bitterly complain that I had opened the windows too wide or that I had failed to turn up the electric blanket.

"It seemed that we disagreed about everything. About our sex life. About the meals. About the proper way of raising children—we have twin daughters who are now in their early twenties. Darn little was exempt.

"I was at the end of my rope as where to turn or what to do. We had tried marriage counselors, encounter groups, transcendental meditation. We even contemplated mate swapping. We talked about divorce and had separated half a dozen times. We always came back because of the children. I had become resigned to a lifetime of fighting. I was convinced that it would only end when one of us was carried out in a mahogany casket.

"It was right after the Bach fiasco that Jeff Miller gave me a paperback copy of *Billy Graham Answers Your Questions*. The book contained some of the replies the evangelist made in his newspaper column. 'This guy has very sound judgment,' Jeff said. 'It might help.'

"Jeff is a senior partner in the law firm I work for. He's very astute and clients pay heavily for his advice. He works very hard. I always felt that he was the most coolheaded of men. He could see how skeptical I was.

" 'Don't let the fact that he's a celebrity fool you,' Jeff said. 'Read the book! Try to pretend that it's research for a lawsuit you're appealing.' To be polite, I put Graham's book in my briefcase.

"When I got home, Myrna was showing the girls how to

75

make fudge. I was given the silent treatment. I didn't much care. Actually, I welcomed it, as it would give me a chance to study some papers I brought home from the office. As I unzipped my case, I noticed the book Jeff had given me. Because I respected him, I thumbed through it.

"I suppose it would make a sensational story if I claimed that I saw the light instantly. And from that moment on my marriage became super-dandy. Well, it didn't happen that way. I'll plead guilty that I found some of the answers provocative, but as a practicing attorney I was prepared to offer a rebuttal. I put the book away. The next morning the Henderson eternal state of war resumed.

"When I got to the office on Monday, I ran into Jeff Miller. He didn't ask me if I had liked the book. That's not his way. I felt that he was waiting for me to offer the first word. He kept looking at me quizzically the rest of the week. I was glad when Friday arrived.

"The next morning Myrna took the girls to the orthodontist. I puttered around in the garden and in my den. The book was on the desk. I picked it up. This time I read it from cover to cover.

"I'm not superstitious, but something happened while I was holding the book. For no reason at all, it suddenly fell to the carpet, landing faceup to this passage:

Q: I expected my marriage to be beautiful and sublime, but it has turned out to be the reverse. . . . Do you think Christ could help me?

A. A family home is intended to be a haven of rest in a world of unrest. And with Christ in the home it can be a refuge from life's storms. Members of a household may be selfish. Our likes

76

and dislikes are not always the same. Tensions are set up and discord follows. Christ has the power to bring peace for He strikes at the center of selfishness. He makes us considerate of others. In His presence, home becomes a place where sharing is an ethic and peace a reality. This is not to say that there is never any discord in a Christian home. But that discord is shortlived and the goal is harmony instead of self-fulfillment.

"I suppose I was 'born again' before it became fashionable," Henderson continued. "Nothing grandiose in its occurrence. An Episcopal clergyman simply welcomed me back. I didn't try to proselytize Myrna. But at times she acted as if she was impressed by what getting religion had done for me. I had learned a very valuable lesson—it takes two to engage in an argument. I stopped rising to her bait. Finally she got tired of provoking me. But it did take almost two years before she was ready to step forward."

Myrna Henderson is the direct opposite of her husband. Whereas he is fragile-looking, she is quite robust. "Her 135 pounds are well distributed," Bradley Henderson said. "Occasionally, our fighting reached the beating-up stage. I must admit she was always the victor."

"It became so obvious," Myrna said, "that some of our friends began calling me 'Myrna, the Goddess of Mars.' At the time I sort of liked the title. However, I do prefer the present one: 'Myrna, the Muse of Mercy.'"

"There's a saying about children being impressionable. It's so true. The twins were the first to notice what religion was doing for their father. They asked if they might go along with him to church. I don't mind admitting that I was plenty peeved. Brad and I always had a definite understanding about the children and religion. We agreed that we would never try to influence them.

"In no uncertain words I reminded him of that commitment. I suppose I stormed and ranted. In his new reasonable way, he calmly told me that it was their own decision. Despite my resentment, I soon realized that he was right—it was solely their own will.

"It probably sounds like a hodgepodge of banality, but I credit our daughters with being the ones that led me to God. I've always described myself as being extremely close to them. The very thought of being an outsider was more than I could stand. Some of my friends felt that I had suddenly become deranged. They'd tell me, 'It was bad enough when Brad did it, but you? We always credited you for having more sense. Can't you see that this Billy Graham character is nothing more than a modern Billy Sunday? That his soft and easy path to heaven is just a camouflaged sawdust trail?'

"They went on and on like that, saving their knockout blow for the very last. 'Wise up, kid,' they'd say. 'Life isn't the simple and sentimental relationship between man and God he speaks of. It isn't that easy! To live in this world you've got to be practical.'

"Dr. Graham's simplicity is what Brad and I admire most. We don't think it's that complicated to realize that we all need someone to cling to. Someone to make life worthwhile. Dr. Graham told us what that someone was. Oh, I know his Ph.D. is honorary. So what? If he had sufficient time I'll wager he could earn a dozen academic titles. I was delighted to learn that he has a degree in anthropology. That was one of my majors in college and I know how valuable the subject is in today's world. I believe that my professors would agree with many of the answers he gave in his book:"

Q: Can having faith in God save our home and turn it into a happy place to dwell?

A: Yes! A home is like a solar system. The thing which holds the solar system together is the fact that a great sun is its center. If it were not for the sun, our solar system would fly to pieces. Well, unless the Son of the living God, the Lord Jesus Christ, is put at the center of your home, it too will fly to pieces.

7
MISSION: TO SAVE
MERRY OLDE ENGLAND

GRAHAM'S FIRST INTERNATIONAL triumph, the spectacularly
successful Greater London Crusade, came in 1954. It was
sponsored by clergymen from more than a thousand local
Protestant churches. They were concerned about diminishing
congregations in the post-World War II period, and turned to
Billy hopefully.

Despite their confidence in the American evangelist, overwhelming defeat was threatened in the outset. As soon as his
ship, the *United States*, docked at Southhampton, he received
a rigorous roasting from the English fourth estate. Ruth, who
had decided to accompany him to offer support, wasn't
spared. Just before the first press conference began, he asked
her to remove her lipstick. It didn't help.

One of the early questions was directed to her. "Is it true
that your husband carries around his own special bottle of
baptism water?" a reporter asked. As she thought of the

appropriate negative reply, another journalist snapped, "Who invited you over here, anyway?"

That evening, London newspapers carried dozens of anti-Graham stories. Typical was the one which appeared in a Fleet Street tabloid: "In America, John the Baptist's name has been changed to Billy. Armed with Bible-sixgun and sombrero-halo he buckles down to his self-appointed mission: snatching sinners from the jaws of hell. Now, he comes to our shores to save Merry Olde England. And Billy Boy claims he's the bloke to do it!"

The People, a weekend gazette with a huge circulation, also lambasted "Silly Billy." Their chief reporter wrote: "Must we be turned better citizens and kinder husbands by the antics of Billy's American hot Gospel circus?" Even the sedate and venerable *Times* speculated, "Is the American revivalist overextending himself?"

Graham had started assembling a team of topflight evangelists to help him spread the Gospel. They urged him to refute all the negative stories. He was unwilling. "I'm not going to answer mudslinging with mudslinging."

The team had rented Haringey Arena, a cavernous hall that was used for boxing matches and greyhound racing. Colorful placards heralding the three-month-long crusade were plastered all over town. United States Senators Stuart Symington and Styles Bridges, who were visiting England at the time, issued press statements stating they would be present at the opening session.

Late in the afternoon, Symington phoned to extend his apologies: "I'm afraid that Styles and I can't make it. An important meeting has just come up." Billy told Ruth it was obvious that the Senators were bowing out because of all the adverse criticism.

As the evangelist and his wife were preparing to leave for the nearby arena, an aide called to tell them it was only a fifth full and that newspaper photographers were snapping pictures of all the empty seats.

"If a devoted mate was ever necessary," Billy recalled, "this was the time. I was a sorry case of nerves. I kept thinking how miserably I had failed. Ruth gave me the sense of confidence I so badly needed. She reminded me that people all over the world were praying for us. That whatever the circumstance of the evening, God would be glorified. I believe that more husbands and wives fail through discouragement than for any other reason."

The Grahams made the short drive to Haringey, which because of heavy traffic took almost half an hour. Holding hands, they entered the lobby—it was deserted. Suddenly a member of the Team rushed up. "It's a miracle!" he shouted excitedly. "Inside, the arena is jammed. Every seat is taken and thousands are standing in the street on the other side of the building!"

He escorted them to a small office. Both Senators were there. As Bridges kissed Ruth's cheek, Symington said, "We're supposed to be having dinner with Anthony Eden, the foreign minister, but we decided we couldn't let you down."

"It turned out to be one of the most glorious nights of my life," Billy said. As he delivered his message, "Does God Matter?", one of the women in the audience shouted, "Billy, you reminded us that He does! God bless you!"

When Billy wound up his sermon, 178 men and women of

all ages marched down the aisles to make their decision. One of them, Charles Parker, a chemist who worked in a Piccadilly pharmacy, told the London *Daily Mirror,* "I suppose you'd call my marriage an acceptable one. Meredith and I rarely clashed—we certainly didn't lead a dog-and-cat existence. Oh, I'm not going to pretend that we had a wildly amorous relationship. We were too self-centered for that. You might say that we suffered from 'waxy tongues of vanity.'

"It was Graham who made me recognize that I was the possessor of a bad case of selfishness. And that selfishness was one of the greatest problems a marriage had to endure. He claimed that when you accepted Christ, the selfishness disappeared, as you now were able to submit your ego to Him. And that's exactly how it happened to me."

Since the crusade meetings were usually held at night, Billy often spoke at schools and hospitals during the daytime. He had been invited to address the students at the London School of Economics. As he was being introduced, one of the professors stood up and in a booming voice bellowed, "This is the first time a clergyman has been allowed to accost us! I object strenuously! I was under the impression that this was a secular school!" The students roared their approval.

Billy smiled and started his talk. Suddenly there was a piercing sound of broken glass. A blond youth in his early twenties had crashed through a window onto the balcony. There, in full view of the other students, he started scratching himself ape fashion. Everyone laughed, including Graham. "That young man reminds me of my ancestors," Billy quipped. The students whistled and applauded. That was when he added, "Of course, all my ancestors came from

Britain." They cheered even louder. After that, everyone listened attentively. Later Billy said, "I don't think I made many converts. But then, who knows? God does move mysteriously!"

Later, he spoke to a large group of upperclassmen at Cambridge University's School of Divinity. It was obvious their orientation was far more liberal than his, and they had come to heckle. As is his custom, Billy prefaced his remarks with "The Bible tells us . . ." One student was so indignant that he shouted, "Really—you can't expect us to swallow that nonsense! Assuredly, even you are aware that man has progressed far beyond."

He was silenced, but it was very apparent that many of the others shared the accuser's viewpoint when they yelled, "Hear! Hear!"

Billy remained composed. There were a few more interruptions—several students rattled their chairs and issued some bland catcalls. However, most of them decided to listen quietly. Near the end of his talk, the American evangelist said, "I assume we are all Christians. And as Christians we love one another. A minister is not a minister unless he is winning people to Christ. If theological students don't think they can do that, they should quit studying for the ministry."

When he finished, they applauded and cheered for five minutes. This time their "Hear! Hear!" was intended for him.

By the end of the crusade's first week, newspapers reported that people were fighting for tickets. Police estimated that it was not unusual to have crowds of 25,000 or more standing outside the arena. Billy was flattered when he was invited to take tea at Lambeth Palace with the Archbishop of

Canterbury: "I was so jittery that Ruth had to pull me up short. In her practical way she said, 'Any man who has six sons, even if he's an archbishop, has to be an ordinary man.'

"He was far from ordinary," Billy said. "But upon meeting him, he instantly made me feel at ease."

Ruth spent most of her days in London assisting her husband and counseling converts. Those who discovered that she was Mrs. Billy Graham wanted to know the secret of her happy marriage. Repeatedly, she told them, "Bill and I live for each other, and together for God."

On one occasion her participation was not ecclesiastical. It happened near the Hyde Park corner. Ruth was on her way back to the hotel when it started to rain. She hadn't taken her umbrella, so she ran for shelter. Suddenly, a young man appeared at her side.

"You look like somebody badly in need of help," he said. "Why don't we wait out the rain over a cup of tea?"

"No, thank you," she replied. "I'm on my way back to my hotel."

"You must be an American. Even they can take time out for tea. It's jolly good."

"I simply have to get back. But thanks anyway."

"Well, how about tomorrow night?"

"That would be impossible. I have to be at Haringey for the revival meeting."

"Then the next night?"

"Thank you, but it's off to Haringey again."

"I'm afraid to ask, but I suppose it's Haringey the night after?"

"Yes."

"You wouldn't be connected with Billy Graham, would you?"

"His wife," she replied, laughing. "But I do hope you'll come."

"I . . . might," he grunted as he made a rapid departure.

When Billy learned about the attempted pickup, he was elated that he was married to such an attractive woman. "Ruth gets prettier and prettier with each passing year. I keep telling her that. Everybody loves to get compliments."

One of the born-again Christians whom Ruth counseled was British actress Joan Windmill. "The first thought that came into my mind when I saw her," the stage and screen star said, "was how much sooner people like me would have come to Christ if we had met a few attractive Christians like her . . . and at the time I hadn't known that she was Billy Graham's wife.

"She told me that her Bible is always handy. That when she gets a free moment she turns to it. She said that recently she had been faced with a problem and turned to Psalm 37, which says, 'Trust the Lord.' With great sincerity she explained that, 'I believe I live in that Psalm. We must trust Him. We have to know He loves us and has a wonderful plan for our lives if we give Him a chance. Yes, we must trust in the Lord.'"

More than 2 million people attended the English sessions. Declarations for Christ poured forward from the humble and the mighty. Among the prominent were the First Sea Lord; Sir John Hunt, leader of the expedition that conquered Mt. Everest; and the Admiral of the British Fleet.

One convert who was famous for an entirely different reason was a much-jailed pickpocket. After listening to the American evangelist, he mumbled to the man sitting next to him. "Now I'll have to return your wallet to you; I slipped it out of your jacket pocket a few minutes ago."

Although his conversion didn't last very long—he was shortly apprehended again—Billy claimed that others did. Many asked, "Aren't you afraid that a decision made in a few minutes won't last?"

He had a ready answer: "When I met my wife, I decided in minutes that I wanted to marry her. It was the same way when at sixteen years of age I attended a revival service like this. I walked forward and made a decision. I made a calm, quiet resolve in my heart to live for Him from that moment on. I have lasted. I personally know hundreds of married couples, factory workers, business executives and professional people who have lasted.

"We're not strong enough to hold on to Christ—He holds on to us. There is a doctor back in the States who was on the alcoholic skids until several years ago. His practice was gone and his family had about given up hope for him when he was converted in a campaign. After the decision he did an about-face. His practice is now booming and he has a happy Christian home.

"An acquaintance cornered the doctor recently and said, 'Now tell me the truth, Doc. If you were all alone where there was no possibility of anyone ever finding out, wouldn't you take another drink? Let's be honest with each other.' The doctor thought for a minute before replying. 'Yes, if I were all alone I think I would take another drink.' After a short pause he added, 'But I'm never alone. Christ is always with me.' "

Ruth also had a reply to these skeptics. Indignantly, she said, "People don't crowd around a nursery window and whisper as they gaze at the newborn babies, 'But will they live?' They know that doctors and nurses and mothers and fathers will be trying to make sure they do live.

"Often the reason that some of the 'baby' Christians don't last is that nobody helps them. They are terribly in need of somebody who will teach them how to use stumbling blocks for stepping-stones, somebody who will pick them up and dust them off when they fall. There is a poignant voice in Ecclesiastes 4:10 . . . 'Woe to him that is alone when he falleth.'

"Yes," she continued, "there are those who do not last—as surveys have revealed. But no survey can ever show how the zeal of one Christ-dedicated life touches another and another and goes on and on!"

After the new disciples march down the aisles, churches of their choice are notified. If the minister dallies too long—the Team checks—the name is sent to another church. During the greater London crusade, the Archbishop of Canterbury was making his rounds. In one Church of England he visited, the minister told him that he had received the names of two would-be members from the American Evangelical Team.

"You had better call on those people right off," the Archbishop cautioned. "If you don't, Billy Graham will send their names to a Baptist church."

Now that Billy was an international celebrity, his presence

was eagerly sought. The House of Commons gave a luncheon in his honor. Queen Elizabeth and Prince Philip requested that the Grahams dine at Windsor Castle.

Ruth relished telling an anecdote about the royal meeting: "Bill was so excited that upon entering the palace he heartily shook the hand of the liveried man who opened the door. It was the butler."

A short while later he committed the same *faux pas*. This time he and Ruth were guests of the Duke and Duchess of Hamilton, the Queen's representatives to the Church of Scotland. The evangelist rented formal clothes for the occasion. After being introduced to the other guests, he found himself facing a very distinguished-looking gentleman. Bowing low, Billy said, 'How do you do, your grace? I don't believe we've met.' "

The startled man stepped back. "I am your waiter, sir," he muttered haughtily.

Graham admitted that he was very embarrassed, but later when he told friends about the incident he asked, "After all, wasn't he also created in God's image?"

Near the conclusion of the crusade, Billy, who had been trying to arrange a meeting with Winston Churchill, was summoned to No. 10 Downing Street. They shook hands. Then the aging Prime Minister, holding an unlit cigar, stared silently at his visitor. Suddenly he pointed to three newspapers lying on a table. "Look at them," he said sadly. "They carry headlines about murder, robbery and rape. I'm an old man without any hope for the world. What hope do you have for the future?"

"Mr. Prime Minister, I'm filled with hope," Graham replied

as he withdrew a small Bible from his jacket pocket. "Life can be exciting. This book tells of God's plan for the future—and it's wonderful!"

Again, Churchill was silent. Then he mumbled, "Yes, what you say may be our only hope."

The next time they met, Churchill wasn't so pessimistic. "Billy," he said, "the people certainly believe in you. I don't think Marilyn Monroe or any other Hollywood celebrity, performing in London free-of-charge, could draw bigger crowds than you did!"

Billy was asked to conduct rallies at Hyde Park and Trafalgar Square. The throngs were so overwhelming that on the last day of the crusade it was decided to hold rallies at two mammoth stadiums: Wembley, London's largest outdoor arena (capacity 120,000) and White City (70,000) were selected. They are several miles apart, and Billy managed to shuttle back and forth through tremendous mobs. Ticket demands were so great that large numbers of people camped all night.

The Lord Mayor and members of Parliament were present at Wembley, and the Archbishop of Canterbury gave the benediction. When Graham started to preach, there was a sudden stillness. "You couldn't hear any other sound—no one coughed—no one moved," reported the *News of the World*, a Sunday newspaper that claimed the largest circulation in the western world. "There was no emotional hysteria, no tension . . . only a very deep reverence. Within minutes of his windup, thousands of men and women and teenagers were moving to the track. They were of all ages, of all classes of society. Husbands and wives were hand in hand with their children."

The Archbishop was so touched that he said, "We'll never see such a sight again until we get to heaven." Grady Wilson, one of Billy's chief associates, put his arm around the prelate and hugged him. "Brother Archbishop, you're so right!" he said joyfully.

Most of the English newspapers sharply altered their opinions of the American evangelist before he left their country. William Connor (who signed himself "Cassandra"), a popular columnist for the London *Daily Mirror,* had been among the most vitriolic journalists. He often referred to Billy as the "the dollar-loving blighter from North Carolina."

As the crusade drew to a close, Graham agreed to dine with him in The Baptist's Head, a well-known London pub. After the meeting, Connor wrote: "He came into The Baptist's Head absolutely at home—a teetotaler and abstainer able to make himself completely at ease in the spit and sawdust department, a most difficult thing to do. . . .

"Billy Graham looks ill. He has lost fourteen pounds in this nonstop merciless campaign. But this fact he can carry back to North Carolina with him. It is that in this country, battered and squeezed as no victorious nation has ever been before and disillusioned almost beyond belief, he has been welcomed with an exuberance that almost makes us blush behind our precious Anglo-Saxon reserve.

"I never thought that friendliness had such a sharp cutting edge. I never thought that simplicity could cudgel us sinners so damned hard. We live and learn."

8
THEN, NEW YORK CITY

FOR YEARS, BILLY'S burning desire was to carry the Gospel to New York City, which he felt to be sorely in need of spiritual revival. Finally, in 1957, his wish was granted. The Protestant Council of the City of New York, representing 1700 churches of thirty different denominations, asked him to come.

"I go in fear and trembling," he told Ruth. "I'm prepared to be crucified by my critics, but I feel I must go."

Dr. Reinhold Niebuhr, the respected liberal theologian, claimed that Billy would invade New York promising a "new life" to his converts, "not through painful religious experiences but merely by signing a decision card."

However, Graham's most hostile belittlers were extreme fundamentalists like Dr. Bob Jones, Sr. (the same man who years earlier had told Billy that he'd be a misfit anywhere), who attacked Billy for "inviting modernists to kidnap him."

Jones was reported to have posted a notice in his school warning students not to hold prayer meetings that "beseeched God to render Billy's New York Crusade a success."

Graham said, "As Ruth had done so many times before, she gave me the strength I needed. She instilled so much confidence in me that when I was handed the anticipated seven-figure budget I wasn't a bit worried. I thought, 'If a big corporation can spend millions of dollars on a campaign to sell a bar of soap, why can't far less than that be spent to tell the message of God's promise of salvation?' "

He formed an executive committee of prominent New Yorkers to help supervise the crusade. Among those selected were Dr. Norman Vincent Peale, the internationally known Protestant minister; Captain Eddie Rickenbacker, World War I flying ace; Ogden Reid, editor of the New York *Herald Tribune;* and Roger Hull, president of Mutual Life of New York. They leased Manhattan's largest indoor arena, Madison Square Garden, for sixteen weeks. When Billy heard about it, some of his doubts returned. Ruth reminded him, "With God, all things are possible."

The Grahams accepted an offer to be the guests of a leading hotel. Norman "Red" Pearson, the bellman who escorted them to their room, recalled, "I showed them in first, then went outside to get their luggage. When I got back, what do I find? The two of them bending down to pray. I can spot phonies right off—those two weren't!

"They didn't even seem bashful that I caught them. Instead, Billy tells me, 'Praying makes me feel good all over. Does it do the same to you?' I answered, 'I'm afraid it's not for me—I lean to winning on the ponies.' He and his wife laughed. She said something about God giving out with sure winners.

"Just about that time it hit me who I'm talking to. But there weren't any airs about them. Billy handed me two tickets for his opening night. 'Bring your wife,' he said.

"I did. All through Billy's sermon I kept nudging her. 'Imagine, he talked directly to me!' It was the same with the gas station I deal with. They gave out free bumper stickers that advertised the crusade. As I took one, I said, 'Yeah, I know Graham personally. He's a good friend of mine.' "

That quality formed the lead paragraph of a story that appeared in the New York *Journal American:* "Billy Graham, the Southern evangelist, has learned a most profound secret: You feel his piercing eyes riveted on you and his heart with you. . . . Instantly you become his friend."

Dorothy Kilgallen, a columnist for the newspaper, prepared an affectionate five-part biography. In one of the installments she referred to Billy and his wife as a "dazzling advertisement for the state of matrimony." Kilgallen said that when she next saw Ruth, she was told, "Bill and I aren't so unique. Every marriage that admits God can become a dazzling advertisement for matrimony."

Ruth also spoke about Kilgallen's reference to Billy's constant jumping to his feet every time a woman entered the room. The reporter, who had visited the Graham's home in Montreat, counted twelve separate occasions in a single hour. "You've made poor Bill so self-conscious," Ruth said, "that to be on the safe side he now stands all the time. To give him some much-needed rest I purposely keep out of his way."

The *Herald Tribune,* which had recently started using

pictures of pretty girls on their front page, decided that Billy's visit was an excellent opportunity to run a large photograph of his attractive wife. A reader wrote, "At long last I have a pinup that I think the Lord approves of."

Another newspaper, the comprehensive *New York Times*, faced a special problem—how to address the evangelist properly. They disliked using diminutives, but felt his formal name: William Franklin Graham, might cause some confusion. After several meetings, the editors settled for "the Rev. Dr. Billy Graham." They also decided to publish the entire forty-five-minute text of his first sermon. This was not an easy task, as Billy was speaking ad-lib. He took his text from Isaiah: "Ah sinful nation, a people laden with iniquity. . . . Your country is desolate, your cities are burned with fire: your land, strangers devour it in your presence. . . . If ye be willing and obedient, ye shall eat the good of the land. . . ."

Then he told the hushed crowd, "We have not come to put on a show or an entertainment. We believe that there are many people here tonight that have hungry hearts—all your life you've been searching for peace and joy, happiness, forgiveness. I want to tell you, before you leave Madison Square Garden this night, you can find everything that you have been searching for, in Christ. . . ."

When Ruth read the sermon in the next day's newspaper, she remarked, "Seeing this in print makes me sad I'm a Christian."

A shocked Billy asked, "Why?"

"It would be so wonderful to make a decision after hearing you," she replied.

"I'm merely God's messenger," he reminded her humbly.

"Bill's humility is truly heartfelt," Ruth said. "Here he was a celebrity in his own right. Yet, he was so thrilled when Ethel Waters, the Negro blues singer, started attending the crusade sessions, and referring to him as, 'my child.' One night he asked me in complete sincerity, 'Do you think Miss Waters would regard me as being too pushy if I asked her for an autographed picture?'"

Midway through his appearance at Madison Square Garden, a reporter from *Look* magazine wanted to write a story about him from the angle of the handsome Hollywood type who became the world's leading evangelist. "Billy promptly refused," recalled an aide. "He told me that he certainly wasn't a handsome Hollywood type."

Sonja Henie, the Norwegian ice skater who later became a leading actress, attended the New York crusade. "Billy could easily have become a famous star," she said. "He is good-looking enough. And it is clear that he has much talent. I once asked him why he hadn't gone to Hollywood and made himself a fortune. 'With your reputation,' I said, 'you could easily demand big, serious roles.'

" 'But I do play a big role,' he answered. 'And one of the most serious ones in the world.' "

The *Herald Tribune* called his preaching "A rich mixture of solemnity and humorous anecdote." One night Billy told his audience about "some Texans who decided to play a practical joke on a fellow Texan. We've been hearing a great deal about how everything in that part of the country is on a grand scale. Well, recently some mighty rich Texas oil men dropped a pack of sedatives in the coffee of a fellow Texan. The victim passed out immediately. They carried him to a newly dug grave and left him there in a fancy, custom-made coffin. The next morning when the hungover man awakened he felt the satin in the casket and wondered where he was. He stood up to find out. That's when he saw all the tombstones. And all of a sudden he exclaimed, 'Hallelujah! It's Resurrection Morning and a Texan is the first up!' "

Quickly, Graham raised a forefinger and asked, "Where will you be on Resurrection Morning? It's coming! Will you be an unredeemed sinner condemned to hell? I want you to listen tonight not only with your ears, but the Bible teaches that your heart also has ears. Listen with your soul tonight. Forget me as the speaker, listen only to the message that God would have you to retain from what is to be said tonight.

"Few people really want to do wrong. But they do it. Few people want to be sinners. But they are. What is wrong? The Bible calls it sin. I know we don't like to admit it. We would like to give it some other terminology; that would be easier on our egos. But during this crusade I am going to use Biblical terminology. I do not intend to beat around the bush and skirt the basic issues of life and death!"

He didn't.

Billy has always had the ability to use simple but firm language. When he is commended for it, he often tells listeners about Dr. Karl Barth: "Some years ago the outstanding Swiss theologian—perhaps the greatest of his generation—was lecturing in the United States. He was asked by a young divinity student what was the supreme single thought that ever crossed his mind. Dr. Barth bowed his head and puffed on his pipe. He didn't speak for several minutes—it was very apparent that he was giving the question a great deal of thought. Then he slowly lifted his shaggy head. The audience were on the edge of their seats prepared for some tremendous statement. 'The greatest ever,' he told them, was: *Jesus loves me, that I know, for the Bible tells me so'.*

"Now that's profound," Billy adds. "But it is also very simple. I think this was the secret of the teachings of Jesus. He talked to people who were illiterate, but they understood him. He used little stories—everyday happenings to illustrate great spiritual truths. He made it so simple that all the people could understand him. I think this is the kind of preaching and teaching we need today in the field of religion."

"Billy follows that example," said Dr. Koji Honda, a leading Japanese evangelist. "Even children understand what he's saying and are not bored by him."

Donna Wannamaker, of White Plains, New York, was thirteen years old when she attended the Garden meeting. "I came with my sitter," she said. "My parents are divorced and my mother hired Mrs. Reiss to take care of me while she worked or went out on a date. I lived most of the time with my mother. Every other weekend and the Christmas and Thanksgiving holidays I spent with my father. I did a lot of shuffling around. But it wasn't so bad. In fact, at the time I thought it a pretty neat arrangement. I remember that I shamefully played one parent against the other. It worked. I'd tell my father about the big doll my mother just gave me and he'd buy me an even bigger one. Or I'd say to my mother, 'Daddy is so nice. He lets me stay up until 10 o'clock!' She'd try to outdo him and wouldn't put me to bed until 10:15. But despite all of that

I felt that something important was lacking. Don't for a minute think that young children aren't aware of that.

"Billy Graham had such an effect on me. It's not fair to dismiss it as some childish notion. It was far removed from that. At the end of the evening, he said, 'Your whole life can be completely changed if you come to Christ! Come now!'

"I did. There were temporary moments when I retreated back to the way I was. But it was only temporary. For the most part, I think I've remained a good Christian."

Other than a few minor incidents, the New York crusade was declared a huge success.

One occurred when a retired mathematics teacher shouted, "Dr. Graham, even my students would realize your counting is faulty! You said, 'Christ came on this earth 2000 years ago.' That's wrong. It was 1957 years ago!"

Billy chuckled at the interference. "Whatever the exact year was, we should be forever thankful that He made His appearance." Then he resumed his sermon. "If church people would start living as Christ taught, we would have a spiritual revival that would move the whole world. We have the power to do it!"

When the evangelist finished speaking, he was besieged by autograph hunters. After signing a great many books, an aide called a halt and whisked him out through a side door.

"I worry about that," Billy said. "Did I hurt someone's feelings? This always nags at me. When I'm out I think that I should have smiled at somebody or perhaps have stopped to offer some help."

He recalled walking along a New York street and seeing a

drunkard lying on the sidewalk. "I passed right on. But I kept thinking how Jesus would have stopped and taken time with that forlorn man. I felt terribly guilty."

So guilty that he backtracked. He found a telephone and arranged to pay $75 for an ambulance that took the man to a Salvation Army shelter. The following day he visited him.

Walter Winchell, the late gossip columnist, learned about the incident. He telephoned the evangelist to get more details. "All Billy would tell me," Winchell said, "was that sometimes we forget that we are all part of God's family."

9
MY HUSBAND IS BILLY GRAHAM

THE EVANGELIST WAS away from home for weeks and months at a time. "Neither Ruth nor I enjoyed being separated any more than other couples who are in love," he said. "After much prayer, we both felt that we could take no other course. Being away from her was the most difficult thing I've had to do. After she'd leave me at the train station or airport, I'd feel like crying. I just couldn't bear to think of being three or four weeks without her."

His wife has often been asked if the prolonged absences made her lonely. "Occasionally," she confessed, "I went to bed with his tweed jacket for company. But there was little opportunity for self-pity. Little Grahams were constantly underfoot. I don't think God ever really called me to be a missionary. It was like when Bill was young and dreamed of becoming a big-league ballplayer. We all have a dream. But it worked out very well because later when he started traveling around the world, instead of resenting his going, I got a tremendous vicarious thrill out of what he was doing."

Early in the marriage, Ruth tried to spend a few days at each of her husband's crusades. However, as the family grew, she decided that her first duty was to the children: "If at all possible, a mother's place should be in the home. Children are perceptive. They know if their mother is working for an extra color TV set or because the family cannot do without the money she earns. A mother has to remember that she has the most enviable position in the world. Rearing children is a tremendous responsibility and an enjoyable job. I feel that we mothers are homemakers by divine appointment. We are put here by God to perform a divinely appointed task."

Women's liberation groups might take sharp issue with Ruth's position on the female role. "Marriage is the greatest career a woman can have," she insists. "Her home should be her primary interest. In a Christian marriage, the responsibility falls on the wife's shoulders to adjust to her husband."

To many, this attitude would appear to be extremely far behind the times. "She is extreme in only one area," said Dr. Lois Ferm, a longtime family friend and director of the Billy Graham Oral History Program. "And that is her deep love of God. With all heart and soul she believes that God created woman to be an helpmeet. She is that helpmeet's most sincere defender. Once when Billy asked her what she thought of a sermon he had just delivered, she replied, 'It was fine except for the timing.' He wanted to know what she meant. 'You preached eleven minutes on a wife's duty to her husband and only seven minutes on a husband's duty to his wife.' "

During the 1954 crusade in London, Ruth was browsing through the stacks of secondhand religious tracts in Foyle's, a large bookstore. A distressed-looking clerk darted out from behind the shelves. "Aren't you Mrs. Billy Graham?" he asked. "I desperately need your help!" He poured out his story: a marriage that was breaking up, a wife who was uncertain of her role, unhappy children, and a job that was threatened by his discontent.

Ruth determined that the man was an absentee husband and an absentee father. She urged him to attend the revival services Billy was conducting. As she was about to leave she told him, "You have to be prepared to work for happiness!"

A year later, Ruth, who has a passion for old books, was again shopping at Foyle's. She met the same clerk. This time he was beaming. He had taken her advice and had gone to the revival meeting and there made a declaration for the way of Christ. He was happy to report that his marriage had improved tremendously: "My wife has never been in more cheerful spirits. My children are thriving."

Some years later, the Grahams visited London once again for a series of religious meetings. At one of them a man approached Ruth. She instantly recognized the Foyle's salesman. This time he introduced her to his family, who were all then engaged in "doing God's work."

"Mrs. Graham," his wife said, "you were so right when you told my husband, 'You get out of marriage what you are prepared to put into it.' "

Ruth was pleased that she was credited with providing help. "But," she said, "it was clearly visible when I first talked to him that he and his wife so badly needed to believe in Jesus Christ. They just weren't aware of it. Too often, people aren't."

When someone compliments Ruth, she quickly changes the subject or offers some amusing anecdote. "That clerk in the bookstore was one of the few people in London who didn't have a title," she joked. "Over there, all we met seemed to be lords and ladies. Everybody with some lofty rank—and me with a homemade dress that had zipper trouble!"

Her sense of humor is always evident. When Billy was courting her, he said he would like to meet Dr. and Mrs. Bell. He telephoned for directions from the village. Ruth, who had warned him that the area was filled with hillbillies, pulled down her long, dark hair, blacked out a tooth, took off her shoes and walked down the road barefoot to meet him. She had disguised herself so well that he drove right by.

She enjoys poking gentle fun at people who take themselves too seriously. One dinner guest who insisted on endless bragging about his achievements was served tadpoles swimming in muddy water for the soup course. He was about to hold forth on his favorite subject—himself—when he noticed the strange contents of his bowl. He put down his spoon, gulped several times and remained silent the rest of the evening.

At Thanksgiving some years ago, Ruth felt some members of her family weren't paying proper attention to the significance of the holiday. She substituted shaving cream for whipped cream on the pumpkin pie—after that, everyone was very aware of that special day.

"It's amazing how little she worries about what people think," said a former neighbor. "She believes in trying to do what she knows is right and not wasting time caring what people are saying. Once I attended a school meeting with her. Most of the well-to-do mothers were all for buying fancy

104

Christmas presents for the teachers. Ruth said it sounded more like a bribe. And she didn't mince words when she expressed her feelings although she said them calmly.

"This refusal to be provoked," the neighbor continued, "seemed to release great spurts of energy. She'd write poetry, build stone walls and kill ever-present rattlesnakes. She'd go around in blue jeans and flat sandals. Once she told me the reason for that was because she could never tell when an emergency would occur. 'So I dress accordingly,' she explained."

When Ruth Graham goes out in public, her picture is completely different. She carefully coiffes her hair, puts on lipstick and dons fashionable clothes. A Hollywood reporter who interviewed her when she attended the Tournament of Roses in Pasadena wrote, "Billy Graham's wife fits perfectly into our neighborhood. She could easily be mistaken for a movie star."

Her husband was proud of the description, but he said, "That newsman is only half right. I agree that Ruth's pretty as an actress. Why, she even gets whistles at Bible colleges. But she possesses far more than just physical beauty. Something many Hollywood stars don't have—a special radiance that comes from the love of God!"

There is admiration for each other's appearance. Ruth once told her mother, "Bill looks now just the way I used to think my ideal man would be. He certainly didn't look like that when I married him. Do you remember what a beanpole he was then? But he's filled out over the years. When he's home, I often find myself looking at him with intense pride and pleasure."

Thirty-eight-year-old Harvey Cutler, a salesman for an

Atlanta, Georgia, mobile home company, claims that this mutual esteem played a large role in returning him to the Lord: "I guess you'd call me a confirmed look-away southerner. We always had a Confederate flag flying in front of our house and a large picture of Robert E. Lee in the living room. My mother tells me that I could sing 'Dixie' long before I learned 'The Farmer in the Dell.' So you see that good manners and courtesy went down along with hog and hominy.

"I was considered a crackerjack salesman. True, everything I said and promised customers wasn't exactly the complete truth, but it did get results. Because of my sales record I won a free trip to Florida for two—all expenses paid. My wife, Edna, and I were on our way back when the Grahams got on the same plane and sat down right in front of us. 'With them here,' I kidded Edna, 'there can't possibly be a crash. God just wouldn't allow something bad to happen to Billy!'

"I eyed the Grahams' every move. He bowed all over the plane when he gave his wife the window seat. She kept on thanking him. Then he made sure she was comfortable. I'm pretty tall and could see them perfectly. He put his arm around her and they kissed. I knew they weren't exactly spring chickens, but they acted that way. I don't mean they did anything raunchy, but it was pretty clear they liked each other a whole lot.

"During the flight they did a great deal of talking. I leaned forward so I could hear them better. They discussed the Bible, money, hunger, people who were not able to read. Even animals. She told him she thought one of their dogs needed tender loving care. He asked her a great many questions, then he'd listen respectfully, nod and say, 'Honey, you're quite right,' or 'Dear, now it's clear to me.'

"When it came time to get off the plane, he waited until she was in front of him. He put his hand on her shoulder as if to keep trouble away. It had been a long while since I saw such consideration and good manners. I was right behind him and shook his hand as we waited for the door to open. Billy introduced me to his wife and I did the same. Mrs. Graham, who looks like a shorter version of her husband, said, 'I see you also had a vacation. It does help to wind down.'

"Edna and I went to church regularly, but it never really made much of an impression. Now it seemed different. We told our pastor about meeting the Grahams. He wanted to know all the details and had me speak to the entire congregation. Edna and I were so moved by the whole thing that we both decided to accept the Lord again.

"It probably sounds like a silly reason and that we did it because of an ego trip. We've talked about it a great deal. I think what really pushed us forward was something Mrs. Graham told Billy. He asked her if she was sorry the vacation was over. 'Not for a moment,' she answered. 'It will be such a joy to return to the serenity of our home.'

"You see, we didn't feel that way—we never had a real home!"

Some visitors would regard the Grahams' household as anything but tranquil. "One of the peculiar things about living in a preacher's family," said Ruth, "is the way strangers expect to see halos. For all our striving to make God the center of our home, life in the Billy Graham household is not a matter of uninterrupted sweetness and light."

She once described it as "Noah's Ark of happy confusion." Billy felt that keeping a large variety of pets provided an excellent opportunity for teaching their children the facts of life. His wife agreed but said wistfully. "Why can't I just tell them and save us a lot of bother and money?"

She has always managed the family's finances. In the early days of their marriage, it presented some problems, as she was frequently overdrawn on her checking account. She recalled, "Whenever I heard that nice Mr. Hickey from the bank say over the phone, 'Ruth, this is Bill Hickey, uh—how are you?' I'd know it's not my health that concerned him. I'd reply, 'Oh, dear, have I done it again?' He was always patient. Eventually I learned to add and subtract."

Josephine Haggerman certainly couldn't be considered a leading exponent of Ruth's theories on the female role. She is married but uses her maiden name. She has a four-year-old son who attends a day care center while his mother serves as a primary school teacher. "Yet," she said recently, "after listening to Ruth Graham on the Phil Donahue television show where she made a guest appearance and reading her book of poetry—I've become impressed by her understanding of our problems.

"We don't live too far away from the Grahams and occasionally I'd see her when I was out shopping. I went to school with her son Franklin. So it was with special interest that I watched her on television. When she was asked if she was a liberated woman, she smiled and said, 'Yes, I am. I'm liberated from having to earn a living so I can devote my time to my family and home.' She told him that before Jesus came along women didn't have a chance. She said that she regards the Bible as the best book ever written on women's liberation as well as child-rearing.

"I was moved by her utter sincerity. I reasoned that any woman who can be such an exceptional wife and mother has to have pretty sound ideas. Especially when she said that love between family members should include a large measure of respect—that deference for each other is a very necessary ingredient. I gathered that the Grahams are very much a mutual admiration society." Then she added, "But on second thought I guess they're more than that—a mutual admiration society for all Christians—that is those they believe are truly Christians."

Billy is frequently asked, "What is a Christian?" He often replies in a Socratic fashion by posing his own query. "Do you think it is a person who is born in a Christian home?" Before the individual can reply, he thunders, "No! I could be born in a garage, but that doesn't make me an automobile! You can be born in a Christian home and have fine Christian parents, but it does not automatically make you a Christian. You cannot inherit Christianity!"

10
OUR DADDY IS
BILLY GRAHAM

JUST AS THE shoemaker's children are proverbially barefoot, it is a cliché that the sons and daughters of evangelists come to grief. And suicide, constant brushes with the authorities, violent marital discord and exceedingly antisocial behavior are certainly more noticeable when the culprit is a minister's child.

One young man, whose revivalist father tirelessly preached salvation to sinners, was accused of theft. Bitterly, he told the police, "Sure, I'm guilty as all hell. But then so are my parents! My mother felt her place was always alongside my old man, who was forever rescuing others—never had a minute left to provide their own kids with a normal home."

The five Graham children are leading happy and productive lives. Virginia and Anne, the two oldest children, were quickly joined by Bunny and Franklin; Ned, the youngest, was born six years later in 1958. Adults now, they are an exceptionally appealing-looking clan, and practice the religious routines of worship that they were taught at home.

"Their well-being is all due to Ruth," Billy acknowledges. "While I was on the go, she remained at their side. When they needed her, she was there. Ruth feels strongly that a mother's job is the most important one in the world, and that no preacher ever gets as close to anyone as a mother does to a child she holds on her lap.

"She often emphasized this viewpoint with a story Dwight Moody, an earlier famed evangelist, used to tell. He was once approached by a mother of six who said she suddenly had the call to preach. 'You certainly have,' Moody agreed fervently. 'And your congregation is waiting—all six of them!' "

Ruth, in turn, credits her husband for the Graham children's equanimity. "Despite Bill's frequent absences," she insists, "he was a far better father than many male parents who are always home for dinner. He made sure that they knew what his values were. Not just by telling them, but by showing them. He taught them how to grow up loving the Lord.

"When they were very young, Bill managed to enter their make-believe world with enthusiasm as great as theirs. Oh, I know it wasn't always easy. But then, Christ never promised that it would be easy."

"Right from the start," observed a neighbor, "it was pretty evident that the Grahams intended to use the Bible for their Dr. Spock. At the time I was pregnant with my first, Gigi [Virginia] Graham was two years old. She was a lovely little girl. So, as a matter of course, I turned to Gigi's mother for child-rearing instruction. I remember Ruth saying to me that Proverbs 22:6 offered the greatest advice she had ever discovered. It certainly worked wonders for her brood":

> Train up a child in the way he should go: and when he is old, he will not depart from it.

Virginia

The eldest Graham child is married to Dr. Stephen Tchividjian, a psychologist of Armenian descent. They were wed in an ancient stone church overlooking Lake Geneva in Clarens, Switzerland. She was seventeen, the bridegroom twenty-three. Billy performed the service. He told reporters, "Stephen is one of the most dedicated young Christians I have ever met. He is the only man in the world to whom I'd give my daughter in marriage at her age."

Virginia recalled, "When my sisters and I were growing up, Daddy took us to a remote mountain spot and told us to pray for the boys we would eventually marry. 'You're still quite young,' he said. 'But God has already made the selections.'

"At the time some of us may have thought it silly, but I realize now how fortunate I was to be born in a family that believed so strongly in the power of prayer. My parents prayed and loved me before I ever entered this world. Once, when Stephen and I and our children visited Montreat, Daddy said, 'Remember, the most important thing in rearing a family is each person's relationship to the Lord. All things flow from that."

She describes herself as a Christian, a wife, a daughter, a mother and a friend. Ruth endorses that characterization. "Gigi is grand in all five categories," she says.

The editor of a national magazine once tried to hire the Grahams' eldest child for his cover. "She has all the requirements to be a top professional model," he said. "Pretty, tall and curvy."

"All the credit belongs to my parents," Virginia told a journalist. "The only thing they didn't do enough of when we children were young was to argue in front of us. We never heard a cross word. One result was that when I married and my husband and I had our first argument, it shook me up, because I thought that wasn't supposed to happen. But then as Stephen and I got older, we realized that they had had their arguments, but they kept them from us. In every other area they were excellent examples.

"I was always aware of how much love existed between Mother, Daddy and God," she says. "Stephen and I have tried to pass it on to our children. Once we asked them what they thought marriage was. Our oldest, who was quite young at the time, exclaimed, 'It's when you find somebody you want to keep!' "

Ruth believes that every parent should have one Virginia to raise: "She was a terror one moment and an angel the next. One time she got into some mischief and when I questioned her about it, she replied, 'Mother, you can't blame me. It wasn't my fault. It was the devil! He's the one that got into me and made me do it!' All of a sudden she noticed the expression on my face and said, 'But, Mother, as soon as he saw you coming, he left.' "

When Virginia was pregnant with her second child, Ruth composed a poem in her honor and sent it to her as a Mother's Day gift:

It seems but yesterday
you lay
new in my arms.
Into our lives you brought
sunshine
and laughter
play—
showers, too,
and song.
Headstrong,
heartstrong,
gay,
tender beyond believing,
simple in faith,
clear-eyed,
shy,
eager for life—
you left us
rich in memories,
little wife.
And now today
I hear you say
words wise beyond your years;
I watch you play
with your small son,
tenderest of mothers.
Years slip away—
today
we are mothers
together.

Anne

A member of the Bible study class the second Graham

daughter teaches said, "Not only is Anne lovely-looking and brainy, she is also so sincere in her love of God that it's practically impossible not to be affected by that love."

Anne Morrow Graham Lotz was born in 1948. She is married to Dr. Daniel Lotz, a former star basketball player who became a dentist. Together with their children they live in Raleigh, North Carolina. She was about to enter college when she asked her parents' permission to be allowed to drop out of school in order to marry Lotz, eleven years her senior.

"She was very young," said Ruth, "but Bill and I realized how much they loved each other. We agreed that it would be foolish to make them wait. Besides, some of the most interesting people I know never went to college. They made up for it by reading. And some of the dullest I have met graduated cum laude."

"Our middle daughter was usually the kindest of children," Billy recalled. "However, one afternoon her mother heard her shouting orders, followed by moans. It was coming from the kitchen. Ruth rushed in to find five-year-old Anne slapping her two-and-a-half-year-old sister in the face. After stopping the one-sided brawl, she demanded to know what was going on. Anne replied sweetly, 'It's all right, Mother. I'm just teaching her the Bible—how to turn the other cheek.'"

Anne looks and sounds like her father. She is tall and long-legged; she possesses many of his mannerisms, including his speaking ability. There is frequently an extensive waiting list for her Bible class. She takes her religion seriously and has the skill to make it interesting. It was due to her urging that Billy conducted a crusade in Raleigh, her adopted home-town.

She values privacy and doesn't often discuss her family. "Daddy is sharing everything else with the world," she said. "This part of his life is ours alone. People may think it's because we're not a close family, since we're awfully spread out, mileage-wise. But we're close in spirit and we absolutely adore our parents. They set the tone of our lives by the way they lived theirs. Their dependence on God was obvious—Mother's light would be on late at night and early in the morning as she studied her Bible and prayed. And Daddy, even though the world acclaimed him as a great man, and so many sought him for advice, would still get on his knees and humbly ask the Lord for guidance.

"Through all of this we learned that seeking God was not a sign of weakness but a sign of strength and knowledge of ourselves—we are not complete persons until we allow Him to take control; then we become that for which we were created. This wasn't taught to us in a dry pious manner, but with an abundance of happiness."

A local minister, writing in his church bulletin, once castigated Billy for harboring reactionary ideas. Anne quickly dashed off a letter to a Raleigh newspaper, stoutly defending her father. "The naiveté of this type of criticism amuses me," she wrote. "This critic assumes that because Dr. Graham is a friend and spiritual counselor to kings, queens, presidents and leaders, that he sanctions their various policies and practices of government."

Anne does have one wryly amusing story about her father. Some years ago she drove him to the Asheville, North Carolina, airport. It was extremely crowded and as usual dozens of people came up to greet him. When the time came

to board the plane, Anne turned to hug him. That was when
the preoccupied evangelist reached for his daughter's hand,
shook it firmly and murmured, "It was so nice to meet you."

Bunny (Ruth)

"It is not surprising that my first memory is of my family
kneeling in the living room for prayers," recalled the Graham's middle child, who was born in 1950. "Prayers were
held during or after breakfast and again at supper. To be
honest, there were times we groaned when we heard the
familiar call, 'Prayers.' But today each one of us children has
family prayers in our own homes.

"Many people pray as if God were a big aspirin pill. They
pray only when they are hurt. But Mother and Daddy taught
us to pray about everything. Daddy has said, 'The Lord is not
so busy with great affairs of the universe that He cannot
bother about these little lives of ours.'

"In a world where there is so much insecurity and no
absolutes and so much confusion, there is no greater assur-
ance than to know that we can always be in touch with the
King of Kings, Lord of Lords, and Ruler of the Universe."

It's likely that a listener would get an unflattering impression of any person who mouthed such lofty phrases. Joan
Ratner Heilman, who interviewed her for *Good Housekeeping*
magazine, said, "She isn't the dowdy and oppressively pious
stereotype one might expect in a preacher's daughter. She's a
strikingly pretty woman. Tall and slender, with long blonde
hair, porcelain skin and deep blue eyes. She wears lipstick,
blue eye shadow and swinging clothes."

Ruth endorsed the description. She objected, however, to one of the words: "The clothes are not *swinging*," she said. "They are *stylish!*"

Like her two older sisters, Bunny is greatly in demand to teach Bible classes. The minister of a church she attended said, "Billy's daughter has a special gift of communicating God's word. I've listened to her and found myself thrilled at her skill in making the Bible come so alive."

Bunny's husband, Ted Dienhart, is an advertising executive for a firm that lists the Billy Graham Evangelistic Association as one of its largest clients. "People call at all hours begging to get in my wife's Bible class," he said.

"From the moment Bunny arrived," Ruth recalled, "she was good. I feel that God realizes that exhausted parents occasionally need one like her. She'd play happily in her crib for hours. Rarely cried. She was the sort of a child who did things without being nagged. She always had a wonderful disposition and would make us laugh with her sense of the ridiculous."

One day Bunny's mother discovered that the youngster had a great many coins in the tiny purse she had been given at Easter. "This was very strange," Ruth said, "since she only received an allowance of twenty-five cents a week. I questioned her about it. She cheerfully admitted, 'Nice people give me money to stand still while they snap my picture. If I smile a lot they give me a nickel extra. So I always smile.' "

There were times when the laughter gave way to tears. "Children have very real problems," Billy said. "They worry deeply about them. To them it's just as important and far reaching as an adult facing a major crisis. Unfortunately, I

118

wasn't home often enough to offer my full support. But when I was there I tried so very hard to be a good listener. Over the years I've discovered how necessary it is to listen respectfully when a child is despondent. And not to dismiss their complaints as nonsense."

Once the evangelist returned briefly from Washington, D.C., where he'd met with the President of the United States. He was exhausted. He wanted to shave and change his clothes before leaving for an important meeting. Bunny intercepted him with a serious worry. She threw her arms around him as she poured out her woes.

"We talked for a long time," Billy said "I was late for my meeting, but I'm glad I knew where the priorities were."

Bunny well recalls that occasion. "Busy as Daddy was, he spent time, he loved me, he prayed with me, he cried with me. That will always be a very special memory, that Daddy would take time from his busy and tiring schedule to share his daughter's burden."

Franklin

William Franklin Graham III, son and namesake of the world-renowned evangelist, said, "My father accepted God because he chose to do so. I had to do the same—my way."

The first three Graham children were girls. Billy and Ruth hoped the next one would be a boy. When he was about to arrive, the evangelist was conducting a crusade in Texas. Informed that his wife was in the early stages of labor, he rushed back to Montreat in time to escort her to the hospital. He was with Ruth until she was wheeled into the delivery room. A short while later, a nurse told him that his wife and new son were doing fine.

"I was so excited," Billy recalled, "I jumped high in the air and let out a happy yell that you could hear all over the hospital."

Ruth insisted on naming the infant William Franklin Graham. Billy reluctantly agreed, with the provision that the boy would be called Franklin. In Boone, North Carolina, where he and his wife, the former Jane Austin Cunningham, and their three sons make their home, he is known as "Frank Graham, the fun-loving doer of good."

He is considered one of the town's leading citizens. He heads a nonprofit missionary organization, World Medical Mission, which among its many overseas pursuits recruits physicians for Third World countries. Recently, he was ordained into the ministry, which started rumors, that he had been chosen to succeed his sixty-five-year-old parent. "God gave my father a special talent," he said. "One that he can't pass on by his own choice."

Billy also discounted the reports about his son's being groomed to take over: "Franklin has repeatedly told the press that he would never follow in my footsteps. He's very much his own man and makes his own decisions. Besides, I have no plans for retirement."

Nevertheless, he and his wife were overjoyed when Franklin was ordained. Billy embraced his son and pronounced the occasion "a culmination of my life."

Ruth, merrily, but with visible relief, jested, "In case anyone worries about a son being away from God, stop fretting. Nobody is hopeless."

Although Franklin made his first decision for Christ at the age of eight, he had strayed far afield in the course of growing up.

At the time Ruth observed, "I think Franklin is rebelling against being a preacher's son. Especially that the preacher happens to be a famous one."

Adverse publicity arrived only too soon. A popular columnist wrote: "The handsome son of evangelist Billy Graham was out nightclubbing until the wee hours with the pretty daughter of songstress Lena Horne!" At the time Franklin was only nine years old. Although the columnist printed a retraction, it was an accurate forecast of what was to come.

"We prayed," Billy recalled, "that until Franklin realized he was wrong and came back to spiritual living, our love would hold him up."

When Franklin's third child was born, Ruth wrote a poem about her son's early days:

> God,
> look who my Daddy is!
> He is the one
> who wore his guardian angel out
> (he thought it fun).
> First, it was bikes:
> he tore around those hills
> like something wild,
> breaking his bones
> in one of many spills;
> next, it was cars:
> how fast he drove (though well)
> only patrolmen
> and his guardian angel knew;

the first complained,
the second never tells . . .
Not long ago
You touched him,
and he turned,
Oh, Lord, what grace!
(And how quizzical the look
upon his angel's face:
a sort of skidding-to-a-stop
to change his pace.)

And know, he just had me:
which only shows
who needs a little angel of his own
to keep him on his toes.
Oh, humorous vengeance!
Recompense—with fun!
I'll keep *him* busy, Lord.
Well done! Well done!

Ned

Billy was present during the birth of his younger son. The evangelist was very moved by the experience. "How can anyone doubt God's presence after witnessing such a miracle?" he asked. "The infant's first cries are the language of beauty, order, perfection and intelligence—God's work!"

The new baby was named Nelson Edman for his maternal grandfather, Dr. Nelson Bell, and for Dr. Raymond Edman, president of Wheaton College, where the infant's parents had met.

"From his earliest days Ned showed a passion for the out-of-doors," said his mother. The angelic-looking, blond, blue-eyed youngster was always wandering in the woods. "I knew where to find him. He'd be out collecting rocks or leaves or wild flowers. It seemed that he had a different hobby each week, all somehow connected to nature."

The older Graham children had attended local schools, but Billy and Ruth decided to send Ned to a very austere English boarding school. "It was so strict," the boy's father said, "they made the unruly students strip down and sit in ice cold water for an hour whenever they broke a rule."

Ned was brought back to the States after a year and sent to a private school in Stonybrook, New York. An excellent swimmer, Ned won several cups in school competitions. His coach felt that with more experience he could make the Olympic team, but Ned quickly dismissed the idea. "I don't plan on staying in the water for eight hours at a stretch!" he said.

Ned took a year's sabbatical to think things through. He got a job as a salesman in a sporting goods store that specialized in rock-climbing equipment. "Ned is an expert in that field," said his mother. "Also in tennis and karate." She believes that his temporary academic recess helped him sort things out. "His relationship with the Lord is solid," she feels. "If anything, it's increasing. He's a very devoted young man." Presently, Ned is working on his bachelors degree. He and his wife, Carol, a nurse, live on the west coast. They met when she treated him for a leg injury.

"God was very wise when he made that selection," said the proud father-in-law. "I'm certain that Carol will bring as much happiness to Ned as Ruth has given me."

In his sermons, Billy frequently refers to his children. "They often help me make a point," he says. During a crusade in Houston, he told his audience, "One day I was walking along the road with my son Ned, who was then five years of age. We stepped on an anthill. We killed a lot of ants and wounded many others. 'Wouldn't it be wonderful,' I said to him, 'if we could go down there and help those ants rebuild their house and bury their dead, take care of their wounded?'

"He looked up at me. Then he said, 'But, Daddy, we are too big. We can't get down there and help those ants.'

"I thought for a moment. 'Wouldn't it be wonderful if we could become an ant and live in an ant world?' And that is exactly what God did. God Almighty decided to become a man and that is who Jesus Christ was. My young son seemed to understand what I was saying."

Several years before Ned was born, the Grahams decided they needed living quarters that provided more privacy, for Billy's fame was rapidly growing. Streams of the curious drove up to their very accessible home and gawked. They peeked in the kitchen window to see what Ruth was cooking, gathered flowers for souvenirs, took photographs of the children.

"It was terribly annoying," Ruth recalled, "but I felt we had learned to cope with the lack of privacy. It got to be a family joke. I'd claim that if the sightseeing cars drove quickly by, they were probably from the Episcopal center. If they slowed down, they were Presbyterians. Then there were the ones that actually stopped, got out of their cars and wandered all over. They were the Baptists. Bill used to kid me that I was prejudiced against the Baptists. But that's the way they were. They were so friendly. Sometimes, too friendly!"

The Grahams wished to continue living in the Montreat area and looked at many remote land parcels. They particularly liked a 200-acre plot located at the edge of the Blue Ridge Mountains. A narrow, winding, single-lane road, practicable only by Jeep, led to it. That suited them very well. The evangelist said, "The land was very cheap—$13 an acre. However, the owner wanted to sell the entire tract. We decided, reluctantly, that it was too costly."

One day when Billy was on the west coast a very determined woman, armed with a large box camera, knocked on the Grahams' back door. When she learned that several of the children were taking afternoon naps, she demanded that they be awakened so she could get a group snapshot.

"That did it," Ruth said. "I felt something had to be done immediately. I borrowed money from the bank and bought that terrific piece of Blue Ridge land we had both liked so much."

With help from friends they built a house with a superb mountain view. A stream was dammed to make a swimming pond for the children. "I thought our wish for privacy might hurt them," Billy said. "Granted, there weren't many playmates around, but they did have each other and that seemed to be enough. They were always doing something. Sometimes too much!"

The Graham children were physically punished for willful misbehavior, for the evangelist and his wife believe that sparing the rod spoils the child. They feel that parental responsibility involves giving the youngster what he or she needs—and frequently that need means physical discipline. "Coddling children," Billy said, "avoiding correction, is one of the primary causes of delinquency. The parent who takes the time and the trouble to discipline his child loves him far more than does the namby-pamby parent who sows the seeds of delinquency in overlooking and tolerating antisocial action. Children actually welcome being disciplined."

Once, when the Graham children were still quite young, the usually mild-mannered Anne told her mother, "You aren't such a sweet person. You spank people."

"Mother has to do that," Virginia quickly said. "If she doesn't spank us when we are bad, God will punish her."

Three-year-old Franklin had other ideas. Billy disciplined him for striking one of his sisters. "Now, if you had a little boy who was mean to his sister, what would you do?"

Franklin, always able to think rapidly, replied, "I would not spank him!"

Father and son talked about children hitting each other. Then Billy suggested that he and Franklin pray over the offense. They knelt down. The youngster's prayer was: "Dear God, please forgive me for hitting my sister. And forgive her for all the times she has hit me."

While most of the discipline problems were easily solved, Ruth was always afraid that one of them would surely find its way to the newspapers. During a crusade in Florida, she brought her two older daughters for a brief visit. While she was resting in a Miami hotel room, the girls were amusing themselves on the roof garden. Suddenly Billy burst in.

126

"Looks like we have a lawsuit on our hands!" he shouted. "The girls have been throwing rocks and the desk clerk just told me they hit a woman on the head!"

Aware that a reporter who had written several unfavorable crusade stories was in the lobby, Ruth rushed out to find her daughters. They had disappeared from the roof garden. After a great deal of searching, she discovered them locked in a tiny broom closet. Despite her pleas, they refused to leave their hiding place. In desperation, Ruth found an electric cord, which she shoved under the door. After several thrusts, the girls decided that their mother was really enraged and reluctantly came out.

Ruth was convinced that the journalist would uncover all the details and print a disapproving story. She could imagine the headline: EVANGELIST'S WIFE BEATS DAUGHTERS WITH ELECTRIC CORD!

Although the children occasionally sported slightly red backsides, they vigorously endorse their parents' discipline theory. "It worked because Mother and Daddy were just and firm," said Bunny. "Rules were carefully spelled out. If they were broken, punishment followed swiftly. Usually a shoe tree applied to the bottom by Mother. She did most of the disciplining. But neither ever punished in anger.

"I can remember distinctly that Daddy only spanked me three times. All for very good reasons: once for lying, once for kicking Franklin in the head, and once for telling Mother that I hated her. But when it was all over, we'd pray together and ask for guidance, and Daddy would always gather me in his arms and tell me that he loved me. Mother would do the same."

Ruth drew up a list, prompted from Proverbs, entitled "A mother must . . ."

1. Walk with God.
2. Put happiness in the home before neatness.
3. Not be the victim of her own disposition.
4. Make her tongue the law of kindness.
5. In discipline, be firm but patient.
6. Teach that right means behaving as well as believing.
7. Not only teach, but live.
8. Not only speak, but listen.
9. Realize that to lead her child to Christ is her greatest privilege.

People who know the evangelist's wife regard her as a very practical person. "She tells it as it is," said a storekeeper who has done business with the family for years. "I remember the time she gave one of my customers quite a tongue lashing. This other lady came in with a dog on a leash. He was very frisky and knocked over several unopened cartons. That's when his owner beat him real hard. It got Mrs. Graham very angry."

Ruth loves dogs and has owned and appreciated many of them. Recently she said, "Dog trainers seem to know more about child-rearing than some parents. In many households the dogs are better trained than the children." She says quite seriously that every parent should get hold of a good book on dog obedience. "Follow the rules," she advises. "They are very simple."

1. Keep commands at a minimum. One word to a command and always the same word.
2. Be consistent.

3. Be persistent. Never give a command without seeing it obeyed.
4. Offer praise when the command is carried out.

"It's not true that Bill and I had no major problems with our children," she admits. "Each crisis has taught us so much of God and also compassion and understanding for each other. Granted there were headaches and heartaches, but they were far overshadowed by all the joys our children brought. Who can forget Franklin's first night when he decided to camp out on our front porch? In the morning I asked the youngster if he hadn't been worried that the polecat might come around.

" 'No, ma'am,' he replied.

'Why not?' I asked.

'I had my gun with me.'

'Honey, that wasn't a real gun!'

'But, Mom, the polecat didn't know that!' "

Her husband shares her thoughts on children. Several years ago he told a crusade audience that he wouldn't want his daughters to meet Elvis Presley for fear of contamination. Hearing of this, Presley was deeply hurt. "I admire Billy a whole lot," the singer said. "I wouldn't dream of putting a finger on anyone from his family."

To which Graham replied, "That's good, since I regard every child as part of my family."

"Ruthie feels exactly the way her husband does," said Ethel Waters. The late black songstress and actress frequently performed at Billy's revival meetings. "I learned what love really is from that precious child," she told a *New York Times* reporter. "I'll never forget the night when I was with the crusade in London. At the time I had a bad foot and was trying to leave before the huge crowds started pouring out. That's when I ran into her on the stairway. She was holding on to a teenaged girl who was so drugged, her eyes were rolling—she was really on a trip. Somehow the girl had gotten into the meeting and had almost passed out.

"There was delicate little Ruthie, half-carrying, half-dragging this girl who was twice her size. She was a dirty, hippie type—smelled like she hadn't taken a bath in months. But that didn't seem to bother Ruthie. She was soothing this girl. Embracing her. Showing her the love of God. Showing her that someone cared."

Ruth spends a great deal of time counseling troubled young people. Once when she talked to a group of inmates at a reformatory, a pretty fourteen-year-old brunette, who had been committed for habitual shoplifting, told her, "More than anything else I'd like to be part of a happy home."

"What's your definition of a place like that?" Ruth wanted to know.

"It's where the mother and father like each other and also their kids," the delinquent girl replied. "And are not afraid to show it." Then she added wistfully, "But I guess that's expecting too much—homes like that happen only in the movies." The other girls nodded in agreement.

"I don't want to blame parents for all of society's ills," Billy said. "But shouldn't every child be entitled to a happy home? In today's world too many of our youngsters are 'orphaned' by the total disintegration of the family. Millions of mothers and fathers have abdicated their proper parental roles."

The Grahams are both of the opinion that a truly satisfying

home has to be based on disciplined and obedient children. "I've often said that the reason our own children turned out well," Billy observed, "was because their mother managed them with a Bible in one hand and a rod in the other. Of course, punishment must be meted out carefully and compassionately in the spirit of love. However, I've discovered that a great many parents are confused when it comes to discipline. They are afraid physical punishment will bring on hate. As a matter of fact, the reverse is true. A child that's permitted to defy convention constantly, often grows up to be a discontented adult, bringing grief to himself, his mother and father.

"Not long ago a woman complained to me about her unruly son. 'I can't understand his rebellious behavior,' she confided. 'All I ever do is give him a pat on the back.' I quickly replied, 'Madam, perhaps that's where the trouble lies. Why don't you try applying your pat lower down?'

"Young children," Billy added, "will invariably talk, walk, think, respond and act like their parents. Give them a target to shoot at. Give them a goal to work toward. Give them a pattern which they can see clearly and you give them something that gold and silver cannot buy."

11
CHRISTMAS
AT MONTREAT

Christmas love is close at hand,
About to embrace all the land.
The holy days are here we know,
When comes forth Billy's TV show.

Several years ago this bit of doggerel appeared in a weekly
New Hampshire newspaper, heralding the start of the holiday
season. Whenever his frenzied schedule allows, the evangelist tries to share Christmas with television viewers. On the
evening of December 24, millions of people around the world
ardently watch Billy and Ruth, the Graham children and their
spouses, grandchildren and friends, who are all on camera
sitting in front of the large, stone fireplace in the living room
of the evangelist's home. Billy often wears a red sweater;
Ruth, a green dress. "For us it's the most thrilling time of the
year," Graham said. With a grandchild perched on his lap, he
reads from the Bible the story of the advent and birth of

Jesus. The reading is followed by prayers and the singing of carols and hymns.

"Billy has a special gift of making Christmas meaningful," observed country singer Johnny Cash, a frequent visitor to their home. "He makes you feel you can almost touch the miracle."

Soon after the program is aired, many ministers report sharp increases in born-again Christians who attribute their renewed conviction and dedication to the Billy Graham show. Here are three case histories:

"I guess for people like me," said Pete Horton, a very fat, very bald and very bowlegged construction worker, "that program officially starts Christmas. This may sound like I'm some kind of unbeliever, which I'm definitely not. But it's like Billy's the baseball umpire who waves his hand and yells, 'Play ball!'

"As a matter of fact, isn't life sort of a ball game? There are winners and losers. Me, I was always on the losing end. It started from the time I was born. I never knew who my parents were. They probably weren't married—leastway, not to each other. Until I was sixteen, I lived in an orphan asylum. Foster homes weren't yet popular in my town. Oh, I'm not going to complain that everything was terrible. That's not true. Just most things!

"Anyway, when it came time to leave the orphanage, they got me a job as maintenance boy in a factory that made paintbrushes. For a while it was okay, but then the whole plant moved to another state. I was out of a job. After a lot of searching I managed to get work in a printshop sweeping and cleaning—things that I had done before. But they had to shut down from lack of business. It went on like that. Nothing lasted.

"I got so disgusted that I joined up with the Army. They made me a cook. Why, I'll never know. Maybe they figured that was the best thing for a bandy-legged GI. My buddies used to say, 'Pete's scrambled eggs taste like poured cement!' Despite that, when I was discharged, I managed to become a fast-order cook—for a single week. But when they started getting complaints about my cooking, I was given the gate. It seemed that no one in his right mind wanted me.

"Then a fellow I knew in the Army told me about a civil service opening for a park attendant. At the time I was living in Boston. I applied and was hired. I was tickled pink. Here was a steady lifetime job that even carried a pension.

"Rita, that's my wife, worked in the park department office as a file clerk. I met her there. I discovered that we had a lot in common—she had also grown up in an orphanage. We started going around steady, then got married. It was good having a regular home and having somebody that cared if you lived or died. The only real trouble we faced was when Rita had a miscarriage. But right after she became pregnant again—the doctor felt it was too soon. Anyway, this time she carried it through and we had a son. He was some kid—weighed almost ten pounds right off. Rita said he was my spitting image. We named him after me.

"Things looked better than ever. There was talk of me becoming a foreman. Then it happened. Two weeks after I got my promotion, young Petie dropped dead in his sleep. We were told it was from a rheumatic heart condition. A doctor once said that Petie's heartbeat was a little off, but claimed we shouldn't worry—that it wasn't serious. He made it sound like it was really nothing.

"Petie's death changed everything. Rita and me started fighting all the time. She blamed me. That I couldn't wait to demand sex right after her miscarriage. It became a regular hang up with her. I tried to tell her that the doctor had assured me that it had nothing to do with it. But that didn't help. Sometimes she'd get me so mad that I'd call her every name in the book and belt her. Rita didn't exactly take it lying down. She'd scratch and kick me. I still have bruises. It got to be such a regular habit that the only thing left was to call it quits—which we did.

"I thumbed my way all over the country—been to forty-five of the fifty states. To earn enough money I'd find small, part-time jobs like parking cars or washing dishes. It was in Eugene, Oregon, that I saw Billy Graham's Christmas Show. Looking at his healthy grandchildren didn't exactly make me happy, but somehow his message got through to me: *that I had another chance!*

"At the orphanage they used to make us go to church. I guarantee that no one listened to what the preacher was saying—least of all me. I never went much for religion and I hadn't looked at a Bible in years. Now, it seemed to matter. Tears started streaming down my cheeks as I thought about how I had messed up my life. I counted the number of commandments I had broken. Billy was saying that at times like this families should be together.

"Wouldn't you know it? That was exactly when the television set broke down. I shook it real hard. Nothing happened.

So I shook it even harder. This time it went back on just as he was saying that to feel alive you had to reach out to God. That with Him in your corner you would wipe out the past. That God loves you and will forgive you.

"For over a month I thought about what Billy Graham had lectured about, but kept putting off making a decision. I guess I was too stubborn to go forward and admit that I desperately needed God's help. But no matter how hard I tried I couldn't put it out of my mind. Over and over I kept thinking about what Graham had said. Finally, I took the plunge and walked into a small Baptist church in Albuquerque, New Mexico. You may find this hard to swallow, but I swear that when I came out I felt different—it was as if a 500-pound weight had suddenly been lifted.

"I hitchhiked back to Boston, where Rita was still living. She wasn't at all happy to see me. The honest truth, she was downright unhappy that I was there. She told me to get lost—that she never wanted to see any part of me again. I remember one time she said, 'Why don't you join the French Foreign Legion? But on second thought, they wouldn't even have you. Peter Horton, you stink out loud!'

"If this had happened earlier, I'm sure I would have blown up and given her a few slaps. This time I didn't take her flat-out. Sure, I was hurt, but I kept coming back. Finally she realized that I was a changed man—that the bad things had left me. We've been back together for five years. Have two healthy and happy children. And, best of all, a healthy and happy marriage. All thanks to Billy Graham and his Christmas Eve Show. I wrote and told him about what he done for one American family."

Everett McCauley's life was also radically altered by Billy's television program. However, his story is very different from the previous one. McCauley is in his late forties. He has often been told that he resembles Cary Grant. The comparison delights him, but he quickly dispells any notion that he's a movie type.

"I prefer the legitimate stage," he said loftily. "What's more, I'm the vice-president and comptroller of a small insurance company. And there's probably nothing more prosaic than that.

"It's the only company I ever worked for; came here immediately following my college graduation. I was earning $48 a week when Elizabeth and I were married. We didn't have much money, but it always was a most satisfactory union. I don't think that during the sixteen years we were man and wife we ever had a serious quarrel.

"There weren't any children. Not that we didn't want any; we tried for years. Medical authorities convinced us that it was impossible. Elizabeth was infertile because of an ovarian tumor. It wouldn't respond to any treatment. We discussed adoption. However, I fear it was only talk. Instead, we got increased pleasure out of each other's company. Selfish pleasure.

"We traveled extensively. Twice a year we'd get to New York to see hit plays. Whenever I had to go out-of-town on business, she'd come along. We spent an inordinate amount of time together. I was pleased when the working day ended so that I could be with her.

"Well, it was too good to last. Shortly after our sixteenth wedding anniversary she had a mastectomy. There was a malignant tumor in her breast. Two months later she died.

"I'm not overstating when I say I became deranged. After her death I didn't go to the office for weeks. Just sat in the house and stared into space. When I finally dragged myself into the office, I just sat there and did some more staring. My associates suggested a long holiday—perhaps a trip around the world. At first I was annoyed at the recommendation. But when our firm's president repeated the suggestion, I took a round-the-world cruise.

"It failed completely. In every exotic port the ship docked, I'd think how Elizabeth would have reacted. It got so bad that I actually started engaging her in conversation. Once, a fairly attractive divorcée invited me to go sightseeing with her. 'Are you husband-shopping?' I asked belligerently. 'I've got a wife!'

"I was glad when the voyage ended. I came to the conclusion that I'd led a good and happy life, but the major part of it was over. The time had come to resign myself to that fact. Nothing could be done to bring Elizabeth back.

"Now everything revolved around the company. Insurance all day long. I would get to the office early and stay late. When I'd get home, I'd turn on the television set and sit there for hours. I'd drift off to sleep in the midst of the late show and wake up, still dressed, to the early-birds' program.

"On Christmas Eve it seemed that all the programs revolved around the holiday. I found myself watching Billy Graham and his self-satisfied-looking family. I rotated the dial, but kept coming back to the Grahams. In spite of my displeasure, I was intrigued. It was so apparent they were a happy group. I noticed the decorated tree in the corner of his living room and it brought back memories of the times Elizabeth and I decorated ours, laughing and throwing on the tinsel. I remembered that I still had all the ornaments stacked away. They hadn't been opened in a long while. This made me quite disturbed. I kept seeing the ornaments glittering through newspaper wrappings.

"The more I watched the show, the more restless I became. But it wasn't a hopeless kind of upset—I find it difficult to describe the feeling. I suppose it was like a swimmer who is about to go down for the third time who suddenly realizes there are things he can do to save himself.

"I didn't rush out to find Jesus Christ. Although Elizabeth and I couldn't be called regular church attenders, we still thought of ourselves as proper Christians. We had never renounced the church. I had been christened soon after my birth. I felt I hadn't strayed. That I was still a Christian. But the Graham Christmas TV Show did something for me—it made me realize that I no longer wanted to be alone. That Elizabeth wouldn't think me evil if I found someone else to share my life. Three years ago I took a new wife. It, too, has been a good marriage."

Paul Atwood's Yuletide transformation was more subtle, but equally as meaningful. Atwood is the forty-three-year-old manager of a supermarket in a large middle-class suburb of Philadelphia. He is proud of serving as a commander in the Naval Reserve. He looks trim in his blue uniform, although his wife recently had to let out the waistband of his trousers two inches.

"It was my daughter, Barbara, who begged us to watch the

show. She had seen it the previous year and thought we should look at it. Kids these days seem to be real interested in religion. So to please her, we did. My wife, Catherine, sat on the couch. Naturally, I sat on the chair the family calls 'Pop's Super Special.' It's a tattered but really comfortable Morris chair that leans all the way back. Barbara and my other daughters, Laura and Nancy, sat on the rug.

"When I took over the supermarket we were at the bottom in volume of business. There are seven food markets in our town—we ranked seventh. Now we are in third place, and, believe me, we're not going to stop there. I make a fairly good salary, but Catherine decided to go back to work after Nancy entered junior high. My wife's a dietician. She got a job in a nearby hospital. I didn't exactly like the idea of her returning to work, but I didn't argue. The money was useful. And besides, Catherine is pretty strong-willed.

"Not that much of what she said affected me. And vice-versa. We went mostly our separate ways. I don't mean to imply that we had one of those modern-style open marriages. I'm sure another man never entered her mind. And I certainly didn't think that way. Except if you count that checkout clerk that kept giving me the eye. We had coffee together a few times, but that's all.

"I can't say that because of Catherine's job the house was sloppy or that the meals came out of cans or that the girls were not cared for adequately. Things seemed to fall into place, but despite that, they didn't seem just right. That Christmas, Billy Graham showed us what was missing. A relationship with God.

"We've become a family. We're really interested in all the

other members. Rod, the butcher in my store, said to me a couple of months ago, 'Paul, I don't know what it is, but you've become more alive.'

"He was so right. I have. I guess you might call me a living, breathing Billy Graham Christmas miracle!"

A cameraman's helper who once worked on the show recalled, "Billy happened by while I was checking some of the equipment. He asked me if I thought he was coming across properly. I told him that I wasn't the best person to ask since I considered myself a dyed-in-the-wool, irrevocable atheist.

"My remark seemed to intrigue him rather than anger him. Respectfully, he wanted to know more about my antireligious sentiments. That's when I said that people who claim there are no atheists in foxholes are off their rocker. I pointed to myself as one of the exceptions. 'When I was in Nam,' I told him, 'and the shells flying all around, I'd just close my eyes and think of a juicy steak smothered in onions. It always worked. I don't think they served juicy steaks in Bethelem.'

"Graham smiled and said, 'That makes me think of something that occurred a few years ago when most of the family visited. On Christmas morning we have breakfast before going to the living room to open the presents. Ruth always serves oyster stew—it's a Bell family tradition. I fear we two are the only ones who like it. As soon as the breakfast meal was over, I thought we should have a prayer. It was longer than I intended. Prayer once started is not within human limits. My grandchildren became impatient. When it was finished, they immediately started running for the living room. My daughter Anne called a halt. She asked them to walk very slowly because she had a movie camera and wanted to take pictures. That's when my oldest grandchild muttered, 'I'm sure Bethlehem was never as miserable as this!'

"As Billy headed back to his seat, he turned toward me and called out, 'Perhaps not juicy steaks, but something far better for the soul!' I suppose a good evangelist has to be quick on his feet. He sure is."

Once, in the midst of a sermon Graham was delivering in Sydney, Australia, a group of teenagers attempted to disrupt the service by tossing a smoke bomb. The auditorium was soon engulfed in fumes. To avoid confusion, Billy quickly said, "There goes the old devil doing his dirty work. But this book will soon clear the air." Vigorously he waved his Bible back and forth.

As the audience cheered, he continued, "It reminds me of the time some other mischief-makers, dressed all in red and armed with pitchforks, charged screaming into a small church back home. They looked and sounded so frightening that everybody rushed for the exit. That is everybody but one sweet old lady who was sitting in a front pew. The ringleader approached her and said, 'Don't think this red outfit makes me Santa Claus! I'm the devil! Aren't you scared of me?'

" 'I know full well who you are,' she replied. 'No, I'm not one bit afraid. After all, I've been on your side for years!' "

At the conclusion of Billy's sermon, hundreds of converts marched down the aisles—including one of the smoke-bomb throwers.

12
ALL THE
PRESIDENTS' MEN

ACTOR-PHILOSOPHER Will Rogers was known for his genial ridicule of governments and political systems. On pork-barreling, he said, "Being a friend of a President of the United States not only puts a feather in your cap, but miraculously helps you feather your nest."

Over the years, seven American presidents have regarded the evangelist from North Carolina as a special friend. Dwight D. Eisenhower was one of them. "It is very clear," he said, "that Will Rogers wasn't talking about someone like Billy Graham when he made that statement. In all the times it was my good fortune to have Billy visit the White House, he never once asked me for a single, solitary thing for himself. To my wife and myself he gave a great deal."

However, Graham's initial encounter with a Chief Executive was an unfortunate experience. A congressman from Massachusetts had arranged a meeting between Billy and Harry Truman. Graham was dressed in a white linen suit, hand-painted tie and spotless white buck shoes. He said he was dressed that way because in summer months Truman wore similar clothes and he wanted to fit right in.

"I was plenty scared," he told a reporter from the *Washington Star*. "Here, I was the son of a simple dairy farmer, face to face with an American president. I tried to reassure myself that he was a former haberdasher, but that fact didn't help much. Everything in the Oval Office looked so majestic!"

Truman quickly announced that the contents of the meeting was strictly off the record. Then he said that he too was a God-fearing Baptist but had qualms about mixing religion with government. He added that he had to be extra cautious because the press was after him, especially "that damn Drew Pearson."

Billy asked if they might have a prayer together. "I suppose there can't be any harm in that," Truman said. Whereupon the evangelist bowed his head and prayed that God would bless the President and give him of His wisdom in dealing with all the difficulties in the country and the world.

Although Graham left by a side door, he was immediately accosted by reporters and photographers, who demanded that he give them all the details. When they learned he had prayed with the President, he was asked to kneel down and repeat the prayer. Obligingly, Billy fell to his knees on the White House lawn while the photographers snapped away. Truman was outraged when he saw the story in evening newspapers. "I never want to see that s.o.b. again!" he angrily told members of his staff. "And you better not invite him to this house or you'll never see me again!"

As soon as Graham got back to Montreat he told Ruth all

about the Truman catastrophe. "I discovered long ago," he said, "how important it is to let your mate know the bad as well as the good. I learned that confiding helps the marriage considerably. Keeps it honest."

The Truman debacle was the only defeat an American president ever handed the evangelist. All succeeding Chief Executives went out of their way to inform the public· that Billy Graham was not only their friend, but a close friend. Eisenhower frequently told audiences, "I always keep the Bible that Billy gave me close to my bedside. Mamie says that I won't be without it because he was the one who gave it to me. She's right. I can't think of another person who has a closer ear to the Lord than Billy."

Eisenhower once wrote Graham a letter telling him how he felt: ". . . not only my congratulations on what you are doing, but my hope that you will continue to press and fight for the old-fashioned virtues of integrity, decency and straight-forwardness in public life. I thank the Almighty that you are ready to give full time and energy to this purpose."

The General and the evangelist first met in 1952 at the SHAPE base of operations located near Paris. During a two-hour conversation, Eisenhower repeatedly questioned Billy about his religious philosophy. After getting answers, the future President said sadly, "Those are the same values my mother and father held. I'm afraid being in the Army has made me forget some of them."

Immediately after his nomination, Eisenhower sent for Graham. When the evangelist arrived at Ike's headquarters in Chicago's Blackstone Hotel, Eisenhower wanted to know if Billy had any special suggestions that should be included in the campaign. "I'm not partisan," Graham replied. "As a matter of fact, I'm a Democrat. But I do believe that the country is badly in need of a spiritual revival." He urged the candidate to include this message in his speeches.

Eisenhower did so. Soon after being declared the victor, he again asked Billy for advice. This time the President-elect said that he planned on using a biblical phrase in his inaugural address. Graham suggested several. He also helped Ike decide on a church to join. The five-star military officer confided that during his long years in the Army he had never thought about which Protestant denomination was his.

When Billy asked him which one he'd like to be affiliated with, he replied, "My wife is a Presbyterian. I suppose I would like to be the same."

"There are two Presbyterian churches in Washington I would highly recommend," Billy said. "One is the National Presbyterian and the other is the New York Avenue Presbyterian." The new President eventually joined the former.

During Eisenhower's eight years in the White House, and upon his retirement to Gettysburg, Pennsylvania, Billy was frequently invited to call on him. After one of the visits, the irritated General told an inquisitive reporter, "Billy Graham is my friend. And a friend is supposed to visit! Period!"

The evangelist was one of the last persons to speak to Eisenhower as he lay dying in the Walter Reed Hospital. They discussed heaven and prayed together. The General wanted to know if his sins would be forgiven and if Billy thought he was going to heaven. When the evangelist finished providing answers, the former President said, "Thank you. I'm ready."

On the day of the funeral, Mamie Eisenhower invited Graham to her house. She later told a journalist, "My husband would have wanted me to do exactly that. He so regarded Dr. Graham on such a lofty plane."

John Kennedy, Eisenhower's successor, had been warned by his father to be very leary of the evangelist. "You have to be nice to Billy because of all the adulation part of the public gives him," he cautioned. "But be careful! He's another one of those Protestant preachers who desperately tried to keep Catholics out of the White House."

The newly elected President discovered that his father wasn't completely accurate. Although Graham had been involved in the Roman Catholic controversy, he had played a minor role. In the summer and fall of the campaign, when the religious issue was being hotly discussed, Billy was prudently out of the country.

He returned to the United States in time to hear leading Protestant clergymen predict that the Pope would be one of the President-elect's first visitors. They were astonished when Billy accepted a Palm Beach golf invitation from JFK. Kennedy was intrigued by a story he'd heard about a golf game the evangelist had played at St. Andrews, Scotland. He told Lyndon Johnson about it.

"It seems," Kennedy said, "that Billy hit his ball into a trap called Hell's Bunker. It's fifteen feet below the surface and all sand. Instead of taking penalty strokes and slipping back, he got a ladder and climbed down into the bunker. He desperately tried to hit the ball back to the green, but he kept sifting the sand. Finally, on his fifteenth try, he succeeded. As he came up, he said proudly, 'I couldn't let something called hell defeat me. Now, could I?' "

Kennedy grinned and added, "I figure I have to meet someone with such fierce determination." The meeting had to be canceled because of the birth of the new President's son. It was rescheduled.

"I was impressed by his charm," the evangelist said. "He revealed a restless, probing interest in theology and must have asked me more than a hundred questions about my opinions and attitudes, including the second coming of Jesus Christ and the future triumph of the Kingdom of God. From that day on we became friends."

Shortly after John Kennedy's assassination, Billy told a southern audience that the slain President and he had agreed on many important lessons. Among them were the desperate need for racial harmony and religious tolerance, the dire necessity that the world learn to live in peace, and the brevity of life. "His premature death was a terrible thing. But sometimes we must have a terrible shock to rouse us out of our spiritual neglect and apathy."

Graham recalled that he used the White House as a hotel when Lyndon Johnson, Kennedy's Vice-President, moved in. "He was always trying to keep me there—wouldn't let me leave."

The new President, who described himself as a "deeply religious Texan," was the great-grandson of an evangelist who had brought frontier hero Sam Houston to Christ. Johnson was very proud of that conversion and frequently boasted about it. He felt that with Billy's help he could give the

American people "shots of godliness they so badly needed." Presidential appointments are usually scheduled for fifteen minutes. Billy's first meeting with the new Chief Executive lasted five hours.

A story the President enjoyed repeating concerned a joint press conference that he held with Graham shortly before the 1964 national election. Billy told reporters that although he enjoyed Johnson's company, he was going to remain politically neutral. This didn't stop the President from proclaiming that the evangelist was the greatest religious leader alive. Graham felt that he had to return the compliment and said that Johnson was the greatest political leader of the twentieth century.

A few days later, one of Billy's daughters announced that she was going to support Johnson's Republican opponent, Barry Goldwater. The President read about the endorsement and immediately telephoned Graham. "You may be an outstanding religious leader," he said, "but you can't even influence your own family in politics."

Several weeks went by and Johnson's younger daughter declared that she intended to become Roman Catholic. This time it was Billy who telephoned. "You may be a great political leader," he told the President, "but you don't seem to have much influence over your family's religious life."

Johnson was delighted by the phone call and assigned an airplane to transport Billy to his Texas ranch. There the evangelist was asked to conduct services, causing the President to remark proudly, "I personally have the best preacher in all of Christendom."

Billy and Ruth were guests of the Johnsons on the last

weekend the President and Lady Bird occupied the executive mansion. The President, who had a premonition of death, secured a promise from the evangelist that he would preach at his funeral. (Billy kept that vow.) He also handed Billy a note that read: "Your prayers and your friendship helped to sustain a president in hours of need. No one will ever know how much you helped lighten my load or how much warmth you brought into our house."

Many people would rate Billy's friendship with Richard Nixon as his major presidential association. Graham said, "I've known him for a long time—for many years. He was a close friend. I feel that I didn't misjudge him, but I misjudged what he would do under pressure. I think there came a point when he cracked under all those pressures and was no longer the Nixon I had known and admired."

Billy met the future President when Nixon was a member of the U.S. Senate. The two men became good friends, played golf and exchanged family visits. They became even more intimate when Nixon was chosen as Vice-President. In 1960, the controversial political figure decided to seek the top office and asked the evangelist to be his running mate. Graham said he was flattered but quickly replied, "God has called me to preach the Gospel, and I consider that the highest calling in the world."

Later, Nixon claimed that the offer was made in "pure jest." However, a close aide said, "He wasn't exactly kidding. He figured with Billy Graham's name on the ticket, he'd be a certain shoo-in."

Nixon lost that election but was victorious eight years later when he defeated Hubert Humphrey. Shortly after the final vote was counted, the President-elect proposed that Billy join his cabinet or become an ambassador to a major country. Again, Graham refused. "I respect him for his answer," Nixon told reporters. "But I have to say that the country is the loser. Billy is truly one of the giants of our time."

The press was aware of the President's awe of the evangelist. One columnist referred to Graham as "Nixon's man behind the scenes." Billy contends that his influence was highly exaggerated. "I actually saw less of him than I had of Eisenhower or Johnson."

This may be accurate, but as Gerald Strober, one of Billy's chroniclers, pointed out, "There is little doubt that Graham's friendship with Nixon deepened during the Californian's first term in office. Graham was reported as saying, 'It is wonderful for a clergyman to have a friendship with a president.' "

Strober, a reputable, skilled journalist who has spent considerable hours with the evangelist, said, "The two men met and talked with each other often. During one thirty-seven-week period in the spring of 1969, Graham flew with Nixon in Air Force One to a dedication ceremony, took part in a meeting of the Richard Nixon Foundation, stayed at the western White House in San Clemente and was one of the two clergymen invited by Nixon to attend a dinner honoring the astronauts. He also golfed with the President."

During the early days of Watergate, Billy defended Nixon. He told one television interviewer, "His moral and ethical principles wouldn't allow him to do anything illegal like that. I've known him for a long time and he has a very strong sense of integrity."

As more and more evidence began to pile up, the evangelist started expressing doubts. He kept repeating, "There must be two men there!" Finally, in May of 1974, there was no further question about Nixon's complicity. Graham released a statement that appeared on the front page of the *New York Times:* "What comes through in these tapes is not the man I've known. . . . Our repudiation of wrongdoing and our condemnation of evil must be tempered by compassion for the wrongdoers. Many a stone is being cast by persons whose own lives could not bear like scrutiny. Therefore we dare not be self-righteous."

Ruth said, "Watergate was the hardest thing that Bill ever went through personally."

Graham knew Gerald Ford when he was a member of the House of Representatives. "I always thought a lot of him," said the man who succeeded Nixon. "But my admiration grew when I moved into the White House. Not only does Billy love his country, but all the people in it."

The evangelist was very pleased when Ford granted a full pardon to his predecessor. "It was a wise decision. Watergate has already done irrevocable harm. Keeping it alive might well have split the nation into two warring camps."

In the spring of 1975, Graham was to give the benediction at a Bicentennial celebration that featured an address by Ford. Ruth was in the audience and became enraged when a twenty-seven-year-old demonstrator waved a sign that blocked out her view of the President. She grabbed the poster which read: EAT THE RICH. DON'T TREAD ON ME.

When Ford was told of her action, he said, "Mrs. Graham,

like her husband, reveres the office of the President of the United States." He was amused when he learned that she had later handed the young man a Bible.

"Instead of carrying that ridiculous sign," she had said, "I suggest you spend your time reading these marked passages."

Jimmy Carter, who replaced Ford, met Billy during a Georgia crusade. He had personally invited the evangelist. "I know from firsthand experience the great beneficial impact of your crusades for Christ," Carter wrote. "It would be a meaningful experience for the people of Georgia if you came here to share with us your commitment to our Lord."

The evangelist agreed to preach. He tried to get a prominent Georgian to serve as chairman. More than a dozen VIPs were approached. They all refused because Billy insisted that the crusade be fully integrated. Carter had to do the presiding.

When he became President, he promptly invited Graham to the White House. Billy went, but ever since the Nixon experience he had been extremely careful not to be accused of doling out secular advice. He was determined to limit his discussions to religious matters only. He and Carter had long talks about the strong need of Americans to seek God. "I value Billy's counseling on Jesus Christ," the southern President said. "I'm grateful that I have been privileged to know him."

Billy was equally impressed. He told a reporter from the *Washington Post,* "I think President Carter's bringing a new spirit to the country. God has a place of honor in the White House."

Ronald Reagan, the current occupant of the executive mansion, is also an old friend. He, too, admits to having a very high opinion of the evangelist: "And why not? I had decisive evidence of his tremendous effectiveness when I was governor of California."

At the time, Reagan discovered that one of his aides was having severe marital problems. After listening to the troubled husband, he advised him to read Billy's book *The Secret of Happiness*. "It may sound like too simple a solution," Reagan said. "But with my own eyes, I saw how well it worked. That man and his wife were surely headed for the divorce courts. Now they are enjoying an excellent marriage. I give a great deal of credit to Billy's book."

Though mixing closely with assorted American presidents, Billy has retained some of his early roots. Marshall Frady, author of one of the most comprehensive Graham biographies, best described this phenomenon: "From his boyhood on his father's farm, there still seems a quality about him, like a lingering ambiance from all those years of milking twenty cows every day, of fresh cream and butter and custard, a certain pasteurized dairy-like mildness."

Harry Truman, several months before his death, said he was quickly aware of that farm background: "You may think you're taking the country out of the boy, but you can never fool another farmer—he knows right off. The minute I laid eyes on Billy I could detect where he grew up. He'll carry that hay and straw smell with him to the grave. The ministry needs people who come from the soil."

Not everyone can readily spot Billy's rural origins. Ruth

once attended a luncheon where her husband was the guest of honor. When he finished his speech, the woman sitting next to her whispered, "I'm very surprised to learn that he milked cows when he was a boy." Then she gushed, "He's so eloquent and handsome. To think he was raised on a farm! With that background isn't it a shame that he isn't in politics?"

"Maybe the Lord thought politics had its share and decided to give the ministry a break," Ruth replied.

Recently, John Robinson, a reporter for the Raleigh *News and Observer,* asked Billy to describe himself. "I'm a little bit lazy," the evangelist replied. "Totally dependent upon God because I know I have so little to offer myself. A little shy, which people don't see probably, but I am. I have a hard time just going up to somebody and introducing myself and speaking to them."

13
TO RUSSIA
WITH LOVE

MANY OF GRAHAM'S staunchest supporters felt that his influence as an evangelist ended when he returned from his 1982 trip to Moscow. Even the White House condemned the mission. He was accused of ignoring the plight of Soviet Christians and Jews and telling the Russians that religious freedom existed in their country.

What he actually said was that he himself did not observe any lack of religious freedom in the Soviet Union. His remarks were poorly reported and quickly misrepresented. Typical was a headline that appeared in a Virginia newspaper: BILLY HOODWINKED BY COMMUNISTS!

The usually sympathetic *Time* magazine questioned the wisdom of his visit: "Graham seemed oblivious to the precarious role of religion in a country that endorses scientific atheism and outlaws public evangelism."

Conservative columnist George Will called Billy "America's most embarrassing export."

The New York *Daily News*, a long and loud advocate of Billy's crusades, reported, "Graham displayed an extraordinary combination of innocence and ignorance."

Yet, three months later the evangelist's crusade in New England drew overflow crowds. Charles Woodring, a divinity student, attended several of the revival sessions. "Although," he said, "I go to a school that is considered liberal, I certainly don't regard myself as a fellow traveler. Quite the contrary, my classmates know how deeply I'm opposed to anything Red. They claim that I'm so paranoid on the subject that I'm forever seeing radicals under the bed—that I won't even order a cherry soda because of the color.

"However, after hearing Dr. Graham speak, I genuinely believe that he went expressly to spread the love of Jesus Christ to people behind the iron curtain. I think he succeeded despite what all the newspapers printed. It's ridiculous to think for one minute that he was hoodwinked by the Communists. He's much too smart for that. I'm sure the reason for his actions was that he wanted to be invited back to preach a full-scale Crusade for Christ throughout Mother Russia. It seems to be working out exactly the way he planned. Almost immediately after his pilgrimage to the Soviet Union he was asked to make religious trips to East Germany and Czechoslovakia, which he did.

"I only hope that someday I'll be one-tenth as good a servant of God as he is."

At a press conference in New York City, Billy defended the remarks he made in Russia. "If there had been any restrictions on what I wanted to say, I would not have gone," he told reporters. "I would not, of course, pretend in the least to be an expert on the Soviet Union after only five and one-half days in Moscow. I received many impressions that I will, I am sure, be reflecting upon for some time to come. However, my primary goal in going was to preach the Gospel, as I have done all over the world for so many years. I had more opportunities than I ever expected to accomplish this goal. . . .

"Before going I prayed a great deal about it and felt that God had led me. Upon my return I feel even more certain that I was doing His will. It may be some time before the full results of my visit can be evaluated, but even the short-term results are gratifying. . . . After all, the more contact we have, the better."

There is little doubt that over the years some of Graham's views have altered sharply. In 1964 he wrote, "Either Communism or Christianity must die, because it is actually a battle between Christ and anti-Christ." However, in 1982, not only did he deliver an hour-long sermon to a thousand Russians in Moscow's only Baptist church, but he met with several high-ranking members of the Central Committee of the Communist Party.

This ability to reshape his thoughts has attracted many diverse people. Among them was twenty-three-year-old Jonathan Ferris. He, like Charles Woodring, is a divinity student. But unlike Woodring, he considers himself to be "somewhat unorthodox theologically." He explained, "Whereas Charlie is a dyed-in-the-wool fundamentalist who takes every word and comma and period literally, I must confess that I have other interpretations. And listening to Billy Graham hasn't convinced me otherwise. But I will admit that I'm moved by his candidness in owning up to a shift in his social thinking. Hearing him speak made me aware of one very important fact—a person grows—including Christian clergymen.

"I didn't start out to become a minister. If you had asked me when I was a tiny child what I intended to be, I'd immediately reply, 'A doctor.' But when the medical schools I applied to hung out no admission signs, I soon forgot that wish. Instead, I joined the Peace Corps. At the time I was really down on Billy. He had called the Peace Corps a materialistic outfit and said that it couldn't possibly succeed because it didn't have God at its center. I understand he later retracted his statement, but when he said it, he sure got a lot of people irritated.

"You can see that I always had this desire to help. Many's the time I've been called a professional do-gooder. It was in the Virgin Islands, where I was assigned, that I got the idea for the ministry. There was a local Roman Catholic priest who was the most dedicated person I'd ever met. Although I wasn't of his faith, we had long talks. It was he who convinced me that I could perform no greater service. I didn't change my religion, but I figured that becoming a Protestant clergyman would also give me the opportunity to benefit mankind. You may think me silly, but I still feel that way. That is if man doesn't blow himself up before I get ordained.

"Shortly before Billy flew to Moscow, he spoke at Harvard. He talked about many things, including the arms race and the importance of an international meeting that would lead to the destruction of all nuclear weapons. He told us that he intended to spend the rest of his life not only preaching the

Gospel, but working for peace among nations.

"I remember him saying, 'As I searched the Scriptures, my responsibility dawned upon me, and I began to speak out on the subject of peace.' Then he told us that he was still learning. 'The more I learn,' he said, 'the less dogmatic I become.'

"This reached me. I go along with Dr. Harvey Cox, a theology professor at Harvard who is considered one of the outstanding religious thinkers in our country. He said, 'It should give all of us courage that a man in his sixties can grow this way.' "

When the Reverend Jim Jones persuaded 919 of his disciples to drink cyanide-spiked Kool Aid, many people confused the mass suicide with Christianity. Billy was quite concerned. In a widely quoted Op Ed article that was printed in the *New York Times*, the evangelist said, "We have witnessed a false messiah who used the cloak of religion to cover a confused mind filled with a mixture of pseudo-religion, political ambitions, sensual lust, financial dishonesty, and apparently even murder. None of this has anything to do with true faith in God.

". . . as long as man's heart remains unchanged, this type of tragedy will continue to occur—whether in the cold-blooded murders that plague every American city, or the frightening terrorism that stalks so much of the world, or through the wholesale deception of false messiahs like Jim Jones."

Soon after the message appeared, the evangelist received thousands of approving letters. Typical was one from an elderly woman in Arizona who wrote, "Billy, I have to confess that I was pretty confused by those deaths. I kept wondering how a Christian could commit such atrocities. But like always, you made me think twice and then set my mind at ease."

The Reverend Leighton Ford, who is married to Graham's sister Jean, said, "The reason Billy has remained so popular is because he has never stopped growing and closed himself off from new ideas." Ford, who is also a well-known evangelist, adds, "He has maintained the simplicity of his basic message and he has developed greatly in terms of his practical wisdom."

Billy gives a great deal of the credit to Ruth. He has repeatedly stated that one of the functions of a good wife is to aid her husband in maturing. "Ruth's done exactly that," he said. "She has always helped me to think clearly."

An interview the evangelist recently had with journalists Wes Michaelson and Jim Wallis of *Sojourners* magazine, a liberal religious monthly, best reveals that maturity:

Sojourner: How would you describe changes in your thinking on the nuclear arms question, and what factors would you cite as important in prompting those changes?

Graham: It has only been recently that I have given as much attention to this subject as it deserves. I suppose there have been a number of reasons why I have come to be concerned about it. For one thing, during my travels in recent years I have spoken to a number of leaders in many countries. Almost to a person they have been concerned and pessimistic about the nuclear arms race. Second, I think also that I have been helped by other Christians who have been sensitive to this issue. I guess I would have to admit that the older I get the more aware I am of the kind of world my generation has helped shape, and the more concerned I am about doing what I can to give the next generation at least some hope for peace. I ask myself, "What kind of world are my grandchildren going to face?"

Third, I have gone back to the Bible to restudy what it says about the responsibilities we have as peacemakers. I have seen that we must seek the good of the whole human race, and not just the good of any one nation or race.

There have been times in the past when I have, I suppose, confused the kingdom of God with the American way of life. Now, I am grateful for the heritage of our country, and I am thankful for many of its institutions and ideals, in spite of its many faults. But the kingdom of God is not the same as America, and our nation is subject to the judgment of God as much as any other nation.

I have become concerned to build bridges of understanding among nations and want to do whatever I can to help this. We live in a different world than we did a hundred years ago, or even a generation ago. We cannot afford to neglect our duties as global citizens. Like it or not, the world is a very small place, and what one nation does affects all others. That is especially true concerning nuclear weapons. . . . I know one thing—the ultimate hope of the world is the coming of the Prince of Peace—when war shall be no more. Even so, come, Lord Jesus.

Billy has said, "If the Gospel is not more powerful than any ism, I ought to quit preaching."

Some people feel he should. A postcard addressed to the evangelist bore an imperious, one-line scrawl: *"Dear Pope Billy, get lost!"*

Ruth resents anyone speaking unkindly about her husband. "She is not at all defensive about herself," said a family friend. "You can say anything about her you want and she won't take it personally. But when it comes to Billy, it's a totally different story."

Ruth was enraged when all the criticism arose over his trip to Russia. She had to be restrained from offering caustic rebuttals to detractors. One vociferous fault-finder was told about an archeologist she once knew whose hobby was mending broken china and pottery. "He'd spend hours gluing cracked pieces together," she said. "That man reminded me of something God does all the time—carefully and lovingly takes broken pieces of our lives and puts them back together." Then she stared at the person who had the effrontery to attack her Bill. "And that is why my husband went to the Soviet Union," she said indignantly. "To tell the Communists that God will do it for them."

However, she feels quite free to do the dissenting herself. "Both Bill and I speak up for what we think is right," she says. "I fear something is very wrong with a marriage when one of the partners is always in fear of expressing his or her thoughts."

Fraye Gaillard, an editorial writer and columnist for the Charlotte *Observer*, has interviewed both of the Grahams. "In some areas," he said, "she is more conservative than her husband. She offers her thoughts with characteristic bluntness, challenging without apology the flow of his thoughts. They seem to be accustomed to this give-and-take. Their disagreements seem devoid of either coddle or sulk, and he gently hurls the challenge back in her direction.

" 'I'm for capital punishment,' she announces with a tone of finality. 'I think it is a deterrent. I know in countries where they have it, I feel safer walking down the streets.' "

" 'Darling,' Billy replies, 'there are countries where they have executions in which I don't feel safe at all.' "

He has avoided taking a public stand on capital punishment. "I have to be very careful what I say about a great many things," he explained. "My main focus is in the Gospel. But I'm greatly troubled over capital punishment. True, we live in a time of horrible and hideous crime. Is capital punishment the answer? The system has always been one-sided. Most people on death row are poor people who couldn't afford good lawyers. A disproportionate number of them are black. An execution makes it so final."

The evangelist has said repeatedly that when he finds some important issue troubling him, he discusses it with his wife. "That's the way marriage should be. Ruth's often my bell-wether. We lie in bed close together and have long conversations. Those are some of the finest moments."

Ruth likes being Mrs. William Franklin Graham. "In addition to being honored to be Bill's wife, I so enjoy being married to him," she said. Ruth feels that it's within a wife's jurisdiction to poke good-natured fun at her mate. She teases Billy about the time they were vacationing in the south of France. "I looked up the beach," she recalled, "and there was this tall, skinny man wearing red boxer shorts. These were about as common on French beaches as a wedding dress. He had on laced-up Hush Puppies, yellow socks, a baby-blue windbreaker, immense sunglasses and a denim hat pulled down over his ears.

"I thought, 'That's about the weirdest-looking man I've ever seen.' But as he got closer, I moaned, 'Oh, my goodness, he's mine!' "

When she feels that his vanity needs deflating, she delicately yanks him back. "Oh, Bill," she said after he proudly told her about the public embrace he got from the President of

Mexico. "Don't feel too flattered. After all, I saw on television where he did the same thing to Castro."

"There are no airs about her," said a friend. "Some years ago, just before Christmas, she came down with a bad case of the flu. Billy had to take over some of the household chores. Dishwashing included. He wasn't very adept at it—broke several plates. His solution was to give his wife a large, white Christmas present—a shiny new electric dishwasher.

"That was when Ruth told me, 'I always wanted one. What some wives will do to maneuver their husband!'

"How can you avoid loving that woman?"

14
SEX AND MARRIAGE

RECENTLY, A PROFESSOR of psychology at the University of Southern California queried his students about how they rated the sex lives of practicing Christians. Two classifications were offered: "Dull" and "Lively." A decided majority of those interviewed felt the first category gave an accurate description. Typical replies were:

"Sex is unimportant to those people."

"They rarely discuss it."

"When they do have sex, it's not very satisfactory."

"They feel it's sinful to enjoy sex—only dirty old men do."

Billy sharply disagrees: "Sexual pleasures exist lifelong in a good marriage. However, Christians do feel that sex is sacred, not an instrument of self-indulgence to satisfy your appetite like a fast-food hamburger."

His sermons frequently deal with the subject. Sex, he has said, is the act by which all life on this earth has been created. It should be the most wonderful, the most meaningful, the most satisfying of human experiences. However, it has been made low and cheap and filthy. Too often there is the sly, secret, embarrassed, let's-pretend-it-doesn't-exist attitude. Used rightly, it is a servant of love, to be used as a sensual expression of true unity between husband and wife.

He told one audience, "A man prominent in public life planned the seduction of a beautiful young woman. When she rejected him, he raped her. The wife of a government figure tried to seduce her husband's young associate. When he refused to succumb to her wiles, she charged him with attempted rape, causing his imprisonment.

"Are both of these incidents taken from today's newspapers? No! Though they have a very modern ring, they are taken from the Bible. A book that has never gone out of date, the Bible could properly be called the world's most reliable textbook on sex. No book deals more forthrightly with the subject. As history, it records without distortion the sexual aberrations of its times. As biography, it refuses to gloss over the sins of its heroes, but details them with straightforward explicitness. As philosophy, it sets forth the changeless standards of God. . . .

"Nowhere does the Bible suggest that the battle between the flesh and the spirit is easy. Neither does it suggest that to be tempted is sin. God does not hold you responsible for seeing something which might engender impure thoughts. He holds you responsible for the second look.

"The Bible teaches by precept and example that there are spiritual resources we can use to overcome our illicit urges. . . . For all those caught in a web of sexual confusion and guilt, that there is still the Divine Word. The fact that immorality is rampant throughout the nation doesn't make it right; the fact that some clergymen may condone it doesn't make it right.

"When sex occurs outside wedlock," the evangelist warns, "it only contributes to unhappiness. The adulterer or adultress may boast, 'I cheat on my mate all the time and I don't have any hangups.' Perhaps not yet, but one day soon I guarantee it will take its toll. Misused sex becomes a terrible tyrant!"

Graham has repeatedly pointed out that satisfying sex doesn't just happen. "You have to work at it," he says. "You have to want to make it satisfying. You have to be willing to communicate with your wife or husband. Your mate will never know what pleases you unless you do communicate. I'm not offering you a mess of lofty platitudes. Christian psychiatrists, psychologists, sociologists, marriage counselors, back up what I'm saying. They have all discovered that sexual freedom outside marriage leads to chaos."

Even before turning to God at age sixteen, Billy held that view. His parents told him that the sexual act should be postponed until after the wedding. He is glad they did and happy that he listened. "I shall be eternally grateful. Some of the other fellows in town may have thought me a square. But they were really the squares. All around me I see the misery caused by the wanton use of free sex."

Shortly after Graham became a full-time evangelist, an elderly revivalist told him, "Billy, you better be constantly on your guard. You're young and virile and women are attracted to evangelists—I know."

Many women have tried to place Graham in a compromising position, and he is very careful to leave his door open or to have an associate present whenever he talks to someone of the opposite sex. These precautions are occasionally insufficient. One brazen divorcée attempted to remove her clothes as she loudly announced that she would "gladly sacrifice all privacy for the privilege of serving the evangelist." He fled before she reached her slip.

In the course of a visit to East Berlin, a newspaper reported that a drunken Billy was making the rounds of nightclubs with a blonde draped on each arm. When the revivalist was shown the story, he said, "That poor reporter sure goofed. The night I was supposed to have been whooping it up happened to be the one I was rolling in agony with a kidney stone in the Frankfurt army hospital."

Ruth is not deceived by any of these false plots. "A successful marriage has to be built on mutual trust," she said, "and I know fully that Bill's values coincide with mine."

15
TEN COMMANDMENTS FOR A HAPPY MARRIAGE

EACH YEAR Billy Graham receives thousands of letters from husbands and wives seeking help for love and marriage problems. The writers complain that romance has fled the home, that controversy and dissent occur daily. They are fearful that their marital unions are sentenced to death.

The evangelist replies that if you really want to save your marriage, you can. He points out that despite the alarming divorce statistics, many good marriages do exist. He asks why some work marvelously while others seem to be nothing short of a battleground.

He believes the reasons are not as obscure as some authorities assume and that no dispute exists that cannot be resolved. Billy recalls that when he and Ruth were about to celebrate their thirty-fifth wedding anniversary, a friend wanted to know if the evangelist had ever seriously considered divorce. "No," Graham replied truthfully. "It never even entered my mind."

The next question asked was, "What's your secret?"

Billy said that God has given us certain guidelines for marriage, and when they are neglected, the likelihood of marital difficulty is greatly increased. For years he and Ruth have followed what may be called *The Grahams' Ten Commandments for a Happy Marriage*.

1. *Put God in your marriage.* I mention this first because I am convinced that this is the most important key for a solid marital union. It must have a solid rock upon which to build—it cannot be half and half. If you want certain discord in your home, have deep-seated religious differences. There must be a spiritual understanding.
2. *Learn the art of mutual acceptance.* Respecting each other without constantly wishing things were different is crucial. That doesn't mean a husband or wife simply relaxes and casually decides it is unimportant to change. If the couple honestly wants to improve their marriage, they will seek to overcome irritants. Frustration, disappointment and sorrow are an inevitable part of life. Happiness is hoped for but not promised. It must be merited.
3. *Accept your individual responsibilities.* Not only should the mates accept each other, but they should accept the responsibilities each has as husband and wife. Obvious? It is surprising how many letters I get groaning about these failures—each blaming the other. Self-righteousness is a menace to marriage.
4. *Communicate.* This is essential. One of the saddest things I have heard married people say is, "We don't really have anything to talk about anymore." I know of couples who remain silent with each other the entire day. In the restaurant, just look at a table next to you shared by a husband and wife. Often, nothing is said during the entire meal. A wonderful way to rekindle conversation is by discussing the Bible.

5. *Take time with each other.* For two people to get married only to go their separate ways is illogical and against God's plan for marriage. Modern life may appear to require perpetual running—I urge you to slow down.

6. *Give attention to the little things.* What do I mean by "little things"? It may be removing the curlers from your hair before your husband comes home. It may mean taking out the trash without protesting. *Simple things,* but oh so important.

7. *Beware of pitfalls and learn to forgive.* Each marriage is unique, and each faces its own peculiar problems. Recognize them and try to avoid them. But if they do occur— forgive. To have a successful marriage you need two good forgivers.

8. *Recognize the greatest enemy of your marriage—selfishness.* Have you ever asked yourself what the opposite of love is? Many of us would say, "hate." But this is an incomplete answer. The real opposite of love is selfishness. Being aware of this fact is an important step in the right direction. A happy marital partnership has to be dominated by love— two people seeking out ways to do what is best for the other.

9. *Learn to grow—together.* Too often one mate has matured remarkably but the other one is left far behind. Ruth and I have learned to listen carefully and respectfully to the other's point of view. We find it healing to kneel together at least once a day. I pray for her and she in turn prays for me. Let not the sun go down upon your wrath.

10. *See your marriage as an opportunity to serve.* God has not given us marriage just to be selfishly enjoyed. He wants us to use our marriage to benefit others. You will feel enriched when you do.

Billy stresses that each of the ten marriage commandments is only a starting point. "They can help prepare you for everlasting joy," he says. "That is, if you let them. Sadly, in our mixed-up system of values there is so much turmoil regarding the proper roles for husband and wife, father and mother. It's gotten so complicated that many couples do not know which way to turn. They regard the Bible as a stumbling block when it says, 'Wives, submit yourselves unto your husbands.'

"I try to tell them that 'submit' is only part of the passage. The full sentence is: 'Wives, submit yourselves unto your husbands, *as unto the Lord*.' I ask them to consider the word 'submit.' It means yield to authority and judgment of another. Its ancient root includes the implication that the partners are to adapt themselves to each other '*in the Lord*.'

"If the husband is 'in the Lord' his mind will be that of Jesus. Thus a husband is never first in the human family; that position rightfully belongs to God. The husband and wife have different functions but are equals in mind and conscience, position and privilege, freedom and happiness. Instead, many couples ignore that and battle about supremacy."

16
LIVING FOR EACH OTHER AND TOGETHER FOR GOD

"I LOVE RUTH far more now than I did when we were married," Billy confided. The evangelist and his wife believe without reservation that there is a simple explanation for their continuing ecstasy. To the Grahams, wedded bliss means *to live for each other and together for God*.

"A successful marriage is a triangle," Ruth says. "It consists of the husband, wife and the Lord. With that combination, marriage is made. It has been that way for me. Now that the children are grown and have families of their own, Bill and I are getting to spend more time together."

Recently, she joined her husband in London, where she watched Prince Philip award him the coveted $200,000 Templeton Prize in Religion. A usually reserved British journalist covering the posh event, which was held in Buckingham Palace, muttered, "Mrs. Graham should be emulated by all other wives. It's rather obvious that my wife didn't ogle me in that manner when I was named our borough's Outstanding Father of the Year."

That opinion is shared by many people who have observed the pair. Golda Meir, the late Premier of Israel, considered herself a good friend of the evangelist. "If he wasn't such a *goy*," she said jestingly when she was in her mid-seventies, "I'd try to catch him for a husband. But I'm afraid that Ruth would object, and I know what a hopeless job it would be to yank them apart. He gets stars in his eyes whenever he talks about her."

Billy has made many trips to the Holy Land, where he is held in high esteem by prominent Israeli officials. He disarmed them quickly by saying, "I'm very pro-Jewish. I feel close to the Jewish people. Christianity was built on Judaism. After all, we Christians have committed our lives to a Jew. . . . Whenever any group suffers injustice and oppression, the potential of a new holocaust exists. It would be blind optimism to declare it couldn't happen again."

Teddy Kollek, the fiery mayor of Jerusalem, said, "I know of no other Christian who is more dedicated an ally to us. I remember a trip I made with him to the Wailing Wall, the only surviving part of the Second Temple. We watched the *yarmulka*-wearing worshipers praying. Some of them were very, very old. There were tears in Billy's eyes."

Graham was extremely upset about the slaughter of Lebanese civilians by Christian Phalangist militiamen. He immediately told reporters that Israel should conduct a complete inquiry to determine how it was allowed to happen. He added that Americans should realize that the soldiers who committed the atrocity "are not Christians in our sense of the word." He emphasized that Christian Phalangist is a political term and not a religious name.

In between crusades the Grahams enjoy sitting on their porch and gently swaying in the handcarved rocking chairs President Johnson presented them. As they gaze across the valley 3600 feet below, to high mountain peaks, they frequently discuss world problems. Currently, the Middle East occupies a great deal of their concern. Ruth, who also feels close to the Jewish people, dangles a tiny lavaliere that she often wears. It's inscribed in Hebrew: "Pray for the peace at Jerusalem." She has stated repeatedly, "I simply can't understand how anyone who calls himself a Christian could be remotely anti-Semitic!"

Billy is not as worried about the United States or the Soviet Union dropping the atomic bomb as he is with the possible menace of a hostile and ambitious small country. "It's the tiny nation that is headed by an unstable leader that I fear the most."

He says that he gets some of his best thoughts during conversations with his wife: "I so look forward to spending quiet moments alone with her," he said recently. "Especially in our mountain home that seems so far removed from the hurry-scurry of the outside world. I've found that periods of tranquillity are so necessary for everyone's well-being. That's one of the things wrong with modern marriage—too much of 'you step on it, I'm in a hurry!' "

Billy has always liked to take long walks in the woods accompanied by one of his pet dogs. Belshazzar, a Great Pyrenees, was often at his side, and upon returning would boldly follow his master into the house. "That dog would never do that when Bill was away on a crusade," said Ruth. "But with Bill home, it was a completely different story. He idolized him—wouldn't leave his side. Why, he would get so jealous that once he ripped the coat of a visitor who had the effrontery to shake Bill's hand. Sometimes I wish there was such a thing as getting a dog converted."

A narrow, twisting, single-lane road winds up to the Graham's ten-room, cabin-style home. It was built of local hand-hewn logs and is encircled by an eight-foot electrified fence. Additional protection is provided by a sturdy iron-grille gate and three German shepherd police dogs. Ruth admits the security measures make her think of a concentration camp. "I always feel like apologizing to our guardian angels," she said.

J. Edgar Hoover recommended the high barrier and attack dogs when the evangelist and his family received kidnap threats. "In one week's time, five people tried to break into Billy's house," the F.B.I. director told a reporter from the *Washington Star*. "That's when I advised him that he better do something before tragedy struck. I proposed a sign saying: *Trespassers will be eaten*."

Johnny Cash is a close friend of the Grahams. "I'm afraid these safeguards are very necessary," he said. "My wife, June, and I also have been forced to install some precautions. Once you get past the ones Billy and Ruth have, you immediately think of heaven on earth. It's one of the most peaceful places June and I have ever visited. Simple, but at the same time inspiring. . . . Billy and Ruth are very serious about a German inscription that's burned into the mantel of their huge living room fireplace: *Ein feste Burg ist unser Gott*. It means, 'A mighty fortress is our God.' "

One intruder, a wild-eyed and disheveled man in his early twenties, managed to get into the house. He found Billy alone in the study. "I've come to kill you!" he shouted as he charged at the evangelist.

Graham wrestled him to the floor. Suddenly, the would-be assassin began to sob and babble unintelligible phrases. Billy realized that his unwelcome guest was mentally deranged. After calming him down and calling the authorities, he and the sick young man knelt down and prayed together.

An immense kitchen is the heart of the house. It, too, has a large fireplace. The walls and ceiling, like all the other rooms, have exposed timbers. The living room, dining room, book-lined study, and bedrooms are furnished with primitive mountain pieces now rated valuable antiques. "They are very rugged and have withstood the onslaught of energetic children and pets," Ruth said. "If we had bought delicate modern things, they would have worn out long ago. I was lucky to get them at a time when they were still available for insignificant sums. Today, we couldn't afford them."

She traveled the countryside, looking for mountain furniture, old beams and bricks. While saying, "Fill 'er up," she asked gasoline attendants if they knew of any abandoned cabins. The owner of a service station near Montreat recalled, "Mrs. Graham sure has a lot of native grit. She'd pounce on the slightest suggestion. One time I told her I thought a wooden bench was available down the road. I barely had time to get the nozzle out of her gas tank before she took off."

Several years ago Muhammad Ali visited the Grahams' mountain home. For more than five hours the former heavyweight boxing champion talked about what it was like to be a Muslim and discussed his fighting career. "I liked those two," Ali says. "But they are full of surprises. It started at the airport. I expected to be chauffeured in a Rolls-Royce or at least a Mercedes. But we got into this old American car and Billy drove it all by himself. The house also caught me by surprise. It's not a fancy mansion with crystal chandeliers and gold carpets. Just made out of plain old logs. Billy could probably make even more money than me, but I guess he likes what he's doing."

There has been widespread speculation about the value of the Graham estate. Estimates have ranged from $100,000 to several million. The evangelist shrugged his shoulders when replying. "The bank helped us raise money for the land. Book royalties and friends helped us build the house."

Early in Billy's career he decided to refuse the love offerings that traditionally provided income for traveling revivalists. By 1950 he had become a household name. For the past thirty years pollsters have rated him as one of the Ten Most Admired Men in the World. He was advised by Dr. Jesse Bader, Secretary of Evangelism for the National Council of Churches, to set up a nonprofit organization.

"What set me off," Graham recalls, "was two photographs in an Atlanta newspaper. One showed me waving good-bye to a crusade audience and the other showed a box of money the ushers had collected. They were featured side by side. The inference was pretty plain—I was conducting a racket. The image of Elmer Gantry was still large in many minds.

"I wanted no mistakes like that. So, to avoid any possible suspicion, I took Dr. Bader's advice and set up a corporation called the Billy Graham Evangelistic Association. I got a very competent board of directors, made the finances public and put myself on a straight salary. . . . I fear it's not enough to allow my family to sit back and enjoy a large inheritance."

The evangelist's initial salary was $15,000 a year. Currently he earns $39,500. He also receives royalties from his books. These funds are held in trust for Ruth and the children. The Grahams resolved they would never live higher than the pastor of a large city church. Close friends say that they have kept that vow (The $200,000 Billy received when he was awarded the Templeton Prize was promptly donated to relief organizations and to schools which train evangelists.)

Shortly after Billy appeared on the cover of *Time* magazine, one of the children was asked, "Now, that your father is so famous, I suppose he'll buy you a large, talking doll."

The youngster shrugged her shoulders. "Who do you think he is," she replied, "Rockfeller?"

Whenever possible the Grahams visit their fifteen grandchildren. Several years ago Ruth was putting up a swing for her eldest daughter's youngsters. She leaned too far forward and fell out of a tall tree, which resulted in a concussion, memory loss and other severe injuries. Her right hip had to be reconstructed and surgery was performed on her wrist. For months she was forced to use a cane. She has abandoned motorcycle riding and hang-gliding, both sports she took up after reaching her fiftieth birthday.

Doctors restrict her to less vigorous activities. Among them are composing poetry, gardening, painting, sewing and traveling with her globe-trotting husband. Shortly after an earthquake struck Guatemala City, she and Billy flew there to coordinate relief work. Together they helped rebuild the devastated region. When they returned to the United States, the evangelist told a reporter, "I'm indeed fortunate to be married to a wife who has such deep-seated passion for people who aren't as lucky as we are. But then, many married men have wonderful helpmeets—they simply fail to recognize it. It doesn't have to be something as spectacular as an earthquake to make them realize their blessing."

Ruth has had a chronic cough for the past twenty years; it used to keep Billy awake. Not long ago she moved into a bedroom which adjoins his, but shyly admits that she's often in her husband's room. "Married couples need many moments together," she says.

Although the evangelist looks in splendid health, he has been hospitalized many times and suffers from a number of ailments. He has frequent disability from kidney stones, recurrent backache, high blood pressure and insomnia, and is subject to attacks of flu. Recently, he and his wife were scheduled to dine at the White House with President and Mrs. Reagan. The invitation had to be postponed when he slipped on a mountain ledge in Spokane, while hiking with his son Ned, and injured his lower back.

"A lesser man would have slowed down long ago," said one of his associates. "Doctors have warned him to take it easy. But not Billy Graham! He declared that God entrusted him with a mission and he's determined to carry it out no matter what. That man is a human spiritual dynamo—always on the move—always trying to operate full force. We have to constantly shield him or he'd attempt to work twenty-four hours a day. The president of the Southern Baptist Convention realized this when he said, 'I'm awfully glad the Lord is easier to get to than Billy is.'"

Dr. Martin Buehler, a distinguished Dallas physician, tried to impress upon the evangelist the pressing need to take better care of himself: "I insisted that he required more time off to rest and relax. I explained to him that no human body or mind could take the tremendous burden that he was constantly imposing on himself. I fear, however, that he listened with half an ear."

Billy did agree to make one concession: try and keep in shape by performing regular exercise. He run-walks every afternoon, and when he's at home during the warm weather, swims in a small pool that Ruth has built for him. "It's next to his bedroom," she explained, "and he doesn't have to walk far to use it. Not very big—four strokes by two strokes. He complained about the cost, but I told him that it's cheaper than a funeral."

Each September, Billy and Ruth take a two-week vacation. "It has become a ritual," says the evangelist. "We try to let nothing interfere with it. We go down to a little island in the Caribbean—St. John in the Virgin Islands. Believe me, by September we badly need the rest."

Several years ago their annual holiday afforded more than tranquillity and relaxation. Norman Lawrence, a fifty-one-year-old realtor from Maryland, tells why: "Marion, my wife, and I were vacationing at the Rockefeller place in St. John.

It was our twenty-fifth wedding anniversary, but it felt more like a hundred. To put it mildly, we weren't very contented with our lives.

"Not that we argued in public. No, we were too civilized for that. We were just plain bored! We'd sit through an entire meal without exchanging a word. It was the same when we were tennis partners or playing bridge. Even something simple like sneezing was ignored. It wouldn't occur to us to say, 'God bless you,' or to offer some other acknowledgment. Where the other one was concerned, we were strictly 'Silent Sam' and 'Silent Sue.'

"It was during one of our mute dinners that we saw the Grahams. Because they seemed so unlike us we kept staring at them. They were so animated. So alive. Then we did something we hadn't done in a long time—we actually talked to one another. We kept speculating why the Grahams liked being together. It was clear they had something we hadn't. It was Marion who suggested it was 'believing in the Lord.' I always wanted to be a good person—doesn't everybody? Perhaps this was the opportunity.

"Well, to make a long story short, we both became 'born-agains.' Marion doesn't like me using those words. She says that 'born-again' sounds like some kind of hellfire revivalism. She prefers 'conversion.' Feels that term is more accurate.

"Whatever you call it, we didn't honestly expect it to make much of a difference in our lives. But it has—honestly it has. It is still working—we're both happy to be in God's world. I don't want to sound saccharine, but I'm actually looking forward to our Golden Anniversary. And to think it all started by watching two people talk to each other!"

Billy is often asked, "Does being a public figure bother you?"

"Yes," replies the evangelist. "One of the most difficult things I have had to face was the loss of personal privacy. I did not seek the publicity, and how it all came about I truthfully don't know. I'd much rather be the minister of a small parish somewhere, but Ruth and I decided long ago that as it was this way, we'd go ahead with it. Years before I discovered that if your wife is behind what you're doing, the path becomes much smoother."

Billy evidenced his marital bliss in a television conversation with David Frost. "If a burglar was to get into your house somehow," asked the British talk show host, "and said he'd leave you one material possession or gift if you asked him nicely, what would you say you wanted to keep?"

Without hesitation, the evangelist replied, "My wife!"

Unmistakably, Ruth feels the same way. Some time ago a woman who was sitting next to her at a crusade gazed tenderly at the evangelist while he was speaking. "I wonder what it would be like to wake up and find yourself married to that man?" she said dreamily.

"You've asked the right person," Ruth replied. "I've been doing it for years. I tell you it's great and gets better all the time!"

BIBLIOGRAPHY

Allan, Thomas. *Crusade in Scotland*. London: Pickering and Inglis, 1955.

Babbage, Stuart, and Siggins, Ian. *Light Beneath the Cross*. Garden City, New York: Doubleday, 1960.

Barnhart, Joseph. *The Billy Graham Religion*. Philadelphia: United Church Press, 1972.

Bishop, Mary. *Billy Graham: The Man and His Ministry*. New York: Grosset and Dunlap, 1978.

Brown, Joan Windmill, editor. *Day by Day*. Minneapolis: World Wide Publications, 1976.

Burnham, George. *A Mission Accomplished*. Old Tappan, New Jersey: Fleming H. Revell, 1955.

————. *To the Far Corners*. Old Tappan, New Jersey: Fleming H. Revell, 1956.

———— and Fisher, Lee. *Billy Graham and the New York Crusade*. Grand Rapids, Michigan: Zondervan Publishing House, 1957.

Colquhoun, Frank. *Haringey Story*. London: Hodder and Stoughton, 1955.

Cook, Charles. *The Billy Graham Story*. Wheaton, Illinois: Van Kampen Press, 1954.

———. *London Hears Billy Graham*. London: Marshall, Morgan and Scott, 1955.

Demary, Donald, editor. *Blow, Wind of God: Selected Writings of Billy Graham*. Grand Rapids, Michigan: Baker Book House, 1975.

Eisenhower, Julie Nixon. *Special People*. New York: Simon and Schuster, 1977.

Frady, Marshall. *A Parable of American Righteousness*. Boston: Little, Brown, 1979.

Frost, David. *Billy Graham Talks with David Frost*. Philadelphia: A. J. Holman, 1971.

Gillenson, Lewis. *Billy Graham and Seven Who Were Saved*. New York: Trident Press, 1967.

Graham, Billy. *The Secret of Happiness*. Garden City, New York: Doubleday, 1955.

———. *The Seven Deadly Sins*. Grand Rapids, Michigan: Zondervan Publishing House, 1955.

———. *Billy Graham Talks to Teenagers*. Grand Rapids, Michigan: Zondervan Publishing House, 1958.

———. *Billy Graham Answers Your Questions*. Minneapolis: World Wide Publications, 1960.

———. *The Challenge: Sermons from Madison Square Garden*. Garden City, New York: Doubleday, 1969.

———. *The Jesus Generation*. Grand Rapids, Michigan: Zondervan Publishing House, 1971.

———. *How to be Born Again*. Waco, Texas: Word Books, 1977.

Graham, Morrow. *They Call Me Mother Graham*. Old Tappan, New Jersey: Fleming H. Revell, 1977.

Graham, Ruth Bell, as told to Elizabeth Sherrill. *Our Christmas Story*. Minneapolis: World Wide Publications, 1971.

————. *Sitting by My Laughing Fire*. Waco, Texas: Word Books, 1977.

————. *It's My Turn*. Old Tappan, New Jersey: Fleming H. Revell, 1982.

High, Stanley. *Billy Graham*. New York: McGraw-Hill, 1956.

Hoke, Donald. *Revival in Our Time*. Grand Rapids, Michigan: Van Kampen Press, 1950.

Kilgore, James. *Billy Graham, the Preacher*. New York: Exposition Press, 1968.

Kooiman, Helen. *Transformed: Behind the Scenes with Billy Graham*. Wheaton, Illinois: Tyndale House, 1970.

McLoughlin, William. *Billy Graham: Revivalist in a Secular Age*. New York: Ronald Press, 1960.

McMahan, Thomas. *Safari for Souls: With Billy Graham in Africa*. Columbia, South Carolina: The State Record Company, 1960.

Mitchell, Curtis. *Billy Graham: The Making of a Crusader*. Philadelphia: Chilton Books, 1966.

————. *Billy Graham, Saint or Sinner*. Old Tappan, New Jersey: Fleming H. Revell, 1979.

Morris, James. *The Preachers*. New York: St. Martin's Press, 1973.

Parrot, L. Lee. *How to Be a Preacher's Wife and Like It*. Introduction by Ruth Graham. Grand Rapids, Michigan: Zondervan Publishing House, 1956.

Paul, Ronald. *Billy Graham: Prophet of Hope*. New York: Ballantine Books, 1978.

Poling, David. *Why Billy Graham?* Grand Rapids, Michigan: Zondervan Publishing House, 1977.

Pollock, John. *Billy Graham*. New York: McGraw-Hill, 1966.

————. *A Foreign Devil in China*. Minneapolis: World Wide Publications, 1971.

————. *Billy Graham, Evangelist to the World*. New York: Harper and Row, 1979.

Settel, T. S., editor. *The Faith of Billy Graham*. Anderson, South Carolina: Droke House, 1968.

Shea, George Beverly, with Bauer, Fred. *Then Sings My Soul*. Old Tappan, New Jersey: Fleming H. Revell, 1968.

Smart, W. J. *Six Mighty Men*. London: Hodder and Stoughton, 1956.

Strober, Gerald. *Graham: A Day in Billy's Life*. Garden City, New York: Doubleday, 1976.

————. *Billy Graham: His Life and Faith*. Waco, Texas: Word Books 1977.

Tchividjian, Gigi Graham. *Thank You Lord, for My Home*. Minneapolis. World Wide Publications, 1980.

Wilson, Grady. *Billy Graham as a Teenager*.

Wirt, Sherwood Eliot. *Crusade at the Golden Gate*. New York: Harper and Row, 1959.

Index

Note: No attempt has been made to record references either to Billy Graham (William Franklin Graham, Jr.) or to Ruth Bell Graham

MADRID

| CONDENSED |

 sally o'brien

LONELY PLANET PUBLICATIONS
Melbourne • Oakland • London • Paris

contents

Madrid Condensed: 1st edition – March 2003

Published by
Lonely Planet Publications Pty Ltd
ABN 36 005 607 983
90 Maribyrnong St, Footscray, Vic 3011, Australia
e www.lonelyplanet.com or AOL keyword: lp

Lonely Planet offices
Australia Locked Bag 1, Footscray, Vic 3011
☎ 03 8379 8000   fax 03 8379 8111
e talk2us@lonelyplanet.com.au
USA   150 Linden St, Oakland, CA 94607
☎ 510 893 8555   Toll Free 800 275 8555
fax 510 893 8572
e info@lonelyplanet.com
UK   10a Spring Place, London NW5 3BH
☎ 020 7428 4800   fax 020 7428 4828
e go@lonelyplanet.co.uk
France   1 rue du Dahomey, 75011 Paris
☎ 01 55 25 33 00   fax 01 55 25 33 01
e bip@lonelyplanet.fr
www.lonelyplanet.fr

Designer Steven Cann Editor Simone Egger Proofer
Adrienne Costanzo Cartographers Andrew Smith,
Jacqui Nguyen, Jarrad Needham & Tony Fankhauser
Cover Designers Annika Roojun & Gerilyn Attebery
Project Manager Charles Rawlings-Way Commission-
ing Editor Heather Dickson Series Designer Gerilyn
Attebery Series Publishing Managers Katrina Browning
& Diana Saad Thanks to LPI, Nikki Anderson & Rowan
McKinnon

Photographs
All uncredited photos by Guy Moberly. Other images
as indicated.

Many of the photographs in this guide are available
for licensing from Lonely Planet Images:
e www.lonelyplanetimages.com
Edward Hopper's 'Hotel Room' image on p17 used
with kind permission of Museo Thyssen-Bornemisza.

Front cover photographs
Top Hats near Puerta del Sol (Christopher Wood)
Bottom Torres Puerta Europa (Donald C. & Pricilla
Alexander Eastman)

ISBN 1 74059 392 8

Text & maps © Lonely Planet Publications Pty Ltd 2003
Grateful acknowledgement is made to World Food
Spain, and for reproduction permission of Metro de
Madrid: Madrid Metro Map ©2001
Photos © photographers as indicated
Printed through Colorcraft Ltd, Hong Kong
Printed in China

how to use this book

SYMBOLS

- ⊠ address
- ☎ telephone number
- Ⓜ nearest metro station
- ▣ nearest Cercanía station
- ▤ nearest bus route
- ⊘ opening hours
- ⓘ tourist information
- Ⓢ cost, entry charge
- Ⓔ email/website address
- ♿ wheelchair access
- ♣ child-friendly
- ✕ on-site or nearby eatery
- Ⓥ good vegetarian selection

COLOUR-CODING

Each chapter has a different colour code which is reflected on the maps for quick reference (eg all Highlights are bright yellow on the maps).

MAPS

The fold-out maps inside the front and back covers are numbered from 1 to 4. All sights and venues in the text have map references which indicate where to find them on the maps; eg, (3, E14) means Map 3, grid reference E14. Although every item is not pin-pointed on the maps, the street address is always indicated.

PRICES

Price gradings (eg $10/5) usually indicate adult/concession entry charges to a venue. Concession prices can include senior, student, member or coupon discounts.

AUTHOR AUTHOR!

Sally O'Brien

Sally first visited Madrid in the '80s as a teen, where she was intrigued by *la movida*, the excellent shoe shopping, the art and the fact that a singing nun forced wine on her during Midnight Mass. An impecunious summer in Madrid in the '90s led to an even greater appreciation of beer, tapas and museum air-conditioning. In the '00s, she sees no reason to change the way she conducts herself, except to take a notebook.

Muchas Gracias: Diana, Gabrielle, Charles, Katrina, Heather, Simone and Steven at LP; Damien Simonis; Martin Hughes – for Condensed advice; Fabi, Marie-Claire, Zoe, Jaime, Janine, Anthony, Marina, Paola and María; Lara, Jody and Gerard.

READER FEEDBACK

Things change – prices go up, schedules change, good places go bad and bad places improve or go bankrupt. So, if you find things better or worse, recently opened or long since closed, please tell us and help make the next edition even more accurate. Send all correspondence to the Lonely Planet office closest to you (listed on page 2) or visit Ⓔ www.lonelyplanet.com/feedback.

facts about madrid

Wanna wake up in a city that never sleeps? Then this is your town. Madrid is like a heady, frothy beer slammed down in front of you. It's sometimes accompanied by a dazzling smile or studied indifference, but always with a small plate of tempting titbits pushed towards you.

This is a place where people aren't fazed by out-of-towners (after all, Madrid's population is full to bursting with people who weren't born here) and pride themselves on an 'anything goes' attitude to other peoples' lives. The harsh repression of the Franco years saw an explosion of extroverted creativity and festivity upon his demise in 1975, and *madrileños* (citizens of Madrid) aren't about to look backwards. Don't be surprised by animated conversations between strangers being struck up around you – join in. Self-consciousness and 'knowing one's place' are not the norm here – enjoying life is, whether it be at a sun-drenched *terraza* (terrace), a spine-tingling flamenco performance, a bloody bullfight, a fevered soccer match, a long lunch, a quick tapas stop, a soul-stirring day in an art museum, early morning dancing in a nightclub or a colourful local fiesta.

With the hours they keep, at first you'll wonder how madrileños have time for business, but you'll soon realise that their business *is* pleasure, and the city's infrastructure has been set up to accommodate this in many ways. As the old saying goes: 'Work to live – don't live to work'. And no other city lives quite like Madrid.

Whose shout? Café Central (p94)

HISTORY

Muslim Influence

Magerit, or Mayrit, as it came to be known, was a fortified garrison against the small Christian kingdoms to the north from 854 until well into the 10th century. Very little evidence survives, although the area between La Latina and the Palacio Real is still known as the *morería*, or Moorish quarter. Magerit was handed over to Christian rule in 1085 in exchange for the preferred area of Valencia.

Royals vs Reality

The royal court sat in Madrid for the first time in 1309, but it wasn't until 1561 that Madrid became the capital of Spain. The place still had unpaved lanes and filthy alleys, and suffered in comparison to other cities of Europe. It had no navigable river, or substantial port, and trade and communications with the rest of the country were difficult. The royal court spent untold sums on its sumptuous existence in an attempt to retreat from the squalid reality that surrounded it. The population swelled with immigrants hoping to gain patronage or a post with the machinery of government.

Caped Crusader

Carlos III's unpopular Italian minister, Esquilache, tried to have long capes declared illegal, arguing that Madrid's cleaner streets rendered them obsolete. After long riots, the notion was repealed, only to be reintroduced peacefully under a less controversial minister!

The mid-1700s was marked by a change in ruling dynasty and resulted in a period of common-sense government, with Carlos III at the helm. Madrid was generally cleaned up and attention turned to public works (with the completion of the Palacio Real and inauguration of the Jardín Botánico) and a fostering of the intellectual life of the city.

Napoleonic Interlude

Around 1805, France and Spain conspired to take Portugal. By 1808 the resulting French presence had become an occupation and Napoleon's brother was crowned king.

On 2 May 1808 townspeople attacked French troops around the Palacio Real and what is now Plaza del Dos de Mayo. The rebels were soundly defeated, but it marked the beginning of the War of Independence, a long campaign to oust the French. In 1812, 30,000 madrileños perished from hunger alone. By 1813, the war (with help from the British and Portuguese) ended.

A Republic or Civil War?

The first attempt at a republic was in 1873. The army had other ideas though, and restored the monarchy. A period of relative stability ensued and it wasn't until 1931 that a second republic was called.

By 1931, the rise of Madrid's socialists and anarchists elsewhere in Spain sharpened social tensions. A coalition of republicans and socialists proclaimed the second republic, which led to some reforms and political confrontation. Street violence and divisions within the left helped a right-wing coalition to power in 1933. Then, in 1936, it was the left-wing Frente Popular's turn to be in power. A violent face-off appeared to be inevitable – either the right-wing army would stage a coup, or the left would have its revolution.

The army moved first, and three years of bloody, horrendous warfare ensued. Franco's troops advanced from the south and were in the Casa de Campo (see p33) by early November 1936. The government fled, but a hastily assembled mix of recruits, sympathisers and International Brigades held firm, with fighting heaviest in the city's northwest. A battered Madrid finally fell to Franco on 28 March 1939.

The Franco Era

In the dark years of Franco's dictatorship, with Western Europe at war, the right-wing Falangist party maintained a heavy-handed repression, at its harshest in the 1940s.

> ### There's a Bear in There
> The symbol of Madrid city is a she-bear nuzzling a *madroño*, or strawberry tree (so named because its fruit resembles strawberries). The symbol is bordered by a frame bearing seven five-point stars and topped by a crown. If you don't believe us, check out the statue at Plaza de Puerta del Sol, near Calle del Carmen.

Look for real madroño trees in the plaza

Thousands of people suspected of sympathising with the left were harassed, imprisoned and subjected to forced labour.

Spain was internationally isolated, which lead to the *años de hambre* (the years of hunger). Only in 1955 did the average wage again reach the level of 1934. By this time, discontent was expressed in the universities and workers' organisations.

The Cold War saw the US grant economic aid to Franco's Spain in exchange for the use of Spanish air and naval bases. An economic boom followed in the 1960s, but clandestine opposition to Franco's rule remained.

Return to Democracy

When Franco died in 1975 trade union and opposition groups emerged from hiding. By 1977 these groups were legalised and elections were held. A centre-right coalition won power, which set about writing a new constitution in collaboration with the opposition. It provided for a parliamentary monarchy with no state religion and guaranteed a degree of devolution of power to the 17 regions into which the country is now divided.

ORIENTATION

Madrid is surprisingly compact. The main north-south artery, Paseo de la Castellana (which becomes Paseo de los Recoletos and Paseo del Prado at its southern end) connects the city's main train stations – Chamartín and Atocha.

The core of the oldest quarters is between Paseo del Prado (east) and the Palacio Real (west). Plaza Mayor is just west of the Puerta del Sol. South of this is the working-class *barrio* of Lavapiés – a vibrant, fascinating district.

West of Lavapiés is La Latina, a slightly more polished version of Lavapiés and a popular night haunt. The most delightful part of the old quarter is just east of the palace, an area known as Los Austrias.

North of Gran Vía, which runs north-east from Plaza de la Cibeles to Plaza de España are the lively 19th-century, slightly grungy *barrios* of Chueca and Malasaña.

East of Paseo de la Castellana are the tony 19th-century neighbourhoods of Retiro (the green oasis of Madrid) and Salamanca, with wide, tree-lined streets and smart shops.

Addressing the Problem

Addresses are frequently abbreviated in Madrid. Here's a key to deciphering some of the most common usages:

Av or Avda	Avenida
C/	Calle
Gta	Glorieta (roundabout)
Pº or Po	Paseo (parade/avenue)
Pl or Plz	Plaza
Pte	Puente (bridge)
s/n	*sin número* (without a number)
2º, 3º etc	2nd, 3rd floor etc

ENVIRONMENT

The usual big-city problems of air pollution are present, despite the fact that many of the streets in Madrid's older quarters have restrictions on parking and driving. The best solution for expanding your lungs with something other than traffic fumes is to head to one of Madrid's larger parks, such as the Parque del Buen Retiro or the Casa de Campo.

Plastic – not native to Río Manzanares

Rubbish disposal and collection remain a rather haphazard affair. Large, brightly coloured containers are scattered about the city for separated rubbish collection, but it's up to the locals to make use of it!

Noise pollution is a chronic problem for Madrid's citizens and visitors. Traffic, late-night partying and rubbish collection, sirens, loud conversations across inner court-yards in apartment blocks and barking dogs all assault the ears. Despite numerous protests by residents in town (look for the banners hanging off apartment balconies near the 'party plazas'), madrileños are frequently subjected to noise levels of around 80 decibels or more.

GOVERNMENT & POLITICS

Three governments rule from Madrid. The national government sits in the *cortes* (parliament), divided into the Congreso de los Diputados (lower house) on Carrera de San Jerónimo and the Senado (senate) on Plaza de España.

The city government, or *ayuntamiento*, is led by the mayor (*alcalde*) – the Partido Popular's (PP's) José Maria Alvarez del Manzano in 2002. Elections are due in 2003, with the main opposition, the Partido Socialista Obrero Español (PSOE; Spanish Socialist Workers' Party) looking strong as we went to press. The PP candidate is Alberto Ruiz-Gallardón.

> ### Did You Know?
> - Madrid's population is 3.03 million
> - The average annual salary in Madrid is €19,413
> - Madrid is the highest capital city in Europe at 650.7m above sea level

The regional government also sits in Madrid. Until the death of Franco, the province of Madrid remained a part of Castilla La Nueva (New Castille), the predecessor of today's Castilla-La Mancha. With 1983's devolution, Madrid province became a separate autonomous region, governed by a council (*consejo gobierno*), whose actions are controlled by the regional parliament (Asamblea de Madrid). Its president in 2002 was the PP's Alberto Ruiz-Gallardón.

For administrative purposes, Madrid is divided into 21 districts, each with its own local council (*junta municipal*).

ECONOMY

Madrid and its surrounding region are home to a big range of farming and industrial activities. Crops of wheat, barley, corn, garlic and grapes (among others), plus livestock, boost agriculture. Principal industries include metallurgy, chemicals, textiles, tobacco, paper and some foodstuffs. As the Spanish capital, Madrid itself is largely given over to services and big business. It's worth keeping in mind that Madrid was slow to develop during what was for many other cities the Industrial Revolution, and only really developed a middle class from the 1830s onwards.

Eternal rival Barcelona has watched with dismay as Madrid appears to grow in stature and become the prime financial and economic mover of Spain, shedding its previous image as a bureaucratic deadweight. Although unemployment fell steeply in the

Detail of the Stock Exchange building

second half of the 1990s, it still outstrips EU averages, and while the Spanish economy has been doing well in the 21st century, rising house prices are forcing the average madrileño family to spend 62% of its income on housing purchases.

SOCIETY & CULTURE

Madrid receives huge numbers of tourists every year, but it doesn't seem to phase the locals one bit. You'll find many people who speak English, particularly in the hotel and restaurant trade, but even a smattering of Spanish (officially known as *castellano*) will be patiently and warmly received, so learn a few basic phrases and don't be shy.

Born & Bred

True-blue, dyed-in-the-wool madrileños are known as *castizos* or *chulapos* (generally abbreviated to *chulos* – although the word can have some negative connotations, so perhaps it's best not to bandy it about). Occasionally you'll hear working-class men and women of Lavapiés referred to as *manolos* and *manolas* respectively.

About 185,000 migrants live in the city: Ecuadorians, Colombians and Moroccans comprise the majority, with Pakistanis, Africans, Chinese and Latin Americans filling the ranks. Many 'madrileños' also hail from elsewhere in Spain, making for a lively mix of cultures and accents.

Most madrileños profess to be Catholic, although this is often little more than lip service on a day-to-day basis. Still, passion remains strong for Easter processions and local fiestas for patron saints.

Etiquette

Madrileños can be economical with etiquette such as *por favor* and *gracias*, but don't take this as a sign of rudeness. That said, it's customary when in a bar or small shop to wish everyone a hearty *'Buenas días'* when you enter and *'Adiós'* when you leave. It's perfectly acceptable to attract the attention of the waiter or barstaff with *'oigo'* (literally, 'hear me') and the norm to respond to thanks with *'de nada'* (it's nothing).

The standard form of greeting between men and women is a light kiss on each cheek, from right to left. Men seem to take or leave handshakes on informal occasions, but they're pretty much standard in a business context. Women who are meeting for the first time – except in business situations – will generally kiss each cheek.

The Spanish concept of time is more relaxed than some other countries, but things that need a fixed time get one and it's generally adhered to. Littering is the norm, and in bars it's perfectly acceptable to chuck paper, toothpicks, cigarette butts etc onto the floor, but it's best to suss out what others are doing first.

Los Gatos (cats) - the place, not the order

ARTS

Architecture

Madrid is bereft of signs of the earlier stages of Spain's architectural history. Only a stretch of wall remains to indicate Madrid's status of early Muslim outpost, and the bell towers of the Iglesia de San Pedro El Viejo and Iglesia de San Nicolás de los Servitas are the only survivors of the Mudéjar style, which features a preponderance of brickwork. The much-interfered-with Casa de los Lujanes is the sole example of late-Gothic architecture.

Juan de Herrera (1530–97) was the greatest figure of the Spanish Renaissance, and developed a style that bears almost no resemblance to anything else of the period. His great masterpiece was the palace-monastery complex of San Lorenzo de El Escorial. Even after his death, Herrera's style lived on in Madrid. Termed *barroco madrileño* (Madrid baroque), his stern style is fused with a timid approach to the voluptuous ornamentation inherent in the baroque period. Buildings that fall into this category include the Real Casa de la Panadería, the Basilica de San Isidro, the *ayuntamiento* (town hall) and the Convento de la Encarnación. The last two were designed by Juan Gómez de Mora (1586–1648).

One of Madrid's greatest architects of the late 18th century was Ventura Rodríguez (1717–85), who designed the interior of the Convento de la Encarnación and the Palacio de Liria, in a style heading towards neoclassicism. His main competitor was the Italian Francesco Sabatini (1722–97), who finished the Palacio Real.

Neoclassicism was best executed by Juan de Villanueva (1739–1811), who designed the building now called the Museo del Prado. The 19th century saw the use of iron and glass becoming more commonplace – best exemplified by the Palacio de Cristal and train stations. The neo-Mudéjar style became *the* style for bullrings, with Las Ventas, finished in 1934, a prime example.

In the 1920s, the newly created Gran Vía provided the perfect opportunity for new building, and a number of Art Deco caprices still line the boulevard.

Madrid is a relatively modern city, which means that much of it has been constructed in the last 100 years or so. Still, few recent edifices display the sparkle of 'great architecture', although the leaning Torres Puerta Europa on Plaza de Castilla demonstrate some bold experimentation.

Palacio Real ceiling – a real palace

Painting

Madrid wasn't a centre of artistic production until 1561, when Felipe II moved the royal court here. Even so, the bulk of artists who lived and worked here came from elsewhere. Perhaps the most extraordinary of these was the Cretan-born Domenikos Theotokopoulos (1541–1614), popularly known as El Greco. He chose, however, to settle in Toledo and met with relative indifference from the court of Felipe II.

The golden age of Spanish art had few figures from Madrid, although there's plenty of great art from this period to see in the city. An extensive collection of José de Ribera's (1591–1652) works are in the Prado, as are some from Bartolomé Esteban Murillo (1618–82), while Francisco de Zurbarán's (1598–1664) work can be seen in the Real Academia de Bellas Artes de San Fernando. The great star of this time, however, was Velázquez (1599–1660), who moved to Madrid to be court painter. His eye for light and detail, plus the humanity that he captured in his subjects, are unmatched. His works can be seen at the Prado, including the masterpieces *Las Meninas* and *La Rendición de Breda*.

A parade of late-baroque artists working over the course of the 17th century has been loosely lumped together as the Madrid School, with some of them actually born and raised in Madrid.

Velázquez outside Museo del Prado – oh the humanity!

Antonio de Pereda (1608–78) and Fray Juan Rizi (1600–81) both have paintings in the Real Academia de Bellas Artes de San Fernando, while madrileño Claudio Coello (1642–93) has large-scale works displayed in San Lorenzo de El Escorial.

The 18th century saw Bohemian Anton Raphael Mengs (1728–79) as court painter, and it was his encouragement that inspired Francisco José de Goya y Lucientes (1746–1828) to begin a long and varied career. Goya is recognised as Spain's greatest artist of the 18th (and even the 19th) century. His early pieces had some of the candour of Hogarth and betrayed the influence of Tiepolo. He was appointed Carlos IV's court painter in 1799, and his style grew increasingly merciless. Masterpieces at the Prado by Goya include *La Maja Vestida* and *La Maja Desnuda* (see p15), along with *Los Caprichos* (The Caprices), a biting series of 80 etchings lambasting court life.

Madrid-born Juan Gris (1887–1927) flew the Cubist flag during his short life, and while the 20th century's greatest artist Pablo Picasso (1881–1973) was born in Málaga, he did study in Madrid for a time at the Escuela de Bellas Artes de San Fernando from 1897 (it didn't thrill him though). His most powerful work, *Guernica*, can be seen in the Centro de Arte Reina Sofía.

highlights

With some of the world's truly great museums (which are reason enough for coming), buildings that span the centuries, and atmospheric neighbourhoods brimming with character, Madrid has plenty of sights to keep you occupied. The highlights listed here are a combination of absolute must-sees and a few lesser-known favourites. Madrid's compact nature and excellent metro system are great for visitors.

Stopping Over?

Day One Take Madrid's pulse at Plaza de la Puerta del Sol, then listen to its heartbeat at Plaza Mayor. Spend at least half a day at the Museo del Prado before lunching at a traditional restaurant in the Los Austrias area. After lunch, take a walk in Campo del Moro before visiting the Palacio Real. Start the night sampling some tapas at any of the bars in Huertas and around Plaza de Santa Ana.

Day Two Start the day with a tour of Real Monasterio de las Descalzas Reales before heading to the Museo Thyssen-Bornemisza for a few hours. Refuel in Salamanca, then stroll through the Parque del Buen Retiro. Indulge in a glass of *cava* (champagne) at Café del Círculo de Bellas Artes before an evening stroll among the twinkling lights and grand buildings of Gran Vía.

> ### Madrid Lowlights
> Every city has its bits and pieces that it and you could do without – here are the things we didn't dig:
>
> - the pimps and customers of the hookers on Calle de la Montera, just off Puerta del Sol
> - the crowds on 'Free for EU citizens' Wednesday and Sunday
> - roadworks, roadworks, roadworks
> - the August exodus of locals
> - good local bars polluted by *tragaperras* – pokie machines
> - noise pollution and the lax attitude to street litter

Day Three Time for the Centro de Arte Reina Sofía, followed by a walk through the authentically gritty Lavapiés *barrio* and La Latina, over to the Basílica de San Francisco El Grande. Take lunch at one of Chueca's smart restaurants, then a post-prandial chill-out session is in order at the Real Jardín Botánico. When it starts to get dark, head to Malasaña for dinner and drinks.

Caminan en el Campo del Moro

MUSEO DEL PRADO   (3, H14)

In a city with three truly great art museums, the Museo del Prado sits at the top of the heap for most visitors – indeed, the Prado is a reason in itself for many to come to Madrid. Don't despair if you feel as though you haven't absorbed everything in this extraordinary collection – common wisdom suggests you need more than one visit here, and at *least* four hours on your first!

The building itself – completed in 1785 – served as a natural history museum and laboratories, and as a cavalry barracks before its conversion in 1819 as a repository of Spanish art held in royal collections. The collection has over 7000 works, with less than half on display. A grand extension (to be completed in late 2003 at a cost of €43 million) will allow visitors greater access to the treasures.

The Prado's three floors are organised as follows: the ground floor contains 12th- to 16th-century Spanish painting, 15th- to 16th-century Flemish and German painting, 14th- to 17th-century Italian painting, and sculpture from Ancient Greece and Rome; the 1st floor contains 17th- to 18th-century Spanish painting and 17th-century Flemish, Dutch and French painting; the 2nd floor has 18th-century Spanish, British, French, German and Italian painting, with sculpture, drawings and exhibition rooms. If your time is very limited, the strongest collections are the 17th- and 18th-century Spanish paintings.

Highlights of the ground floor include the *Annunciation* by Fra Angelico, and *The Story of Nastagio degli Onesti* – a perplexing work by

The pillars of artistic integrity

DON'T MISS
• the Casón del Buen Retiro (the one-time ballroom)
• rehydrating and resting in the cafeteria

Sandro **Botticelli** – both in Room 49. *The Triumph of Death* by Pieter **Brueghel** the Elder, *The Garden of Earthly Delights* by Hieronymous **Bosch** (El Bosco in Castillian) reside in Room 56a. *Auto da fé with Saint Domenic of Guzmán* by Pedro **de Gerruguete** is in Room 57b, **Titian's** *Danaé and the Shower of Gold* in Room 61b, and **Tintoretto's** *Christ Washing the Disciples' Feet* in Room 75. The works of **El Greco** can be seen in Rooms 60a, 61a and 62a; of particular note is his striking *Crucifixion*.

INFORMATION

- ⊠ Edificio Villanueva, Paseo del Prado
- ☎ 91 330 28 00
- e http://museoprado.mcu.es
- Ⓜ Banco de España
- ⊘ Tues-Sat 9am-7pm, Sun & hols 9am-2pm; closed 1 Jan, Good Friday, 1 May & 25 Dec
- Ⓢ adult/concession €3/1.50
- ⓘ booklets €1
- ♿ good
- ✗ cafeteria and restaurant

On the 1st floor, unmissables abound: *Atalanta and Hippomenes* by Guido **Reni** is in Room 5 (see also Plaza de la Cibeles, p31), and *The Three Graces* by **Rubens** in Room 9. *Christ Embracing Saint Bernard* by Francisco **de Ribalta** hangs in Room 24, and José **de Ribera's** sweet-eyed *Magdalen* is in Room 25. A collection of **Velázquez'** paintings (that any museum would kill for) is housed in Room 12; his innovative depiction of *The Triumph of Bacchus* competes with *Las Meninas*, which is perhaps the most extraordinary painting of the 17th century. It depicts Velázquez himself (on the left) painting a portrait (it is assumed) of King Felipe IV and Mariana of Austria (visible in the mirror) while the Infanta Margarita and her *meninas* (maids) enter the room, in the company of dwarves. Cheeky Velázquez depicts himself with the cross of the Order of Santiago on his breast – years before it was granted to him. The mathematical composition of the painting and use of perspective is a singular great achievement in Spanish painting. Other works by Velázquez are in Rooms 14, 15, 15a and 16.

Masterpieces by **Goya** can also be found on the 1st floor (Rooms 32 & 34–9). These last rooms contain his haunting *Pinturas Negras* (Black Paintings), including the truly disturbing *Saturn Devouring his Children* (Room 39). Also in Room 39 are *The 2nd of May* and *The 3rd of May*, which portray the 1808 anti-French revolt in Madrid and the repercussions of it, respectively. On the 2nd floor, which devotes its whole southern wing to Goya, you'll find the charming *La Maja Vestida* and *La Maja Desnuda*, both portraits of the same woman – one clothed, one nude.

DON'T MISS
- the *Tesoro del Delfín* in the basement
- suss out the copyists replicating the masters

MUSEO THYSSEN-BORNEMISZA   (3, G13)

In 1994, Madrid succeeded in getting the art collection that everyone wanted: that of Baron Thyssen-Bornemisza – an avid and voracious collector of predominantly European art who was happiest when buying a painting a week! The neoclassical Palacio de Villahermosa was overhauled to house the 800-odd piece collection, and in 2000 two adjoining buildings were acquired to hold a further 300 paintings, which should be open by late 2004.

Start perusing the collection on the 2nd floor, where you'll find a remarkable series of medieval triptychs and paintings of Italian, German and Flemish origin; Room 3's minuscule *Our Lady of the Dry Tree* demands a closer look. Room 4 highlights 15th-century Italian art, including works by Paolo **Uccello** (1397–1475). Hans **Holbein** the Younger's (1497–1543) wonderful *Henry VIII* can be found in Room 5 among an assortment of early Renaissance portraiture. Room 6 (known as the Villahermosa Gallery) hosts a sampling of Italian masters such as Lorenzo **Lotto** (c 1480–1556), **Raphael** (1483–1520), **Titian** (c 1490–1576) and **Tintoretto** (1518–94), and a darkly beautiful *Saint Casilda* by **Zurbarán**. Rooms 7 to 10 are devoted to 16th-century works from Italy, Germany, and the Netherlands. Four pieces by **El Greco** are displayed in Room 11, while a wonderful portrait of *Saint Catherine of Siena* by **Caravaggio** (whose influence on José de Ribera is obvious) is in Room 12. Rooms 13 to 15 display Italian, French and Spanish works of the 17th century, followed by 18th-century Italian work in Rooms 16 to 18, with some wonderful views of Venice by **Canaletto** (1697–1768). **Rubens'** *The Toilet of Venus* dominates the 17th-century works of Flemish, Dutch and German origin found in Rooms 19 to 21, with Anton **van Dyck**, Jan **Brueghel** and **Rembrandt** also represented.

Baron Hans Heinrich Thyssen-Bornemisza

The good baron, one of *the* great art collectors, died on 27 April 2002. In 1993, he wrote: 'An artist's talent is a gift to the world. When I began my collection, my eyes were my principal asset, and these are a gift from God. Painters do not create their works for one person alone. My legacy as a collector is to share my collection and I can only return God's gift by making it possible for more than one person to see it and to appreciate the artist's talent'. There's a full-length portrait of the baron on the museum's ground floor – don't forget to say thanks!

The 1st floor continues with the 17th-century Dutch theme from Rooms 22 to 26, with some still lifes in Room 27. Room 18 gives 18th-century art a look-in with **Gainsborough** (1727–88). Other continental artists from before the 19th century (North American and European) take over Rooms 29 to 31, with John Singer **Sargent** (1856–1925), John **Constable** (1776–1837) and Gustave **Courbet** (1819–77). Lovers of impressionism and post-impressionist works will be delighted by the museum's collection in Rooms 32 to 33, with paintings by **Renoir**

(1841–1919), **Degas** (1834–1917), **Manet** (1832–83), **Monet** (1840–1926) and **Van Gogh** (1853–90). Then, in a flurry of colour, Rooms 34 to 40 highlight Fauvist and Expressionist art in all their coruscating brilliance, with Egon **Schiele** (1890–1918), Henri **Matisse** (1869–1954), Edvard **Munch** (1863–1944) and **The Blue Rider** school (1911–14) founded by Wassily Kandinsky.

INFORMATION

- ⊠ Paseo del Prado 8
- ☎ 91 369 01 51
- e www.museothyssen.org
- Ⓜ Banco de España
- ◷ Tues-Sun 10am-7pm
- ⑤ adult/concession €4.80/3, temporary exhibitions €3.60/2.40, combined ticket €6.60/3.60, free under-12
- ⓘ guided handsets €3
- ⏜ excellent
- ✕ cafeteria

On the ground floor, visitors are given a powerful dose of the 20th century, from cubism to pop art. The experimental avant-gardes have commandeered Rooms 41 to 44, with **Picasso** (1881–1973) and Juan **Gris** (1887–1927) flying the Spanish flag, and Georges **Braque**. In Room 45, European expressionism prepares you for the next room's focus on works from the USA, with paintings by Jackson **Pollock** (1912–56), a stunning Mark **Rothko** (1903–70) and Georgia **O'Keefe** (1887–1980). For the last two rooms, it's late-surrealism to pop art, with one of our faves from Room 47 being Edward **Hopper's** *Hotel Room*. Lucien **Freud's** wonderful *Portrait of Baron Thyssen-Bornemisza* in Room 48 gives the visitor a chance to compare the complexity of the sitter's face as depicted here with the full-length portrait of the museum's namesake hanging near the entrance.

Part of the pleasure of a visit here lies in the methodical organisation and layout of the museum, which is easy to navigate and therefore makes it easy to appreciate its treasures. There are also such thoughtfully amusing touches as the fact that even the 'no smoking' signs are small canvases!

'Hotel Room' by Edward Hopper

CENTRO DE ARTE REINA SOFÍA (2, O5)

The expansive Centro de Arte Reina Sofía was adapted from the remains of the 18th-century San Carlos hospital with the intention of presenting the best Madrid has to offer in 20th-century Spanish art. The occasional appearance of non-Spanish artworks provides some useful comparisons between the Iberian works and the outside world. The museum's position in bohemian Lavapiés contrasts nicely with such space-age touches as the shiny steel-and-glass external elevators.

The museum's permanent collection is displayed over the 2nd and 4th floors. The 1st and 3rd floors are used to stage some excellent temporary exhibitions, and the 1st floor also boasts a bookshop and pleasant cafeteria.

Floor Plan Tips

The Centro de Arte Reina Sofia uses the US-style floor numbering system, which can cause a little confusion for first-time visitors. All you need to keep in mind is that the ground floor is known as the *primera planta* (1st floor) and so on.

Room 1 (2nd floor) gives visitors an introduction to Spanish painting at the turn of the 20th century, which tended to be dominated by the Barcelona scene. Among the artists featured are Santiago **Rusiñol** (1861–1931), Ramón **Casas** (1866–1932), and Isidro **Nonell** (1873–1911), along with the important Basque painter Ignazio **Zuloaga** (1870–1945).

Room 2 concentrates on *madrileño* José Gutiérrez **Solana** (1886–1945), whose dark-hued *La Tertulia de Café de Pombo* depicts an intellectual gossip session typical of 1920s Madrid. Room 3 presents a mix of Spanish and foreign painters whose work came before, during and after cubism, best exemplified by the works of Juan **Gris** in Room 4. Bronze and iron sculptures by Pablo **Gargallo** (1881–1934) are on display in Room 5.

The massive Room 6 is devoted to **Picasso** and dominated by the extraordinary *Guernica*. The painting (which is the sole reason many visitors come to this museum) is surrounded by a plethora of Picasso's preparatory sketches, and was commissioned by Spain's republican government for the Paris Exposition Universelle in 1937. That was the year that the German Condor Legion (working for Nationalist forces) bombed the Basque town of Gernika (Guernica), provoking outrage in Spain and abroad. The 3.5 by 7.8m painting, which Picasso did not want in Spain during the Franco dictatorship, was only returned from the USA in 1981. The breathtaking force of the work, the fact that it's one of the most famous paintings of the 20th century – and one of the starkest depictions of war's brutality – leaves much of the museum's collection for dust.

After such an experience, Room 7 showcases the primary-coloured works of Joan **Miró** (1893–1983), which are interspersed with a collection of twisting bronzes (and some sketches) by Juan **González** (1876–1942). Those with a penchant for surrealist extravaganzas will love Room 10, with Salvador **Dalí's** (1904–1989) *The Great Masturbator* (1929) and the disconcertingly straightforward *Girl at the Window* (1925). Rooms 11 and 12 have other surrealist works, including films by filmmaker Luis **Buñuel**, while Room 13 hosts works by artists active in the turbulent 1920s and

1930s. Luis **Fernández**, Benjamin **Palencia** and sculptor Alberto **Sánchez** are represented in Rooms 14 and 15, with Joan **Miró** sculptures in Room 16.

INFORMATION

✉ Calle de Santa
   Isabel 52
☎ 91 467 50 62
🖎 http://museoreina
   sofia.mcu.es
Ⓜ Atocha
🕐 Wed-Sat & Mon
   10am-9pm, Sun
   10am-2.30pm
💲 adult/concession
   €3/1.50
ⓘ guided handsets
   €2.40
♿ excellent
✕ cafeteria

The 4th floor comprises artworks created after the civil war – in an atmosphere of Francoist repression – to the present day, starting with Juan Manuel Diáz **Caneja** (1905–1988) landscapes in Room 18. In Room 19, works by two important post-WWII groups are presented – Pórtico and Dau al Set. Barcelona's Antoni **Tápies** (born in 1923) is one artist from the latter group – his textural explorations are worth noting. Abstract painting comes to the fore from Rooms 20 to 23, with members of the Equipo 57 group on display. From Room 24, the 1960s and 1970s are given an airing, with foreign references provided by Francis **Bacon** and Henry **Moore**. The present day, from Room 38, is given over to works by Eduardo **Arroya**, while sculptures by Eduardo **Chillida** fill Rooms 42 and 43.

The great glass elevators of Centro de Arte Reina Sofía

PLAZA MAYOR (3, G8)

The Puerta del Sol may feel like the hub of Madrid, but its imperial heart beats loudest at Plaza Mayor – the town square designed in 1619 by Juan Gómez de Mora. In the Middle Ages this area was positioned outside the city walls and known as Plaza del Arrabal. Traders liked the location as it enabled them to peddle their wares free from intramural taxation. The *alhóndiga del pan* – where wheat and flour to make bread were sold – was located here (to be replaced by the **Real Casa de la Panadería**, or royal bakery) along with butchers' stalls, fishmongers, wine stores and more. There are still plenty of shops in the plaza, and they're often good places to pick up local craft objects.

In 1673, food vendors raised tarpaulins above their stalls, thus protecting their wares (and themselves) from the refuse that people habitually tossed out of their windows from above. A fire in 1790 destroyed much of the plaza, but with Juan de Villanueva's supervision, a more-or-less faithful reproduction was soon delivered to the people of Madrid.

In the past, the plaza was the site of royal festivities, autos-da-fé (the ritual condemnation and burning of heretics) and bullfights. These days it's largely given over to those fancying an alfresco drink or snack, or wanting to meet up with people in an obvious location (some get really specific – 'under the testicles of the sculpted horse that Felipe III sits astride'). And if you think the murals adorning the Real Casa de la Panadería look a little modern, you're right. They're a 1990s addition, and a surprising success.

Felipe III oversees Plaza Mayor from atop his horse

DON'T MISS
- a morning coffee at any of the cafés
- the Sunday morning stamp and coin collectors' market
- buying a lurid 'your name here' bullfighting poster

PALACIO REAL   (3, F5)

Madrid's alcazar (fortress) burned down in 1734, giving King Felipe V the chance to really make his mark in the city with a dose of architectural splendour.

Felipe didn't live long enough to see the fruits of architects Filippo Juvara and Giovanni Batista Sacchetti's labours. Construction of the Italianate baroque palace lasted 26 years, by which time King Carlos III was in charge, and much of the palace's interior reflects his predilections. There are 2800 rooms, of which you can visit around 50.

Access to the apartments is from the northern end of Plaza de la Armería, where you'll ascend the grand stairway to the **Halberdier's rooms**, before entering the sumptuous blood-red and gold **Throne Room** with a Tiepolo ceiling. After this, you'll enter the **rooms of Carlos III**. His drawing room features a vault fresco, *The Apotheosis of Trajan* by Anton Raphael Mengs. The blue antechamber, decorated in the neoclassical style also has ceiling work by Mengs, this time depicting the *Apotheosis of Hercules*; there are also four portraits by Goya.

The **Gasparini Room** features an exquisite stucco ceiling and walls of embroidered chinoiserie silk. The extraordinary **Porcelain Room** (the name says it all), has elaborate details climbing every surface. Many of the rooms are awash with a predominant colour (yellow, green, blue or red), and in the midst of such luxury comes the sumptuous **Gala Dining Room**, with seating for what seems like thousands, and some staggering examples of tapestry work.

INFORMATION

✉ Calle de Bailén
☎ 91 454 88 00
ℰ www.patrimonio
nacional.es
Ⓜ Ópera
◷ 1 Apr-30 Sep Mon-Sat 9am-6pm, Sun & hols 9am-3pm; 1 Oct-31 Mar Mon-Sat 9.30am-5pm, Sun & hols 9am-2pm
⑤ adult/concession €6/3, free under-5 & Wed for EU citizens
ⓘ guided tours €7
♿ good
✗ cafeteria

Imposing Palacio Real

DON'T MISS
• the Armería Real (Royal Armoury) • the Farmacia Real (Pharmacy)
• the changing of the guard (1st Wed of every month Sept-June)
• the view from Plaza de la Armería over the parkland to the west

REAL MONASTERIO DE LAS DESCALZAS REALES   (3, F8)

The Real Monasterio de las Descalzas Reales is an oasis of calm in the heart of frenetic Madrid. This unmissable treasure trove of art exists thanks to Doña Juana of Austria, Felipe II's sister who converted the former palace into a Franciscan convent (there are still 23 nuns cloistered here) in the mid-16th century. She was followed by the Descalzas Reales (Barefooted Royals), a group of illustrious women who became Franciscan nuns, bringing some extraordinary works of art with them.

The convent's centre features a small garden with orange trees and a fountain, its simplicity in marked contrast to the elaborate Renaissance stairway, which features lavish fresco work and a painted vault by Claudio Coello. A portrait of Felipe II and three royal children looks down at visitors from the top of the stairs – with a suitably sombre and inbred cast to their features.

There are 33 (Christ's age at death) chapels in the convent, and a compulsory tour takes you past several of them. The first contains an eerily realistic recumbent Christ. The tombs of Doña Juana and Empress Maria of Austria are in the choir, which has 33 stalls (the convent's maximum capacity is 33 nuns). The convent also contains an extraordinary collection of 17th-century **tapestries** from Brussels, which are kept in the former sleeping quarters. Along the way, try spotting works by Rubens, Titian and Brueghel (you might need to if you're following a Spanish-language tour and don't speak Spanish).

INFORMATION

- ✉ Plaza de las Descalzas 3
- ☎ 91 542 00 59
- e www.patrimonio nacional.es
- Ⓜ Sol or Callao
- ⏰ Tues-Thur & Sat 10.30am-12.45pm & 4-5.45pm, Fri 10.30am-12.45pm, Sun & public holidays 11am-1.45pm
- Ⓢ adult/concession €3.45/1.80, free under-5 & Wed for EU citizens, combined ticket (valid 7 days) with Real Monasterio de la Encarnacion (see p40) €6/3.30
- ⓘ compulsory guided tour (English available) included in entry fee
- ✖ see Sol & Gran Via p87

A treasure trove of art awaits

Neil Setchfield

DON'T MISS
- the Bosch-style painting of the *Ship of Salvation*
- Pedro de la Mena's *Dolorosa*

PLAZA DE LA VILLA   (3, H6)

It is thought that this plaza was chosen to be the city's permanent seat of government in the late Middle Ages. It's one of Madrid's most beautiful spots, with a sense of history and some damn fine architecture.

The oldest structure is the early-15th-century **Casa de Los Lujanes**, with an exquisite tower, Gothic portals and Mudéjar arches. The tower is said to have held the imprisoned French monarch François I and his sons after they were captured during the Battle of Pavia in 1525.

The **Casa de Cisneros** was constructed in 1537 by the nephew of Cardinal Cisneros, who was a key adviser to Queen Isabel. It is *plateresque* (Spanish Renaissance) in inspiration, although it was much restored and altered at the beginning of the 20th century. The most obvious signs of the Renaissance style are visible in the main door and window above. It now serves as the *alcalde* (mayor's office) – lucky him!

A marvellous enclosed bridge links the Casa de Cisneros building with Madrid's 17th-century **ayuntamiento** (town hall), which stands on the western side of the plaza. This building is a wonderful example of the *barroco madrileño* (Madrid baroque) style, with Herrerian slate-tile spires. It was originally planned by Juan Goméz de Mora to be a prison, but ended up serving as both a prison and a town hall.

INFORMATION

Ⓜ Ópera
ⓘ free guided tours of the *ayuntamiento* (Spanish) on Mon 5pm & 6pm (arrive 10mins before)
♿ good
✗ see Los Austrias pp82-4

Plaza de la Villa

A Tight Budget

The austere demeanour of Madrid's *ayuntamiento* is due to the scarcity of funds for municipal buildings during the 17th century. As a matter of fact the *consejo* (town council) had met for the previous three centuries in the Iglesia de San Salvador (no longer standing), which once faced the plaza on Calle Mayor.

REAL JARDÍN BOTÁNICO (3, J15)

Meticulously maintained, the real Jardín Botánico is a must-visit for those seeking some green respite. Originally created in 1755 under orders from King Fernanado VI on the banks of the Río Manzanares, the gardens consisted of over 2000 plants.

In 1774, King Carlos III decided that the garden should be moved to Paseo del Prado, which was completed in 1781. The **Pabellón Villanueva**, designed by Juan de Villanueva, was constructed and botany classes were taught here in the early 19th century. Today it is used to display free art exhibitions.

The 1808 War of Independence wasn't kind to the gardens, with little money being set aside for maintenance and development. In the 1850s though, the garden was renovated and a zoo was established (now at Buen Retiro). The enormous Ministry of Agriculture building swallowed two hectares of the garden's space (leaving a total of eight) in 1882, and a cyclone in 1886 battered over 500 trees. After generations of serious neglect, the gardens were closed to the public in 1974, and extensive renovations carried out that – after seven years – saw the gardens restored to their former glory. For some unknown reason, you'll generally encounter few people as you stroll through the charming canopied pathways, admire the plots and statues of famous botanists, and the sounds of chirping birds. At these times, the chaos of Paseo del Prado seems miles away.

INFORMATION

- ✉ Plaza de Murillo 2
- ☎ 91 420 30 17
- e www.rjb.csic.es
- Ⓜ Atocha
- 🚌 10, 14, 19, 24–7, 32, 34, 45, 54, 57, 140 & Circular
- ⊙ Nov-Feb 10am-6pm, Mar 10am-7pm; Apr-Oct 10am-8pm
- ⑤ adult/concession €1.50/75c, free under-10 & over-65
- ⓘ art exhibitions (free, same hours as gardens) in the Pabellón Villanueva
- ♿ excellent

Steamy Real Jardín Botánico

DON'T MISS
- The muggy Exhibition Greenhouse • The plot of old roses
- The plots of medicinal, aromatic and culinary plants

GRAN VÍA (3, C7–E12)

Madrid's mighty boulevard cuts a southeastwards swathe through the city from Plaza de España to Calle de Alcalá. It is in parts tacky, energetic, elegant and garish. You'll find luxury hotels, *hostales,* fast-food joints, sex shops, chain stores, elegant fashion houses, banks, Internet cafés, cinemas, theatres and nightclubs, and a lot of people and vehicles!

The Gran Vía was constructed in the first decades of the 20th century, when over a dozen streets were discarded and entire neighbourhoods bulldozed, all to be replaced by grand architectural piles. Spain's neutral status in WWI made Madrid a prosperous city when other European capitals were riven with poverty.

Keep your eyes peeled for some buildings of note situated along Gran Vía (it can be tricky when there's so much throbbing life at ground level!), which provide a progressive tour through the 20th century's architectural trends. At Gran Vía 1 there's the **Edificio Grassy** (see p43). At No 2, **La Gran Peña** is a curved wedding cake of a structure. At No 10, **Edificio Estrella** is an excellent example of Madrid's ability to blend neoclassical influences, while No 12 is an Art Deco delight of a bar, the **Museo Chicote** (see p92). Gran Vía 28 is the site of Madrid's first skyscraper, the **Telefónica** building (see p45), while the intersection at Plaza Callao is rich in Art Deco-era cinemas (and human traffic!).

Gran Vía - the grand way

Big Guns

During the civil war, the length and breadth of Gran Vía made it perfect for artillery shells to thunder in from the front lines around the Ciudad Universitaria to the north. Gran Vía was subsequently nicknamed 'Howitzer Alley' (after the cannon).

PARQUE DEL BUEN RETIRO (2, N6)

Madrid's magnificent green lungs began life as the Real Sitio del Buen Retiro, or palatial grounds of King Felipe IV (1621–65). After Isabel II's ousting in 1868, the park was opened to one and all, which is exactly what you'll find on any weekend in this busy, vital and beautiful spot. Buskers,

INFORMATION

☉ Observatory Mon-Thur 9am-2pm, tours Fri 11am

Ⓜ Retiro, Ibiza or Atocha

♿ good

hawkers, fortune-tellers, potheads, families, lovers, puppeteers, cyclists, joggers, and tourists all soak up the leisure options and add to the atmosphere – particularly on a Sunday morning, or after Sunday lunch.

The artificial lake (*estanque*) is watched over by the massive structure of Alfonso XII's mausoleum. The western side of the lake features the **Fuente Egipcia** (Egyptian fountain), where legend says a fortune was buried (unfortunately not true).

South of the lake you'll find the **Palacio de Velázquez** and the **Palacio de Cristal** (Crystal Palace), which were both built by Ricardo Velázquez Bosco. The Palacio de Cristal, a particularly charming metal-and-glass structure, was built in 1887 as a winter garden for exotic flowers. Occasional exhibitions are held here and in the Palacio de Velázquez.

The very southern part of the park's borders contains one of Madrid's loveliest examples of 18th-century architecture – the **Observatorio Astronómico** (Astronomical Observatory), designed by Juan de Villanueva for King Carlos III.

Don't throw stones in crystal palaces – the Palacio de Cristal

DON'T MISS

- the Casón del Buen Retiro – the only remnant of the original palace (see also Museo del Prado, p14)
- *El Ángel Caído* (The Fallen Angel) – a statue of Lucifer

EL RASTRO (3, K8)

Sunday morning may seem quiet in other parts of Madrid, but in the area around Calle de Embajadores things are positively humming by 9am, buzzing by 11am and exploding by 2pm. El Rastro flea market has been given mixed coverage of late, with some believing it's not as good as it used to be, and that it caters mostly to tourists nowadays. Rubbish! On any given Sunday you'll find the streets choked with madrileños, tourists, a few pickpockets (watch your bags) and a cornucopia of stalls selling whatever you fancy – clothes, accessories, electrical goods, music, plants, furniture, art, food, drink and general junk.

The main action takes place from Plaza de Cascorro, down Calle Ribera de Curtidores, although it's always worth wandering off into the sidestreets and perusing the makeshift stalls that are set up on blankets and sheets placed on the ground. The less-transient shops of the neighbourhood are also doing a roaring trade, with second-hand shops (often specialising in particular goods) staying open on what's supposed to be a day of rest. Calle de Arganzuela, for example, seems to be *the* place if you're into military antiques and old office goods. The cafés, bars and restaurants of the neighbourhood provide sustenance for those who need re-fuelling (some of the streets are quite steep). Places to eat generally get really crowded from 2pm – when the market is at its peak and people start to think about lunch.

Treasure hunt at El Rastro

INFORMATION

- ✉ from Plaza de Cascorro, down Calle Ribera de Curtidores
- Ⓜ La Latina, Puerta de Toledo & Embajadores
- ⊕ Sun & hols 8am-3pm
- ✗ see La Latina to Lavapiés pp81-2

What's in a Name?

Wondering where the market gets its name from? It comes from the fact that the area was a meat market in the 17th and 18th centuries – *rastro* refers to the trail of blood left behind when animals were dragged down the hill.

CAMPO DEL MORO (2, M2)

The exquisite Campo del Moro (Moor's Field) is aptly named, as it was here that an Almoravid army, led by Ali ben Yusef, set up camp beneath Madrid's walls in 1110 in the hope of retaking the town (they were unsuccessful). In medieval times, the area was used for jousting tournaments among knights. The park was not laid out as it now appears until 1844, with further alterations in 1890, when it was used as a playground for royal children. The 20th century saw the park open to the public under the second republic of 1931, and closed under the dictatorship of Franco. King Juan Carlos I declared the park open to the public in 1983, although you could be forgiven for thinking that not everyone had been told, as this beautiful spot often seems devoid of people.

INFORMATION

✉ Paseo de la Virgen del Puerto

☎ 91 542 00 59

Ⓜ Ópera or Príncipe Pío

🕐 Mon-Sat 10am-8pm, Sun & hols 9am-8pm

Quiet time at Campo del Moro

As you enter the park (from the gate at Paseo de la Virgen del Puerto) and head down the charming rockery stairs, aspects of the park's English style become apparent. Among all the greenery, you'll find winding paths, verdant canopies, many neatly laid-out flowerbeds and two delightful fountains. The fountain known as **Fuente de las Conchas** was designed by Ventura Rodríguez in the 18th century. The other, **Fuente de los Tritones**, was made in the 17th century for the grounds of Aranjuez. Also on the grounds is the Museo de los Carruajes (Museum of Carriages), which has been closed for some time and doesn't look like opening anytime soon.

DON'T MISS

- the peacocks, peahens and ducks that rule this particular roost
- the morning quiet
- inspecting the curious little English-style cabins that dot the grounds

BASÍLICA DE SAN FRANCISCO EL GRANDE (3, K4)

According to legend, Saint Francis himself built a chapel on the site of this basilica in 1217, hence the name. The present building is one of the city's biggest churches, and was completed under the watchful eye of Francesco Sabatini in 1784, after the original architect, Francesco Cabezas, had difficulty with the enormous expanse of the 33m-diameter dome. And indeed, it's an enormous place of worship, parts of which have been nicely restored in recent years.

INFORMATION

✉ Plaza de San Francisco

☎ 91 365 38 00

Ⓜ La Latina

🕐 Tues-Sat 11am-1pm & 5-7pm

⑤ 60c

✗ see La Latina to Lavapiés pp81-2

The elaborate interior decorations are the result of restoration work carried out in 1878. At the entrance, the building arcs off in both directions in a flurry of columns. Upon entering you will probably be directed to a series of corridors lined with artworks behind the church's glittering high altar. A guide will take you to the sacristy, which features fine Renaissance *sillerís* (sculpted walnut seats where the church's superiors would meet). Walnut is a feature of the church's seven doors, which were carved by Juan Guas. Take note of the lovely frescoed cupolas and chapel ceilings by Francisco Bayeu (yes, it does seem that almost everyone who worked on the building had a variation on the name of the patron saint).

The chapel on your left as you enter the building has a **Goya**

Basílica de San Francisco el Grande

painting of *The Sermon of San Bernardino of Siena*, while the adjoining chapel has a startling depiction of Christ. Extensive restoration over the years means that a visit often includes some scaffolding.

Grande Plans

One grand 19th-century idea that never left the drawing board was the ambitious plan to create a linking plaza supported by a viaduct between the basilica and the Palacio Real. The mind boggles…

REAL MADRID (2, E6)

There may be a lot of Catholic highlights on the peninsula, but to many Real Madrid is the real sacred turf of Spain. A powerhouse of Spanish, European and international football, Real Madrid was named Team of the Century in 1998 by FIFA, and the club's list of achievements is long and impressive: 28 Spanish League titles, 17 Spanish Cup titles, 9 European Champions Cup titles and 2 UEFA Cup titles – among others.

INFORMATION

- ✉ Paseo de la Castellana 144
- ☎ Exposición de Trofeos 91 457 06 79, tickets 91 398 43 00
- e www.realmadrid .com
- Ⓜ Santiago Bernabéu
- 🚌 No 27
- ⏰ ticket office and Exposición de Trofeos Tues-Sun 10.30am-7.30pm (closed 2hrs before kick-off on match days)
- Ⓢ Exposición de Trofeos adult/concession €3.50/2.50
- ✗ see Chamberí pp75-6

The club celebrated its centenary in 2002 (its name was changed from Madrid Foot-Ball in 1920, thanks to King Alfonso XII), and the excitement can be savoured in a visit to the stadium, Estadio Santiago Bernabéu, named after the club's most illustrious president, who served from 1943 for 32 enviable years. While a trip to the Exposición de Trofeos (trophy exhibition) is a poor second to catching a match in the 85,000-seat stadium against arch-rivals FC Barcelona, it's much easier to organise. You'll see the silverware and some boots of note, plus a video presentation of the club's glorious victories.

Smoking is not allowed, but you definitely get the feeling that a lot of people want a post-coital cig when Queen's *We are the Champions* goes into overdrive at the conclusion of one video. Expect to be joined by excited kids, misty-eyed men and football-loving women. For about €60 you can get a Real Madrid strip (club colours) at the attached shop (if you want a strip with a name and number, you'll pay about €72).

That other place of worship – the stadium

DON'T MISS
- a look at the green, green grass of Real Madrid's pitch
- squatting down and having your pic taken in front of a life-size photo of the team

PLAZA DE LA CIBELES   (3, E14)

At the intersection of Paseo del Prado and Calle de Alcalá, this glorious fountain is one of Madrid's most enduring symbols and recognisable monuments. The fountain at the centre of this busy junction depicts the Ancient Greek goddess of nature, Cybele, in a chariot drawn by two lions. The story behind this myth is as follows: Cybele had Atalanta and Hippomenes (a match made by none other than Aphrodite herself) turned into lions and shackled to her chariot for having profaned her temple. Aphrodite had tricked them into this, due to her displeasure at the couple's apparent ingratitude for her good work.

INFORMATION

Ⓜ Banco de España
✕ see Chueca pp76-7 or Salamanca & Retiro pp85-6

The fountain was erected in 1780 by Ventura Rodríguez and José Hermosilla. As befits a monumental fountain, it is surrounded by some appropriately monumental architecture: the 1904 Palacio de Comunicaciones (see p44), the 1873 Palacio de Linares, the 18th-century Palacio Buenavista and the 19th-century Banco de España.

King Carlos III thought the fountain was so beautiful that he wanted to have it moved to the gardens of the Granja de San Ildefonso, on the road to Segovia, but this idea did not meet with the approval of locals. On the eve of big Real Madrid matches, the fountain is boarded up in an effort to protect it from idiotic fans (see boxed text).

Lapping it up

When Real Madrid wins a big match, the club's supporters like to commandeer the fountain for their festivities. The entire plaza and surrounding streets can get *packed* with revellers, and the damage to the fountain and litter left behind is not a pretty sight.

Giddy up – Plaza de la Cibeles

IGLESIA-CATEDRAL DE SAN ISIDRO
(LA COLEGIATA)   (3, J8)

1767 was not a good year for the Jesuit order, as it was the year when King Carlos III had them expelled from Spain. This meant that this austere, sturdy-looking baroque basilica (designed by Pedro Sánchez) underwent a few changes from its status as Colegio Imperial (from which it gets it nickname, La Colegiata). Originally built in the 1620s, Carlos III decided that Ventura Rodríguez should remodel the interior, and an elaborate job was done, with a lavish altar drawing the attention of visitors.

INFORMATION

- ⊠ Calle de Toledo 37
- ☎ 91 369 20 37
- Ⓜ La Latina or Tirso de Molina
- ⏰ 8am-noon & 6-8.30pm
- ✕ see La Latina to Lavapiés pp81-2

The building's name was also changed to Catedral de San Isidro, after Madrid's patron saint. His remains were moved here in 1769 (in the third chapel to the left from the entrance) after resting in the Iglesia de San Andrés (see p40). He's been taken out of the basilica twice (1896 and 1947) to encourage the heavens to open up and rain. No matter what the weather is like, it's pretty unlikely that such an event will take place when you're visiting Madrid!

During the reign of King Fernando VII (1814–33), the basilica was returned to the Jesuit order, and from 1885 until 1993 it served as Madrid's 'temporary' cathedral, while the construction of the Catedral de Nuestra Señora de la Almudena (see p39) was carried out.

Iglesia-Catedral de San Isidro

A Leading School

Jesuit schools have a reputation for academic and moral rigour. It's no surprise then to learn that the **Instituto de San Isidro**, next door to Iglesia-Catedral de San Isidro, was the place where many of Spain's leading figures were educated from the 16th century onwards. You can wander in and look at the elegant courtyard, although the rest remains closed.

CASA DE CAMPO   (3, E1)

Casa de Campo is a huge expanse of scrubland spreading west of the Río Manzanares for 1740 hectares. This semi-wilderness was in royal hunting hands until 1931, after which the second republic made it accessible to the public. It's certainly not as attractive as the Parque del Buen Retiro, but it is effective as a mini-getaway for those who are finding Madrid a little congested, and there is plenty on offer.

INFORMATION

☎ 91 463 63 34
Ⓜ Batán, Lago or Norte

During the civil war, many of Franco's troops used the area to shell Madrid, and trenches are still scattered about the park. You can enter at the metro stop Lago or by air with the Teleférico de Rosales (see p46), and indulge in a little R&R, thanks to Casa de Campo's swimming pools, tennis courts and lake (see pp49–50). The park is also a popular spot for cyclists and joggers, and er, other types (see boxed text).

For the littlies, there's the **Parque de Atracciones** (see p47). It's also a popular past-time to hang out with a coffee or linger over lunch at some of the *terrazas* (outdoor cafés) that skirt the lake's edge. If you enter via the Batán metro stop, you'll be close to Madrid's zoo and aquarium (see p48). This stop is also close to the Andalucian-style ranch (known as Batán) that houses the bulls des-

Ladies of the Night (and Day)

Day or night, parts of Casa de Campo can seem a little more clogged with traffic than they should be. If you enter the park during the day, you'll notice that a lot of the winding roads are crawling with cars steered by solo men. And that a lot of scantily clad women seem to be just hanging around. During the evening, business really hots up, with prostitutes and punters jockeying for position around the lake. If you're taking the kids here, maybe it's best to do so during the day.

tined to go crazy at a red rag – China shop-style – in the bloody spectacle known as the Fiestas de San Isidro (see p89).

Casa de Campo from the teleférico

MUSEO SOROLLA   (4, G7)

Built in 1910, the former home of Valencian artist Joaquín Sorolla is a must-see. Left largely as it was in 1923 (the year of his death), the stunning house now holds an impressive collection of his light-filled impressionist works, plus articles and collections (tiles and ceramics) acquired by the artist during his lifetime. The ground floor gives a great idea of the manner in which Sorolla lived and worked, with a sun-drenched studio (courtesy of some judiciously placed skylights) and a neat little spot for him to take a nap on a Turkish bed. This is also the area where his various collections are displayed.

The first floor (the former sleeping quarters) takes you to the gallery that houses works from the 1890s onwards. Sorolla's work is dominated by an easy-on-the-eye style of portraiture and landscape. You won't need to whip out your dictionary of art theory to decipher these attractive scenes of pretty ladies at rest or various Spaniards at their leisure or toil. However, the art is arranged chronologically, which makes Sorolla's earlier works easily recognisable for their dark tones. They're especially dark for someone who was renowned for his mastery of depicting light.

There's a heavenly Moorish-style garden on the grounds too, which was designed by the artist himself. Spending some time here will make you forget that you're in one of Europe's most frantic cities.

INFORMATION

- ✉ Paseo del General
  Martínez Campos 37
- ☎ 91 310 15 84
- e www.mcu.es/
  nmuseos/sorolla/
  index.html
- Ⓜ Rubén Darío or
  Iglesia
- ⏱ Tues-Sat 10am-3pm,
  Sun 10am-2pm
- ⓢ adult/concession
  €2.40/1.20, free
  under-18 & over-65

The must-see Museo Sorolla

Better Than Ever

Behind closed doors, the museum has recently been spruced up. It was in fact closed at the time of research, but should be ready and raring to go by the time you read this, so go!

sights & activities

NEIGHBOURHOODS

South of Gran Vía and west of Paseo de la Castellana is the area that will take most of your attention. West of the Palacio Real lies the **Los Austrias** *barrio* (neighbourhood), sometimes called the *morería*, or Moorish quarter, with charming narrow streets and traditional restaurants.

West of this, from Calle de Toledo, are the **La Latina** and **Lavapiés** *barrios*, which are rich examples of *castizo* (distinctly Madrid) life mixed with new waves of immigration.

Huertas and **Santa Ana** are *the* eating and drinking zones, with thousands of bars and big crowds at night. It was also the scene of the literary golden age in the 17th century.

North of Gran Vía lies the pink barrio of **Chueca**, a respectable 19th-century area that fell on hard times and has been rejuvenated by the gay community. West of this is **Malasaña**, a working-class district popular for nightlife, with a bohemian feel. Further west, you'll find **Argüelles**, with pleasant *terrazas* (outdoor cafés) and a distinctly untouristed feel. North of Malasaña is the area known as **Chamberí**, which underwent development in the second half of the 19th century but still retains a *castizo* air and a family atmosphere, despite not being in the oldest part of the city.

Off the Beaten Track
The areas that feel most touristy in Madrid tend to surround Plaza de la Puerta del Sol and Plaza Mayor, or the 'big three' art museums. For the most part, La Latina, Lavapiés, Chueca and Malasaña remain faithfully local haunts, except at night, when Madrid becomes a mobile party town. The city's parks are also good places to escape to during the week.

East of Paseo de la Castellana is the stylish **Salamanca** *ensanche* (extension), constructed on a grid during the late 19th century. Its tree-lined streets play host to some of the fanciest shops in Madrid. South of this, bordering the Parque del Buen Retiro, the **Retiro** neighbourhood feels less exclusive but is still pleasant, thanks to its greenery.

View from El Viajero Terrace (p91)

MUSEUMS & GALLERIES

Biblioteca Nacional & Museo del Libro

(3, C15) The Biblioteca Nacional was commissioned in 1865 by Isabel II and completed in 1892. Inside you'll find some cleverly arranged collections on the history of writing and the gathering of knowledge. The *museo* is bibliophile heaven – with Arabic texts, illuminated manuscripts, and centuries-old Torahs.

✉ Paseo de Recoletos 20, Salamanca ☎ 91 580 78 00 e www .bne.es Ⓜ Colón ◷ Biblioteca Mon-Fri 9am-9pm, Sat 9am-2pm; museo Tues-Sat 10am-9pm, Sun 10am-2pm Ⓢ free ⓺ good

Casa de la Moneda

(2, L9) Numismatic maniacs can revel in coins from throughout the ages at this slightly down-at-heel museum in the National Mint. It runs the gamut from Ancient Greek coins to the poor old peseta, which was relegated in 2002 to the fiscal dustbin.

✉ Calle del Doctor Esquerdo 36, Retiro ☎ 91 566 65 44 Ⓜ O'Donnell ◷ Tues-Fri 10am-2.30pm & 5-7.30pm, Sat, Sun & hols 10am-2.30pm Ⓢ free

Casa de Lope de Vega

(3, H12) Felix Lope de Vega was one of Spain's leading golden-age writers, and he moved to this austere-looking house in 1610, remaining here until his death in 1635. You wouldn't really know he's no longer with us though, as it's filled with memorabilia pertaining to his life and times, giving a wonderful insight into life in Madrid in the 17th century.

✉ Calle de Cervantes 11, Huertas ☎ 91 429 92 16 Ⓜ Antón Martín ◷ Tues-Fri 9.30am-2pm, Sat 10am-noon Ⓢ adult/concession €1.50/90c

Ermita de San Antonio de la Florida

(2, K1) This small hermitage has two small chapels: the southern one contains a magnificent dome fresco by Goya depicting the miracle of St Anthony. The crowd of people swarming around the saint are interesting not just for Goya's extraordinary skills, but also because they've been placed in the dome, an area usually reserved for heavenly subjects.

✉ Glorieta de la Florida 5, Argüelles ☎ 91 542 07 22 e www.munimadrid .es/ermita Ⓜ Príncipe Pío ◷ Tues-Fri 10am-2pm & 4-8pm, Sat & Sun 10am-2pm, closed hols Ⓢ adult/concession €1.80/90c, free Wed & Sun

Museo de San Isidro p37

Fundación Juan March

(4, J11) Businessman Juan March established this cultural and scientific foundation in 1955, and the modern facilities house a permanent collection of contemporary Spanish art, including some way-out sculptures on its grounds. Temporary exhibitions and concerts are also held here on a regular basis (see also p96).

✉ Calle de Castelló 77, Salamanca ☎ 91 435 42 40 e www.march.es Ⓜ Núñez de Balboa ◷ Mon-Sat 10am-2pm & 5.30-9pm, Sat, Sun &

hols 10am-2pm ⓢ free
& good

Museo de América

(2, H1) When the Spaniards weren't loading their ships with Latin American gold, they found a bit of room for transporting ceramics, statuary, jewellery, hunting implements and a few shrunken heads from indigenous cultures. Some good temporary exhibitions with Latin American themes are also held in this interesting museum.

✉ Avenida de los Reyes Católicos 6, Moncloa ☎ 91 549 26 41 Ⓜ Moncloa ☉ Tues-Sat 10am-3pm, Sun & hols 10am-2pm ⓢ adult/concession €3/1.50

Museo Arqueológico Nacional

(3, C15) Founded by royal decree in 1867, this is one mother of a royal collection, with goodies from prehistory to Ancient Egypt, Greece and Rome, up to Mudéjar Spain. Among other things, keep an eye out for the sarcophagus of Amemenhat (Room 13), the Lady of Elche (Room 20), Livia (Room 21), Recesvinio's crown (Room 29) and the Aljafería arch (Room 30).

✉ Calle Serrano 13, Salamanca ☎ 91 577 79 12 ℮ www.man.es Ⓜ Serrano or Colón ▣ Recoletos ☉ Tues-Sat 9.30am-8.30pm, Sun 9.30am-2.30pm, closed Mon & hols ⓢ adult/concession €3/1.50; free under-18, over-65, Sat 2.30-8.30pm & Sun 9.30am-2.30pm & good

Museo de Cerralbo

(3, C5) This is the former 19th-century home of the 17th Marqués de Cerralbo – politician, poet, archaeologist, as well as avid collector. The collection has been kept close to how the Marqués lived, and according to his wishes. It includes religious paintings (El Greco's *Éxtasis de San Francisco* is stunning), clocks, suits of armour, jewellery and books. Most of the opulent rooms are fascinating – you'll feel like a right sticky-beak at times.

✉ Calle de Ventura Rodríguez 17, Argüelles ☎ 91 547 36 46 Ⓜ Plaza de España or Ventura Rodríguez ☉ Tues-Sat 9.30am-2.30pm, Sun 10am-2pm ⓢ adult/concession €2.40/1.20; free under-18, over-65, Wed & Sun

Museo del Ejército

(3, G15) This army museum is housed in what was the Salón de Reinos del Buen Retiro in one of the few remaining parts of the Palacio del Buen Retiro. There's a room devoted to the nationalist campaign in the civil war and the Sala Árabe room contains the sword of Boabdil – who was the last Muslim ruler of Granada. Apparently this museum is going to be shifted to the alcázar in Toledo (see p56), but we didn't see any signs of movement at the time of research.

✉ Calle de Méndez Núñez 1, Retiro ☎ 91 522 89 77 Ⓜ Banco de España ☉ Tues-Sat 10am-2pm ⓢ adult/concession 60c/30c, free seniors & Sat

Museo de San Isidro

(3, J6) Madrid's patron saint has a tastefully renovated museum named after him, where you can see various archaeological finds from old Madrid, including mosaic fragments from the Roman villa in Carabanchel (now a southern suburb). The building also has a 16th-century courtyard, a 17th-century chapel and some very interesting displays based on the history of Madrid.

✉ Plaza de San Andrés 2, Los Austrias ☎ 91 366 74 15 ℮ www .munimadrid.es/museo sanisidro Ⓜ La Latina or Tirso de Molina ▣ 3, 17, 18, 23, 35, 60 ☉ Tues-Fri 9.30am-8pm, Sat & Sun 10am-2pm ⓢ free & good

Baroque doorway, Museo Municipal de Madrid p38

Museo Lázaro Galdiano

(4, G9) A rich collection of delightful works by artists such as Van Eyck, Bosch, Zurbarán, Ribera, Goya, Gainsborough and Constable are held here, with ceilings painted according to the

Real Academia de Bellas Artes de San Fernando

room's particular function. It was closed in 2002 for renovations.

✉ **Calle de Serrano 122, Salamanca** ☎ **91 561 60 84** e **www .flg.es** Ⓜ **Rubén Darío or Gregorio Marañón** Ⓢ **free**

Museo Municipal de Madrid (3, B11)

A restored baroque entrance greets visitors to this museum, but unfortunately, that's all we got to see – restoration works should be finished by the time you read this, with some interesting maps and manuscripts on display. The building was founded in 1673 and retains its original chapel and some decent

paintings, which are also worth seeing.

✉ **Calle de Fuencarral 78, Chueca** ☎ **91 588 86 72** e **smuseosm @munimadrid.es** Ⓜ **Tribunal** ◷ **Tues-Fri 9.30am-8pm, Sat & Sun 10am-2pm** Ⓢ **adult/ concession €1.80/90c** ♿ **good**

Museo Nacional de Artes Decorativas

(3, F15) Spread over five floors, this museum presents a fascinating collection of glassware, ceramics, furniture, fabrics and utensils in an attractive setting, plus some well reconstructed rooms. Our favourite was the *alcoba*, a room used for 'conjugal unions'. But we also loved the parquetry

floors and the detailed ceilings – and the fifth floor's tiled 18th-century kitchen.

✉ **Calle de Montalbán 12, Retiro** ☎ **91 532 64 99** Ⓜ **Banco de España** ◷ **Tues-Sat 9.30am-2pm, Sun 10am-2pm** Ⓢ **adult/ concession €2.40/1.20; free under-18, over-65 & Sun**

Museo Romántico

(3, B11) A minor treasure trove of mostly 19th-century paintings, furniture and porcelain. The downstairs rooms contain a variety of books, photographs and documents relating to the life of the Marqués de la Vega-Inclán, while his personal collection is upstairs. It's an interesting insight into what upper-class houses were like in the 19th century. The *museo* was closed for renovation when we visited, so check.

✉ **Calle de San Mateo 13, Chueca** ☎ **91 448 10 45** Ⓜ **Tribunal** ◷ **Tues-Fri 9am-3pm, Sat, Sun & hols 10am-2pm** Ⓢ **free**

Real Academia de Bellas Artes de San Fernando (3, F11)

This was founded by King Fernando VI in the 18th century as a centre to train artists; this rather fusty gallery can boast that both Picasso and Dalí studied here. Spanish artists of note displayed include José de Ribera, El Greco, Bravo Murillo, Goya and Sorolla.

✉ **Calle de Alcalá 13, Sol & Gran Vía** ☎ **91 524 08 64** Ⓜ **Sevilla** ◷ **Tues-Fri 9am-7pm, Sat-Mon 9am-2.30pm** Ⓢ **adult/concession €2.40/1.20**

CHURCHES & CATHEDRALS

Basílica de San Miguel (3, H7)
This basilica stands on the site of an earlier Romanesque church. The present edifice was built between 1739 and 1745 and is an interesting example of late baroque. The interior (no photos allowed) is a mix of rococo and the contemporary.
✉ **Calle de San Justo 4, Los Austrias** ☎ **91 548 40 11** Ⓜ **Ópera or La Latina** ⊘ **Mon-Sat 11am-12.15pm & 5.30-7pm** Ⓢ **free**

Catedral de Nuestra Señora de la Almudena

Capilla del Obispo
(3, J6) This chapel is a rare example of the transitional style from Gothic to Renaissance. Built to house San Isidro's remains (which are no longer here) by the Vargas family, it's a tricky proposition to get inside. You'll probably have to ask at a tourist office if a temporary exhibition is on.
✉ **Plaza de la Paja, Los Austrias** Ⓜ **La Latina** Ⓢ **free**

Catedral de Nuestra Señora de la Almudena (3, G5)
Just south of the Palacio Real, Madrid's cathedral is externally grand and internally bland. It was finally completed in 1993 after a good 110 years of construction – the Spanish civil war was a major interruption. The present place of worship may well be a new building, but this site (and the areas nearby) have served a religious purpose in one way or another since the city's earliest settlement.
✉ **Calle de Bailén, Los Austrias** ☎ **91 542 22 00** ⓔ **www.patrimonio nacional.es** Ⓜ **Ópera** ⊘ **Sep-Jun 9am-9pm;**

Jul & Aug 10am-2pm & 5-9pm Ⓢ free ♿ good

Iglesia de San Ginés
(3, F8) One of Madrid's oldest churches, San Ginés has been here in some shape or form since the 14th century. There's also speculation that pre-1085, when Christians arrived in Madrid, a Mozarabic community (Christians in Muslim territory) had its parish church on the site. The dark interior is ideal for contemplation of matters both spiritual and artistic (note the El Greco painting).
✉ **Calle de San Martín, Los Austrias** Ⓜ **Ópera or Sol** ⊘ **8.45am-1pm & 6-9 pm** Ⓢ **free**

Doorway detail, Iglesia de San Jerónimo el Real p40

Iglesia de San Andrés (3, J6)

San Andrés suffered severe damage during the civil war, but its exterior looks as neat and shiny as a new pin now. The interior features some baroque decorative touches and a lovely dome, with plump cherubs running riot in a sea of colour.

✉ Plaza de San Andrés, Los Austrias Ⓜ La Latina ⏰ 9am-1pm & 6-8pm Ⓢ free

Blink and You'd Miss It ...

You could easily be forgiven for failing to notice the small brick structure on the corner of Calle de Fuencarral and Calle de Augusto Figueroa in Chueca (3, C11). It's Madrid's tiniest church, and has little more than a crucifix and diminutive altar.

Iglesia de San Jerónimo el Real

(3, H15) This church was constructed in the 16th century and was once the nucleus of the extremely powerful Hieronymite monastery. The interior structure is a 19th century remodelling that gives more than a nod to the Monasterio de San Juan de los Reyes in Toledo. King Alfonso XIII was married here in 1906, and King Juan Carlos I was crowned here in 1975.

✉ Calle del Moreto 4, Retiro ☎ 91 421 35 78 Ⓜ Banco de España ⏰ 9am-1.30pm & 6-8pm Ⓢ free ♿ good

Iglesia de San Nicolás de los Servitas (3, G6)

A few periods are represented in this church (which is considered the oldest surviving church in the city), from the 12th-century Mudéjar bell tower, to the church itself, which dates in part from the 15th century – note the late-Gothic interior vaulting and timber ceiling. There are 18th-century baroque touches too.

✉ Plaza de San Nicolás, Los Austrias ☎ 91 559 40 64 Ⓜ Ópera ⏰ Mon 8.30am-2pm, Tues-Sat 8.30-9.30am & 6.30-8.30pm, Sun 10am-2pm & 6.30-8.30pm Ⓢ free

Iglesia de San Pedro El Viejo (3, J6)

Those wanting to see one of the few remaining examples of Mudéjar architecture should raise their eyes to San Pedro's bell tower, which dates from the 14th century.

✉ Costanilla de San Pedro, Los Austrias ☎ 91 365 12 84 Ⓜ La Latina Ⓢ free

Iglesia de Santa Bárbara (3, C14)

This large baroque church was built between 1750 and 1757 for Bárbara de Braganza, the wife of Fernando VI. External design was left in the capable hands of François Carlier, while the splendid interior is the work of Doménico Olivieri. It features a painting by Corrado Giaquinto and is also the final resting place of Fernando VI himself.

✉ Calle del General Castaños 2, Chueca

Ⓜ Alonso Martínez or Colón ⏰ Mon-Fri 9am-1pm & 5-9pm, Sun & hols 10am-1pm & 5-9pm Ⓢ free

Oratorio de Caballero de Gracia

(3, E11) This charming oratory was designed in the neoclassical style by Juan de Villanueva in 1795 and declared a national monument in 1956. The interior features some fine paintings and a stunning altar.

✉ Calle Caballero de Gracia 5, Gran Vía Ⓜ Gran Vía or Sevilla ⏰ unreliable, check with tourist office Ⓢ free

Real Monasterio de la Encarnación (3, E6)

This enclosed Augustine convent has some decent royal portraiture (it was founded by Felipe III and Margarita of Austria in 1611). However, the real reason for visiting is the jam-packed *reliquario*, which has over 700 assorted skulls and bones, bits of the True Cross and a vial of St Pantaleón's blood – which liquefies on the night of 26 July.

✉ Plaza de la Encarnación, Sol & Gran Vía ☎ 91 454 88 00 ✉ www.patrimonio nacional.es Ⓜ Ópera ⏰ Tues-Thur & Sat 10.30am-12.45pm & 4-5.45pm, Fri 10.30am-12.45pm, Sun & hols 11am-1.45pm Ⓢ adult/concession €3.45/1.80 (free under-5 & Wed for EU citizens), combined ticket (valid 7 days) with Real Monasterio de las Descalzas Reales (see p22) €6/3.30

PLAZAS & PARKS

Parque del Oeste
(2, J1) Nestled between the university and Moncloa metro station, this large park is a surprisingly tranquil and beautiful place to get some green in Madrid. The park is the site of the deaths of many locals at the hands of Napoleon's army in 1808, and in recent times an on-off 'beat' for transexual prostitutes and their customers at night.
Ⓜ Moncloa

Big on Botero
Plaza de Colón's most attractive artwork is the sculpture by Fernando Botero of *Man on a Mule*. Also look out for his delightfully cheeky *Reclining Woman* on Paseo de la Castellana.

Plaza de Chueca
(3, C12) This party-loving plaza is named after a composer of *zarzuelas* (light opera) and is at its best late at night. Locals, gays, party types and anyone else hangs out at the tables, benches and chairs and on the ground. It's flanked by Calle de Gravina, Calle de Augusto Figueroa, apartments and more than a few banners protesting about the racket.
Ⓜ Chueca

Plaza de Colón
(3, B15) As an inspired memorial to Christopher Columbus and his discovery of America, this plaza makes a great transport hub. The *Monumento a Colón* (statue of Colombus) ain't too bad, but the big slab known as the *Monumento al Descubrimiento* (Monument to the Discovery) has a distinctly 1970s cobbled-together feel about it. Still, there's a cultural centre (Centro Cultural de la Villa) underneath it all (see p96), which offers lots of entertainment potential.
Ⓜ Colón or Serrano

Plaza de España
(3, C6) Not as grand as you'd think, given its name, but this plaza is a popular meeting spot for plenty of *madrileños* and has some welcoming seats under trees for hot days. Its north side faces the bombastic Edificio de España, but its centre has a charming bronze statue of Miguel de Cervantes, with his famous characters Don Quixote and Sancho Panza at his feet.
Ⓜ Plaza de España
♿ good

Plaza de la Paja
(3, J6) This plaza's name translates to Straw Square, and it was once the hub of Madrid in medieval times. It's been lovingly restored over the years, and affords some attractive views of surrounding buildings.
Ⓜ La Latina

Plaza de Neptuno
(3, H14) Officially known as Plaza de Cánovas del Castillo, but more readily referred to as 'the roundabout with Neptune near the Prado'. The sculpture of the sea-god is, for the record, by Juan Pascal de Mena. Atlético Madrid fans flock here when their team is victorious, halting traffic.
Ⓜ Banco de España

Neptune, Plaza de Neptuno

Plaza de Olivade
(4, H4) You won't find anything of historical interest here but we think it's one of the city's most pleasant afternoon/evening spots. There's a large open area, plenty of small bars with outdoor seating, some pretty rose bushes and an authentically local feel, with few tourists disturbing the social intercourse.
Ⓜ Bilbao, Quevado or Iglesia

Plaza de Oriente
(3, F6) Between the Palacio Real and the Teatro Real is one of Madrid's loveliest plazas, which gets its French feel from Joseph Bonaparte's rule in the early 1800s. It contains an equestrian statue of Felipe IV and statues of ancient monarchs that were supposed to adorn the Palacio Real but were deemed too heavy.
Ⓜ Ópera ♿ good

Plaza de San Andrés to Plaza de la Cebada (3, K6)

This area is a conglomeration of tiny plazas that comprise one of Madrid's most pleasant spots to unwind. Plaza de San Andrés sports the church of the same name and some nice community murals. Other mini-plazas flanking it are plazas de los Carros, de Puerta de Moros and del Humiladero. Plaza de la Cebada has a market and some of the best nighttime terraces in Madrid.

Ⓜ **La Latina**

Plaza de Santa Ana

(3, H11) You can thank Joseph Bonaparte for this square, as he demolished the 16th-century Convent of Santa Ana to make room for its construction. A long-famous drinking haunt, it's been tarted up recently and many feel it has lost its earthy charm and now has an antiseptic feel. Still, it's buzzing every afternoon and night of the week, and

there's even play equipment for the kids (see boxed text below).

Ⓜ **Sevilla or Antón Martín** ♿ **good**

Lorca statue, Plaza de Santa Ana

Plaza del Callao

(3, E9) On Sundays madrileños like to go to the movies, and this plaza (at the intersection of Gran Vía and Calle de Preciados) is where the hordes come. There are seven cinemas here (films are dubbed into Spanish if they're foreign), with some eye-catchingly garish advertising billboards and banners, giving the place a lively feel.

Ⓜ **Callao**

Plaza del Dos de Mayo (3, A9)

This square gets its name from the heroic last stand that madrileños took against Napoleon's troops on 2 May 1808. All that's left of the barracks that were here at the time is an arch. In more recent times, the plaza has had a reputation as the party spot for underage drinkers, although recent legislation has curbed the booze-and-hormone explosion.

Ⓜ **Noviciado or Tribunal**

Plaza de Santo Domingo (3, E7)

Named after a huge Dominican monastery that once stood here, this plaza's missing namesake is a telling indication of the power of anticlericalism in 19th-century Spain. There's not much to see though.

Ⓜ **Santo Domingo**

Plaza de la Puerta del Sol (3, G9)

This is Madrid's most central point and the psychological centre of town. Check out the small plaque on the southern side that marks km 0, the point from which distances are measured along the country's highways. A good meeting point is the bronze statue of a bear nuzzling a *madroño* (strawberry tree).

Ⓜ **Sol**

Playtime

Madrid tries not to forget the civic needs of even its tiniest citizens by including play equipment in some of its plazas. You can check out Plaza de Santa Ana or the more restrained Plaza de Olivade in Chamberí (among others) for slides and other kiddies' things.

Hangin' with the Play Set

NOTABLE BUILDINGS & MONUMENTS

Azca (4, B8)

This development goes by the nickname 'Little Manhattan', and construction started in the late 1960s. The 1980s saw it come into its own though as the epicentre of yuppie life, with big corporations, shops, restaurants and plenty of glass, concrete and steel. The most notable features of the complex are the Torres Puerta Europa and Picasso skyscrapers, designed by Miguel Oriol e Ybarra (1982) and Minoru Yamasaki (1989), respectively.

✉ **Paseo de la Castellana 95, Coplejo Azca** Ⓜ **Lima or Nuevos Ministeríos** ♿ **good**

Edificio de España

(3, C6) For some strange reason, this building, which towers over Plaza de España, is not as hideous as you'd expect fascist-era architecture to be. The building was constructed between 1947 and 1953 when Spain was not on friendly terms with the rest of the world. Needless to say, it became a symbol of the 'we don't need them' school of thought for the Franco era. It looks best at sunset.

✉ **Plaza de España, Sol & Gran Vía** Ⓜ **Plaza de España**

Edificio Grassy

(3, E12) Look for the Piaget sign to identify this, one of Gran Vía's most elegant buildings. It was built in 1916 (Spain had money for such things thanks to her neutrality in WWI) and has a circular 'temple' as its crown. Given the presence of the Piaget sign, it's only fitting that there's a museum of timepieces in the basement.

✉ **Gran Vía 1, Gran Vía** ☎ **91 532 10 07** Ⓜ **Banco de España** ⏰ **museum Mon-Sat 10am-1pm & 5-8pm**

Edificio Metropolis

Edificio Metropolis

(3, F12) You could be forgiven for thinking you're in Paris when you catch sight of this magnificent building. It was designed by Jules and Raymond Février and was completed in 1910 (although the victory statue was only placed on top in 1975). Note the four allegorical sculptures that represent Agriculture, Commerce, Mining and Industry, and the beautiful dome with gilded details.

✉ **Calle de Alcalá 39, Gran Vía** Ⓜ **Banco de España or Sevilla**

Faro de Madrid

(2, H1) It may look like an air traffic control tower, but the *faro* (literally, 'lighthouse') exists just to provide a panoramic view of Madrid from 92m up. The views *are* good, though the tower's lacking in the usual touristy facilities (no café or restaurant). Look southeast towards the city centre and you'll see the Arco de la Victoria – the archway built to celebrate Franco's victory in the civil war.

✉ **Avenida de los Reyes Catolicos, Moncloa** ☎ **91 544 81 04** Ⓜ **Moncloa** ⏰ **Tues-Sun 10am-2pm & 5-9pm** ⑤ **adult/concession €1/50c**

La Corrala (2, O4)

Yep, it's a tenement block, but it's not going to scare you. La Corrala is a great example of 19th-century timber-framed apartment

In-your-face edifice: Edificio de España

complexes that were constructed in Madrid. It was declared a historic monument in 1977, and has been restored (though it still has an unfinished feel about it), enabling it to be used as a backdrop for summertime performances.
✉ **Calle de Mesón de Paredes 65, Lavapiés** Ⓜ **Lavapiés**

Muralla Árabe

(3, H5) This is a fragment of the city wall built by Madrid's early medieval Muslim rulers. The earliest sections date from the 9th century, while others date from the 12th and 13th centuries. The council organises open-air theatre and music performances here during summer.
✉ **Cuesta de la Vega, Los Austrias** Ⓜ **Ópera**

Palacio de Comunicaciones

(3, E14) This must be one of the most elaborate post offices in the world, and the word 'palace' is not misplaced. Some find it much too grandiose, while others enjoy the sense of occasion that comes with buying a stamp. It was built in 1904 by Antonio Palacios Ramilo, in the North American monumental style, and has Gothic and Renaissance touches.
✉ **Plaza de la Cibeles**
☎ **91 396 26 79**

Ⓜ **Banco de España**
🕐 **Mon-Fri 8.30am-9.30pm, Sat 8.30am-2pm**

Palacio de Liria

(3, A6) This fabulous 1780 palace is home to works by masters including Titian, Rembrandt, Rubens, Goya and El Greco, but there's a slight catch: it's still owned by a duchess, and to get a peek inside you'll need to apply in writing to: Don Miguel, Calle de Princesa 20, 28008 Madrid, to request a visit (which is possible Fri 11am & noon). Then you'll have a *long* wait (of at least six months). It's just as well that the view from the

The monumental Plaza de Toros Monumental de las Ventas p45

grounds' gates is so impressive.

✉ **Calle de Princesa 20, Malasaña**
☎ 91 547 53 02
Ⓜ Ventura Rodríguez

Plaza de Toros Monumental de Las Ventas (2, J10)

This is the biggest and most important bullring in the world, and it's suitably impressive in appearance. Built in 1929 in the neo-Mudéjar style and featuring some lovely tilework, it has the capacity to hold over 20,000 spectators. It's worth a visit, even if you're not seeing a bullfight.

✉ **Calle de Alcalá 237, Las Ventas**
☎ 91 356 22 00
ⓔ www.las-ventas.com
Ⓜ Las Ventas

Puente de Segovia

(3, H1) This fine nine-arched stone bridge was constructed in 1584 by Juan de Herrera for Felipe II, as a means of making San Lorenzo de El Escorial (see p55) more accessible. It runs from Calle de Segovia, heading west, and is worth crossing, though the river beneath (Río Manzanares) isn't much chop.

Ⓜ Puerta del Ángel
♿ good

Sala del Canal de Isabel II (4, E4)

This 1911 water tower was built in the neo-Mudéjar style, and ceased active water service in 1952. However, photographic exhibitions are sometimes held here, so it's worth checking listings and making the trip.

✉ **Calle de Santa Engracia 125, Vallehermoso** ☎ 91

445 10 00 Ⓜ **Rios Rosas** ⏰ Tues-Sat 10am-2pm & 5-9pm, Sun & hols 10am-2pm
⑤ free ♿ good

Sociedad General de Autores y Editores

(3, B12) You'll have to admire this modernist architectural confection from the outside, which is no trouble, as it resembles a half-melted ice cream cake and is hard to miss. It was designed by José Grasés Riera in 1902 for the banker Javier González Longoria. Now it's the home of Madrid's book nerds' society.

✉ **cnr Calle de Pelayo & Calle de Fernando VI, Chueca** ☎ 91 349 95 14 Ⓜ Alonso Martínez

Teatro Real (3, F6)

Re-opened in 1987 and an opulent mix of state-of-the-art theatre technology and Palacio Real-style grandeur (although some sections are reminiscent of imposing-but-insipid big hotels), a tour of the Teatro Real is nifty for those who want a peek inside without seeing a performance. There are guided tours (in Spanish, approximately 1hr).

✉ **Plaza de Oriente, Los Austrias** ☎ 91 5 16 06 96 ⓔ www .teatro-real.com
Ⓜ Ópera ⏰ guided tours Tues-Sun 10.30am-1.30pm
⑤ €3/1.80, free under-7 ♿ good

Telefónica (3, E10)

This colossus was constructed in the 1920s with the formation of the national phone company. Designed by US architect

Louis S Weeks, it was the tallest building in the city for years. During the civil war, its prominence made it a constant target for nationalist artillery.

✉ **Gran Vía 28, Gran Vía** ☎ 91 522 66 45
Ⓜ Gran Vía ♿ good

Templo de Debod

(3, C3) The Templo de Debod is something of an attention-catcher, not only for its prime position in the Parque de la Montaña, but also for the fact that it's a 2200 year-old Egyptian temple, gratefully transported to Spain in 1968 as a gesture of Egyptian thanks for Spain's help in building the Aswan High Dam.

✉ **Paseo del Pintor Rosales, Argüelles**
☎ 91 366 74 15
Ⓜ Plaza de España
⏰ 1 Apr-30 Sep Tues-Fri 10am-2pm & 6-8pm, Sat & Sun 10am-2pm; 1 Oct-31 Mar Tues-Fri 9.45am-1.45pm & 4.15-6.15pm, Sat & Sun 10am-2pm ⑤ adult/concession €1.80/90c, free Wed & Sun
♿ good

Torres Puerta Europa

(2, C6) The leaning Torres Puerta Europa are a remarkable addition to Paseo de la Castellana, mostly because they stand 115m high and have a 15-degree tilt. Designed by John Burgee to symbolise a gateway to Europe, they are probably the most impressive modern structures in Madrid. Film buffs will remember them from the closing scenes of *Abre Los Ojos*.

✉ **Plaza de Castilla, Chamartín** Ⓜ Plaza de Castilla ♿ good

QUIRKY MADRID

Chocolatería de San Ginés (3, G8)

You may not think that a shop specialising in *churros y chocolate* sounds very quirky, but just look at the opening hours. If you've been partying till the early hours of the morning, this place is a rite of passage.

✉ Pasadizo de San Ginés, Los Austrias ☎ 91 365 65 46 Ⓜ Ópera ⏰ 6pm-7am

Museo Erótico de Madrid (3, H9)

Madrid now has a sex museum, where you can peruse all manner of resolve-stiffening devices, images and a S&M room. It's probably not suitable for the kids though, unless you're trying to scare them.

✉ Calle del Doctor Cortezo 2, La Latina ☎ 91 369 39 71 Ⓜ Tirso de Molina ⏰ Tues-Sat 11am-2pm & 6-9pm, Sun & hols 11am-2pm & 5-9pm ⑤ €5.10/3.90

Museo de Esculturas al Aire Libre (4, H9)

A space you might stumble upon and one that's often ignored by residents of Madrid, this open-air museum lies under the bridge connecting Paseo de Eduardo Dato and Calle de Juan Bravo. There are sculptures from prominent 20th-century Spanish artists (including Miró, Sánchez and Chillida) that enliven a space that's normally little more than an eyesore in most cities.

✉ Paseo de la Castellana 41 ☎ 91 588 86 72 e www.munimadrid .es/museoairelibre Ⓜ Rubén Darío ⏰ 24hrs ⑤ free

Museo Naval (3, F14)

This *museo* is a sea-dog's paradise in landlocked Madrid, and boasts dazzlingly well-crafted models of ships that'll have you itching to get out the hobby glue. Also worth noting is the surprisingly accurate parchment map (dating from 1500) of the 'known world' (it wasn't flat!), and the beautiful reproduction of the *Sala del Patronato*.

✉ Paseo del Prado 5, Retiro ☎ 91 379 52 99 Ⓜ Banco de España ⏰ Tues-Sun 10.30am-1.30pm ⑤ free

Museo Taurino (2, J10)

On the right-hand side of Las Ventas, this place is steeped in bull. It's small and modern, with displays (English- and Spanish-language) devoted to the art/sport of man fighting bull. You'll see busts and paintings of famous bullfighters, the bloody suit worn by Manolete when he was killed by 'Islero' in 1947 and six enormous bulls' heads mounted on the wall.

✉ Plaza de Toros Monumental de las Ventas, Las Ventas ☎ 91 725 18 57 Ⓜ Ventas ⏰ Mon-Sat 9.30am-2.30pm, bull-fight days 10am-1pm ⑤ free

Teleférico de Rosales (2, K1)

To put it bluntly, this cable car is no great shakes in the excitement stakes, but it is an interesting way to enter Madrid's Casa de Campo, plus you'll get to see from on high the baffling amount of traffic crawling along the park's roads. The reason? Prostitutes work in the area. It makes for Madrid's quirkiest traffic jam.

✉ cnr Paseo del Pintor Rosales & Calle del Marqués de Urquijo, Argüelles ☎ 91 541 74 50 e www.teleferico .com Ⓜ Argüelles or Ventura Rodríguez ⏰ Mon-Fri 11am-3pm & 5-9pm; Sat, Sun & hols 11am-9.30pm ⑤ one way/return €2.80/4

Get initiated at Chocolatería de San Ginés

MADRID FOR CHILDREN

There's plenty to keep the little ones occupied in Madrid, from performance artists and buskers in plazas, parks and streets to attractions specifically aimed at children. Locals certainly don't ascribe to the 'children should be seen and not heard' philosophy, and you'll find kids taking part in plenty of late-night dinners surrounded by grown-ups, without a whiff of condescension or irritation. Look for the 🐾 with individual reviews in the Places to Eat, Entertainment and Places to Stay chapters for more child-friendly options.

Museo de Cera
(3, B15) If spending your time and money guffawing at waxen representations of the rich, famous and infamous is your thing, then this is your place. Adults will need to use their imagination for some of the depictions, but kids are quite happy to wax lyrical about the pseudo celebs and ride the Tren de Terror.
✉ Paseo de Recoletos 41, Chueca ☎ 91 308 08 25 Ⓜ Colón ◷ 10am-8.30pm ⑤ full visit (museo, Tren de Terror, Simulador) adult/concession €12/7; museo only €9/5

Museo del Ferrocarril
(2, P6) About 500m south of Atocha station, you'll find around 30 pieces of rolling stock at this train museum, housed in the disused 1880s Estación de Delicias. Adults will enjoy the café in the 1930s dining car, and kids will love everything, especially the chance to plead for train-related toys from the shop.
✉ Paseo de las Delicias 61, Delicias ☎ 902 22 88 22 ⓔ www.museodel ferrocarril.org Ⓜ Delicias ◷ Tues-Sun 10am-3pm ⑤ adult/concession €3.50/2, free Sat ♿ good

Museo Nacional de Ciencias Naturales
(4, E8) Kids and adults alike will love this place! Fascinating permanent and temporary exhibitions cover topics as cool as the history of the earth and all natural sciences, plus kids' programs on weekends.
✉ Calle de José Abascal 2, Salamanca ☎ 91 411 13 28 ⓔ www.museociencias .com Ⓜ Gregorio Marañón ◷ Tues-Fri 10am-6pm, Sat 10am-8pm, Sun & hols 10am-2.30pm, ⑤ adult/concession €3/2.40

Parque Biológico
(1, E4) The 'Biological Park' is a recent arrival on Madrid's scene of animal distractions. Here you can promenade from one thematic area to the next: they include an aviary, an insectarium, a penguin parade, a jungle scene and performing dolphins. It lies east of the M-40, well out of the centre.
✉ Avenida de la Democracia 50 ☎ 91 301 62 10 Ⓜ Valde-bernardo 🚌 Nos 8 & 130 ◷ 10am-9pm ⑤ adult/concession €16.20/11.40 ♿ good

Parque de Atracciones
(2, M1) This is a monster-sized theme park with rides and plenty of other diversions for the kiddies, plus some noisy, colourful shows during the summer months. Those who have easily rattled tummies should beware.
✉ Casa de Campo ☎ 91 526 80 31

Babysitting & Childcare
Larger hotels (especially deluxe and top-end) will often have an in-house babysitting service, and even medium-sized places have a reliable contact for such things, starting at about €10 an hour and available at your hotel room. There is a nursery (for children under six) at Barajas airport (T2) from 8am to 8pm. There are also numerous advertisements for multilingual babysitters in the English-language *In Madrid* publication.

Carousel Carousing

There's a carousel outside the El Corte Inglés department store at Calle Serrano 47. If you've dragged them to all the fine shops of Salamanca, don't they deserve a turn at something? €1.50 a pop. Big kids are allowed on too.

✉ www.parque deatracciones.es
Ⓜ Batán ⏲ noon-10pm Ⓢ €4.50

Parque Juan Carlos I (1, E4)

This is a large green space that's perfect for families with kids. It's located west of the Parque del Capricho, and has well-kept gardens dotted between fields. You'll see people flying kites, riding bikes, sailing remote-control boats on the water and just generally hanging out. From Tues-Fri in the evening, and on weekends and hols, there

are train and catamaran rides (€3).
☎ 91 722 04 00
Ⓜ Campo de las Naciones

Warner Brothers Movie World (1, E4)

About 25km south of central Madrid, this corporate entertainment festival (enter via Hollywood Boulevard) gives movie-savvy kids the chance to frolic with their celluloid pals.
✉ San Martín de la Vega ☎ 91 821 12 34
e www.warnerbros park.com ⏺ San Martín de la Vega
⏲ Wed-Sun 10am-midnight Ⓢ adult/concession €32/24 for two consecutive days
♿ good

Zoo Aquarium Casa de Campo (2, M1)

Madrid's good zoo, housed in Casa de Campo, has over 3000 animals (there are even koalas!) and a decent aquarium with a better-than-average dolphin show. At night,

there are guided tours of the aquarium and sound-and-light shows.
✉ Casa de Campo
☎ 91 512 37 80
e www.zoomadrid .com Ⓜ Batán ⏲ Sun-Wed 10.30am-sunset, Thur-Sat 10.30am-midnight Ⓢ adult/concession €12.15/ 9.80, free under-3
♿ good

Festival de Titeres

If you're in Madrid in July, and your kids are itching for a bit of culture, check out the great Festival of Puppet Theatre, with shows in the Parque del Buen Retiro (Ⓜ Retiro) held throughout the month at 7.30pm & 10.30pm. Further information can be found at tourist offices (it's part of the Veranos de la Villa program) or by calling
☎ 610 38 51 98.

Something for the littlies at Parque de Buen Retiro p26

KEEPING FIT

Despite their love of food and drink, madrileños make looking good an artform, and are prepared to exercise to keep themselves easy on the eye. The city itself, with its parks, pools, gyms and golf courses is a good place to keep your fitness regimen going. For more information, it's a good idea to contact the **Oficina de Información Deportiva** (☎ 91 540 39 39) or the **Consejo Superior Deportes** (☎ 91 589 67 00).

Cycling

'Madrid', as Fernando Martínez-Vidal (the city councillor in charge of traffic issues) once commented, 'is not a city for bicycles', but if you really need to get some pedal power, you can try the Parque Juan Carlos I (see p48), Casa de Campo (see p33) or the Parque del Buen Retiro (see p26).

Karacol Sports (2, O6; ✉ Calle de Tortosa 8, Huertas ☎ 91 539 96 33 [e] www.karacol.com) rents out mountain-bikes for €12 per day, and staff can help with information on spots outside of Madrid, where cycling is more of an attractive option. You'll need to bring photo ID with you to hire a bike.

Golf

Spaniards are golf-crazy, and it can be tricky to get a game on weekends and holidays. The peak season is October to March. Some clubs don't accept casual visitors.

Golf Park (1, D4; ✉ Parque Empresarial de la Moraleja ☎ 91 661 44 44 [e] www.golfpark.es, 9 holes from €17) is open to all comers and is in a business park north of the city along the N-I highway, beyond Paseo de la Castellana. Your own transport is the best way to get out here, otherwise grab a taxi.

Gym

Many of Madrid's deluxe and top-end hotels have work-out facilities for guests. Grab a list of *polideportivos* (sports centres) that have gyms from one of the tourist offices. The Chueca neighbourhood has a handful of gay-friendly gyms that accept casual visitors. Maps from the Berkana bookshop (see p61) have further details. The sports centres attached to the municipal swimming pools listed on the following page also offer casual aerobics classes and gym use.

Jogging

Madrid's parks have plenty of paths that can be used by joggers. Our favourite is the Campo del Moro (see p28), not just for its beauty, but also because it seems relatively undiscovered. Other parks that are popular with joggers include the Retiro (see p26), which has a designated jogging path; and the Casa de Campo (see p33), which is at its best early in the morning.

Swimming

Outdoor pools are open from June to September in several locations. During the rest of the year, indoor pools operate, as do some private pools that allow casual visits.

Piscinas Casa de Campo (2, M1; ⊠ Avenida del Ángel, Casa de Campo ☎ 91 463 00 50, ⓢ adult/concession/over-65 €3.20/1.60/80c) has a great vibe, with all types jostling for space – families, preening narcissists, fitness fanatics and old folks taking a dip and a bit of sun (topless permitted).

Instalación Deportiva Municipal Chamartín (2, D8; ⊠ Plaza de Perú ☎ 91 350 12 23, ⓢ adult/concession/over-65 €3.20/1.60/80c) has an indoor Olympic-sized (50m) swimming pool, although its location isn't particularly convenient for those staying centrally.

Hotel Emperador (3, D8; ⊠ Gran Vía 53, Gran Vía ☎ 91 547 28 00, ⓢ Mon-Fri €19 Sat & Sun €29) is easily the city's swankiest place to swim, located on the rooftop and with marvellous views of the city. Non-guests are allowed to swim here.

Into the blue at Hotel Emperador

Tennis

Contact the organisations mentioned in this section's introduction (p49) for further details of public courts. Bringing your own equipment is a good idea.

Tennis Casa de Campo (2, M1; ⊠ Casa de Campo ☎ 91 464 96 17, ⓢ adult/concession/over-65 €4.40/2/1) has extensive, quality tennis facilities. Courts can get heavily booked at weekends, so weekdays are a better idea.

Watersports

Madrid's landlocked status doesn't mean you can't partake in watersports – and thank heavens for that in summer!

Aquópolis (1, D3; ⊠ Avenida de la Dehesa ☎ 91 815 69 11 ℮ www.aquopolis.es, ⓢ adult/child €12.85/8.45), on the way to San Lorenzo de El Escorial (see p55), is a very large spot to indulge in waterslides, wave pools and other aquatic pursuits. Catch the bus from Moncloa. The park is in the suburb of Villanueva de la Cañada.

Boating Casa de Campo (2, M1; ⊠ Casa de Campo ☎ 91 464 96 17, ⓢ €3.60 for up to 4 people for 45mins) is on the lake in this park. It has facilities for small boats, and is a relaxing way to get some peace and quiet. Ask at the information office near the lake for information about conditions and other details.

Flotarium (2, A8; ⊠ Avenida Burgos 44, Chamartín ☎ 91 383 97 28 ℮ www.flotarium.com, ⓢ €30 for 1hr 20mins) is a very relaxing form of sensory deprivation if Madrid's feast for the senses gets a little too overwhelming. It's probably not a great idea if you suffer from claustrophobia, however. Other relaxing treatments are also available.

out & about

WALKING TOURS
Los Austrias Stroll

From the grand 17th-century Plaza Mayor ❶, exit from the northwest corner and head left down Calle Mayor to historic Plaza de la Villa ❷, with Madrid's 17th-century *barroco madrileño* (Madrid baroque) *ayuntamiento* ❸ and Gothic-Mudéjar Casa de Los Lujanes ❹, one of the city's oldest surviving buildings. Follow cobbled Calle del Cordón to Calle de Segovia, where almost in front of you is the 15th-century Iglesia de San Pedro El Viejo ❺, with its Mudéjar tower. Walk down

distance 1.5km **duration** 2½-3hrs
▶ **start** Ⓜ Sol (Plaza Mayor)
⬤ **end** Ⓜ Sol (Plaza de San Miguel)

Walk this way: the back of Plaza Mayor

Costanilla de San Pedro to nicely restored Plaza de San Andrés ❻, which is the site of the Iglesia de San Andrés ❼. In nearby Plaza del Humiladero ❽, relax with a drink and snack, or take refreshments at any one of the tapas bars or traditional restaurants on Calle de la Cava Baja ❾, an atmospheric old street that follows the line of the city's former 12th-century wall, before venturing through Plaza Conde de Barajas. From the plaza, head up Calle de Miranda, finishing at the wrought-iron Mercado de San Miguel ❿ in Plaza de San Miguel.

Paseo del Prado

From Plaza de la Cibeles ❶, which separates Paseo del Prado from Paseo de los Recoletos and is encircled by the Palacio Buenavista ❷, the Banco de España, the Palacio de Linares ❸ – which once belonged to the prominent Alba family – and the Palacio de Comunicaciones ❹ – Madrid's impressive post office – head south on the left-hand side before turning left at Calle de Montalbán, where you'll find the Museo Nacional de Artes Decorativas ❺, former home of the Duchess of Santoña. Head back to Paseo del Prado, continuing south to Plaza de la Lealtad, where more grand architecture awaits, with the

Purpose-built Westin Palace

distance 1km **duration** 1½-2hrs
▶ **start** Ⓜ Banco de España
(Plaza de la Cibeles)
● **end** 🚉 Atocha
(Real Jardín Botánico)

city's *bolsa* (stock exchange) and the plush Hotel Ritz ❻, a heady example of early 20th-century style. A little further down, you come across the Plaza de Neptuno ❼ (so-named for its statue of the mythological sea king), which is bordered by the Museo Thyssen-Bornemisza ❽ as well as the mammoth Westin Palace ❾, which was built for the wedding of Alfonso XIII. From the plaza, you're within striking distance of the Museo del Prado ❿, with the Real Jardín Botánico ⓫ just across Plaza de Murillo, at the Prado's southern end.

Lavapiés

Not chock-full of tourist attractions, but filled with authentically grungy sights, sounds and smells, this is one of Madrid's most interesting neighbourhoods. Start at Plaza de Cascorro ❶ (once the scene of public executions) and walk south down Calle de Ebajadores. You'll pass El Rastro flea market, and soon come across the Iglesia de San Cayetano, a baroque church built over many years between the 17th and 18th centuries. Continuing down this street, turn left at Calle Sombrerete, then right at Calle de Mesón de Paredes, where you'll see the famous 19th-century tenement building of La Corrala ❷. Back on Calle Sombrerete, continue through to Plaza de Lavapiés – one of the best places to witness the festivities that take place in the neighbourhood for the Fiesta de la Virgen in August. From here, walk down Calle de Argumosa, a pleasant, tree-lined street with lots of nibbling options – we recommend the Casa de Tostas ❸. After this, turn left into Calle Dr Fourquet, then right at Calle de Santa Isabel.

SIGHTS & HIGHLIGHTS

La Corrala (pp43–4)
Casa de Tostas (p81)
Centro de Arte Reina Sofía (pp18–19)

Not a very hip flask – El Rastro market

Check out the barbershop tiles at No 22, then head south for the revamped hospital that now serves as the Centro de Arte Reina Sofía ❹.

distance 1.5km **duration** 1½hrs
▶ **start** Ⓜ La Latina (Plaza de Cascorro)
● **end** Ⓜ Atocha (Centro de Arte Reina Sofía)

Malasaña

Start this walk at the gates to the Palacio de Liria ❶, a glorious 1780 palace. From here, walk up Calle de Conde Duque, dominated by the enormous Centro Cultural Conde Duque ❷. Turn right at Plaza Guardia de Corps, into Calle Cristo, before turning left at Calle Bernardo López García, which will take you to Plaza de las Comendadores ❸ which has a cool Saturday afternoon market and the fine 17th-century Iglesia de las Comendadores de Santiago. From here, walk along Calle de Quiñones, turn left at Calle de San Bernardo and continue to Glorieta de Ruiz Jiménez, where you walk east to Glorieta de Bilbao. Pop into the Café Comercial ❹ to wet the whistle. That done, head down Calle de Manuela Malasaña, named after the local 19th-century seamstress who was a heroine of the city's brief 1808 anti-French uprising. Turn left at Calle de San Andrés, where you'll find some choice tilework, the best of which can be seen in the lively depictions of pharmaceutical cures at the corner of this street and Calle de San Vicente Ferrer. Hang a right at this last street and continue down Calle del Dos de Mayo to Plaza del Dos de Mayo ❺, the scene of fighting between angry *madrileños* and Joseph Bonaparte's troops on 2 May 1808.

SIGHTS & HIGHLIGHTS

Palacio de Liria (p44)
Centro Cultural Conde Duque (p96)
Plaza de las Comendadores (p69)
Café Comercial (p84)
Plaza del Dos de Mayo (p42)

USAD CONTRA LAS DIARREAS
DIARRETIL
PRECIO
0'40 CENTIMOS
JUANSE
REGISTRADO EN LA DIRECCIÓN GENERAL DE SANIDAD CON EL N° 4632

Um, what are you doing son?

distance 1.75km **duration** 2hrs
▶ **start** Ⓜ Ventura Rodríguez (Palacio de Liria)
● **end** Ⓜ Tribunal (Plaza del Dos de Mayo)

EXCURSIONS
San Lorenzo de El Escorial   (1, D2)

Sheltering against the protective wall of the Sierra de Guadarrama and enjoying a healthy climate, the magnificent palace/monastery complex of San Lorenzo de El Escorial is a must-see. Felipe II had the complex built in the latter half of the 16th century, consisting of a huge monastery, royal palace and mausoleum (for his parents Carlos I and Isabel), all under the watchful eye of architect Juan de Herrera.

The main entrance lies on the west side. Above the gateway, a statue of San Lorenzo stands watch. Enter the Patio de los Reyes, which houses the statues of the six kings of Judah. Directly ahead lies the sombre basilica with its dark interior and wonderful statue of a crucified Christ, by Benvenuto Cellini.

Go back through the patio, turn right and follow the signs to the monastery and palace quarters. There are several rooms containing tapestries, one of which has El Greco's depiction of the martyrdom of San Mauricio. You'll soon reach the stupendous Hall of Battles, a long room with extraordinary depictions of military events running the length of the room and a beautiful barrel-vaulted ceiling painted in 1584. After this, go to the Palacio de los Austrias where you'll be able to imagine how Felipe II and his children lived. You then descend into the Panteón de los Reyes, where almost all of Spain's monarchs have been interred with their spouses. In the southeastern corner of the complex, the chapterhouses contain a minor treasure-trove of works by El Greco, Titian, Tintoretto and Bosch.

The orderly gardens just south of the monastery can also be visited.

INFORMATION

50km northwest of Madrid

🚊 line C-8a from Atocha to El Escorial (€2.40 one way, 70mins, up to every 30mins), then 🚌 L1 (Circular) to San Lorenzo (95c, 5mins)

🚌 661 (€2.70 one way, 1hr, every 20mins or so from Moncloa)

☎ 91 890 59 02

e www.patrimonionacional.es

ⓘ guided tour €6.90, audioguide €1.80; tourist office (☎ 91 890 53 13; Calle de Grimaldi 2; open Mon-Thur 10am-6pm, Fri-Sun 10am-7pm).

⏱ 1 Apr-30 Sept Tues-Sun 10am-9pm; 1 Oct-31 Mar Tues-Sun 10am-5pm

$ adult/concession €6/3

✕ in town

The green, green gardens of San Lorenzo de El Escorial

Toledo   (1, G2)

Once set to become the capital of a united Spain, Toledo is a remarkably beautiful city, and *the* place to come for architectural history. With evidence of the Jewish, Muslim and Christian presence (all of whom lived in relative harmony), and such a concentration of Spain's artistic legacy, Toledo really does knock your socks off.

INFORMATION

70km south of Madrid
- 🚊 Chamartín or Atocha stations (€4.80 one way, 8 to 10 daily)
- 🚌 Galiano Continental buses from Estación Sur (€3.65 one way, 50mins, every hour or so from 6.30am-10pm)
- ⓘ tourist office (☎ 925 22 08 43; fax 925 25 26 48; open Mon-Sat 9am-7pm & Sun 9am-3pm), just outside the Puerta Nueva de Bisagra; information office (open Mon 10.30am-2.30pm, Tues-Sun 10.30am-2.30pm & 4.30-7pm) in the *Ayuntamiento* (town hall)
- ✕ in town

The city is built on a hill around which the Río Tajo flows on three sides. Modern suburbs spread beyond the river and walls of the old town *(casco antiguo)*. However when you arrive, sooner or later, you'll end up at Plaza de Zocodover, the main square of the old town, from where a medieval labyrinth of streets spreads out in a confusing manner.

Just south of the plaza is the alcazar – originally a Muslim fortress in the 10th century, and later rebuilt as a royal residence for Carlos I. Just outside what were once the Arab walls, you'll find the **Museo de Santa Cruz** (☎ 925 22 10 36, Calle de Cervantes 3, open 10am-2pm, €2) a 16th-century former hospital that holds several El Greco paintings. And if that whets your appetite, you should head to Toledo's stunning **cathedral** (☎ 925 22 22 41; Calle de Cardenal Cisneros; open 10.30am-6.30pm, €4.80) an essentially Gothic structure that (in the 13th century) replaced the central mosque. Inside you'll find the Capilla de la Torre and the sacristy, where another collection of El Greco's works exists. El Greco's masterpiece *The Burial of the Count of Orgaz* can be seen in Iglesia de Santo Tomé. And if that's still not enough, go to the **Casa y Museo de El Greco** (☎ 925 22 40 46; Calle de Samuel Levi; open Tues-Sat 10am-2pm & 4-6pm, Sun 10am-2pm; €1.20).

Toledo town

Real Palacio de Aranjuez   (1, F4)

Aranjuez is something of a haven from the capital. Once a royal playground, the palace and its meticulously maintained gardens are accessible to the public and make a popular weekend getaway. The town of Aranjuez is pleasant too, and has a reputation for producing juicy strawberries, which are sold throughout town.

The palace started life as a relatively modest summer residence for Felipe II, and was converted into an architectural extravaganza by the 18th century. With Versailles (the palatial benchmark for much of Europe) in mind, the palace has over 300 rooms and lots of glitz. Rooms of note include one covered in mirrors and a stunning octagonal smoking room kitted out 'Alhambra-style'. Don't forget to wander around the gardens either – a nice natural antidote to decor overload.

INFORMATION

48km south of Madrid
- 🚆 line C3 from Atocha to Aranjuez (€2.60 one way, 45mins, at least hourly), then a signposted 10min walk
- 🚌 Autominibus Urbanos (☎ 91 527 12 94, €2.60 one way, 1hr, every 30mins or so)
- ☎ 91 891 07 40
- ⓔ www.patrimonionacional.es
- ⓘ tourist office (☎ 91 891 04 27; ⓔ www.aranjuez.net; Plaza de San Antonio 9; open 1 Oct-31 Mar Tues-Sat 10am-1pm & 3-5pm, Sun 10am-2pm; 1 Apr-30 Sept Tues-Sat 10am-2pm & 4-6pm, Sun 10am-2pm)
- 🕑 1 Oct-31 Mar Tues-Sun 10am-5.15pm, 1 Apr-30 Sept 10am-6.15pm
- ⓢ adult/concession €4.80/2.40, free under-5 & Wed for EU citizens
- ✕ in town

Real Palacio de El Pardo   (1, D3)

This is the nearest regal retreat to Madrid, with a large palace that seems almost deserted much of the time. The site was attractive to Madrid's monarchs due to its excellent hunting (you'll see plenty of animal-related traffic signs on the trip out here), and made even more attractive by the royal palace constructed for King Felipe II. The current palace was designed by Francesco Sabatini after the original was destroyed by fire in the 18th century. It was used as a residence by General Franco until his death, and there are compulsory tours (Spanish-language) of the interior. State rooms are the usual mix of

INFORMATION

15km northwest of Madrid
- 🚌 601 (€1, 25mins, every 15 mins from Moncloa)
- ✉ Carretera de El Pardo
- ☎ 91 376 15 00
- ⓔ www.patrimonionacional.es
- 🕑 Mon-Sat 10.30am-6.45pm, Sun & hols 9.30am-2.30pm
- ⓢ adult/concession €3/1.50, free under-5 & Wed for EU citizens
- ✕ in town

gilt, tapestry, silk and chandeliers, but Franco's brown-hued bathroom would have to be one of the more interesting stops.

ORGANISED TOURS

The **Patronato Municipal de Turismo** organises myriad walks around Madrid. You can get information about them from any Caja de Madrid bank and its office at Plaza Mayor 3 (3, H8; ☎ 91 588 16 36; **e** infor turismo@munimadrid.es;), as well as information about other organised tours throughout the city. Keep your eyes peeled for privately run tours and the services of guides in the local press.

Bravo Bike (3, F10)
Fancy a bike tour of Madrid, or further afield? Bravo Bike can help you out. The one-day tour is a nice blend of the urban and the outdoors.
✉ **Calle de la Montera 25** ☎ 91 640 12 98
⑨ from €55

Madrid Vision
Backed by the *ayuntamiento*, these red double-decker buses show visitors the sights. There are three routes, frequent stops and you can buy tickets on board.
☎ 91 779 18 88
⏲ late-Jun–late-Sep 9.30am–midnight
⑨ adult/concession €9.60/4.80 (€1.20 surcharge weekends & hols)

Paseo por el Madrid del Capitán Alatriste (3, H8) Fans of swordwielding 17th-century

literary hero Capitán Alatriste will enjoy discovering his haunts. The tour is conducted in English and Spanish. Buy tickets 30mins before.
✉ **Plaza Mayor 3**
☎ 91 588 16 36 ⏲ Fri 9.30pm ⑨ €3

Paseo por el Madrid de los Austrias
(3, H8) This handy tour (in Spanish and English) is organised by the *patronato*, and is a great introduction to Habsburg Madrid's sights. Buy tickets 30mins before the tour departs.
✉ **Plaza Mayor 3**
☎ 91 588 16 36
⏲ Sat 10am ⑨ €3

Paseo por el Parque del Retiro (2, M6)
This is a good group stroll through Madrid's green lung. There's commentary in English and Spanish, and it's all under the aegis of the *patronato*. Buy tickets

30mins before from Caja de Madrid or information offices.
✉ **Puerta del Alcalá entrance** ☎ 91 588 16 36 ⏲ Fri 10am ⑨ €3

Pullmantur (3, F6)
Mainstream tours are offered, with daytime jaunts, night tours, dinner-and-show trips, as well as excursions further afield; they can also organise a bullfight visit for you.
✉ **Plaza de Oriente 8**
☎ 91 541 18 07
⑨ from €12

Tapas Walking Tour (3, J14) One interesting guided tour is this tapas crawl, run by Olé Spain. Various other tours (group and individual) are offered that go to a range of other cities.
✉ **Paseo Infanta Isabel 21** ☎ 91 551 52 94

Don't forget to duck – Madrid Vision bus

shopping

Madrid's shopping, whether you intended to indulge or not, will compete with many of the city's famous sites for your attention. From small local-craft shops and slick modernist fashion temples to old-fashioned food stores and full-to-bursting department stores and malls, Madrid will impress you with the quality of goods on offer, the generally reasonable prices and the courteous service that never descends to obsequiousness. Prepare to stretch your credit card and those airline baggage restrictions to the limit!

Chueca is an excellent shopping precinct, with Calle del Almirante, Calle de Fuencarral and Calle Piamonte full of fashionable shops. **Salamanca** is like Chueca's grown-up sister, with more expensive, conservative (yet still chic!) tastes catered for, especially on Calle de Serrano.

For gifts and items typical of Madrid, the shops around Plaza Mayor and Plaza de Puerta del Sol have some colourful window displays and a wealth of goodies. And of course, there's always the famous El Rastro.

Opening Times

Most shops are open Monday to Saturday 10am to 2pm and 5 to 8pm, although many businesses only open for the morning on Saturday. Traditional shops almost always observe the siesta, while modern ones and those on main shopping streets stay open all day. Almost all shops are closed on Sunday, unless they sell items of 'cultural significance', such as books. Some stores in the city centre operate on a rotating system of Sundays, with times signposted in the window.

ANTIQUES & CRAFTS

Agustin (3, K8)

A delightful trip back in time, Agustin is a tiny shop that sells antique *trajes de luce* (bullfighter suits), bullfighting posters, gloriously colourful capes and shawls, and quaint postcards. It's handy to the Rastro markets too, and noticeably more peaceful.

✉ Calle de Rodas 28, La Latina ☎ 91 467 87 50 Ⓜ La Latina
🕐 Mon-Fri noon-2.30pm & 6-8.30pm, Sat & Sun noon-2.30pm

Antigua Casa Talavera (3, E7)

Talavera is a Castilian town famous for its ceramics, and there are plenty of examples of the town's talent here, as well as from other parts of Spain. It's absolutely full to bursting with breakables, so don't act like a bull in a china shop.

✉ Calle de Isabel la Católica 2, Sol & Gran Vía ☎ 91 547 34 17

Ⓜ Santo Domingo
🕐 Mon-Fri 10am-1.30pm & 5-8pm, Sat 10am-1.30pm

Galerías Piquer

(3, K8) If you'd like to do the bulk of your antique shopping under one roof, this centre is a good start. There are about 70 antique shops here, of varying quality and scope, but handy to El Rastro on Sunday. Hours may differ from shop to shop, with some closing for August.

✉ cnr Calle Ribera de Curtidores & Calle de Rodas, La Latina
Ⓜ Puerta de Toledo
🕐 Mon-Fri 10.30am-2pm & 5-8pm, Sat & Sun 10.30am-2pm

La Pepa (3, D13)

A lavender-tinted jewellery box of a store, La Pepa is charming for its cuteness and its stock, which consists of old-fashioned trinkets in very good knick: hats, ashtrays, baubles and

> **VAT Refund**
> Value-added tax (VAT) is known as IVA in Spain. On accommodation and restaurant prices, it's 7% (usually included in prices). On retail goods it's 16%, and you're entitled to a refund of the 16% IVA on purchases from the one retailer totalling more than €90, if you take the goods out of the EU within three months. Ask for a Cashback form when you make a purchase, show your passport and then present the form at the customs booth for IVA refunds when you depart Spain. You'll need your passport and proof that you're leaving the EU.

all sorts of gifts with a difference. Service comes with a smile and a *violeta* (lolly).
✉ Calle de Gravina 12, Chueca ☎ 92 532 18 48 Ⓜ Chueca 🕐 Mon-Sat 11am-2pm & 5-9pm

Lladró (4, J9)

That much sought-after and coveted Lladró figurine your mum's been aching for can be found here. A veritable menagerie of lonely shepherds, imploring children and beatific virgins awaits placement in the *objets d'art* cabinet.
✉ Calle de Serrano 68, Salamanca ☎ 91 435 51 12 Ⓜ Serrano or Nuñez de Balboa
🕐 Mon-Sat 10am-8pm

Got to get past the rhino at Galerías Piquer

BOOKS

Berkana (3, C11)
With a strong selection of gay literature, gifts and videos, Berkana is a must-visit, with lots of good information about Madrid's gay scene available, plus a café.
✉ **Calle de Hortaleza 61, Chueca** ☎ **91 522 55 99** Ⓜ **Chueca** ⏲ **Mon-Fri 10.30am-9pm, Sat 11.30am-9pm & Sun noon-2pm & 5-9pm**

FNAC (3, E9)
This large, French-owned store not only stocks a very solid range of Spanish-language books of all descriptions, but also has French- and English-language publications, CDs and concert/event tickets.
✉ **Calle de Preciados 28, Sol** ☎ **91 520 00 00** Ⓜ **Callao** ⏲ **Mon-Sat 10am-9.30pm, Sun & hols noon-9.30pm**

The International Bookshop (3, E7)
If you're after second-hand books that you won't mind disposing of or that you might like to add to your collection, The International Bookshop has loads, predominantly in English.
✉ **Calle de Campomanes 13, Sol & Gran Vía** ☎ **91 541 72 91** Ⓜ **Santo Domingo or Ópera** ⏲ **Mon-Fri 11am-2.30pm & 4.30-8.30pm, Sat 11am-2.30pm & 4.30-7.30pm**

La Casa del Libro
(3, E10) Madrid's leading bookshop stocks a wide selection of books on all manner of subjects, with some in French, some in English, and plenty in Spanish.
✉ **Gran Vía 29–31, Gran Vía** ☎ **91 521 22 19** Ⓜ **Gran Vía** ⏲ **Mon-Sat 9.30am-9.30pm**

Librería Booksellers
(4, F7) You'll find plenty of English-language titles here, which is probably the best place for books if English is your mother tongue. Helpful staff will ease any decision-making dilemmas.
✉ **Calle de José Abascal 48, Chamberí** ☎ **91 442 79 59** Ⓜ **Alonso Cano** ⏲ **Mon-Fri 9.30am-2pm & 5-8pm, Sat 10am-2pm**

Librería de Mujeres
(3, G9) There's a good range of literature by women, books dealing with feminism, and plenty of non-fiction titles about women's issues here.
✉ **Calle de San Cristóbal 17, Los**

FYI: FNAC

Local Books
The immensely popular Arturo Perez-Reverte has written a few books set in Madrid, which make great accompaniments to a visit. Try *The Flanders Panel*, an art-world thriller; *The Fencing Master*, a historical mystery; or the trilogy based on the adventures of the sword-fighting 17th-century Capitán Alatriste.

Austrias ☎ **91 523 23 20** Ⓜ **Sol** ⏲ **Mon-Fri 10am-2pm & 5-8pm, Sat 10am-2pm**

Panta Rhei (3, B12)
This friendly bookshop has a plethora of tomes specialising in art, design, illustration and photography – and they look good enough to eat. You can also view well-selected drawings in the gallery.
✉ **Calle de Pelayo 68, Chueca** ☎ **91 319 89 02** Ⓜ **Chueca** ⏲ **Mon-Fri 10.30am-2.30pm & 5-9pm, Sat 10.30am-2.30pm & 5-8pm**

Second-hand Bookstalls (3, K15)
Just near the Real Jardín Botánico, this is not a bad little strip to bag some interesting reading. It can be a bit of a trash-or-treasure hunt.
✉ **Cuesta de Claudio Moyano, Jerónimos** Ⓜ **Atocha** ⏲ **10am-2pm & 5-8pm**

DEPARTMENT & CONVENIENCE STORES

ABC Serrano (4, H9)
Housed in a beautiful Mudéjar-style building in fashionable Salamanca, this excellent mall has five levels of shops (men's and women's fashion, homewares, gifts) and a space for eating.
✉ **Calle de Serrano 61, Salamanca** ☎ **91 577 50 31** Ⓜ **Rubén Dario** ⏰ **Mon-Sat 10am-8.30pm**

El Corte Inglés (3, F9)
Behold the mother lode! A national institution and the embodiment of the one-stop shop, El Corte Inglés deserves a round of applause for seeming to stock everything you could possibly think of. Clothes, underwear, footwear,

ABC Serrano

books, music, tickets for various events, electrical appliances and furnishings are all represented, and there are well over a dozen branches throughout town.
✉ **Calle Preciados 1, Sol** ☎ **91 418 88 00** Ⓜ **Sol** ⏰ **Mon-Sat 10am-10pm**

El Jardín de Serrano
(2, L6) As shopping malls go, this one's in the small but perfectly formed category. It's high-end stuff, and mostly covering the fashion side, with a smattering of accessories. Pop into the Mallorca café to refuel on tea and cakes, all while gazing at the garden.
✉ **Calle Goya 6, Salamanca** ☎ **91 577 00 12** Ⓜ **Serrano** ⏰ **Mon-Sat 10am-10pm**

Marks & Spencer
(4, K9) Marks & Spencer is a popular spot for homesick English expats and *madrileños*. You'll find the usual M&S goodies, plus foodstuffs. It's not quite in the same league as El Corte Inglés, though.
✉ **Calle de Serrano 52, Salamanca** ☎ **91 520**

00 00 Ⓜ **Serrano** ⏰ **daily 10am-8.30pm**

Moda Shopping
(4, A8) There are plenty of boutiques here to get you outfitted for whatever Madrid's weather dishes out. There's also a strong showing from some of the nicer homeware chains.
✉ **Avenida del General Perón 40, Complejo Azca** Ⓜ **Santiago Bernabéu** ⏰ **Mon-Sat 10am-9.30pm**

VIPS (3, D8)
You might shudder at the idea of coming to a shopping mecca like Madrid and having to visit a convenience store, but hey, we've all got to do it at some point. VIPS branches are scattered throughout the city, with a range of items. This is where you'll find those damn toenail clippers you forgot to pack.
✉ **Gran Vía 43, Gran Vía** ☎ **91 559 66 21** Ⓜ **Callao or Santo Domingo** ⏰ **Mon-Fri 8am-2am; Sat, Sun & hols 9am-2am**

El Jardín de Serrano

DESIGN, HOMEWARES & GIFTS

Alambique (3, E6)

The sort of people who can't get enough gadgets and utensils in their kitchen will love this place. You can find glassware, pots, pans and cutlery. Cooking classes can also be arranged – great if you speak Spanish.

✉ Plaza de la Encarnación 2, Sol & Gran Vía ☎ 91 547 42 20 Ⓜ Santo Domingo or Ópera ⏰ Mon-Sat 10am-2pm & 5-8pm

A teaser of what's in store - Objetos de Arte Toledano

Listas de Boda

Listas de boda (wedding registries) are wedding-happy Madrid's answer to nuptial gift-giving dilemmas. Many of the city's stores display a sign advertising the service, and these shops can be excellent places to look for homeware-related presents for yourself (and anyone else).

Batavia (3, A12)

Batavia brings a world of stylish furniture and homewares to Madrid, particularly from Asia. Countries of origin include China, Indonesia, India and Vietnam. There are also paintings, silk fabrics and porcelain objects in both antique and modern designs.

✉ Calle de Serrano Anguita 4, Chueca ☎ 91 448 75 63 Ⓜ Alonso Martínez ⏰ Mon-Fri 10am-2.30pm & 5-8.30pm, Sat 10.30am-2pm & 5-8pm

Casa Yustas (3, G8)

Gift shopping can be a real pain. Buy something practical or buy something emblematic of where you've been? You can actually cover both bases here, with cute *castizo* (true-blue *madrileño*) caps in all sizes and ceramic homewares. You can also find some laughably kitsch stuff if you want to provoke hilarity back home.

✉ Plaza Mayor 30, Los Austrias ☎ 91 366 50 84 Ⓜ Sol ⏰ Mon-Sat 9.30am-9.30pm, Sun & hols 11am-9.30pm

Fann (2, L7)

Fann is a bright and colourful shop that specialises in prints and posters and a range of beautifully coloured stationery.

✉ Calle de Velázquez 24, Retiro ☎ 91 435 72 23 Ⓜ Velázquez ⏰ Mon-Sat 10am-2pm & 5-8pm

Musgo (2, L6)

Something of a riot of colour and texture, Musgo shops stock bohemian-inspired homewares and gifts, with plenty of soft furnishings in natural fibres. There are also shoes, bags and clothes for sale.

✉ Calle de Serrano 18, Salamanca ☎ 91 575 33 50 Ⓜ Serrano ⏰ Mon-Sat 10.15am-8.30pm

Objetos de Arte Toledano (3, H13)

An enormous emporium of Spanish arts, crafts and kitsch awaits shoppers just near the Prado. Yep, it's touristy, but it's also fun and the range is huge.

✉ Paseo del Prado 10, Huertas ☎ 91 429 50 00 Ⓜ Banco de España ⏰ Mon-Sat 9.30am-8pm

Stone Designs (3, H6)

This perky, airy studio contains some of Madrid's spaciest and out-there homewares and gifts. Colours are bold, designs are beautiful, yet everything has a purpose, and prices are more than reasonable.

✉ Calle del Cordón 10, Los Austrias ☎ 91 540 03 36 Ⓜ Ópera ⏰ Mon-Sat 10am-2pm & 4-8pm

FASHION, CLOTHES & SHOES

Adolfo Dominguez
(2, L6) When we popped in, Adolfo Dominguez was doing a brisk trade with those wanting well-made, stylish clothes in natural fibres, with the odd twist thrown in. The shop itself is akin to an airy temple of minimalism.
✉ Calle de Serrano 18, Salamanca ☎ 91 577 82 80 Ⓜ Serrano ◷ Mon-Sat 10am-8.30pm

Camper
(3, D8) Fight the hordes of Spaniards seeking comfort, and American college students seeking cool, to get to these shoes. With innovative designs, sturdy construction and all the colours of the rainbow represented, a visit here ensures you're a happy Camper. There's also a branch at Calle de Preciados 23.
✉ Gran Vía 54, Gran Vía ☎ 91 547 52 23 Ⓜ Sol ◷ Mon-Sat 10am-2pm & 5-8.30pm

Cortefiel
(2, L7) Cortefiel is good for clothes more suited to business than pleasure. Clothes maintain a fashionable edge to stop them looking too conservative, and a good range of accessories and leather goods can help with outfit-update crises.
✉ Calle Goya 29, Retiro ☎ 91 577 55 05 Ⓜ Velázquez ◷ Mon-Sat 10am-8.30pm

Dresscode
(3, D12) Not for shy and retiring types, the *haute* end of men's fashion gets a serious work-out here (as do credit cards), with beautifully cut garments for those who like to be noticed.
✉ Calle de Augusto Figueroa 16, Chueca ☎ 91 531 64 79 Ⓜ Chueca ◷ Tues-Sat 11am-2pm & 5-9pm, Mon 6-9pm

Ekseption
(2, K7) Spain's most exclusive boutique has all the big names that 'fashionistas' love: Marni, Prada, Chloe, Dries Van Noten, Jean-Paul Gaultier and Dolce & Gabbana. You enter via a sleek Zen-style pebbled walkway and you depart with a serious case of fashionitis.
✉ Calle Velázquez 28, Retiro ☎ 91 577 45 53 Ⓜ Velázquez ◷ Mon-Sat 10.30am-2.30pm & 5-9pm

Excrupulous Net
(3, D13) The shoes here tend towards the very well-made and the imaginative, with a great range from the excellent Muxart (Barcelona) brand. There are shoes for men and women, plus a range of bags too.
✉ Calle Almirante 7, Chueca ☎ 91 521 72 44 Ⓜ Chueca ◷ Mon-Sat 11am-2pm & 5.30-8.30pm

Farrutx
(2, L6) The antithesis of Camper shoes, Farrutx is where you come for flashy, killer heels that make you wonder if you'll be able to walk more than five metres once they're on. There's a range of bags on offer as well, and a few party-pooping flats.
✉ Calle de Serrano 7, Salamanca ☎ 91 577

Need a H.A.N.D? p65

09 24 🚇 Retiro
🕐 Mon-Sat 10am-2pm
& 5.30-8.30pm

H.A.N.D (3, D11)
Short for Have A Nice Day
(shudder), but not at all
cheesy. The clothes here
lean towards the smarter
end of whatever's in fashion in France at this very
minute. It's a nice-looking
shop too, with some interesting colours and textures
scattered about.
✉ **Calle de Hortaleza
26, Chueca** ☎ **91 521
51 52** 🚇 **Gran Vía**
🕐 Mon-Sat 11am-9pm

Lanikai (4, K3)
A three-storey palace of
street-, skatewear and
snowboarding gear.
Trainers (often limited edi-
tion) are bountiful, and you
can also buy records and
CDs here.
✉ **Calle Alberto
Aguilera 1, Malasaña**
☎ **91 591 34 13**
🚇 **San Bernardo**
🕐 Mon-Sat 10.30am-
9pm

Lo Stivale (3, C13)
Men who want good qual-
ity shoes should head
straight here, where some
very stylish Italian numbers
jostle for your attention. The
store itself is very attractive
too, which makes it easier
for anyone in your company
who's hanging around waiting for a decision.
✉ **Calle de Piamonte
14, Chueca** ☎ **91 531
18 01** 🚇 **Chueca**
🕐 Mon-Sat 11am-2pm
& 5-9pm

Matane (3, B13)
Matane is a groovy little
shop with some interesting
design touches, but of
greater interest is the

Clubbing Clobber

Calle de Fuencarral is easily *the* place to get kitted out
for Madrid's clubs. There are dozens of shops, many
featuring very little in the way of natural fibres or
sombre colours. The shops themselves are easy to find
– they sound just like the nightclubs and are just as
loud. Check the quality of some of the garments, as
they can get quite pawed. The best place to look is
Mercado Fuencarral, which stocks better-quality stuff.

selection of Europe's riskier
designers. The accessories
are excellent too.
✉ **Calle de
Campoamor 9, Chueca**
☎ **91 319 19 90**
🚇 **Alonso Martínez**
🕐 Mon-Fri 10.30am-
2pm & 5-8.30pm, Sat
11am-2pm & 5-8.30pm

Mercado Fuencarral
(3, C11) A one-stop collection of shops for those
itching to get their hands
on streetwear and rave-
friendly fashions. Shoes,
tops, bottoms, jewellery,
sunglasses, bags and music
can all be found, and a

range of budgets can be
catered to. Plus, it beats
some of the tackier outlets
on this particular strip.
✉ **Calle de Fuencarral
45, Chueca** ☎ **91 521
41 52** 🚇 **Tribunal**
🕐 Mon-Sat 11am-9pm

Mitsouko (3, C11)
Billing itself as a
'fashion/press/music/design/
cafe' sort of place,
Mitsouko has some slick
designer clothes for club-
bing or chilling out, coffee-
table books on fashion and
photography, and a little
bar with an espresso
machine and bottles of

Made for walkin' – Mercado Fuencarral

Busy, busy Zara

Purificación Garcia
(2, L6) The business-like clothes (albeit featuring interesting fabrics and colours) are allowed to shine in this modern lay-out. It's a good place for quality, special-occasion outfits.
✉ Calle de Serrano 28, Salamanca ☎ 91 435 80 13 Ⓜ Serrano
🕒 Mon-Sat 10am-8.30pm

Sportivo (3, A7)
Label-lovin' casuals will want to move in here. Labels include Duffer of St George, Oeuf, Burro and Pringle. The range of shirts is particularly appealing, as is the decor.
✉ Calle de Conde Duque 20, Malasaña ☎ 91 542 56 61 Ⓜ Noviciados 🕒 Mon-Sat 10am-2pm & 4-9pm

The Deli Room
(3, C10) With goods dis-played like, you guessed it, a deli, we were hooked from the first moment. The stock consists of cutting-edge Spanish designers out to make a statement. Look out for the Ailanto label in particular.
✉ Calle de Santa Bárbara 4, Malasaña ☎ 91 521 1983 Ⓜ Tribunal
🕒 Mon-Fri 10.30am-2pm & 5-9pm, Sat 11am-2pm & 5-8.30pm

Underground (2, O3)
With that authentic vintage-clothing store smell, Underground is a groovy place to scour the racks for preloved ball-gowns, suede jackets, old-fashioned heels and funky tops. You'll find fashions

from the 1950s to the very recent for men and women alike, plus some new stuff.
✉ Calle Mira el Río Baja 14, Rastro ☎ 91 364 15 46 Ⓜ Puerta de Toledo 🕒 Mon-Fri 10am-2.30pm & 5.30-8.30pm, Sat 10am-2.30pm, Sun & hols 10.30am-3.30pm

Zara (3, E10)
This chain has branches all over Madrid. Zara's recipe for success involves churn-ing out fashion-conscious knock-offs of designer col-lections for men, women and children at very afford-able prices, without the stain of sweatshop labour. The store's popularity means that items can get severely mauled, so before you buy check things such as buttons, collars, zips and seams.
✉ Gran Vía 32, Gran Vía ☎ 91 522 97 27 Ⓜ Gran Vía
🕒 10am-8.30pm

alcohol; it has other branches too.
✉ Calle de Fuencarral 59, Chueca ☎ 91 701 08 35 Ⓜ Tribunal
🕒 Mon-Sat 10.30am-9pm

Pedro del Hierro
(2, L6) The typical Pedro del Hierro look revolves around elegant, low-key designs (for men and women) with high-quality fabrics and finishes. This shop is also a good spot for ties, shoes and bags.
✉ Calle de Serrano 24, Salamanca ☎ 91 575 69 06 Ⓜ Serrano
🕒 Mon-Sat 10am-8.30pm

Rebajas!
Anyone with an eye for a bargain will be salivat-ing if they visit Madrid during sale time. Look for the word *rebajas* and get ready to exer-cise those credit cards. Everything is marked down from around mid-January to the end of February, and from the beginning of July until the end of August, with the discounts increasing as the sales draw to their conclusion (al-though the really good stuff gets snapped up very quickly!).

FOOD & DRINK

Bombonería Santa
(4, K9) A sweet tooth should be indulged at regular intervals, and this lovely shop will give you (and your dentist) plenty to work with. Selections can be packaged in gift boxes, which are almost as edible-looking as their contents.
✉ **Calle de Serrano 56, Salamanca** ☎ **91 576 86 46** Ⓜ **Nuñez de Balboa** ⊙ **Mon-Sat 10am-2pm & 5-8.30pm**

Casa Mira (3, G11)
Turrón, a nutty nougat treat that's queued for at Christmas-time, can be tracked down here. Locals say it's the best, and we're inclined to agree, as the business has been in the same family's hands since 1842.
✉ **Carrera de San Jerónimo 30, Huertas** ☎ **91 429 88 95** Ⓜ **Sevilla** ⊙ **10am-2pm & 5-9pm**

La Bio Tika (3, J12)
Attached to the restaurant of the same name, La Bio Tika stocks macrobiotic grains, nuts and cereals. There are also soy products, plus a range of gluten-free edibles.
✉ **Calle Amor de Dios 3, Huertas** ☎ **91 429 07 80** Ⓜ **Antón Martín** ⊙ **Mon-Fri 10am-11.30pm; Sat, Sun & hols 1-5pm & 7-11.30pm**

Lavinia (4, J10)
This capacious, well-equipped store will set you right in your search for the perfect Spanish drop. You can also find wines from around the world. If you've

mmmm Mallorca

remembered to pack your own bottle opener, you might like to wander to the park for an alfresco tipple.
✉ **Calle de José Ortega y Gasset 16, Salamanca** ☎ **91 426 06 04** ⊙ **Mon-Sat 10am-9pm**

Mallorca (4, K10)
A fantastic spot to pick up delicious goodies as gifts or as snacks on the run, Mallorca has a great range of cheeses, meats, pastries, alcohol and some mouth-watering tapas. You pay for your goods at the cash register, handing over a small plastic board where purchases have been recorded. Ingenious!
✉ **Calle de Velázquez 59, Salamanca** ☎ **91 431 99 09** Ⓜ **Núñez de Balboa** ⊙ **9.30am-9pm**

Museo del Jamón
(3, G10) Only the Spanish can call a ham shop a 'museo', but then again, it looks like every single pig

in Spain has donated a leg. There are branches throughout the city, and it's a good place to assuage hunger pains (vegetarians look elsewhere!) or ponder how to get a big fat pig leg through customs.
✉ **Carrera de San Jerónimo 6, Huertas** ☎ **91 521 03 46** Ⓜ **Sol** ⊙ **Mon-Sat 9am-midnight, Sun 10am-midnight**

Patrimonio Cultural Olivarero (3, B12)
Pedro Rodrigo knows his oil, and so will you if you spend enough time here. Bottles of golden and green olive oil from all over Spain are all you'll find here. It almost makes you wish you'd smuggled in some bread.
✉ **Calle Mejia Lequerica 1, Chueca** ☎ **91 308 05 05** Ⓜ **Alonso Martínez** ⊙ **Mon-Fri 10am-2pm & 5-8pm, Sat 10am-2pm**

FOR CHILDREN

Caramelos Paco
(3, J8) Much as you tell them 'it'll rot your teeth', kids will be drawn to this treasure-trove of sweets, sweets and more sweets. And they are indeed delicious, although anyone who dreads putting kids to bed in the midst of a sugar rush might want to time their visit here accordingly.
✉ Calle de Toledo 53, Los Austrias ☎ 91 365 42 58 Ⓜ La Latina ⏱ Mon-Sat 9.30am-2pm & 5-8.30pm

Dideco (2, O3)
Stock up on kids' toys (many of which may appeal to grown-ups) at Dideco, where you'll find everything from mini-roller skates, inflatable pools, educational games, bath toys and art supplies. There are two other branches in Madrid.
✉ Mercado Puerta de Toledo, Ronda de Toledo 1, Rastro ☎ 91 365 02 40 Ⓜ Puerta de

Toledo ⏱ Tues-Sat 10.30am-9pm, Sun 10.30am-2.30pm

El Tintero Niños
(3, C12) Hunt out imaginative and colourful slogan T-shirts and romper suits for the baby or wee nipper in your life. Our favourite? A red romper suit emblazoned with the phrase 'Enfant Terrible'. Grownups can shop at No 5.
✉ Calle Gravina 9, Chueca ☎ 91 310 44 02 Ⓜ Chueca ⏱ 10.30am-2pm & 5-9pm

Fiestas Paco (3, K7)
Jam-packed with all the prerequisites for a rip-snorter of a party, this is *the* place to come for lurid wigs, games and other sundries that will keep the littlies distracted for 10 minutes or so.
✉ Calle de Toledo 52, Los Austrias ☎ 91 365 27 60 Ⓜ La Latina

⏱ Mon-Fri 9.30am-2pm & 5-8.30pm, Sat 9.30am-2pm

Marquitos (4, J9)
Kids' feet grow so fast, and if a Bigfoot-in-the-making is on holiday with you, you can snap up snazzy little shoes at this shop.
✉ Calle de Serrano 70, Salamanca ☎ 91 576 33 84 Ⓜ Nuñez de Balboa or Serrano ⏱ Mon-Sat 10am-2pm & 5-8.30pm

Prénatal (4, J3)
Madrid loves kids, and there are several branches of this popular chain throughout the city (including Calle de Goya 99). It's a good place to find colourful kids' wear, plus mothering essentials and mother-to-be products.
✉ Calle de San Bernardo 97, Chamberí ☎ 91 594 24 00 Ⓜ San Bernardo ⏱ 10am-8pm

JEWELLERY, PERFUME & ACCESSORIES

Carrera y Carrera
(2, K6) Providing chunky diamonds and other precious-stone jawbreaker rings and jewels to the good ladies of Madrid since 1885, this store is known for service that is so silky smooth that staff will always be courteous and charming even if you're obviously in the 'just looking' demographic.
✉ Calle de Serrano 27, Salamanca ☎ 91 577 05 72 Ⓜ Serrano ⏱ Mon-Sat 10am-2pm & 4.30-8.30pm

Mott (3, C13)
Run by stylish and sweetly patient young women, who never get exasperated – no matter how many times you change your mind – this is a small haven for quirky and well-made accessories such as bags, jewellery and belts. It's obvious everything's been chosen with great care, which is refreshing.
✉ Calle del Barquillo 31, Chueca ☎ 91 308 12 80 Ⓜ Chueca ⏱ Mon-Sat 10am-2pm & 5-9pm

Piamonte (3, C14)
Even repressed women have been known to climax at the sight of so many fantastic handbags, available in all shapes and sizes and in any colour you care to mention. There's a great range of jewellery on offer too, as well as a judicious selection of just-so shoes that will go perfectly with the bag.
✉ Calle de Piamonte 16, Chueca ☎ 91 522 45 80 Ⓜ Chueca ⏱ Mon-Sat 10.30am-2pm & 5-8.30pm

Sephora (3, G10)
Feeling less than fragrant? Or looking for a mother lode of make-up? Sephora is a smartly black-and-white kitted-out store with all the big cosmetic ranges and what seems like 1000 smells.

✉ Puerta del Sol 3, Sol ☎ 91 523 71 71 Ⓜ Sol ⏱ Mon-Sat 10am-9pm

Women' Secret
(2, K7) Hankering to be taken for a madrileña? Then you'll have to start with the basics. Spanish women love their scanties, and this groovy, up-to-the-minute store (part of a chain) has plenty, plus swimwear.

✉ Calle de Velázquez 48, Salamanca ☎ 91 578 14 53 Ⓜ Velázquez ⏱ Mon-Sat 10am-8.30pm

shhhh - Women' Secret

MARKETS

Mercadillo Marqués de Viana (2, C5)
A less touristy flea market than El Rastro is this Sunday morning shopping fest, held in and around the street of the same name in the Tetuán *barrio*. You'll find fresh produce, second-hand clothes and stacks of fun junk.

✉ Calle de Marqués de Viana, Tetuán Ⓜ Tetuán ⏱ Sun & hols 9am-2pm

Mercadillo Plaza de las Comendadores
(3, A7) Madrid's markets usually take place in the morning to early afternoon, but this one allows the night-owl to get among it

and sort through some trash and treasure. There are plenty of handicrafts of varying quality.

✉ Plaza de las Comendadores, Malasaña Ⓜ Noviciados ⏱ Sat 6-10pm

Mercadillo de Sellos y Monedas (3, G8)
Every Sunday sees Madrid's coin and stamp sellers hawk their wares to Madrid's coin and stamp collectors. Start your day with a coffee in the plaza and check out a slice of local life.

✉ Plaza Mayor, Los Austrias Ⓜ Sol ⏱ Sun & hols 9am-2pm

Mercado de San Miguel (3, H7)
If you're self-catering, then this is the market for you. This place, which is quite small, is not a bad spot to seek out fresh fruit and vegetables. It's also a good place to pick-up a quick lunch or just have a look at some rather attractive produce. If you're not hungry or not planning to shop, the building itself, a well-restored wrought-iron structure is worth checking out – even if it's closed.

✉ Plaza de San Miguel, Los Austrias Ⓜ Sol ⏱ Mon-Fri 9am-2.30pm & 5.15-8.15pm, Sat 9am-2.30pm

MUSIC

El Flamenco Vive
(3, G6) Flamenco aficionados and novices alike take note: this store devotes itself to the subject of flamenco dance and music. There are books, CDs, instruments and costumes.
✉ **Calle de Conde de Lemos 7, Los Austrias** ☎ **91 547 39 17**
e www.elflamenco vive.com Ⓜ Ópera
☉ **Mon-Sat 10.30am-2pm & 5-9pm**

El Real Musical
(3, F6) Its location near the Teatro Real should be a giveaway as to what kind of musical tastes are catered for here. Yep, it's classical all the way, with sheet music, CDs, books and instruments temptingly arranged.
✉ **Calle de Carlos III 1, Los Austrias** ☎ **91 541 30 07** Ⓜ **Sol**
☉ **Mon-Sat 10am-2.15pm & 4.30-8pm**

Garrido-Bailén
(3, H5) If Spain has inspired you to take up an instrument, or you're looking to upgrade your existing one, then this shop will please you – it has just about every kind of instrument, plus sheet music and other musical sundries.
✉ **Calle Mayor 88, Los Austrias** ☎ **91 542 45 01** Ⓜ **Ópera**
☉ **Mon-Fri 10am-1.30pm & 4.30-8pm, Sat 10am-1.45pm**

Loud Vinyl (3, A10)
Perhaps you already have a vinyl addiction. Perhaps Madrid's DJs have turned you on to nonstop beats. Either way, Loud Vinyl can help, with European and US releases, and not a CD in sight.
✉ **Calle de Velarde 16, Malasaña** ☎ **91 446 41 92** Ⓜ **Tribunal**
☉ **Mon-Sat 10am-2.30pm & 5-9pm**

Madrid Rock (3, E10)
There's a good selection of music in this store. There's also the added bonus that you can purchase concert tickets here too. Cash only is accepted for ticket purchases. And if you can't get here, there's also a second branch, known as MR Overstock, at Calle de San Martín 3.
✉ **Gran Vía 25, Gran Vía** ☎ **91 521 02 39** Ⓜ **Gran Vía**
☉ **10am-10pm**

Tipo (3, E10)
This hip and happening Malasaña/Chueca record store sells CDs and T-shirts as well as hosting CD signing sessions by performers.
✉ **Calle de Fuencarral 4, Gran Vía** ☎ **902 10 38 21** Ⓜ **Gran Vía**
☉ **Mon-Sat 10am-2pm & 5-8pm**

Garrido-Bailén

SPECIALIST STORES

Amantis (3, C12)
With a wide variety of lubricants, condoms, underwear, games, books and penisy things, Amantis is a popular sex shop with the gay crowd of Chueca and the brown-paper-bag brigade.
✉ **Calle de Pelayo 46, Chueca** ☎ **91 702 05 10** Ⓜ **Chueca**
☉ **Mon-Sat 11am-10pm, Sun 6-10pm**

Capas de Seseña
(3, G10) Madrid's winter will get you in the mood to rug up, and this shop will make nothing less than the best seem a necessity. The capes here are beautifully made and, despite Esquillace's 1766 attempt to make capes (at least long ones) illegal in Madrid, you'll attract nothing but envious glances if you don one. Even Hillary Clinton bought one from here.
✉ **Calle de la Cruz 23, Huertas** ☎ **91 531 68 40** Ⓜ **Sol** ☉ **Mon-Fri 10am-2pm & 4.30-8pm, Sat 10am-2pm**

Casa Exerez (4, J9)
Get those shoes you've been punishing repaired here. This a curious, old-

world throwback on a street known for five-star fashion.

✉ **Calle Jose Ortega y Gasset 11, Salamanca** ☎ 91 431 63 07 Ⓜ Núñez de Balboa ⏰ Mon-Sat 10am-1.30pm

Casa Jiménez (3, E9)
It's easy to fall under the spell of Madrid's beautiful embroidered *mantones* (shawls), and even easier to succumb if you wander into this shop, which specialises in these as well as lace wraps.

✉ **Calle de Preciados 42, Sol** ☎ 91 548 05 26 Ⓜ Sol or Callao ⏰ Mon-Sat 10am-1.30pm & 5-8pm

El Templo de Fútbol (3, E9) For those who eat, sleep and breathe football, and have the appropriate outfit for it. On offer are strips from many clubs, footy boots and some gear from other sports thrown in for good measure.

✉ **Gran Vía 38, Gran Vía** ☎ 91 701 02 41 Ⓜ Callao ⏰ Mon-Sat 10am-9pm

La Cuenta (3, D13)
A tiny, stark-white box with hundreds of different types of beads displayed in jars, this shop gets filled to the brim with crafty types looking to make their own jewellery, and parents looking to occupy their children. Books on making beaded jewellery are also available.

✉ **Calle del Almirante 6, Chueca** ☎ 91 524 01 26 Ⓜ Chueca 🚇 Recoletos ⏰ Mon-Sat 11am-2pm & 5.30-9pm

Loewe (2, L6)
If you're *really* into leather and like combining it with the high end of things, Loewe's your store. With a long-standing international reputation for buttery soft bags, wallets, belts and some seriously elegant fashions, you need never be out of leather if your heart so desires.

✉ **Calle de Serrano 26 (men's at No 34), Salamanca** ☎ 91 426 35 88 Ⓜ Serrano ⏰ Mon-Sat 9.30am-8.30pm

Marihuana (3, K8)
Forgotten to pack your bong? Then Marihuana may be of help. Packed to the gills with smokers' requisites (mostly of the dope-smoking variety) and rock T-shirts, it attracts big crowds when El Rastro's on – and complaints of industrial deafness.

✉ **Plaza de Cascorro 6, La Latina** ☎ 91 467 35 92 Ⓜ La Latina ⏰ Mon-Sat 10am-2pm & 5-8.30pm, Sun 10am-2pm

Maty (3, F9)
Everything you could ever need to flamenco can be found here, from heels and ruffled dresses to perform-ance videos for inspiration, as well as information on classes. It's not a bad spot

Going Dotty?
If you're in Madrid dur-ing any of the fiestas that see madrileños don their finest tradi-tional gear, you may develop a taste for a ruffled polka-dot dress, colourful shawls or black-and-white check caps. The area around Plaza Mayor is a good (if a little touristy) source of such gear, but our faves also include **Maty (p71)** and **Casa Jiménez (p71)**. The less extravagant may simply want to tuck a carna-tion behind an ear.

for fellas to pick up some check caps either.

✉ **Calle de Maestro Victoria 2, Sol** ☎ 91 531 32 91 Ⓜ Sol ⏰ Mon-Fri 10am-1.45pm & 5-8.30pm, Sat 10am-2pm & 5-8pm

Sobrinos de Perez (3, G9) This shop can supply you with everything your sacred heart may desire. Everything's got a Catholic edge. If you're looking for kitsch, don't make it too obvious.

✉ **Calle de Postas 6, Los Austrias** Ⓜ Sol ⏰ Mon-Sat 9.45am-2pm & 4.30-8pm

Have you got one in pink? Sobrinos de Perez

places to eat

It's only fitting that Madrid, at the centre of Spain, should offer a distillation of Spanish cuisine of all types. This is thanks to its status as a city of Spanish immigrants bringing with them Asturian, Andalucian, Basque, Navarran, Catalan, Valencian, Murcian and Galician (among others) cooking styles. It also offers some great international cuisines, with French, Mediterranean, Japanese, Thai, Indian, Kurdish, Mexican and North African widely available. Perhaps most surprisingly, Madrid is a great spot for seafood, with ocean catches transported daily to the capital for the hungry hordes!

Grazers will love the ritual of the tapas crawl and sampling titbits in such a social way. Big eaters will love the long, hearty lunches washed down with wine and punctuated by animated conversation.

MENÚ DEL DÍA

Every restaurant in Madrid will have (by law) its version of the *menú del día* – a set-lunch menu offering three courses and a drink. They cost about half as much as three courses and a drink from the á la carte menu, and are a great way to refuel Madrid-style (over about three hours!) for a reasonable price.

Meal Costs

The pricing symbols used in this chapter indicate the cost of a three-course meal with a drink. For tapas joints, it's two portions and a drink.

$	under €10
$$	€11-20
$$$	€21-35
$$$$	over €36

DINING HOURS & BOOKING

Madrileños love to eat and they love to eat late! Most of them will have three or four courses for lunch (*never* before 2pm, and that will generally last until 4pm), and no-one will even consider dinner before 10pm. Get into the rhythm of the city's dining habits and you'll have a lot more fun.

A lot of places close on Sunday (and public holidays) and quite a few places close for part of August – or all of it. Still, there's no reason to think you'll starve. Because dining out is so popular here, you'd be well advised to make reservations for more expensive restaurants, especially at weekends or for lunch. Credit cards are widely accepted, although inexpensive restaurants generally accept cash only.

Madrid's Cuisine

Frankly, it's a good thing that Madrid is filled with dining options from the rest of Spain, as most home-grown cuisine is a little bland for many tastes. Local staples include **cocido a la madrileña** (see Madrid's Dullest Dish p83) and **callos a la madrileña**, which is tripe casserole with chorizo and chillies. You might also sample **sopa de ajo** (garlic soup) or **sopa castellana**, which is a basic broth with an egg floating in it. Hardly inspiring stuff -- but if it's inspiration you seek...

Tapas will provide you with some of your fondest memories of Madrid. Don't go messing with the word and thinking it's a strict definition, with certain requisite ingredients. Tapas are not just things you eat -- they are a way of eating, and therefore a way of socialising and forging (or reinforcing) relationships.

The word itself means lid, or top. The verb form, *tapar*, means to top or to cover, and most people believe that the origin of tapas was in the 18th century, when tavern keepers would place a slice of ham or bread on the mouth of a glass to keep the flies out. It's also the best way of soaking up alcohol on a night out!

You'll find tapas in almost every bar in Madrid (larger portions are known as *raciones*). A few of the most common nibbling options (apart from olives, which you generally receive as par for the course) include:

albóndigas	meatballs
bacalao	cod
boquerones	fresh anchovies marinated in wine vinegar
callos	tripe
chorizo	spicy red cooked sausage
gambas al ajillo	prawns cooked in garlic-laden olive oil
jamón	ham
morcilla	blood sausage (fried)
pulpo gallego	spicy boiled octopus
tortilla española	potato & onion omelette

ARGÜELLES

Cañas y Tapas
(2, G2) $
Tapas
Part of a newish (since 1999) chain specialising in tapas (although full meals are also available), these places are handy ports of call when fatigue and famine get the better of you. They are all over Madrid, and the San Miguel flows freely. Don't worry, locals are happy to come here too.
✉ Calle de la Princesa 76 ☎ 902 18 09 18
Ⓜ Moncloa ⏱ 1.30-4.30pm & 9pm-midnight ♨

Casa Mingo
(2, L1) $
Asturian
Casa Mingo likes to keep things simple: chicken and cider, the Asturian way. It's a cheery, cheap and chipper place to enjoy a hearty lunch, with a bit of history thrown in, as this place has been cidering up beside madrileños since 1888.
✉ Paseo de la Florida 34 ☎ 91 547 79 18
Ⓜ Príncipe Pío
⏱ 11am-midnight

El Molino de los Porches (3, B3) $$$$
Castilian
Roasted meat and fish dishes predominate here, and it does a busy trade, especially when the weather's good, as this means the verdant *terraza* – with Casa de Campo in sight – can be put to good use.
✉ Paseo del Pintor Rosales 1 ☎ 91 548 13 36 Ⓜ Ventura

Rodríguez
⏱ noon-4.30pm & 8pm-midnight ♨

La Vaca Argentina
(2, K1) $$$
Argentinian
Make an enormous deposit in your body's iron bank right here. Slabs of Argentinian meat are the speciality (washed down with Argentinian wine), and while the cowhide walls are verging on overkill, this place is very popular, with numerous branches throughout the city. Try to get yourself a seat outside.
✉ Paseo del Pintor Rosales 52 ☎ 91 559 66 05 Ⓜ Argüelles
⏱ 1-4.30pm & 9pm-12.30am

Diet Dilemmas
Being a vegetarian isn't too difficult in Madrid, although being a vegan will present problems. However, spare a thought for those wanting to keep kosher. Spain expelled its Jews in 1492 and you'd still think that Isabel and Ferdinand were in charge if you scanned many menus: pork and shellfish as far as the eye can see.

CHAMBERÍ

Combarro
(4, A6) $$$
Galician
Combarro offers its diners quality Galician seafood, especially *pulpo* (octopus). It's not a fancy place, but it's popular with businessmen and women on a lunchbreak, so you may have a bit of a wait, which is the perfect excuse to prop up the bar and imbibe, nibble and chat.
✉ Calle de la Reina Mercedes 12 ☎ 91 554 77 84 Ⓜ Alvarado
🕐 1.30-4pm & Mon-Sat 8pm-midnight

El Bodegon
(4, G9) $$$$
Basque
El Bodegon has a strong reputation for excellent Basque cooking and old-fashioned service. Try the *rodaballo* (turbot) if it's on the menu – the traditional approach doesn't mean the chef's afraid to try new ingredients and techniques.
✉ Calle del Pinar 15
☎ 91 562 31 37
Ⓜ Gregorio Marañón
🕐 Mon-Fri 1-4pm & 8pm-midnight, Sat 8pm-midnight

El Doble **(4, F5)** $$
Tapas
Judging by the photos, this busy tapas bar is owned by bullfighting enthusiasts. The tapas and *raciones* are very good – try the *ventresca* (meat from around the stomach of a tuna). Don't panic if you get drunk and think you're seeing double; there are two of these bars on this street with the same name.
✉ Calle de Ponzano 58
☎ 91 441 47 18

Jai Alai (before the hungry hordes arrive)

Ⓜ Alonso Cano
🕐 Mon-Sat 11am-3pm & 6pm-midnight

Jai Alai
(4, B9) $$$
Basque
Every second person will tell you that Basque cooking is the country's best, and this long-running place (with a curious English look to the decor) will often get a mention in the next breath. Among other things, the pork dishes are handled beautifully and service is sterling.
✉ Calle Balbina Valverde 2 ☎ 91 561 27 42 Ⓜ Nuevos

Ministerios 🕐 Tues-Sun 1-4pm & 9pm-midnight ♿

Santceloni
(4, F8) $$$$
Market
This smartly decorated yet comfortable restaurant is in the basement of the Hesperia Hotel. It's the sort of place that chefs, food writers and enthusiasts put ahead of anything else on their 'must do' list for Madrid. Superlatives just don't cut it; suffice to say that chef Santi Santamaría should be made the patron saint of exquisite food. You'd be well advised to

---

Vegetarian Options
Madrid loves its meat, but there are plenty of places to tuck into vegetarian food. Try: **Chez Pomme** (p76), **La Bio Tika** (p80), **El Estragón** (pp81–2), **Isla de Tesoro** (p84) and **Artemisa** (p87) for strictly vegetarian dining. For restaurants with good vegie options, look at: **El Pepinillo de Barquillo** (p76), **Wokcafe** (p78), **El Cenador del Prado** (pp79–80), **La Finca de Susanna** (p80), **La Tentación de San Miguel** (p83), **Mumbai Massala** (p86) and **Thai Gardens** (pp86–7). The **Ⅴ** indicates that a place is either full vegetarian or has an excellent selection of vegetarian dishes.

make a lunch or dinner reservation.

✉ **Hesperia Hotel, Paseo de la Castellana 57** ☎ **91 210 88 40** Ⓜ **Gregorio Marañón** ⏱ Mon-Fri 2-4pm & 9-11pm, Sat 9-11pm

Santo Mauro
(4, J7)   **$$$$**
Basque
If you're staying here, you'll find it hard to leave, so it's fortunate that the restaurant, housed in the former library, is a delight. We

enjoyed both the *bacalao* (cod) and the garden view.

✉ **Calle de Zurbano 36** ☎ **91 319 69 00** Ⓜ **Rubén Darío or Alonso Martínez** ⏱ noon-4pm & 8pm-midnight ♿

CHUECA

Baires Café
(3, C12)   **$$**
Café
Airy, full of light and not a bad spot to refresh yourself with some caffeine (or something stronger) after some busy times in Chueca, this place appeals because the atmosphere's cool but easy-going, and exhibitions or DJs may get thrown into the bargain.

✉ **Calle de Gravina 4** ☎ **91 532 98 79** Ⓜ **Chueca** ⏱ Mon-Sat 11am-2am

---

Market Cuisine
Many restaurants listed in this chapter specialise in 'market cuisine', which means that the day's menu is based on what looked good at the market that morning, rather than a particular style of cooking or category of cuisine.

Café Miranda
(3, C13)   **$$$**
Theatre restaurant
It's a cliché to say that gay places do wonderful things with flowers and lighting, and this place reinforces it. Stunningly attractive, with lovingly presented, well-prepared dishes – and probably the easiest and

most enjoyable way to catch a really good drag act. Reservations advised.

✉ **Calle del Barquillo 29** ☎ **91 521 29 46** Ⓜ **Chueca** ⏱ 9pm-1am

Chez Pomme
(3, D11)   **$$**
Vegetarian
A smart-looking place, with a loyal clientele from the gay community, Chez Pomme serves up tasty vegetarian morsels and substantial mains, all without ramming earth-tones down your throat, like so many healthy places. The *menú del día* is excellent value.

✉ **Calle de Pelayo 4** ☎ **91 531 57 73** Ⓜ **Chueca** ⏱ Mon-Sat 1.30-4.30pm & 8.30-11.30pm Ⓥ

El Pepinillo de Barquillo
(3, C13)   **$$$**
Creative
Humorous touches (such as the giant gherkin hanging from the ceiling) don't detract from the seriously good food, which combines fresh ingredients with some interesting ideas. Apparently, this place is good for star-spotting the odd celebrity but we think it's Ángela, the chef, who's the star.

✉ **Calle del Barquillo 42** ☎ **91 310 25 46**

Ⓜ **Chueca** ⏱ 1-5pm & 8.30pm-2am Ⓥ

La Barraca
(3, E12)   **$$$**
Paella/Valencian
This is an extremely popular spot for locals and visitors, partly because of its inviting atmosphere, with low whitewashed timber rafters, but mostly because it serves up hearty, flavoursome paellas. Try to get in early (before 2pm or 10pm).

✉ **Calle de la Reina 29** ☎ **91 532 71 54** Ⓜ **Gran Vía or Banco de España** ⏱ 1-4pm & 8.30pm-midnight ♿

La Buena Vida
(3, C14)   **$$**
Market
This very smart-looking restaurant features some good modern art on the walls, open spaces and swish bathrooms, and keeps its menu fairly straightforward. Dishes are perfect for a lightish lunch and there's a good bar.

✉ **Calle Conde de Xiquena 8** ☎ **91 531 31 49** Ⓜ **Chueca** 🚇 **Recoletos** ⏱ Mon-Sat 1.30-4pm & 9pm-midnight

La Dame Noire
(3, C11)   **$$$**
French
This lavish, theatrically decorated restaurant (think

flock wallpaper, gilt and candlelight) specialises in wonderfully rich French food (consult your friendly cardiologist if in doubt) and assiduously cultivated service. Oh, and there's a drag-queen floorshow on Thursday. Reservations are recommended.

✉ **Calle de Perez Galdós 3** ☎ **91 531 04 76** Ⓜ **Chueca or Tribunal** ◷ Tues-Thur & Sun 9pm-1am, Fri & Sat 9pm-2.30am

La Gastroteca de Stéphane y Arturo
(3, D12) $$$$
Creative
The 1980s was the decade to come up with some crazy eating ideas, and this place is the spiritual home of Madrid's 'creative' cuisine scene. Specialities include all sorts of things you probably never thought you would eat. For example, the *raya de mantequilla* (stingray). For some diners, things may seem 'out there' just for the sake of it.

✉ **Plaza de Chueca 8** ☎ **91 532 25 64** Ⓜ **Chueca** ◷ Mon-Fri 1-3.30pm & 9-11.30pm, Sat 9-11.30pm

La Panza es Primero
(3, D12) $$
Mexican
Admire the Mexi-kitsch and get yourself settled with a Coronita (or perhaps a tequila) and a plump south-of-the-border taco. Service is friendly and fast, and the tacos are good for kids, as they can be ordered one at a time, with a range of fillings.

✉ **Calle de la Libertad 33** ☎ **91 521 76 40** Ⓜ **Chueca** ◷ 1pm-1am ♿

La Sastrería
(3, C12) $
Café
Whether you're getting in a post-boogie breakfast or kick-starting the night, you'll find plenty of like-minded folks at this popular Chueca hang-out. The name means 'dressmaker' in Spanish, and various decor odds-and-ends reflect this – some of the customers look as though they've come straight from a fitting too.

✉ **Calle de Hortaleza 74** ☎ **91 532 07 71** Ⓜ **Chueca** ◷ 10am-2.30pm

Lombok
(3, D12) $$$
Creative
Lombok was an 'in' destination when we visited, making it tricky to procure a table at times. The restaurant has a lot of white going on, creating an airy, sometimes chilly feel, especially with the stainless steel tables. The food is great though –

fresh and imaginatively prepared.

✉ **Calle de Augusto Figueroa 32** ☎ **91 531 35 66** Ⓜ **Chueca** ◷ Mon-Thur 2-4pm & 9pm-midnight, Fri & Sat 9pm-1am

madrilia
(3, E11) $$$
Mediterranean
The lower-case 'm' should give you a fairly good idea of what you can expect from this place. Modern, creative dishes (the rice dishes are recommended) are served up in slick, blue-lit surrounds to a smart yet hungry set. Reservations for weekend dining are a good idea.

✉ **Calle de Clavel 6** ☎ **91 523 92 75** Ⓜ **Gran Vía** ◷ 1-4pm & 8.30pm-midnight

Stop Madrid
(3, D11) $
Tapas
Stop Madrid from what? Gorging on delicious tapas? Not likely. This

Stop by Stop Madrid

popular local spot gets busy in the afternoon and evening, and has some great wines. There are plenty of yellowing tiles, lots of dark wood and very warm service. Tapas is mostly *jamón-* and *chorizo*-based.

✉ **Calle Hortaleza 11**
☎ **91 523 54 42**

Ⓜ **Gran Via** ⏱ Mon-Sat 12.30-4pm & 6pm-2am

Wokcafe
(3, E12)   **$$$**
Asian
Chueca's always happy to embrace the new, and Wokcafe has proved popular for its quality stir-fries.

There's also a shop, and a bar for coffee or cocktails. The Asian-inspired decor avoids sterility thanks to the triffid-style greenery and beaten-gold wall.

✉ **Calle de las Infantas 44** ☎ **91 522 90 69**
Ⓜ **Banco de España**
⏱ Mon-Sat 10am-2am
♣ V

HUERTAS & SANTA ANA

Asia Society
(3, H13)   **$$$**
Asian
The tiles and blonde wood hail from the world of New York-Pacific Rim fusion, not classic Madrid. Dishes come from Thailand, Korea, Japan and Indonesia, and a lot of groovy *madrileños* tuck in, even at the early hour of 10pm! The green mango salad was a piece of tangy, textural heaven. Book at weekends.

✉ **Calle Lope de Vega 37** ☎ **91 429 92 92**
Ⓜ **Antón Martín**
⏱ Tues-Sat 1-4pm & 9pm-12.30am

Café del Círculo de Bellas Artes
(3, F13)   **$$**
Café/Brasserie
This cavernous *belle époque* (1919) space is marvellous for a caffeine or champagne hit, or a meal while resting weary feet and sussing out the well-dressed patrons from the terrace. To gain access, you'll need a temporary membership token (60c). Definitely the best spot to revel in the monumental architecture of the surrounding area.

✉ **Calle de Alcalá 42**
☎ **91 531 85 03**

Ⓜ **Banco de España**
⏱ Mon-Thur & Sun 9am-2am, Fri & Sat 9am-3am

Café del Príncipe
(3, G11)   **$**
Café
Although it stays open till late, we prefer this place in the morning when you can sit at a window seat, sip a coffee and watch Madrid go by. It's a nice mix of chandeliers, unhurried smiles and a fruit-pokie machine.

✉ **Plaza de Canelejas 5** ☎ **91 531 93 84**
Ⓜ **Sevilla** ⏱ 9am-3am

Eat & Run
Two mobile food options in Madrid are the *barquillo-* (wafer) selling *castizos* who frequent the Parque del Buen Retiro on weekends with their red barrels, and the Chinese hawkers plying ready-made *boccadillos* or simple rice dishes on Gran Vía or around Huertas late at night. The former is a local tradition, the latter attracts the attention of police.

The society of great food

Casa Alberto
(3, H11) $
Tapas

With pics, paintings and tiles on the walls plus fancy woodwork, this place is a great spot to nibble tapas while quenching a beer or *vermut* (vermouth) thirst. Service is courteous and you can eat in the restaurant ($$) at the back if you hanker for something more substantial.

✉ Calle de las Huertas 18 ☎ 91 429 93 56
Ⓜ Antón Martín
🕑 Tuesday-Sunday noon-5.30pm & 8pm-1.30am

Cervecería Alemana
(3, H11) $$
Tapas

A definite stop on the Hemingway pilgrimage, the tapas and beers here attract many tourists at night, but it retains a local feel during the day. Tables have marble tops and there's a lot of brown going on.

✉ Plaza de Santa Ana 6 ☎ 91 429 70 33
Ⓜ Antón Martín or Sol
🕑 Mon, Wed, Thur & Sun 10.30am-1am, Fri & Sat 10.30am-2am

Champagnería Gala
(3, J13) $$$
Paella/Valencian

Make a reservation for this place as soon as you arrive in Madrid. Even so, you might not get a table until about 4pm for lunch, but the rich paella, glass-covered atrium, friendly service and general conviviality of everyone around you make it worth the wait. Credit cards are not accepted.

✉ Calle de Moratín 22 ☎ 91 420 19 50

Swill a cerveza at Casa Alberto

Ⓜ Antón Martín
🕑 2-5pm & 9pm-1.30am

Donzoko
(3, G11) $$$
Japanese

If Spain's (at times) heavy cuisine is holding you back, head for a sushi fix at this popular place with Japanese staples (right down to the tiny Zen-like rock-garden entrance) that are popular with locals and tourists.

✉ Calle Echegaray 3 ☎ 91 429 57 20
Ⓜ Sevilla 🕑 Mon-Sat 1.30-3.30pm & 8.30-11.30pm

East 47 (3, G12) $$$$
Creative

Both a restaurant and a stylish bar, this reflects its parent, the Hotel Villa Real, as it has a feeling of luxury without being predictable. The meat dishes are particularly strong, and the wine list is worth exploring.

✉ Hotel Villa Real, Plaza de las Cortes 10 ☎ 91 420 37 67
Ⓜ Banco de España
🕑 11am-1am

El Caldero
(3, H11) $$
Murcian

All muted earth-tones and cuisine from Murcia, this place does a wicked line of rice-based dishes for two. The *dorada a la sal* (rock-salt crusted Dory – €13.25) or *arroz negro* (rice with squid ink – €20) are excellent choices, but attentive staff will help the indecisive.

✉ Calle de las Huertas 15 ☎ 91 429 50 44
Ⓜ Antón Martín
🕑 Tues-Sat 1.30-4pm & 9pm-midnight, Mon & Sun 1.30-4pm

El Cenador del Prado
(3, H11) $$$
Creative

When your eyes get used to the riot of red, purple and pink near the

Want Smoke With That?

The campaigns against smoking that are par for the course in many countries have had little impact here. In fact, it would seem that most madrileños have a ciggie 'twixt their lips 24 hours a day, only removing them to take a sip or a mouthful of food. Some restaurants have designated no-smoking areas, but these are rarities.

entrance, you'll probably get taken to a cool, light-filled atrium, where exceptionally prescient service awaits, along with a wonderful modern menu and some of the most lavish desserts we've ever seen.

✉ **Calle del Prado 4**
☎ **91 429 15 61**
Ⓜ **Antón Martín or Sol**
🕐 Mon-Fri 1.30-4pm & 9pm-midnight, Sat 9pm-midnight Ⓥ

La Bio Tika
(3, J12) $
Vegetarian
Feeling that your food pyramid's been turned upside-down? Try here – the healthy (and flavoursome) cuisine is vegetarian *and* macrobiotic, service is calm and casual, and the no-smoking policy is a bonus.

✉ **Calle Amor de Dios 3** ☎ **91 429 07 80**
Ⓜ **Antón Martín**
🕐 Mon-Fri 1-4.30pm & 8-11.30pm; Sat, Sun & public hols 1.30-4.30pm Ⓥ

La Dolores
(3, H13) $
Tapas
Great tilework out the front (since 1907) and an ear-splitting crowd inside – an excellent place to refresh yourself once you've done the museum

trawl. While the tapas are very good, a 'world of beer' theme seems to be taking place on the shelves, which is *so* 80s.

✉ **Plaza de Jesús 4**
☎ **91 429 22 43**
Ⓜ **Antón Martín**
🕐 Mon-Thur & Sun 11am-1am, Fri & Sat 11am-2am

La Fábrica
(3, J13) $
Tapas
Close to the Prado and the jumping Santa Ana night-time playground (without the pesky tourist trade), this bar has great tapas (the canapés are from heaven) and a convivial, chatty atmosphere that's hard to beat. There's also room to sit down and take the weight off those aching feet on the back.

✉ **Calle de Jesús 2**
☎ **91 369 06 71**
Ⓜ **Antón Martín**
🕐 Mon-Thur 11am-1am, Fri & Sat 11am-2am

La Farfalla (3, J12) $$
Italian/Argentinian
La Farfalla may not have the greatest Italian food you'll ever have, but the pasta dishes are filling and the steaks are more than substantial. We figure the place's best assets are the

friendliness and very long opening hours!

✉ **Calle de Santa María 17** ☎ **91 369 46 91** Ⓜ **Antón Martín**
🕐 9pm-3am ♿ Ⓥ

La Finca de Susanna
(3, G11) $$
Mediterranean
Incredible value, given the modern, attractive decor and imaginative dishes, but this place is no secret. Get in early, or join a long queue. The *menú del día* is extraordinary for €6.60, but off-the-menu ordering will deliver the same happy surprise.

✉ **Calle de Arlabán 4**
☎ **91 369 35 57**
Ⓜ **Sevilla** 🕐 1-3.45pm & 8.30-11.45pm Ⓥ

Los Gatos (3, J13) $
Tapas
Like a mission-brown explosion in a bullfighting-kitsch factory, this place brings new meaning to the phrase 'cheek by jowl'. If you're lucky, you'll see the overworked grill on fire when tapas overload occurs. A definite fave, especially the *anguilas* (little eels on toast).

✉ **Calle de Jesús 2**
☎ **91 429 30 67**
Ⓜ **Antón Martín**
🕐 Mon-Thur & Sun noon-1am, Fri & Sat noon-2am

La Trucha (3, G10) $
Tapas
This is one of Madrid's best spots for tapas, especially if it's Andalucian that you're after. The seafood nibbles are truly scrumptious, but you can also eat out the back if you're after something more substantial.

✉ **Calle de Manuel Fernández y González 3**

Los Gatos - a firm favourite

☎ 91 429 58 33 Ⓜ Sol or Sevilla ⏰ daily 1-4pm & 8pm-midnight

La Vaca Verónica
(3, J13) $$
Mediterranean
The ladies of La Vaca Verónica understand that good eating lies in the freshest, finest ingredients, simply prepared – our sardines were plump and juicy, and deserved their own postcode. The decor is yellow-hued, with a few chandeliers thrown in, although this little touch doesn't make it feel stuffy. Reservations are advised if you're planning to eat here at the weekend.
✉ Calle Moratín 38
☎ 91 429 78 27

Cervecería Alemana, a nod to German beer-halls p79

Ⓜ Antón Martín
⏰ Mon-Sat noon-4pm & 9pm-midnight

Lhardy (3, G10) $$$$
Tapas/French/Madrileña
A staple of swanky Madrid since 1839, this is the place to come for high-end tapas, French cuisine – including the *perdiz estofado* (stuffed partridge) – and some excellent local dishes, including *callos* (tripe). The setting is impressive too.
✉ Carrera de San Jerónimo 8 ☎ 91 522 22 07 Ⓜ Sol ⏰ Mon-Sat 1-3.30pm & 8.30-11.30pm, Sun 1-3.30pm

LA LATINA TO LAVAPIÉS

Asador Frontón
(3, J9) $$$
Basque
Nostrils and tastebuds start twitching with thoughts of this place, so good are the charcoal-grilled meat and fish dishes. It's hearty food, and while the desserts may be too heavy after such carnivorous festivities, the wine selection ensures you're getting more than just one food group – well, sorta.
✉ Plaza Tirso de Molina 7 ☎ 91 369 16 17 Ⓜ Tirso de Molina ⏰ 1.30-4pm, Mon-Sat 9pm-midnight

Casa de Tostas
(2, O5) $
Tapas
Lavapiés residents know there's no point in socialising without getting stuck into *tostas*, and the ones here are pretty hefty. Generous serves, with a great range of toppings (the *pate de bacalao* is our favourite) and the place is full of a lot of happy munchers.
✉ Calle de Argumosa 29 ☎ 91 527 08 42 Ⓜ Lavapiés ⏰ 1-4pm & 6pm-1am ♿

El Almendro 13
(3, J7) $
Tapas
Don't get people started on the topic of the *huevos rotos* (scrambled eggs) here – they'll never stop. Just get started on the eggs themselves! Excellent tapas, a great atmosphere, and good wines make this place extremely popular.
✉ Calle del Almendro 13 ☎ 91 365 42 52 Ⓜ La Latina ⏰ 1-4pm & 7pm-midnight ♿

El Estragón (3, J6) $$
Vegetarian
With the pleasant Plaza de la Paja as a good spot to start off a social whirl, the mighty tasty food of this firm fave should see you sated. Staff are kind, even if you've shown up a little too late for their liking.
✉ Plaza de la Paja 10 ☎ 91 365 89 82

Coffee Notes
Café con leche (drunk in the mornings only) is about half coffee, half hot milk. A *café solo* is a short black, while a *café cortado* is a short black with a dash of milk. For iced coffee, ask for a *café con hielo*, which will result in a glass of ice and a hot cup of coffee to be poured over the ice.

Focus on the food at Lamiak

La Latina ⏰ 1.30-5pm & 8.30pm-midnight V

La Carpanta (3, J6) S
Tapas
One of the beauties of this place is that it's got more on offer than just beer and olives. The wines are carefully chosen and the canapés moreish. An even bigger bonus? There's room to sit too.
✉ Calle de Almendro 22 ☎ 91 366 57 83 Ⓜ La Latina ⏰ 3pm-2am

Lamiak (3, J6) S
Tapas/Basque
There's also a great restaurant here ($$$), but it was the *pinchos* that left us breathless – they were Basque and they were simply great. The egg-yolk coloured walls had woeful art but who cares when the nibbles are this good and the beer is so expertly poured?
✉ Calle de la Cava Baja 42 ☎ 91 365 52 12 Ⓜ La Latina ⏰ Tues-Sat 1-4pm & 9pm-midnight, Sun 1-4pm

Tía Doly (2, O4) $$
Italian
Tía Doly (Aunt Doly) makes excellent fresh pasta on a daily basis and all in the homely surrounds of this unpretentious Italian restaurant. It's also possible to get meals to take away if you're staying nearby or fancy dining in the great outdoors.
✉ Calle del Amparo 54 ☎ 91 527 33 26 Ⓜ Lavapiés ⏰ Tues-Sat 8.30pm-12.30am, Wed-Sun 1-4.30pm

LOS AUSTRIAS

Casa Ciriaco (3, G6) $$
Castillian
A local eating place that's frequented by families, business folk, and amateur artists (look at the walls), the food here is unpretentious. Cluey waiters wear white jackets; they will even give your shirt a squirt of stain-remover if you've been sloppy with the *sopa di cocido* (€3.50).
✉ Calle Mayor 84 ☎ 91 548 06 20 Ⓜ Ópera ⏰ Thur-Tues 1.30-4.30pm & 8.30-11.30pm

Casa de Santa Cruz (3, H9) $$$
Market
This place certainly isn't lacking in atmosphere, as it's situated in the old Santa Cruz basilica. But you can relax, because despite the setting, it's short on both formality and stuffiness. The food is excellent market cuisine, and the lamb dishes we sampled bring new meaning to the phrase 'lamb of God'.
✉ Calle de la Bolsa 12 ☎ 91 521 86 23 Ⓜ Sol ⏰ 1.30-4.30pm & 8.30pm-midnight

Casa Lucio (3, J7) $$$
Madrileña
Located on a street that's full of good places to eat, Casa Lucio remains a firm favourite for those who like to partake of well-prepared madrileña dishes, such as *arroz con leche* (rice pudding). The place is casual and welcoming, but can get busy, so you might have to stand at the bar for a while and wait for a table to be vacated.
✉ Calle de la Cava Baja 35 ☎ 91 365 32 52 Ⓜ La Latina ⏰ Sun-Fri 1-4pm, 9-11.30pm ♿

Casa Paco (3, H7) **$$$**
Madrileña
This charming old-style place specialises in madrileña cooking, and the meat and egg dishes come highly recommended. You're firmly in *castizo* territory here, so throw out the dietary restrictions and get busy loosening your belt.
✉ **Plaza de Puerta Cerrada 11 ☎ 91 366 31 66 Ⓜ Sol ⊙ Mon-Sat 1.30-4pm & 8.30pm-midnight ♿**

La Cruzada (3, F6) **$$**
Castillian
Not at its original 1827 address, but you'll be glad to know that the original sculpted wooden bar was brought along. This place is nothing flash, but the *raciones* are tasty and filling, and always a good idea as a substitute for 'children's portions'.
✉ **Calle de la Amnistía 8 ☎ 91 548 01 31 Ⓜ Ópera ⊙ Mon-Sat 1-4pm & 8.30pm-midnight ♿**

Las Bravas (3, G10) **$**
Tapas
Bravas specialises in *patatas bravas* (although the other tapas dishes are good too), so much so, that its sauce is patented (No 357492 if you're wondering). The decor is nothing to write home about, but the spuds certainly are!
✉ **Callejón de Álvarez Gato 3 Ⓜ Sol ⊙ noon-4.30pm & 8pm-midnight ♿ Ⓥ**

La Tentación de San Miguel (3, H7) **$$$**
International
Housed in a sensitively renovated building just near Plaza Mayor, this is a wonderful spot to sample a range of cuisines amid elegant, yet unfussy surrounds. We're fans of whatever they're doing to cous cous, but you can also pick up simple and high-quality tapas, while being surrounded by diners of all types.
✉ **Calle de Conde Miranda 4 ☎ 91 559 98 19 Ⓜ Ópera ⊙ noon-5pm & 8.30pm-1.30am Ⓥ**

Posada de la Villa (3, J7) **$$$$**
Madrileña
A wonderfully restored 17th-century inn where all sorts of people, from travelling salesmen to fellows of ill repute were purported to have sought lodging. The food is classic madrileña, right down to the suckling pig.
✉ **Calle de la Cava Baja 9 ☎ 91 366 18 60 Ⓜ La Latina ⊙ 1-4pm, Mon-Sat 8pm-midnight**

Restaurante Julián de Tolosa (3, J7) **$$$$**
Basque
A charmingly rustic atmosphere pervades this eatery – a Basque institution. Think lots of exposed brick and timber and solid batten-the-hatches food. Beans are a big feature on the menu, and if you want something to break up all that fibre, have a *chuletón* (enormous chop).
✉ **Calle de la Cava Baja 18 ☎ 91 365 82 10 Ⓜ La Latina ⊙ Mon-Sat 1-4.30pm & 8.30pm-midnight**

Restaurante Sobrino de Botín (3, H8) **$$$**
Castillian
We wonder if people even notice the food here, so busy are they soaking up all the history. Restaurante Sobrino is dubbed the oldest restaurant in the world. It's also featured in the well-known novels: Pérez

---

Madrid's Dullest Dish?

Those looking for an 'authentic' dish from Madrid may well wish they'd stuck to all the other fine cuisine that's on offer. The most well-known local offering is *cocido a la madrileña*, a hearty stew that's said to be eaten 'from front to back'. Ingredients are generally chicken, chorizo, some ham (or other cured meat), potatoes, cabbage, chickpeas and macaroni (or rice). You start by eating the broth, with macaroni or rice. Then the chickpeas. Then the meat. By this stage, you'll have trouble fitting into your pants and walking at the same time. You'll also have trouble remembering why you ordered it, as a long cooking process often ensures that all flavour and texture have long disappeared. Still, locals love it and it certainly provides good winter fuel. On that level, we'll say it's not Madrid's dullest dish – we'll leave that honour to *churros*, those bland, greasy sticks of batter that require dunking to make them taste of anything.

Galdós' *Fortunata y Jacinta* and Hemingway's *The Sun Also Rises*. Yep, you could say it's a bit of a tourist trap, but it's a good-looking trap all the same.

✉ **Calle de los Cuchillos 17** ☎ 91 366 42 17 Ⓜ **Sol or Tirso de Molina** ⏰ 1-4pm & 8pm-midnight ♿

Taberna La Bola
(3, E6)   **$$$$**
Madrileña
This *taberna* (tavern) is well known locally for its traditional *cocido a la madrileña*, and has been placating hungry madrileño tummies since 1880. There's a very nice old-fashioned atmosphere here, with good old-fashioned service, and the high turnover means that you know you're getting the good, fresh stuff.

✉ **Calle de la Bola 5** ☎ 91 547 69 30 Ⓜ **Ópera or Santo Domingo** ⏰ 1.30-4pm, Mon-Sat 8.30pm-midnight ♿

MALASAÑA & AROUND

Baban (4, K3)   **$$**
Kurdish
Go downstairs once you've found Baban and feast on delicious dips and excellent meat dishes (best shared). It's a casual place, where locals come to have a relaxed meal in still-groovy surrounds (this is Malasaña after all).

✉ **Calle de Manuela Malasaña 20** ☎ 91 594 18 68 Ⓜ **San Bernardo or Bilbao** ⏰ Tues-Sun 1-4pm & 9pm-midnight

Bar Casa do Compañeiro
(3, B9)   **$**
Tapas
The fried *morcilla* (black pudding) here is served with a few hunks of bread. It's plain and a bit stodgy but it certainly did the trick as a stomach liner-meets-iron deposit. It was good

Galician stuff too, and the smile we got warmed our hearts.

✉ **Calle de San Vicente Ferrer 44** ☎ 91 521 57 02 Ⓜ **Noviciado or Tribunal** ⏰ 1pm-2am

Café Comercial
(4, K4)   **$**
Café
A local institution of the best kind! The Café Comercial has been a meeting place, a *tertulia* (chat session) centre and breakfast spot for donkeys' years. Grab a coffee and a pastry or a snack, and people-watch from behind a newspaper. If the food's not enough, come for the decor.

✉ **Glorieta de Bilbao 7** ☎ 91 521 56 55 Ⓜ **Bilbao** ⏰ Mon-Thur & Sun 8am-1am, Fri & Sat 8am-2am

Isla de Tesoro
(4, K4)   **$$**
Vegetarian
This delightful little joint serves heavenly vegetarian food with a great deal of flair, fun and frivolity. The staff are cheery and the crowds are far from pious, plus the 'treasure island' feel of the decor will make you smile. We also dig the big purple-velvet double bass that you'll see just hanging around.

✉ **Calle de Manuela Malasaña 3** ☎ 91 593 14 40 Ⓜ **San Bernardo or Bilbao** ⏰ 1-4pm & 9-11.30pm Ⓥ

La Musa (4, K3)   **$**
Market
A buzzing disco vibe fills this place even at lunch. Lunch also sees a handy *menú del día* that keeps the Malasaña locals full, satisfied and return customers. We had a great beetroot soup that was full of flavour yet light and refreshing. Nights can get overly crowded, but there's always a nearby plaza for recuperation and some fresh air.

✉ **Calle de Manuela Malasaña 18** ☎ 91 448 75 58 Ⓜ **Bilbao** ⏰ 9am-midnight

Take some company to Casa do Compañeiro

Eating with Children

Kids are welcome at the vast majority of restaurants, although it's rare to find special menus, portions and high chairs, and the amount of cigarette smoke can irritate young eyes. Look for the ♣ with individual reviews for more child-friendly options.

Nudel Bar (3, C7) $$
Asian

A new addition to Madrid's Asian eateries, and pretty trendy to boot. Things were still getting ironed out when we visited, but the noodle dishes (from Thailand, Vietnam and India) rise above the self-satisfied air that sometimes fills the place.

✉ **Calle de San Bernardino 1** ☎ **91 548 36 40** Ⓜ **Noviciado** or

Plaza de España
◷ noon-1am ♣

Siam (3, C7) $$$$
Thai

Beautiful decor touches like stone buddha statues and hanging silks will put you in a mellow state of mind while dining here. The food is the genuine Thai article too, with ingredients flown in especially, and Thai chefs in the kitchen.

✉ **Calle de San Bernardino 6** ☎ **91 559 83 15** Ⓜ **Noviciado** or **Plaza de España**
◷ 1-5pm & 8pm-1am

Tété (3, C8) $$$$
Market

Saved by a whisker or two from being chilly in atmosphere. The seasonal ingredients that feature on the menu are used very imaginatively indeed — we certainly wouldn't have created *sopa de piña con espuma de queso y coco*

(pineapple soup with cheese and coconut foam) in our own kitchen, but it works here.

✉ **Calle Andrés Borrego 16** ☎ **91 522 73 91** Ⓜ **Noviciado**
◷ Mon-Fri 2-4pm & 9pm-midnight, Sat 9pm-midnight

Toma (3, B6) $$$
Creative

A rush of red (paint) to the head is what you experience when you walk into this very modern, yet comfy bistro. The chef, Paul Regan, uses his imagination but never brings out the emperor's new clothes. Speaking of which, you may want to don something a little more special to come to this place, even if you're just having a cocktail.

✉ **Calle de Conde Duque 14** ☎ **91 547 49 96** Ⓜ **Noviciado**
◷ Tues-Sat 9pm-1am

SALAMANCA & RETIRO

Café-Restaurante El Espejo (3, C15) $$
Café/Basque/French

This café is an attractive and elegant spot to while away the hours. Despite its turn-of-the-century style, it only opened in 1990. The *pabellón* (pavillion) is one of *the* places to have a tipple in summer, and it's all to a pianist's tinkling accompaniment. The more upmarket restaurant ($$$$) serves good Basque/French cuisine. Dress up and make a night of it.

✉ **Paseo de los Recoletos 31** ☎ **91 308 23 47** Ⓜ **Colón**
◷ 10.30am-1am

Gran Café de Gijón (3, D14) $$
Café/International

This long-time haunt of literary Madrid has been dishing up coffee, good meals and blood-red velvet decor since 1888. In the winter months, the atmosphere is cosy — in summer you should head outside to the swanky terrace area, where a grand piano sits ready to serenade you, and *cava* (champagne) lightly bubbles away ready to quench your thirst.

✉ **Paseo de los Recoletos 21** ☎ **91 521 54 25** Ⓜ **Banco de España** ◷ 7am-2am

Le Divellec (4, J9) $$$$
French

Named after French chef Jacques Le Divellec, this is an excellent choice for those wanting some dining pleasure while they get down to business. Fishy business even, as the food is billed as 'Cuisine de la Mar'. When we visited, chef David Millet was behind the stove, but there were no complaints.

✉ **Hotel Villa Magna, Paseo de la Castellana 22** ☎ **91 587 12 34** Ⓜ **Rubén Darío**
◷ Mon-Sat 1-4pm & 8.30-11.30pm

Mumbai Massala
(3, D15) $$$
Indian

A strong contender for the title of Madrid's prettiest restaurant, the stunning pink, gold and glittery decor *almost* competes with the northeast Indian cuisine. Dishes are packed with flavour and service is a joy. Book for weekends, as opening hours are relatively short.

✉ Calle de Recoletos 14 ☎ 91 435 71 94
Ⓜ Banco de España
🚇 Recoletos ⊕ Sun-Thur 1.30-3.30pm & 9-11pm, Fri 1.30-3.30pm & 9pm-midnight, Sat 1.30-4pm & 9pm-midnight Ⓥ

Wine

The standard accompaniment to any meal in Spain, wine comes in three varieties: *tinto* (red), *blanco* (white) and *rosado* (rosé). It can be ordered by the glass (*copa*) or in measures of 500mL or 1L. *Vino de mesa* (table wine) is perfectly decent in most places, but the area around Madrid is not widely regarded as one of Spain's premier wine-producing regions.

Restaurante Oter Epicure (4, K9) $$$$
Navarran

The food here is upmarket Navarran, with a bit of Basque thrown in to ensure everyone's satisfied. The service is smooth. The presentation reveals much effort, and the wine list is a thing of beauty. You might

With a View to...

Our favourite view in Madrid is from the top-floor terrace of **El Viajero** (p91), with its heart-stirring vista of the historic centre's skyline, although the restaurant is on the ground floor. For views over the Casa de Campo, head to **El Molino de los Porches** (p74), with a lovely terrace. **Café-Restaurante El Espejo** (p85) has a swanky terrace perfect for beautiful people watching, but our advice is to find a plaza you like, plonk yourself on a seat and watch the world go by, which can be as intoxicating as any tourist-geared view.

want to dress up and make a reservation.

✉ Calle de Claudio Coello 73 ☎ 91 431 67 71 Ⓜ Velázquez
⊕ Mon-Sat 1-4.30pm & 8.30pm-midnight

Sushi Itto (3, D15) $$
Japanese

As neat and shiny as a new pin, but also casual enough to lose the 'Japanese shrine' atmosphere that can hamper the fun in many such restaurants, this place does great sushi, which can be shared or hogged according to your mood, or even delivered to your hotel.

✉ Calle de Recoletos 10 ☎ 91 426 21 69
Ⓜ Banco de España
🚇 Recoletos ⊕ Sun-Thurs 1.30-4.30pm & 8.30pm-midnight, Fri & Sat 1.30-4.30pm & 8.30pm-1am ♨

Taberna de Daniela (2, K8) $
Tapas

It's easy to overlook the Goya area if tapas and tipples are on your mind, but at midday, this well-tiled, colourful joint attracts quite a few people, and they all seem to be enjoying what's on offer, despite

the fact that service is patchy at times.

✉ Calle del General Pardiñas 21 ☎ 91 575 23 29 Ⓜ Goya
⊕ 11.30am-5.30pm, Sun-Thur 7.30-11.30pm, Fri & Sat 7.30pm-1am

Teatriz (2, K7) $$$$
Italian

Even the toilets are a theatrical experience here – visitors leave luminous footprints on the floor. You'll be spending more than a penny though at this Philippe Starck-designed restaurant, as this is one of Madrid's grooviest. You'll certainly want to put on your glad rags, and reservations are definitely recommended.

✉ Calle de la Hermosilla 15 ☎ 91 577 53 79 Ⓜ Serrano
⊕ 1.30-4pm 9pm-1am ♿

Thai Gardens (2, L6) $$$$
Thai

This is one of those places where the name says it all really. The better than average food is graciously presented, and set in a lavish garden-atmosphere. Ingredients are fresh (they're flown in on a weekly basis from Thailand)

and skilfully handled, plus there's parking. You'd be well advised to make a reservation, especially at weekends.

✉ Calle de Jorge Juan 5 ☎ 91 577 88 84 Ⓜ Serrano ⏰ 2-5pm, Sun-Thur 9pm-1am, Fri & Sat 9pm-2am Ⓥ

Zalacaín (4, F8) **$$$$**
Creative
The proud possessor of three Michelin stars, Zalacaín is one of Madrid's finest restaurants. It was established by the Oyarbide family in the 1970s, and standards have not slipped, so loosen the belt, unhinge

the wallet and get busy with the menu (after having reserved a table and put on your best duds).

✉ Calle Álvarez de Baena 4 ☎ 91 561 59 35 Ⓜ Gregorio Marañón ⏰ Mon-Fri 1.15-4pm, Mon-Sat 9pm-midnight

SOL & GRAN VÍA

Artemisa (3, E10) **$$**
Vegetarian
This central vegetarian restaurant is good for animal lovers, with a good varied menu that features tasty salads. The *platos al horno* (oven-baked dishes) are recommended.

✉ Calle de las Tres Cruces 4 ☎ 91 521 87 21 Ⓜ Gran Vía ⏰ 1.30-4pm & 9pm-midnight ♿ Ⓥ

Casa Labra (3, F10) **$**
Tapas
Since 1860, madrileños have been squeezing past each other in Casa Labra to get a beer in one hand and some *bacalao croquetas* in the other. Who knows if these *croquetas* were the inspiration for Pablo Iglesias and his comrades to found the Spanish socialist party here over 120 years ago.

✉ Calle de Tetuán 11 ☎ 91 531 00 81 Ⓜ Sol ⏰ Mon-Sat 9.30am-3.30pm & 6-11pm, Sun 1-4pm & 8-11pm

Casa Parrondo (3, E8) **$$$**
Asturian
Asturian cuisine is staple here, which means lots of chorizo and cheese for tapas and some excellent

main courses, with meat lovers relishing the *cabrales* (rare steak). The restaurant resembles an Asturian house in the mountains and, if the photos of the owner killing pigs doesn't turn your stomach, you'll be rewarded.

✉ Calle de Trujillos 9 ☎ 91 522 62 34 Ⓜ Santo Domingo ⏰ Mon-Sat 1-4pm & 8.30pm-2am, Sun 1-4pm

Delfos (3, E7) **$$**
Greek
If the name and the decor didn't clue you in that this is a Greek joint, then the food certainly will. The *moysaka* (mousaka) is damn fine, and suits the casual, friendly feel of the place.

✉ Cuesta de Santo Domingo 14 ☎ 91 548 37 64 Ⓜ Santo Domingo ⏰ Tues-Sun 12.30-4pm & 8.30pm-midnight

Gula Gula (3, E12) **$$$**
Theatre restaurant
Gula Gula's salad buffet is a veritable sea of greenery in an otherwise meat-loving Madrid. The other reason for coming here though is so you can feast on the nightly drag-queen shows, which are spicy, but not so

risqué as to shock the mainstream.

✉ Gran Vía 1 ☎ 91 522 87 64 Ⓜ Banco de España ⏰ Tues-Sun 1-4.30pm, Tues-Thur & Sun 9pm-1.30am, Fri & Sat 9pm-2.30am Ⓥ

Dinner Deals
If you're in Madrid for business, good places to make an impression include: **Santceloni** (p75), **Zalacaín** (p87), **Le Divellec** (p85), **Santo Mauro** (p76), **El Bodegon** (p75), **East 47** (p79) as well as **Restaurante Oter Epicure** (p86).

Restaurante La Paella Real (3, F7) **$$$**
Paella/Valencian
Paella does not originate from Madrid, but many visitors believe that to eat Spanish is to eat paella. Luckily, you can find it here, and no matter where it's from, it's good stuff. This place offers more than paella though, with a large selection for rice lovers.

✉ Calle de Arrieta 2 ☎ 91 542 09 42 Ⓜ Ópera ⏰ 1-4pm ♿

entitlement

The reason it's a cliché is because it's true – *madrileños* really don't end the night until they've killed it. It's the perfect place for making merry, with a plethora of bars (over 20,000!), great gay nightlife, all-night-long dance clubs, and a whirl of flamenco, jazz, salsa and rock venues. If the more old-fashioned arts are your cup of tea, the theatre scene is lively, the opera is sterling, classical music is appreciated and modern dance, well, it's getting there. Locals love nothing more than going to the movies on a Sunday. All this plus local festivals and city-sponsored events means you can be busy indeed.

Locals *are* as passionate about social life as you've heard, and the hours they keep are startling. Don't even think about starting a big night before midnight. Dancing won't begin until around 3am. Bed time? About 6am – well, maybe.

Top Spots

Madrid's top nightlife area surrounds the Plaza de Santa Ana, with literally hundreds of bars and thousands of people, from the young and not-so-young to the avowedly local and a variety of nationalities. Other popular areas include Malasaña, which attracts a grungy, youthful crowd, and Lavapiés, with a good mix of traditional and quirky nightspots. The upwardly mobile set generally frequents the Salamanca *barrio*, while lovers of gay nightlife flock to Chueca.

Tickets & Listings

The weekly *Guía del Ocio* is a must for keeping abreast of what's on. *In Madrid*, a free English-language rag, is also a good source of information, while tourist offices can help with tracking down events and will have information on the arts scene. You can also try *El País* and *El Mundo*, which publish entertainment listings, or the free *El Duende de Madrid*.

Tickets for plays, concerts and other performances can be bought at the theatre concerned, and a few lottery-ticket booths sell theatre, football and bullfight tickets. Madrid Rock (3, E10; ☎ 91 521 02 39) and FNAC (3, E9; ☎ 91 520 00 00) sell tickets to major concerts.

Telephone and Internet bookings are also possible. Try the Caixa de Catalunya (☎ 902 10 12 12, **e** www.caixacatalunya.es), with tickets to many major events and concerts, and Caja de Madrid (☎ 902 48 84 88), which also sells cinema tickets. Like all credit-card bookings, you pay by card and then collect the tickets from the relevant venue.

SPECIAL EVENTS

January *New Year's Eve* – people eat a grape for each chime, for good luck
Día de los Reyes Magos – 6 Jan; a parade of the three kings winds its way around the city to the delight of kids

February/March *Carnevales* – days of fancy-dress parades and merrymaking across the Comunidad de Madrid, usually ending on the Tuesday 47 days before Easter Sunday

May *Fiesta de la Comunidad de Madrid* – 2 May; celebrations are kicked off with a speech by a local personality from the balcony of the Casa de Correos in the Puerta del Sol, and a host of cultural events and festivities follow
Fiestas de San Isidro – 15 May; the big one! Feast day of the city's patron saint followed by a week of partying. The country's most prestigious *feria*, or bullfighting season, also begins now and continues for a month, at the Plaza de Toros Monumental de Las Ventas

June/July *Local Fiestas* – most districts in Madrid celebrate the feast day of one saint or another; ask the tourist office for details of where and when these local knees-ups take place

July–August *Veranos de la Villa* – council-organised arts festival with something for everyone, day and night, whether it be film, dance, music, theatre, photography, art or fashion
Fiestas de San Lorenzo, San Cayetano & La Virgen de la Paloma – 27 Jul-15 Aug; these three local patron saints' festivities (which revolve around La Latina, Plaza de Lavapiés and Calle de Calatrava in La Latina, respectively) keep the central districts of Madrid busy for the best part of three weeks

September *Local Fiestas* – local councils organise fiestas in the first and second weeks of September; these are very local affairs and provide a rare insight into *barrio* life of the average madrileño
Fiesta del PCE – mid-Sept; the Spanish Communist Party holds its annual fundraiser in the Casa de Campo, a weekend-long mixed bag of regional-food pavilions, rock concerts and political soap-boxing

November *Día de la Virgen de la Almudena* – 9 Nov; *castizos* (true-blue madrileños) gather in Plaza Mayor to hear Mass on this the feast day of the city's female patron saint

BARS

Bar Cock (3, E11)

Once a salon for high-class prostitution, Bar Cock retains a gentlemen's club atmosphere, although the crowd is often comprised of resolutely with-it 30-somethings in linen, leather, lace and polo-neck sweaters. You have to knock to get in, and apparently a table stands reserved for the prince.

✉ **Calle de la Reina 16**
☎ **91 532 28 26**
Ⓜ **Gran Vía** ◷ **Mon-Sat 9pm-4am**

Sexy Bodega Melibea

Bodega Melibea

(3, G10) Owned by the same sexy crowd as the Matador Bar (see p91–2), this is *the* place to come if cheap red wine and Sapphic-themed tiles are your thing, you like to watch, or you just appreciate a chatty atmosphere.

✉ **Calle de Espoz y Mina 9** Ⓜ **Sol**
◷ **7pm-2am**

Café Belén (3, C12)

If the streets surrounding this bar are getting a little *too* young for you, then relax. You and your grown-up friends can sit and listen to an eclectic selection of music without shouting at each other, all while enjoying excellent cocktails (especially the *mojitos*).

✉ **Calle de Belén 5**
☎ **91 308 27 47**
Ⓜ **Chueca or Alonso Martínez**
◷ **3.30pm-3am**

Casa Pueblo (3, H12)

The Casa Pueblo is a cosy place where the young-at-heart (but no longer very young) can enjoy a cocktail and listen to jazz, still played on an old reel-to-reel. It's warm, welcoming, and a nice alternative to the Santa Ana scene.

✉ **Calle de León 3**
☎ **91 429 05 15**
Ⓜ **Antón Martín**
◷ **Tues-Sat 10pm-2.30am, Sun 10pm-3.30am**

Del Diego (3, E11)

For a bar with a blonde-wood Art Deco look going on and waiters who appear to have been inspired by the Chris Isaak school of grooming, Del Diego has a surprisingly casual (dare we say ordinary?) crowd piling in for some very smooth cocktails.

✉ **Calle de la Reina 12**
☎ **91 523 31 06**
Ⓜ **Gran Vía** ◷ **Mon-Sat 9pm-3am**

El Café de Shéhérazad (3, J12)

Quite a romantic spot, given the authentic Islamic kit-out (right down to the beautiful stonework and smoking equipment). You can drink mint tea and all manner of alcoholic drinks, and the attentive and charming staff will make you swoon.

✉ **Calle de Santa María 18** ☎ **91 369 24 74** Ⓜ **Antón Martín**
◷ **7pm-3am**

El Eucalipto (2, O4)

El Eucalipto makes some of the best *mojitos* we've ever had, which is saying something in this cocktail-loving town. The vibe is friendly and chatty, partly because this particular street has a reputation for a breezy, unpretentious atmosphere, especially when there's outdoor seating in summer.

✉ **Calle de Argumosa 4** Ⓜ **Lavapiés**
◷ **6pm-2am**

No Smoke Without Fire

Drug laws in Spain were tightened in 1992, and while marijuana (often called *maría*) is legal for personal use, public consumption is not. You may well find people smoking a joint (*porro*) in bars or in plazas, but you might want to think twice before you join in, as most cops won't have a problem with arresting a foolish foreigner. For the record, hash is also known as 'chocolate', which can lead to a little confusion for some.

El 21 (3, H8)
A shoebox of a place that hasn't seen a lick of paint in years, everything here seems stained a rich shade of nicotine. It's charmingly scruffy, with courteous regulars (young and old) and blindingly cheap drinks. We're tempted to make it one of our 'Highlights', but you wouldn't all fit.
✉ Calle de Toledo 21 ☎ 91 366 28 59 Ⓜ La Latina ◷ Mon-Thur & Sun noon-3.30pm & 7-11pm, Fri & Sat noon-3.30pm & 7pm-midnight

El Viajero (3, J6)
The ground floor serves great organic steaks, but we prefer to venture upstairs, where the first floor offers a bar with great music (dub, acid jazz and funk) and the second floor has our favourite terrace in Madrid, with views of the area's skyline. Get in early or book ahead.
✉ Plaza de la Cebada 11 ☎ 91 366 90 64 Ⓜ La Latina ◷ Tues-Sat 2pm-2.30am, Sun 1pm-8pm

La Divina Comedia
(3, K13) A young, attractive crowd drops in here to get its fill of *mojitos* and enjoy a neo-bordello, Frida Kahlo-tribute atmosphere. It's all red walls, a fair few cushions, some tea candles and DJ-spun sounds, which include acid jazz, cruisy house and a bit of reggae.
✉ Calle de Almadén 14 Ⓜ Anton Martín ◷ Tues-Sun 7pm-2am

La Falsa Molestia
(3, J11) Something of a pale-coloured beauty spot for those hanging around this side of town. It's supposed to be Italian-style, and while there are good Italian wines on offer, we're struggling to remember too many bars in Italy that were this attractive.
✉ Calle de Magdalena 32 ☎ 91 420 32 38 ℯ www.lafalsamolestia .com Ⓜ Antón Martín ◷ Wed-Sun 1pm-3am

Los Gabrieles
(3, G11) Bringing new meaning to the phrase 'a night on the tiles', this popular bar has some of the most impressive tile-work in Madrid (check out the skeleton playing guitar). It used to be a brothel and there's free flamenco Tuesday to Thursday in July. What more could you want?
✉ Calle de Echegaray 17 ☎ 91 429 62 61 Ⓜ Sevilla ◷ Mon-Thur & Sun 1pm-2am, Fri & Sat 1pm-3am

Maderfaker (3, B10)
Someone here has seen *Shaft* and really loved it, hence the name of this place (say it with a Spanish accent!). We really love it because it's a lively spot, without being too crowded or brash, and is therefore the perfect spot to psyche yourself up for later on.
✉ Calle de San Vicente Ferrer 17 Ⓜ Tribunal ◷ Tues-Sat 11pm-3.30am

Magic Room (3, C10)
The night-loving hordes of this night-loving district flock here on a regular basis to soak up the spacey-meets-psychedelic ambience and a good amount of booze. The crowd has an anything-goes quality that makes the name pertinent, and the music choices include Latin-house, 70's disco and house on weekends.
✉ Calle de Colón 12 ☎ 91 531 34 91 Ⓜ Tribunal or Chueca ◷ Tues-Sun 11.30pm-5am

Matador Bar (3, G10)
Playing good flamenco music, this popular bar has been going since 1994. The bar staff are on the dishy side, which is a good thing for the young types frequenting this place, although God knows who got the idea that extremely detailed, amateurish drawings of genitalia were good

---

Heady Stuff
If you've arrived from England, Australia, or any country where the head on your beer must be 'just so', Madrid will surprise you. Heads on beer can seem to take up half the glass, especially if you're drinking a *caña* (small glass). While some bartenders will wield a spatula-like utensil to shave off excess, the initial problem seems to stem from a refusal to tilt the glass when pouring. You may also wonder why beers are slammed down in front of you, as though you've incurred the bartender's wrath. Relax, it's to settle the head.

decor practice. Thankfully the staff are good looking.
✉ **Calle de la Cruz 39**
☎ **91 531 89 91**
Ⓜ **Sol** ⏲ **Tues-Sun 7pm-2am**

Mi Gente (3, K10)

Got a grandparent whose garage is chock-full of old furniture, useless knick-knacks and a few items that are unclassifiables? Now add a small bar. A no-frills, no-fuss establishment with an endearingly laid-back, rough-round-the-edges clientele with special appearances by Lucas the dog. The music's cool too –

think flamenco, blues, and, er, The Police.
✉ **Calle de Olmo 3**
Ⓜ **Antón Martín**
⏲ **midnight-erratic**

Museo Chicote

(3, E11) A sense of tradition hangs over this Art Deco bar, which is a remnant from the 1940s and 50s when this was considered Madrid's swankiest watering hole, with the likes of Ernest Hemingway and Ava Gardner stopping by. Service is old-school, and so are the cocktails.
✉ **Gran Vía 12** ☎ **91 532 67 37** Ⓜ **Gran Vía**

⏲ **Mon-Thur 9am-3am, Fri & Sat 9am-4am**

Viva Madrid (3, G11)

A damn fine spot for some early-evening tippling. It's fine too in the late evening, if you enjoy fighting your way through the heaving crowds (locals and tourists), all wanting liquid refreshment. Keep a look-out for the tiles, they're worth the trip alone.
✉ **Calle de Manuel Fernández y González 7**
☎ **91 429 36 40**
Ⓜ **Sevilla** ⏲ **Sun-Thur 1pm-2am, Fri & Sat 1pm-3am**

DANCE CLUBS & DISCOS

Fortuny (4, H8)

If you fancy a nightclub with a little more style than most, Fortuny comes heartily recommended by the *pijos* (yuppies). It's in a renovated palace, but the sometimes-ferocious door policy will keep you out if you chose your shoes mostly for comfort. The music's unadventurous.
✉ **Calle de Fortuny 34**
☎ **91 319 05 88**
Ⓜ **Rubén Darío**
⏲ **midnight-5am**
⑤ **€8**

Joy Eslava (3, F8)

Going strong for 20 years in a building that dates back to 1872, it's something of an institution, and you never know what mix the club's going to attract on any given night. High types, low types, gays, straights, young and old – they all like gilt-tinged decor and a guilt-free boogy. Head to Chocolatería de San Ginés

(see p46) after if you're still going around breakfast.
✉ **Calle del Arenal 11**
☎ **91 366 37 33**
🖥 **www.joy-eslava.com**
Ⓜ **Sol** ⏲ **Sun-Thur 11.30pm-5.30am, Fri & Sat 11.30pm-6am**
⑤ **€12-15**

Kapital (2, O6)

There are seven, yes, seven floors (but no elevator!) of nocturnal entertainment here, ranging from dance music, karaoke, galleries and a cinema, with a writhing, sexily clad crowd lapping it all up. Kapital also runs 'afternoon' sessions for the young folk.
✉ **Calle de Atocha 125**
☎ **91 420 29 06**
Ⓜ **Atocha** ⏲ **early sessions Sat, Sun & hols 5.30-11pm, late sessions Thurs-Sun midnight-6am** ⑤ **€6**

Morocco (3, D8)

Still a popular stop on the night-owl circuit, although

it's getting a little more sophisticated with time. The music is varied and can include anything from disco lip-synch faves to more experimental.
✉ **Calle del Marqués de Leganés 7** ☎ **91 531 31 77** Ⓜ **Santo Domingo** ⏲ **Thur midnight-3am, Fri & Sat 9pm-5.30am** ⑤ **free**

Ohm (3, E9)

A popular night at the Bash Line club for those in the mood to 'wave your hands in the air like you just don't care'. We saw all types letting it all hang out. This is a must for those who like crowds and inclusive DJs.
✉ **Plaza del Callao 4**
☎ **91 531 01 32**
Ⓜ **Callao** ⏲ **Fri & Sat midnight-6am** ⑤ **€10**

Palacio Gaviria (3, F8)

This place really used to be a palace and the luxury trimmings are still evident.

People get pretty dressed up, and the queues can be disheartening. Despite its exclusive overtones, it's not frighteningly posh, with Salsa (Tues), Cabaret (Wed), 'Exchange' (Thur – lots of international snogging) and lots of disco on the weekend. Much fun.
✉ **Calle del Arenal 9**
☎ **91 526 60 69**
e **www.palaciogaviria .com** Ⓜ **Sol** ◷ **Tues & Wed 10.30pm-3.30am, Thur-Sat 11pm-6am, Sun 10.30pm-3am** Ⓢ **€12**

Space of Sound
(2, A7) If you're still going from the night before, then you'll meet plenty of like-minded souls at Space of Sound, where too much house and techno are never enough. And hey, at least you know the metro's started up again, so you can get home easily when you're finally ready to collapse.
✉ **Plaza de Estación de Chamartín**

☎ **91 733 35 05** Ⓜ **Chamartín** ◷ **Sun 9am-7pm** Ⓢ **€6**

Suite (3, F11)
There's a restaurant/café here, and it's not a bad 'quiet drink' spot (especially if you happen to be a devotee of *wallpaper** magazine), but we like it when things kick-off after midnight on weekends – that's when everyone's shaking out the cobwebs on the suspended dance floor to some seriously funky DJ sounds.
✉ **Calle Virgen de los Peligros 4** ☎ **91 521**

---

40 31 Ⓜ **Sevilla** ◷ **Mon-Sat 11.30am-3.30am** Ⓢ **free**

The Room (3, G11)
The Room is absolutely packed by about 3am, so you'll need to arrive well before then to ensure that you get the chance to dance to one of Madrid's best DJs, Ángel García. A vibrant, heady place, with some great visuals, even if you're almost cross-eyed from partying.
✉ **Calle de Arlabán 7**
☎ **91 523 86 54**
Ⓜ **Sevilla** ◷ **Fri & Sat 1am-6am** Ⓢ **€8**

CINEMAS

Standard cinema tickets cost around €5.50, but many cinemas have at least one day set aside as the *día del espectador* (viewer's day) with cut-price tickets (usually about €2 off). You can purchase tickets at the cinemas or in advance (in some cases) on ☎ **902 48 84 88** or online at e **www.guiade locio.com**.

Alphaville (3, C5)
This is the place to come to avoid mainstream foreign fare and mix it with a few arty types, as it shows original-language films with a more independent streak than other cinemas in Madrid. There are four screens, and three theatres have wheelchair access.
✉ **Calle de Martín de los Heros 14** ☎ **91 559**

Cine Doré

38 36 Ⓜ **Plaza de España** ◷ **daily from 4.30pm** Ⓢ **€5.50 (Mon €3.50)**

Cine Doré (3, J11)
The Cine Doré is a delightful old cinema, housing the Filmoteca Nacional (national film library), and you can expect to see classics old and new, in their original languages. There's also a

library and bar/restaurant attached (open 4pm-midnight).

✉ Calle de Santa Isabel 3 ☎ 91 549 00 11 Ⓜ Antón Martín ◷ three sessions from 6pm Ⓢ (1.35, abono (10-ticket pass) €10.20

Imax Madrid (1, E3)
Well, we don't know what the 3D fuss is about, but kids dig it. It's also housed in the same park as the Planetario de Madrid. Prebook at Caixa Catalunya (☎ 902 10 12 12), El Corte Inglés (☎ 902 400 222) or Ⓔ www.telentrada.com (see p62).
✉ Parque Enrico Tierno Galván, Legazpi

☎ 91 467 48 00 Ⓜ Méndez Álvaro ◷ Mon-Fri 1pm-10pm; Sat, Sun & hols noon-11pm Ⓢ one/two sessions €6.60/9.60 (Mon €5.40) ♿

Princesa (3, B6)
This cinema – like its neighbour – is owned by the Renoir group, but it is bigger, with nine theatres (one with wheelchair access) and has a much better selection of films. There are also prebooking possibilities which are the same for Renoir Plaza de España (see following).
✉ Calle de Princesa 3 ☎ 91 541 41 00 Ⓜ Plaza de España ◷ daily from 4pm

Ⓢ adult/concession €5.40/4 ♿

Renoir Plaza de España (3, C5)
This is part of a chain of cinemas that all specialise in original-language films (there is another at Calle de Princesa 5). The theatres all have excellent facilities and you can pre-book your tickets on the Web at Ⓔ www.guiadelocio.com and by telephone on ☎ 902 888 902.
✉ Calle de Martín de los Heros 12 ☎ 91 541 41 00 Ⓜ Plaza de España ◷ daily from 4.15pm (plus 12.30pm Fri & Sat) Ⓢ adult/concession €5.40/4 ♿

LIVE MUSIC VENUES

Café Central (3, H10)
This is probably Madrid's best place to hear live jazz, with both local and international acts deigning to play here. The atmosphere's good too – you're close to the stage without feeling as though you're in a broom closet, and there's an intimate, low-key vibe.
✉ Plaza de Ángel 10 ☎ 91 369 41 43 Ⓜ Sol or Antón Martín ◷ Mon-Thur 1pm-2.30am, Fri & Sat 1pm-3.30am Ⓢ about €10

Café Populart
(3, H11) A small and intimate, yet lively venue with a tiny stage and some pretty smart service. You can enjoy blues, jazz, Cuban, reggae, flamenco and swing here.
✉ Calle de las Huertas 22 ☎ 91 429 84 07 Ⓔ www.populart.es

Ⓜ Antón Martín ◷ shows at 11pm & 12.30pm

Clamores (4, J5)
Away from the throbbing centre of Madrid's nightlife, Clamores gets a well-regarded selection of jazz artists to play here. Another bonus is the

Off-beat Café Central

greater freedom of movement that comes with the non-*centro* premises.
✉ Calle de Alburquerque 14 ☎ 91 445 79 38 Ⓜ Bilbao ◷ Mon-Thur & Sun 6pm-3am, Fri & Sat 6pm-4am, shows at 10pm Ⓢ €3-6

El Sol (3, E11)
Independent bands (local and foreign) get a live airing here before the funk takes over, and it's a bit of a haven for those who want a slightly grungier, crimson-lit atmosphere. Not as important as it was in the 1980s *movida* scene, but still very lively.
✉ Calle de los Jardines 3 ☎ 91 532 64 90 Ⓜ Gran Via ◷ Concerts from 11.30pm, otherwise Tues-Sat 12.30pm-5am Ⓢ €8

Galileo Galilei (4, F2)
Enthusiasts of live Latin music will enjoy a visit here. The music dominates your attention, but there are also photographic exhibitions at times. It's a good space too, with room to breathe and to move (should the mood take you).
✉ **Calle de Galileo 100**
☎ **91 534 75 57**
e **www.salagalileo galilei.com** Ⓜ **Canal**
⏰ **6pm-4.30am**
⑤ **€5-10**

Moby Dick (2, E6)
In the northern part of town and featuring regular shows by local bands, this is a good spot to catch up on your Spanish rock and pop. DJs keep the crowd buzzing after the show's over.
✉ **Avenida del Brasil 5**
☎ **91 555 76 71**

Ⓜ **Santiago Bernabéu**
⏰ **Mon-Sat 10pm-3am**
⑤ **free**

Suristán (3, G11)
Suristán prides itself on offering a variety of live music acts, and the pride is justified. It's a chilled-out, yet lively place to enjoy a

plethora of music styles, including African, Cuban, Celtic and Spanish, and the need to dance hits your feet fast.
✉ **Calle de la Cruz 7**
☎ **91 532 39 09**
e **www.suristan.com**
Ⓜ **Sevilla** ⏰ **10pm-5am** ⑤ **€7**

Popular artists at Populart, p94

FLAMENCO

Café de Chinitas
(3, E6) A cut above many flamenco joints, but you'll need to book to dine and enjoy the shows here. Famous past audience members include Bill Clinton and the King of Spain, and the performers are often well known too.
✉ **Calle de Torija 7**
☎ **91 559 51 35**
e **www.chinitas.com**
Ⓜ **Santo Domingo**
⏰ **Mon-Sat 9pm-2.30am, show at 10.30pm** ⑤ **dinner & show from €66** ♿

Cardamomo (3, G11)
Many locals with a love of flamenco were thrilled when this place opened recently. Performances take place Wed 10.30pm, and there's always good music

on offer even if you miss one of these. It's a dark, stylish and sexy place – the perfect background for the good-looking patrons, staff and performers.
✉ **Calle Echegaray 15**
☎ **91 369 07 57**
Ⓜ **Sevilla** ⏰ **9pm-4am**
⑤ **free**

Casa Patas (3, J10)
This is an excellent and comfortable space to enjoy recognised masters of flamenco guitar, song and dance. Famous faces can often be found both on stage and in the crowd, and you'd do well to book in advance. Courses in flamenco can also be organised and good food is available.
✉ **Calle de Cañizares 10** ☎ **91 369 04 96**

e **www.casapatas.com**
Ⓜ **Antón Martín**
⏰ **Mon-Sat noon-5pm & 8pm-12.30am, shows at 10.30pm Mon-Fri, at 9pm & midnight Sat & Sun** ⑤ **about €15**

Corral de la Morería
(3, J5) This is another dinner-and-a-show tablao (tourist-oriented flamenco), but this one is actually worth considering. It's not as big and flash as some of the others, but the quality's good so you won't feel as though you've just wandered into and been caught in a tourist trap.
✉ **Calle de la Morería 17** ☎ **91 365 84 46**
Ⓜ **La Latina** ⏰ **9pm-2am, show at 10.45pm**
⑤ **from €25**

Las Carboneras

(3, H7) This place is something of a young gun, or rather a young guitar, on the flamenco scene, and has a cosy feel. The stage lies to your right as you enter and you can set your sights on the bar, which is dead ahead. Performers are not from the heady, older stratosphere, but they're pretty good, and always brimming with spunky young energy.

⊠ Plaza del Conde de Miranda 1 ☎ 91 542 86 77 Ⓜ Sol ◷ 8.30pm-2am, show at 10.30pm Ⓢ free

Duende

Duende is the heart and soul of flamenco, but trying to come up with a definitive description of it is no mean feat. It's that moment when a performer seems to disappear into their art. It's what poet García Lorca described as 'black sounds'. The best way we can think of recognising it is when the hairs on the back of your neck stand up, your eyes are pricked with tears, a shiver goes down your spine and the locals are all calling out 'Olé!'.

CLASSICAL MUSIC, OPERA, DANCE & THEATRE

Auditorio Nacional de Música

(2, G8) Don't let the hideously ugly exterior put you off too much. The inside is more than comfortable and, most importantly if you're listening to music, it's great for acoustics. This auditorium is also the home of La Orquestra y Coro Nacionales de España (Spain's national orchestra), which means you can feast on classical music from October to June.

⊠ Calle del Príncipe de Vergara 146 ☎ 91 337 01 39 ☎ box office 91 337 03 07 or 902 488 488 ℮ www.auditorio nacional.mcu.es Ⓜ Cruz del Rayo or Prosperidad ◷ box office Mon 5-7pm, Tues-Fri 10am-5pm, Sat 10am-1pm Ⓢ varies ⚭ rehearsal attendance – check with theatre

Centro Cultural Conde Duque

(3, A6) Also known as the Antiguo Cuartel del Conde Duque, this massive structure has some excellent shows, especially during summer and the Veranos de la Villa festival. The variety of acts on offer is mind-boggling.

⊠ Calle de Conde Duque 11 ☎ 91 588 58 34 Ⓜ Ventura Rodríguez or Noviciado ◷ box office 5pm performance day; centre Tues-Sat 10am-2pm & 5.30-9pm, Sun 10.30am-2.30pm Ⓢ varies ⚭

Centro Cultural de la Villa

(3, B15) If you're having trouble finding this theatre, look under the waterfall at Plaza de Colón. You'll find performances of classical music, comic theatre, flamenco, exhibitions, as well as stuff that'll please the

kids in this 800-plus capacity venue.

⊠ Plaza de Colón ☎ 91 575 60 80 or 902 101 212 Ⓜ Colón ◷ Tues-Sun 11am-1.30pm & 5-6pm Ⓢ varies ⚭ kids' theatre performances

Fundación Juan March

(4, J11) This important foundation has been a boost to Madrid's artistic scene since the 1950s, and apart from hosting exhibitions, it's also a good source of musical performances (for young and old).

⊠ Calle de Castelló 77 ☎ 91 435 42 40 Ⓜ Núñez de Balboa ◷ Mon-Sat 10am-2pm & 5.30-9pm, Sun 10am-2pm Ⓢ free ⚭

Teatro Albéniz

(3, G9) A variety of performances are staged here, from opera and *zarzuela*

(Spanish light opera) to plays and dance (including flamenco). If you're here in August, don't miss the chance to see Alicia Alonso's Ballet Nacional de Cuba perform the ballet classics, which happens every year.
✉ Calle de la Paz 11
☎ 91 531 83 11 or 902 488 488 Ⓜ Sol
⏰ box office 11.30am-1pm & 5.30-9pm
⑤ varies

Teatro de la Zarzuela (3, G12)

The Spanish version of light opera is known as *zarzuela*, and this is the best place to experience it. The theatre, built in 1856 in a vague imitation of Milan's La Scala also stages ballets and music recitals.
✉ Calle de Jovellanos 4 ☎ 91 524 54 00, box office 902 488 488
🅴 http://teatro delazarzuela.mcu.es
Ⓜ Banco de España or Sevilla ⏰ box office daily noon-6pm (to 8pm performance days)
⑤ €10-180 ♿ kids' matinees Wed 6pm

Teatro Español

(3, H11) A theatre has stood on this spot since 1583. Known as the Teatro Español since 1849, the repertoire consists mostly of contemporary Spanish drama and some gems from the 17th century. It's

a beautiful theatre, and worth a visit even if you understand nothing of what's being said.
✉ Calle del Príncipe 25 ☎ 91 429 62 97
Ⓜ Sol or Sevilla
⏰ box office Tues-Sun 11.30am-1.30pm, Tues-Thur & Sun 5-7pm, Fri & Sat 5-6.30pm & 8-9.30pm, shows Tues-Thur & Sun 8pm, Fri & Sat 7.30pm & 10.30pm
⑤ €5-16

Teatro Monumental

(3, J12) A decent theatre, though not in the same league as the Teatro Real. One reason to come here is to hear the RTVE Orquestra Sinfónica y Coro. School groups and children are often allowed in to watch rehearsals on Thursday mornings, but you'll need to book for this.
✉ Calle de Atocha 65
☎ 91 429 12 81 or

902 488 488
🅴 www.rtve.es
Ⓜ Antón Martín
⏰ box office Oct-May daily 11am-2pm & 5-7pm, concerts Oct-May Tues-Thur 8pm
⑤ €5.50-14 ♿ re-hearsals Thur morning

Teatro Real (3, F6)

The grandest stage in the city and one of the world's most technically advanced theatres. Acoustics are superb, seats are comfy and at intermission you can enjoy lovely views over Plaza de Oriente and the Palacio Real. Catch opera, ballet, classical music and flamenco (July) performances here.
✉ Plaza de Oriente
☎ 91 516 06 06
🅴 www.teatroreal .com Ⓜ Ópera
⏰ box office Mon-Sat 10am-1.30pm & 5.30-8pm ⑤ €12-21
♿ matinees

Teatro Español

GAY & LESBIAN MADRID

Cafe Aquarela

(3, C12) The decor here is part colonial gentlemen's club and part opium den. This smallish bar is great to replenish the thirst you've earned after a hard

day; or to start the mood before a big night. The crowd? There are lesbians on first dates, gay men on last dates, as well as everything in between. The bar staff on the night we

went were capable, yet up themselves.
✉ Calle de Gravina 10
☎ 91 522 21 43
Ⓜ Chueca ⏰ Mon-Thur 3pm-3am, Fri & Sat 3pm-4am

El Mojito
(3, K11) Perhaps you're growing tired of the Chueca scene? If so, head to this place, where the Ken and Barbie dolls have been arranged in poses so suggestive and sometimes ludicrous it never fails to raise a smile. And the cocktails are good too.
✉ **Calle del Olmo 6**
Ⓜ **Antón Martín**
🕐 **Mon-Thur & Sun 10pm-2.30am, Fri & Sat 10pm-3.30am** ⑤ **free**

Into the Tank (2, O3)
There's a varied, albeit strict, dress code (leather, latex, skinhead and military) and plenty of casual sex on offer, plus a 'basement'. It's strictly for men only.
✉ **Calle de Calatrava 29** 🅔 **www.into thetank.org**

Gay Pride
Madrid's gay and lesbian pride festival and parade take place on the last Saturday in June. It's known as the *Día del Orgullo de Gays, Lesbians y Transexuales* and the partying is intense, intrepid and inspiring.

Aquarela, p97

Ⓜ **La Latina or Puerta de Toledo** 🕐 **Thurs & Sun 11pm-5am; Fri, Sat & hols 2am-8am**
⑤ **€10**

Mama Inés Café
(3, D11) Come to Mama indeed! Day or night, this is a popular hang-out for the stylish yet casual and mostly gay clientele. During the day, you can treat this place as a café, but things get busier at night, when you can head downstairs and have a dance, or just prop up the well-stocked bar.
✉ **Calle de Hortaleza 22** 🕾 **91 523 23 33**
🅔 **www.mamaines.com**
Ⓜ **Gran Via or Chueca**
🕐 **Sun-Thur 10am-2am, Fri & Sat 10am-3am** ⑤ **free**

Medea (3, J10) Madrid's
gay scene is famously open to all, but for those nights when it's the sisterhood or nothing, you can try Medea. The girl-friendly establishment has good music and a pool table, and none of Chueca's madness.
✉ **Calle de la Cabeza 33** Ⓜ **Antón Martín**
🕐 **Thur-Sat 11pm-5am**
⑤ **free**

Rick's (3, E11)
Sooner or later, everyone comes to Rick's. It's not that it's a particularly great place, it's just that it's a bit of an institution that's popular with local and out-of-town gays (mostly men). Look for the purple and black exterior and dive right in, if you can find space.
✉ **Calle de Clavel 8**
Ⓜ **Gran Via**
🕐 **11pm-late** ⑤ **free**

Shangay Tea Dance
(3, D7) Even the toilets are the last word in style here! Cool Ballroom hosts the Shangay Tea Dance every Sunday. An incredibly good-looking crowd is often entertainment in itself, but the DJs deserve a special mention for dishing up house music that gets you right where you live.
✉ **Calle de Isabel la Católica 6** 🕾 **91 542 34 39** 🅔 **www.coolball room.com** Ⓜ **Santo Domingo** 🕐 **Sun 9pm-2am** ⑤ **€6**

Star's Dance Café
(3, E12) The gay community appreciates the fact that you can eat, drink and dance here till the wee hours. The straight community likes it too. In fact, everyone likes it here, especially because the decor is attractive, the lighting is flattering and the DJs know how to please.
✉ **Calle del Marqués del Valdeiglesias 5**
🕾 **91 522 27 12**
🅔 **www.starscafe dance.com** Ⓜ **Banco de España or Sevilla**
🕐 **Mon-Wed 9am-2am, Thur 9am-3am, Fri 9am-4am, Sat 6.30am-4am**
⑤ **free**

Strong Center (3, F8)
Time to toughen up and get the leather out! For *hombres* only, this place is not for the faint-hearted or faint-cocked. The dark room (intentionally, so that you use other senses) is famous, or infamous, depending on who you're talking to.
✉ **Calle de Trujillo 7**
🕾 **91 531 48 27**
Ⓜ **Callao** 🕐 **midnight-6am** ⑤ **€6**

SPECTATOR SPORTS

See the Tickets & Listings section (p88) for details of buying tickets.

Athletics

Post-Barcelona, athletics has had something of a boost in Spain, and Madrid's bid to host the 2012 Olympics means that facilities are a priority. The **Estadio de la Comunidad de Madrid** (1, E4; ☎ 91 580 51 80; Avenida de Arcentales, Canillejas; Ⓜ Las Musas) is a great high-tech athletics arena, built in 1994 and hosting various events (including the 9th World Cup in Athletics in September 2002). On the last Sunday in April, the Maratón Popular de Madrid is held. You can get information at ⒺI www.maratonmadrid.com.

Basketball

Palacio de los Deportes (2, L9; ☎ 91 401 91 00; Avenida Felipe II, Salamanca; Ⓜ Goya) is the place to see basketball (*baloncesto*). When we visited, it was being rebuilt after a fire, but it should be ready by April 2003, with improved facilities. Madrid's two main basketball teams are Real Madrid (Ⓔ www.realmadrid.es) yes, they play basketball too!) and Adecco Estudiantes (Ⓔ www.clubestudiantes.com). The season takes place from September to May.

Bullfighting

You've got to admit, any life-and-death sport where the manifestation of prowess and skill involves donning pink silk socks and a skin-tight sequined suit is going to be interesting. Worth seeing is the Feria de San Isidro (Festival of San Isidro), which takes place from mid-May and lasts into June. Tickets for this can be hard to come by though. Regular *corridas* (fights) take place from March to October, generally on Sunday at 7pm. Bullfights take place at the beautiful, enormous **Plaza de Toros**

You big bully

Monumental de Las Ventas (see also p45; 2, J10; ☎ 91 356 22 00; Calle de Alcalá 237; Ⓜ Las Ventas). Tickets cost from €3.50 for a spot in the sun *(sol)* to €105 for a spot in the shade *(sombra)*, and can be purchased at the ticket office at the ring (Thur-Sun 10am-2pm & 5-8pm) or at Caja de Madrid (☎ 902 48 84 88).

Cycling

La Vuelta de España (Tour of Spain) finishes its spoke-fest in Madrid (having started three weeks before in Valencia) on the last Sunday of September. In 2002, riders peddled to Estadio Santiago Bernabeu to decide who was best at touring Spain on two wheels. For details, visit Ⓔ www.lavuelta.com.

Football

The biggest spectator sport is, of course, football. Madrid's most glamorous team is Real Madrid, which plays at **Estadio Santiago Bernabéu** (2, E6; ☎ 91 398 43 00 or 902 27 17 07; Paseo de la Castellana 144; Ⓜ Santiago Bernabéu). Other teams are Atlético de Madrid, which plays at **Estadio Vicente Calderón** (2, P2; ☎ 91 366 47 07; Calle de la Virgen del Puerto; Ⓜ Pirámides); and Rayo Vallecano, which plays at **Nuevo Estadio de Vallecas Teresa Rivero** (1, E4; ☎ 91 478 22 53; Ⓔ www.rayovallecano.es; Avenida del Payaso Fofó, Vallecas; Ⓜ Portazgo) – with a reputation for a jovial atmosphere at their games. Tickets for a Real Madrid match will cost from €6 to €40, but can be hard to come by for important matches. Tickets can be bought from stadiums, from ticket offices on Calle de la Victoria or by phone on ☎ 902 32 43 24.

> ### Real Ronaldo
> In September 2002, all of Madrid heard the news it had been waiting for all summer. Yep, Ronaldo would play for Real Madrid. The most famous footballer in the world to play with the most famous team – a match made in heaven.

A mark of Real Madrid's success

Tennis

Madrid now plays host to the Tennis Masters series (which attracts big bucks and bigger names) in October. A new 9000-seat indoor hard court (2, P1; Calle de las Aves; Ⓜ Lago) named **Recinto Ferial** was under construction on the site of the old Rocódomo in Casa de Campo in August 2002. For more information go to Ⓔ www.tennis-masters-madrid.com. Tickets can be purchased from both El Corte Inglés (☎ 902 400 222) or Servicaixa (☎ 902 332 211).

places to stay

Madrid has plenty of places to stay, and plenty of visitors wanting to stay. There are good hotels in every price bracket, but it can be wise to book ahead, as Madrid's capital status makes it a mecca for business travellers and tourists alike.

Madrid has many excellent deluxe hotels that will have you wanting to move in permanently. Styles vary between state-of-the-art minimalist lodgings (straight from the pages of *wallpaper**) to old-world five-star palaces slathered in gilt and laden with chandeliers. Sadly, there's a noticeable decline in imagination from top end hotels – with a grand-but-bland ethos seeming to rule the roost. Madrid's mid-range places often have endearingly kitsch touches clearly intended to inject a bit of 'class' into the lobby or rooms, but frequently remain in the 'try-hard' league. Madrid's budget hotels are often in the noisier parts of town, but while rooms are usually simple, they are generally spotless, with lots of mop-and-bucket work going on every morning.

Room Rates

The prices in this chapter indicate the cost per night of a standard double room and are intended as a guide only. The reviews assess the character and facilities of each place within the context of the price bracket.

Deluxe	over €200
Top End	€100-200
Mid-Range	€45-99
Budget	under €45

Accommodation comes in two categories: hotels (H), and *hostales* (Hs; cheap to mid-range hotels), with signs indicating each place's status. All hotels are subject to the 7% value-added tax known as IVA.

Room with a view at the Hotel Atlántico (p104)

DELUXE

Hesperia Hotel

(4, F8) When a hotel's list of attributes includes a beautiful interior courtyard, one of the city's greatest restaurants and a piano bar with 'Madrid's widest selection of whiskies', then you hardly have to worry about an unpleasant surprise. Everything is good here – from the service to the design (handled by Pasqua Ortega, who remodelled the Teatro Real).

✉ **Paseo de la Castellana 57, Chamberí** ☎ **91 210 88 00 fax 91 210 88 99** e **www.hesperia-madrid.com** Ⓜ **Gregorio Marañón** ✕ **see Santceloni p75**

Hotel Abascal

(4, F6) An ex-embassy building, and mighty attractive to boot, this hotel has been given a modern fit-out that thankfully retains some of the charming period details of its previous incarnation. A good Basque restaurant and a great summer terrace distinguish it from other big business hotels.

✉ **Calle de José Abascal 47, Ríos Rosas**

☎ **91 441 00 15 fax 91 442 22 11** e **nhabas cal@nh-hoteles.es** Ⓜ **Alonso Cano** ✕

Hotel Bauzá (2, L8)

Hotel Bauzá opened in 1999 and revels in its own modern beauty. Everything is stunning here, with not an inch of chintz or a hint of ruffle. Rooms are beautifully decorated and include lots of little luxuries, though we're still not sure what the 'interactive TV' is. But we like the pillow menu!

✉ **Calle de Goya 79, Salamanca** ☎ **91 435 75 45 fax 91 431 09 43** e **www.hotelbauza .com** Ⓜ **Goya** ✕

Hotel Emperatriz

(4, G9) Close to the shopping of Salamanca and with helpful, multilingual staff, the Emperatriz is just dandy for those looking for luxury or needing a place with good business facilities. The lounge areas and rooms are attractive.

✉ **Calle López de Hoyos 4, Castellana** ☎ **91 563 80 88 fax 91 563 98 04**

e **www.hotel-empera triz.com** Ⓜ **Gregorio Marañón** ✕ ♨

Hotel Ritz (3, G14)

The Ritz opened its doors in 1920 under the watchful eye of both King Alfonso XIII and Cesar Ritz, and there's no chance of standards slipping as it approaches 100 years of ritziness. Even the sheets (hand-embroidered) are luxurious; business and fitness facilities are excellent.

✉ **Plaza de la Lealtad 5, Retiro** ☎ **91 701 67 67 fax 91 701 67 76** e **www.ritz.es** Ⓜ **Banco de España** ✕ **Goya** ♨

Hotel Villa Magna

(4, J9) Visually unappealing from the exterior, this place's interior marks it as a five-star festival. Got a rock star with a troublesome hooker in the bathroom? This place can manage it without batting an eyelid. Business people and fitness fanatics are looked after royally too.

✉ **Paseo de la Castellana 22, Salamanca** ☎ **91 587 12 34 fax 91 431 22 86** e **hotel@villamagna .es** Ⓜ **Rubén Darío** ✕ **see Le Divellec p85** ♨ ♿

Hotel Villa Real

(3, G12) Salivating, we decided that this was *the* place to stay if you wanted to absorb both art's Golden Triangle and the nightlife of Huertas and Santa Ana. Service is bend-over-backwards gracious, with everything you could hope

Ritzy Hotel Ritz

The grand Westin Palace Hotel

for, all provided in an enchanting, art-filled setting that manages to avoid the clichés.

✉ **Plaza de las Cortes 10, Huertas** ☎ **91 420 37 67 fax 91 420 25 47** e **villareal@derby hotels.es** Ⓜ **Banco de España** ✕ **see East 47 p79** ♨

Santo Mauro (4, J7)

A stunning hotel, we were seriously tempted to move into the Santo Mauro when told 'is your house' as we were shown the tasteful modern rooms, beautifully renovated common areas, an indoor swimming pool and a delightful garden area where late suppers are served. Sigh.

✉ **Calle de Zurbano 36, Chamberí** ☎ **91 319 69 00 fax 91 308 54 77** e **santo-mauro@ ac-hoteles.com** Ⓜ **Rubén Darío or Alonso Martínez** ✕ **see Santo Mauro p76** ♨

Tryp Reina Victoria

(3, H10) Something of a bullfighters' haunt, this place is really quite soul-less when you take the aforementioned titbit away, but it's smoothly run and

has been restored to wedding-cake glory (along with the sanitised Plaza de Santa Ana).

✉ **Plaza de Santa Ana 14, Santa Ana** ☎ **91 531 45 00 fax 91 522 03 07** e **tryp.reina .victoria@solmelia.com** Ⓜ **Sol or Sevilla** ✕

Westin Palace

(3, G13) Commissioned by none other than King Alfonso XIII himself (who wanted a comfortable place for his wedding guests to stay), this

elegant hotel, built in 1910 on the site of the former palace of the Duque de Lerma, has not let up on the luxury since. No detail has been overlooked, and we love the stunning stained-glass dome, the fancy bathrooms and the sheer 'marblelousness' of the 465-room palace.

✉ **Plaza de las Cortes 7, Cortes** ☎ **91 360 80 00 fax 91 360 81 00** e **www.westin.com** Ⓜ **Banco de España** ✕ **La Cupola or La Rotonda** ♨

Tryp Reina Victoria, Plaza Santa Ana

TOP END

Gran Hotel Conde Duque (4, J2)

Set on a quiet, tree-filled plaza, the Conde Duque appeals to business travellers because of its location and excellent service. Great deals can be negotiated for weekends, and the restaurant has Basque cuisine. Single rooms are very small – doubles are dandy.
✉ **Plaza del Conde Valle Suchil 5, Chamberí** ☎ **91 447 70 00 fax 91 448 35 69** e **www.hotelcondeduque.es** Ⓜ **San Bernardo or Quevedo** ✕

Hotel Alcalá (2, L7)

Despite its size, this hotel retains quite an intimate atmosphere, with kind staff at the front desk and some unusual touches, such as seven suites designed by *movida* queen-turned-fashion-designer Agatha Ruiz de la Prada (remember to wear your sunglasses!). The other rooms are smart, but may be considered a little tame by comparison.
✉ **Calle de Alcalá 66, Retiro** ☎ **91 435 10 60 fax 91 435 11 05** e **www.nh-hoteles.es** Ⓜ **Príncipe de Vergara** ✕ ♿

Hotel Atlántico (3, E9)

The exterior of this hotel resembles a glorious *belle époque* wedding cake. Designed by Joaquín Saldaña in 1920, this place reflects Madrid's and Gran Vía's architectural heyday. The interior? By contrast to the outside, it's subdued, functional and comfortable, with all the mod cons (gym and lounge) and some great views.
✉ **Gran Vía 38, Gran Vía** ☎ **91 522 64 80 fax 91 531 02 10** e **www.hotelatlantico.es** Ⓜ **Gran Vía** ✕ ♿

Hotel Campomanes (3, F7)

A stylish and well-managed addition to Madrid's hotel scene, the Campomanes has a black-and-white decor and a subdued coolness to all of its 30 rooms. A very slick package indeed, in a prime location for sightseeing.
✉ **Calle de Campomanes 4,** ☎ **91 548 85 48 fax 91 559 12 88** e **www.hhcampomanes.com** Ⓜ **Ópera** ✕ ♿

Hotel Carlos V (3, F9)

This is a plushly renovated 67-room hotel with a distinctive, old-fashioned (despite all the mod-cons) feel – right down to the suit of armour in the lobby. The hotel also has a rooftop area – the perfect spot for a leisurely breakfast on a sunny day.
✉ **Calle del Maestro Victoria 5, Sol**

Making waves at Hotel Emperador (p105)

☎ 91 531 41 00
fax 91 531 37 61
📧 recepción@hotel
carlosv.com Ⓜ Sol or
Callao ✗

Hotel Don Pío (2, C8)

Located in the city's north, and totally nondescript from the outside, the Don Pío is quite a surprise inside. There's some very delicate woodwork in evidence and a welcome feeling of space, especially in the central patio area. Business facilities are very good too, and the hotel has parking and fantastic bathtubs to boot.
✉ Avenida Pío XII 25, Chamartín ☎ 91 353 07 80 fax 91 353 07 81 Ⓜ Pío XII ✗ ♿

Hotel Emperador

(3, D8) With rooms full of sumptuous flourishes, this is an ideal place to conduct business if you're out to impress. Quiet, despite the raucous Gran Vía below, you can chill out after a stint in a conference room by swimming in the great rooftop pool, which has city views.
✉ Gran Vía 53, Gran Vía ☎ 91 547 28 00 fax 91 547 28 17 📧 www.emperador hotel.com Ⓜ Callao or Santo Domingo ✗

Hotel Ópera (3, F7)

A strange one this: the location and standards are excellent, and there's nothing to complain about on the decor front, except for the fact that there are no double rooms here – only twins are available. This might be hard for loving couples, but fine for estranged opera buffs.
✉ Cuesta de Santo Domingo 2, Los Austrias ☎ 91 541 28

Breakfast Included

Many *madrileños* aren't big on breakfast, with a coffee and a pastry deemed a sufficient way to start the day. This is one reason to avoid paying exorbitant rates for hotel breakfasts served by a certain hour. Even if they are included in the room rates, they're generally pretty desultory affairs, and not worth the effort. Get outside and go to a café instead.

Coffee at Plaza de Santa Ana

00 fax 91 541 69 23
📧 www.hotelopera
.com Ⓜ Ópera ✗ yes,
but with singing
waiters! ♿

Hotel Suecia (3, F13)

They say: 'We just want to be the nicest' – and they *are* extremely nice here, right down to providing comfortable chairs for those waiting for a taxi. Room standards are high (and particularly good for business travellers), and Hemingway even stayed here in the 1950s.
✉ Calle Marqués de Casa Riera 4 ☎ 91 531 69 00 fax 91 521 71 41 📧 www.hotelsuecia. com Ⓜ Banco de España ✗ yes ♿

Those Precious Zzzzzs

You'll wonder if anyone sleeps in Madrid, and may well go way past your bedtime most nights, but if you're counting on some real shut-eye, it might be wise to avoid hotel rooms that face the street in Madrid's nightlife *barrios* (neighbourhoods). When you add the noise of revelry to the late-night garbage collection, early-morning street cleaning and roadworks, sirens, church bells, barking dogs, howling kids and arguing couples, you get quite a decibel cocktail. Light sleepers beware! Deluxe and top-end hotels will be more familiar with double-glazing on windows than will mid-range and budget hotels.

Yes, you're still in Madrid – Hotel Paris

MID-RANGE

Hostal La Macarena
(3, H7) Housed in a well-groomed building on the western side of Plaza Mayor, this efficient, safe place offers smallish rooms, with bathroom, TV and air-con, plus a hard-to-beat position for those who love this part of town.
✉ Cava de San Miguel 8 ☎ 91 365 92 21 fax 91 366 61 11 Ⓜ Sol ✗ see Los Austrias pp82–4

Hostal Madrid (3, G9)
A real find in this category, the Madrid has with-it management who are really helpful, while the rooms

(less than 20) are a definite cut above the usual, with TV, air-con, phone, hairdryer and safe. You can also self-cater in their mini-apartments, although the proximity to restaurants might put paid to that.
✉ Calle de Esparteros 6, Los Austrias ☎ 91 522 00 60 fax 91 532 35 10 Ⓜ Sol ✗ see Los Austrias pp82–4

Hostal Persal (3, H10)
This place is a lot better than many *hostales*, and even many hotels The Persal is very well run and has clean, simple rooms with bathroom in a central

location. Sometimes Plaza del Ángel can be a little boozy late at night, but it's harmless stuff and you might just sleep through it.
✉ Plaza del Ángel 12, Huertas ☎ 91 369 46 43 fax 91 369 19 52 ℮ hostal.persal @mad.servicom.es Ⓜ Sol or Antón Martín ✗ see Huertas & Santa Ana pp78–81

Hostal Sonsoles
(3, D11) Close to the non-stop party that is Chueca, this gay-friendly two-star *hostal* has pretty good rooms, with bathroom, phone, TV and safe. On top

of this, they can put you in the know about gay venues and they certainly won't have any curfew hang-ups.

✉ Calle de Fuencarral 18, Chueca ☎ 91 532 75 23 fax 91 532 75 22 ✉ sonsodesa@eresmas .net Ⓜ Gran Vía ✕ see Chueca pp76–8

Hotel Europa (3, F10)

With a pleasant little plant-filled courtyard in its centre and some rather alarming synthetic flowers throughout the premises, this place is cute – in a kitsch way. It's also incredibly close to the Puerta del Sol, located on a pedestrianised street, and has decent food in its restaurant.

✉ Calle del Carmen 4, Sol ☎ 91 521 29 00 fax 91 521 46 96 ✉ www.hoteleuropa .net Ⓜ Sol ✕

Hotel Miau (3, H11)

If you want to be close to the nightlife of Plaza de Santa Ana, then this is the place for you. Newly opened in 2002, a genuine effort has been made (with much success) to offer a truly smart alternative to some of the scruffier places in the area. Still, it's a noisy district.

✉ Calle del Principe 26, Santa Ana ☎ 91 369 71 20 fax 91 429 72 37 Ⓜ Antón Martín ✕ see Huertas & Santa Ana pp78–81

Hotel Mónaco (3, D12)

Tell us a place used to be a brothel and we'll want a peek. The laughably kitsch lobby (with indifferent staff) is just a taster, and the rooms (one equipped with a mirrored canopy) are perfect for amateur filmmaking of the trashiest order.

✉ Calle de Barbieri 5, Chueca ☎ 91 522 46 30 fax 91 521 16 01 Ⓜ Gran Vía or Chueca ✕ see Chueca pp76–8

Hotel Mora (3, K14)

This is a good choice in this category, with proximity to the 'big three' and Atocha station a bonus. Rooms are similar to so many others we've seen in Madrid, but you'll get satellite TV, air-con, phone and a tub.

✉ Paseo del Prado 32, Huertas ☎ 91 420 15 69 fax 91 420 05 64 Ⓜ Atocha ✕

Hotel París (3, G10)

With just a touch of faded grandeur, this hotel, smack-bang on the Puerta del Sol and situated under the famous Tío Pepe sign, is a good choice in this area. Rooms have TV, phone, air-con and a lot of fabric details, and the staff are helpful.

✉ Calle de Alcalá 2, Sol ☎ 91 521 54 91 fax 91 531 01 88 Ⓜ Sol ✕ see Sol & Gran Vía p87

BUDGET

Hostal Cantábrico (3, G11)

The clean rooms here look a little uninspired in terms of decor, but by and large, this place has a charming air, thanks to the tiles. There's a nice little patio for dining as well, if you can't be bothered choosing from the hundreds of options in the area.

✉ Calle de la Cruz 5, Huertas ☎ 91 531 01 30 fax 91 532 14 41 Ⓜ Sevilla ✕

Hostal Cruz Sol (3, G9)

On the 3rd floor (hooray for the lift!) of a building that's showing its age, the Cruz Sol, with its immaculately tidy rooms (including bathroom, TV and phone) comes as a pleasant surprise. The staff's kindness is another plus.

✉ Plaza de Santa Cruz 6, Los Austrias ☎/fax 91 532 71 97 ✉ www.hostalcruz sol.com Ⓜ Sol ✕ see Los Austrias pp82–4

Hostal Dulcinea (3, H13)

In a location close to Plaza de Santa Ana, but quiet enough to let you get some shut-eye, the spotlessly clean Dulcinea is a great choice in this range. The owners are courteous and helpful; if it's full they

Budget beds

No fuss San Antonio

can direct you to their other property across the street.

✉ **Calle de Cervantes 19, Huertas** ☎ **91 429 93 09 fax 91 369 25 69** **e** **donato@teleline.es** **Ⓜ Antón Martín** ✕ see Huertas & Santa Ana pp78–81

Hostal Maria Cristina (3, D11) After the hustle of Calle de Fuencarral and a flight of stairs, the lobby – which resembles your grandma's living room in the 1970s – is quite comforting. Creaky parquet floors and a busy-bee approach to cleanliness only reinforce the feeling. Rooms are simple and bathrooms sparkle.

✉ **Calle de Fuencarral 20, Chueca** ☎ **91 531 63 00 fax 91 531 63 09** **e** **www.iespana.es/ hostalmariacristina** **Ⓜ Gran Vía** ✕ see Chueca pp76–8 ♿

Hostal Retiro (2, L8) With a dose of greenery – thanks to the nearby Parque del Buen Retiro – and friendly management, this is the only real way to adhere to this price bracket in this tonier part of town. The rooms are comfortable and in good nick, particularly on the 4th floor, although short on luxuries.

✉ **Calle de O'Donnell 27, Retiro** ☎ **91 576 00 37 Ⓜ Príncipe de Vergara or Ibiza** ✕ see Salamanca & Retiro pp85–7 ♿

Hostal San Antonio (3, H12) A handy place with tidy air-con rooms (all including bathroom) and helpful, straightforward service, the San Antonio gets good recommendations, although Calle de León itself can get *choked* with traffic (pedestrian and vehicular) until the wee hours on weekends.

✉ **Calle de León 13, Huertas** ☎ **91 429 51 37 Ⓜ Antón Martín** ✕ see Huertas & Santa Ana pp78–81 ♿

Hostal Sardinero (3, H12) A stone's throw from beer-loving Plaza de Santa Ana, this 3rd-floor *hostal* has pleasant, handy rooms with air-con, safe, TV and bathroom, although you'll want to ask for a quiet room, bring some earplugs or keep *madrileño* social hours.

✉ **Calle del Prado 16, Santa Ana** ☎ **91 429 57 56 fax 91 429 41 12** **Ⓜ Sol or Antón Martín** ✕ see Huertas & Santa Ana pp78–81 ♿

Hostal Sil & Serranos (3, A10) These two *hostales*, which are under the same management (go to the 2nd floor), have rooms that are nudging their way out of the budget category. The standards are high, with air-con, phone and satellite TV in well-maintained rooms. They're also close to Chueca's and Malasaña's nightlife, without being in the thick of it.

✉ **Calle de Fuencarral 95, Malasaña** ☎ **91 448 89 72 fax 91 447 48 29 Ⓜ Bilbao** ✕ see Malasaña & Around pp84–5 ♿

Children & Hospitality

Apart from top-end and deluxe places, which cater to every whim, Madrid's hotels don't go overboard with family-friendly details. There are often many flights of stairs (or tiny elevators with no room for a pram) and the nightlife outside is generally unmuffled. You can ask for children's cots, and they'll be provided in some places, but it's best to look for the ♿ in our reviews.

facts for the visitor

Cars, bars and plazas

ARRIVAL & DEPARTURE

As the capital of Spain, Madrid is easily accessible by air from anywhere in Europe and North America. The city is also linked to its European neighbours and Morocco by train and bus (more arduous and often no cheaper than flying). Plenty of air, rail and road connections link Madrid to the rest of the country.

Air

Madrid's Barajas airport (1, E4) is 13km northeast of the city centre. There are three terminals: T1 mostly handles intercontinental and some European flights; T2 mostly handles domestic and Schengen-country flights with Spanish carriers; and T3 handles Iberia's Puente Aereo flights between Madrid and Barcelona.

Left Luggage
The *consigna* (left luggage) offices are in T1 (near the bus stop & taxi stand) and T2 (near the metro entrance). Both are open 24hrs and charge €2.60 for 24hrs.

Information
General Inquiries
☎ 91 393 60 00

Flight Information
☎ 902 35 35 70

Hotel Booking Service
☎ 91 305 84 19

Airport Access
There are two main **parking** areas, both short and long term: P1 (outside T1), and P2 (outside T2); the first 30mins are free.

The recently opened **metro** line (No 8) between Barajas and Nuevos Ministerios (4, C8) is the easiest way to travel between the airport and the city. The trip takes 12mins and from here you can easily connect to your final destination. See Metro (p112) for general times and ticket costs.

The airport **bus** (No 89) runs between the airport and central Madrid. It arrives at and departs from an underground terminus at Plaza de Colón (3, B15). The bus runs from 5.15am to 2am daily every 12mins and costs €2.40 one way. The trip takes about 30mins in average traffic.

A **taxi** to/from the airport costs between €15 and €18. Taxis queue outside all three airport terminals.

Train

Madrid's two main train stations are Atocha (2, O6) and Chamartín (2, A7) in the city's south and north respectively. Atocha is the bigger of the two and the majority of trains to/from the south and east of Spain use this station, while international services arrive at and depart from Chamartín.

The variety of fares and services is mind-boggling. National trains are run by Renfe (☎ 902 24 02 02; e www.renfe.es) and tickets can be purchased by phone, online, at stations and at the Renfe booking office (3, F13; Calle de Alcalá 44; open Mon-Fri 9.30am-8pm).

Bus

The main intercity bus terminal is Estación Sur de Autobuses (☎ 91 468 42 00; e www.estaciondeauto buses.com; Calle de Méndez Álvaro), just south of the M-30 ring road. It serves most destinations to the south and many in other parts of the country. Most bus companies have a ticket office here, even if their buses depart from elsewhere.

Herranz buses (2, J2; ☎ 91 896 90 28) depart from under and around Moncloa station for El Escorial and El Pardo.

The major international carrier is Eurolines (ⓔ www.eurolines.com), which often works in tandem with Spanish carriers that depart from or arrive at Estación Sur de Autobuses.

Travel Documents

Passport
Spain is one of 15 countries that are party to the Schengen agreement, and there is usually no passport control for people arriving from within the EU – although you must carry your passport or a national ID card.

Visa
Visas are not required by citizens of the EU, USA, Australia, Canada, New Zealand, Israel, Japan and Switzerland for tourist visits to Spain of up to three months. If you are a citizen of a country not listed here, check with your Spanish consulate before you travel, as you may need a specific visa. If you intend to stay for more than three months you must apply for a resident's card.

Return/Onward Ticket
A return/onward ticket makes entry into Spain easier for non-EU citizens.

Customs & Duty Free

From outside the EU, you can bring in one bottle of spirits, one bottle of wine, 50mL of perfume and 200 ciggies. From an EU country (with duty paid) you can bring in 90L of wine, 10L of spirits, unlimited perfume and 800 ciggies, and really make a party of it.

Departure Tax

Departure tax is pre-paid with your ticket.

GETTING AROUND

Madrid's public transport is reliable, efficient and user-friendly. The metro is by far the best way to get around town; it stops close to most places of interest and doesn't smell like an underground urinal. The metro is complemented by the Cercanías suburban rail system, and an extensive network of local buses.

The main transport system finishes at around 1.30am, which means you'll sometimes need to use taxis to get the most out of Madrid's famed nightlife. And Madrid being Madrid, it can be harder to get a taxi at 4am than 4pm! Maps of Madrid's transport network are available from tourist offices, train and metro stations, and the airport.

Travel Passes

Monthly or season passes (abonos) are only worth buying if you're staying long term and using local transport frequently. You'll also need an ID card (carnet), available from metro stations and tobacconists. Take a passport-sized photo and your passport. A monthly ticket for central Madrid (Zona A) costs €32.30 and is valid for unlimited travel on bus, metro and Cercanías trains.

Metro

Madrid's excellent metro system (see inside front cover; ☎ 902 44 44 03) has 11 colour-coded lines (with extra stops being added all the time!) and runs from about 6am to 1.30am daily. You can buy tickets from staffed kiosks or machines at the stations; a single trip costs 95c and a Metrobús ticket (valid for 10 trips) costs €5. Only some of the newer stations have wheelchair access.

Bus

Buses run by Empresa Municipal de Transportes de Madrid (EMT, ☎ 91 406 88 10) travel regularly along 170 lines, covering most city routes, between 6.30am and 11.30pm daily. A single-trip ticket costs 95c and a Metrobús ticket (valid for 10 trips) costs €5. About half of the buses are *piso bajo* types, meaning they are wheelchair-friendly.

Cercanías

These short-range regional trains are handy for making north–south trips between Chamartín and Atocha stations, and for places like El Escorial and Aranjuez. As this system is operated by Renfe, the national rail network, tickets (single-trip 90c) are not valid on buses or the metro, although most international rail passes are valid.

Taxi

Madrid's taxis (white with a diagonal red stripe) are plentiful and good value compared to other European cities. Make sure the driver turns the meter; flag fall is €1.35 plus 63c per kilometre (81c between 10pm and 6am). On public holidays it's 81c per kilometre (91c between 10pm and 6am).

Supplementary charges include: €4 to/from the airport, €2 from cab ranks at train and bus stations, €2 for travelling to/from Parque Juan Carlos I, and a special charge on Christmas Eve and New Year's Eve.

A green light on the roof, or a sign displayed behind the windscreen with the word '*libre*' means the taxi is available. You can book taxis with:

Radio-Taxi
Independiente   ☎ 91 405 12 13
Radio Teléfono   ☎ 91 547 82 00
Teletaxi   ☎ 91 371 21 31

Car & Motorcycle

Trying to find a park in Madrid will give your thesaurus of swearwords a workout. And driving will be frustrating, not because of the other drivers (although they don't seem to prize road rules much) but for the maze of one-way narrow streets in the older parts of town. The risk of car theft is another deterrent. Motorcycles and scooters are popular modes of transport, but Madrid is not the place to learn how to ride them!

Petrol prices vary, but count on paying about 80c per litre for lead-free (*sin plomo*), 86c for Super 97 (a lead-replacement petrol) or 68c for diesel (*gasóleo*).

Road Rules

Driving takes place on the right-hand side of the road and seatbelts are compulsory, with on-the-spot fines for the unbuckled.

Speed limits are as follows: on *autovías* (motorways) 120km/h; on highways 100km/h; on other roadways 90km/h; on urban streets 50km/h; and in residential areas 20km/h. It's illegal to drive with a blood-alcohol content of 0.05% or higher.

Rental

Car hire is relatively expensive in Madrid and generally ill-advised unless you're planning more than a couple of day trips. All the major car companies have offices in Madrid and at the airport, although smaller firms such as Julià Car (☎ 91 779 18 60) are a bit cheaper. With a firm such as Hertz (3, C6; ☎ 902 40 24 05; Edificio de España, Plaza de España) you're looking at about €136 for their best three-day weekend deal including insurance and 400km per day.

You can rent motorcycles from Moto Alquiler (☎ 91 542 06 57; Calle del Conde Duque 13) costing €360 for a Monday-to-Friday deal, with a €1500 deposit on your credit card.

Driving Licence & Permit

EU member states' pink-and-green driving licences are recognised in Spain. If you hold a licence from another country you are supposed to obtain an International Driving Permit (IDP).

Motoring Organisations

The head office of the Real Automóvil Club de España (RACE; 4, H5; ☎ 902 30 05 05; Calle de Eloy Gonzalo 32) is in Madrid. Its 24hr, countrywide emergency breakdown service is free for RACE members. Your own national motoring organisation may have reciprocal arrangements with RACE. You will generally be provided with a special telephone number to use in an emergency while in Spain.

PRACTICAL INFORMATION

Climate & When to Go

Madrid's continental climate brings scorching hot summers and dry, cold winters. Locals say *'nueve meses de invierno y tres de infierno'* (nine months of winter and three months of hell). This is a slight exaggeration, but the message is clear that at its worst, Madrid can be nastily cold and infernally hot.

July and August are hottest, with temperatures frequently over 30°C and sometimes over 40°C. In winter, temperatures can plummet to freezing at night and might only nudge 10°C during the day. Late April and May are lovely times to visit, as are September and early October (although this month can be rainy). February can be surprisingly nice, with blue skies and sun.

March is often unpredictable, and early April can be wet.

The combination of tourists and business travellers visiting Madrid means that hotels are busy for much of the year. The city is

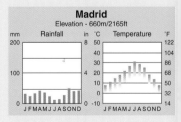

especially crowded during Easter, Christmas holidays and local festivals. Many *madrileños* take holidays in August, which means that the city is noticeably less crowded.

Tourist Information

Tourist Information Abroad
Information on Madrid is available from the following branches of the Oficina Española de Turismo:

Canada
   2 Bloor St W, 34th floor, Toronto M4W 3E2 (☎ 416-961 3131; **e** toronto@tour spain.es)

France
   43 rue Decamps, 75784 Paris Cedex 16 (☎ 01 45 03 82 57; fax 01 45 03 82 51; **e** paris@tourspain.es)

Germany
   Kurfüdamm 63, D-10707, Berlin (☎ 030-882 6543; **e** berlin@tourspain.es)

Portugal
   Avenida Sídonio Pais 28, 1050 Lisbon (☎ 21-354 1992; **e** lisboa@tour spain.es)

UK
   22-3 Manchester Square, London W1U 3PX (☎ 020-7486 8077; **e** londres@tour spain.es)

USA
   666 Fifth Ave, 35th floor, New York, NY 10103 (☎ 212-265 8822; **e** nyork@tour spain.es)

Local Tourist Information
The tourist offices in the city have friendly staff who speak English (among other languages) and can provide maps and information about Madrid and its environs. The email addresses for all the offices (except Plaza Mayor) is **e** turismo@comadrid.es. The Patronato Municipal de Turismo specialises in Madrid-only information. In summer, bright yellow kiosks are established around well-touristed city points, with multilingual staff.

Aeroporto de Barajas
   Ground fl, T1 (1, E4; ☎ 91 305 86 56; 8am-8pm)

Estación de Chamartín
   Estación de Chamartín (2, A7; ☎ 91 315 99 76; Mon-Sat 8am-8pm, Sun & hols 9am-3pm)

Estación Puerta de Atocha
   Estación Puerta de Atocha (2, O6; ☎ 902 100 007; 9am-9pm)

Mercado Puerta de Toledo
   Ronda de Toledo 1, Stand 3134 (2, O3; ☎ 91 364 18 76; Mon-Sat 9am-7pm, Sun & hols 9am-3pm)

Oficina de Turismo Duque de Medinaceli
   Calle del Duque de Medinaceli 2 (3, H13; ☎ 91 429 37 05; Mon-Sat 9am-7pm, Sun & hols 9am-3pm)

Patronato Municipal de Turismo
   Plaza Mayor 3 (3, H8; ☎ 91 588 16 36; **e** inforturismo@munimadrid.es; Mon-Sat 10am-8pm, Sun & hols 10am-3pm)

Embassies

Australia
   Plaza del Descubridor Diego de Ordás 3-2, Edificio Santa Engrácia 120 (4, E5; ☎ 91 441 60 25; **e** www.spain .embassy.gov.au)

Canada
   Calle de Núñez de Balboa 35 (2, L7; ☎ 91 423 3250; **e** www.canadaes.org)

France
   Calle de Salustiano Olózaga 9 (3, E15; ☎ 91 423 89 00; **e** www.amba france-es.org)

Germany
   Calle de Fortuny 8 (4, J8; ☎ 91 557 90 00; **e** www.embajada-alemania.es)

New Zealand
   Plaza de la Lealtad 2 (3, G14; ☎ 91 523 02 26; fax 91 531 09 97)

UK
   Calle de Fernando el Santo 16 (3, A14; ☎ 91 700 82 72)

USA
   Calle de Serrano 75 (4, H9; ☎ 91 587 22 00; fax 91 587 23 83; **e** www .embusa.es)

Money

Currency

The unit of currency is the euro. Notes come in denominations of €500, €200, €100, €50, €20, €10 and €5. Coins come in denominations of €2 and €1, plus 50c, 20c, 10c, 5c, 2c and 1c.

Travellers Cheques

Travellers cheques are useful as they can be replaced if lost or stolen. American Express and Thomas Cook are widely accepted brands. You'll need your passport to cash them; see Changing Money below for more details.

Credit Cards

Credit cards are widely accepted throughout the city. Some places will want to see another form of photo ID, such as a passport or driving licence, but your signature will rarely be checked. For 24hr card cancellations or assistance, call:

American Express	☎ 902 37 35 37
Diners Club	☎ 91 547 74 00
MasterCard/Eurocard	☎ 900 97 12 31
Visa	☎ 900 97 44 45

ATMs

ATMs (*telebancos*) are common throughout Madrid, and as long as you're connected to the Cirrus or Maestro network, you're good to go. It usually works out cheaper than exchanging travellers cheques too, but check first with your bank at home for associated charges.

Changing Money

You can change cash or travellers cheques at most banks (Madrid is swarming with them) and at exchange offices, at bus and train stations and at the airport. Banks tend to offer the best rates, and most have ATMs. Exchange offices (mostly clustered around the Plaza de Puerta del Sol and along Gran Vía), usually indicated by the word *cambio* (exchange), offer longer opening hours and quicker service but have poorer exchange rates. Travellers cheques usually bring a slightly better rate than cash, but always check the commissions.

Bank opening hours are 8.30am-2pm Monday to Friday and 9am-1pm Saturday, although many banks don't bother opening on Saturday during summer.

Tipping

The law stipulates that restaurants include service charges in menu prices, so tipping is very much discretionary. Many people leave small change at bars and cafés (5% is plenty). Hotel porters will be happy with €1 and taxi drivers OK with a round-up.

Discounts

Concessions (up to 50%) are available for youths, students and seniors over 65 years (with identification) at most attractions and on some transport. The most widely recognised student and youth cards are the International Student Identity Card (ISIC) and the Carnet Joven Europeo (Euro <26 card). It's worth carrying photo ID and flashing it wherever possible to see what discounts (which are not always advertised) are available.

Travel Insurance

A policy covering theft, loss, medical expenses and compensation for cancellation or delays in your travel arrangements is highly recommended. If items are lost or stolen, make sure you get a police report straight away – otherwise your insurer might not pay up.

Opening Hours

Office hours are generally Monday to Friday from 9am to 2pm and then 5pm to 8pm. Shops keep similar hours, though they often open at 10am and also on Saturday; some big stores don't close for siesta. Restaurants tend to open from noon or 1pm to 4pm and then 8pm to midnight (after midnight on Friday and Saturday). Many shops close on Sunday, public holidays and for a few weeks in August.

Opening times for tourist sites vary. Museums tend to keep the same hours as shops (often without closing for lunch) but can have a shorter schedule in winter. Virtually all museums close on Monday, and many attractions are open shorter hours (or closed) in August.

Public Holidays

Jan 1	New Year's Day
Jan 6	Epiphany or Three Kings' Day
Mar/Apr	Good Thursday
Mar/Apr	Good Friday
May 1	Labour Day
May 2	El Dos de Mayo
Aug 15	Feast of the Assumption
Oct 12	Spanish National Holiday
Nov 1	All Saints' Day
Dec 8	Feast of the Immaculate Conception
Dec 25	Christmas Day

Time

Madrid is 1hr ahead of GMT/UTC and 2hrs ahead during daylight-savings. Daylight savings is observed for around seven months from the last Sunday in March to the last Sunday in October.

At noon in Madrid it's:

6am in New York
3am in Los Angeles
11am in London
1pm in Johannesburg
11pm in Auckland
9pm in Sydney

Electricity

Spain's electric current is 220V, 50Hz. If your appliances are geared for a different voltage, you'll need a transformer. Plugs are the two round-pin type, so you may also need an adaptor. Adaptors and transformers are best bought in your home country, although they are also stocked in many airport stores.

Weights & Measures

Spain uses the metric system. Decimal points are indicated with commas and thousands with points. See the conversion table (p122) for more details.

Post

Madrid's postal service is reliable and efficient. The main post office is in the Palacio de Comunicaciones (3, E14; Plaza de Cibeles; open Mon-Fri 8.30am-9.30pm & Sat 8.30am-2pm). Stamps are sold at most *estancos* (tobacconists – look for the sign with '*Tobacos*' in yellow letters on a maroon background), as well as post offices *(correos y telégrafos)*.

Postal Rates

A standard postcard or letter weighing up to 20g costs 25c within Spain, 50c within Europe, and 75c to the Americas and Australasia. Aerograms cost 50c to anywhere in the world.

Opening Hours

Most post offices are open Mon-Fri 9am-2pm.

Telephone

The ubiquitous blue payphones are easy to use for both domestic and international calls. They accept coins, phonecards and sometimes credit cards.

Phonecards

Tarjetas telefónicas (phonecards) are sold at post offices, *estancos* (tobacconists) and many news-stands; they come in denominations of €5 and €10. Lonely Planet's ekno Communication Card, which is specifically aimed at travellers, provides competitive international calls (avoid using it for local calls), messaging services and free email. Log on to ⓔ www.ekno.lonelyplanet.com for information on joining and accessing the service.

Mobile Phones

Spain uses the GSM cellular *(movil)* phone system, which works with most phones except those sold in the USA and Japan. To use your phone, you'll need to set up a global roaming service with your service provider before you leave home, or you can buy a Spanish SIM card for around €60.

Country & City Codes

Spain	☎ 34
Madrid	☎ 91

Useful Numbers

Local Directory Inquiries	☎ 1003
International Directory Inquiries	☎ 025
International Operator Europe/North Africa	☎ 1008
International Operator rest of the world	☎ 1005
Reverse-charge (collect)	☎ 900 (+ code of the country you are calling)
Time	☎ 093
Weather	☎ 906 36 53 28

International Direct Dial Codes

Dial ☎ 00 followed by:

Australia	☎ 61
Canada	☎ 15
Japan	☎ 81
New Zealand	☎ 64
South Africa	☎ 27
UK	☎ 44
USA	☎ 1

Digital Resources

Madrid has many Internet cafés, ranging in size from veritable telecommunications palaces with hundreds of terminals to small operations with half-a-dozen terminals. Many of the larger places to stay have facilities for guests for free or for a minimal fee.

Internet Service Providers

Major Internet service providers (ISPs) such as AOL (ⓔ www.aol.com), CompuServe (ⓔ www.compuserve.com) and AT&T Global (ⓔ www.attglobal.net) have dial-in nodes throughout Europe, including Madrid. Download a list of the dial-in numbers before you leave home.

Internet Cafés

If you can't access the Internet from where you're staying, head to a cybercafé:

easyEverything
Calle de Morena 10 (3, F10; ⓔ www.easyeverything.com; open 24hrs; €1 for 30mins-2hrs)

3w.com
Calle de Tetuán 3 (3, F9; Mon-Sat 9-1am, Sun 11-1am; 60c for 30mins)

BBiGG
Calle de Alcalá 21 (3, F11; ⓔ www.bbigg.com; Sun-Thur 9am-midnight, Fri & Sat 9am-2am; €1.20 per 30mins)

Useful Sites

The Lonely Planet website (**e** www.lonelyplanet.com) offers a speedy link to many of Madrid's websites. Others to try include:

Comunidad de Madrid
e www.comadrid.es

Descubre Madrid
e www.descubremadrid.com

Metro de Madrid
e www.metromadrid.es

Renfe
e www.renfe.es

Ayuntamiento de Madrid
e www.munimadrid.es

Doing Business

All the deluxe and top-end hotels have business facilities including conference rooms, secretarial services, fax machines and photocopiers, computers and private office space etc. If they don't provide translation services, they will know someone who does.

Your first port of call (apart from the trade office of your embassy or consulate) should be the Oficina de Congresos de Madrid (Madrid Convention Bureau; 3, H6; ☎ 91 588 29 00; fax 91 588 29 30; Patronato de Turismo office, Calle Mayor 69; open Mon-Fri 8am-3pm & 4-7pm).

Newspapers & Magazines

Madrid's main newspapers are *El País* and *El Mundo*. International newspapers, which include the *International Herald Tribune*, are available at newsstands around central Madrid, especially along Gran Vía and around Puerta del Sol. The *Guia del Ocio* (€1) is a must-read for anyone wanting to sample Madrid's entertainment options, and can be found at any newsstand. *Shangay* is Madrid's free gay paper and is available in many shops and bars, especially around the Chueca neighbourhood. *In Madrid* is a free English-language newspaper with good entertainment listings and classifieds. You can find it in bars and shops around the city.

Radio

BBC World Service broadcasts on a variety of frequencies (6195kHz, 9410kHz and 15,485kHz) depending on the time of day. Likewise, Voice of America can be found on short-wave frequencies at 6040kHz, 9760kHz and 15,205kHz. The Spanish national network, Radio Nacional de España (RNE), operates RNE1 (88.2FM) broadcasting general interest and current affairs. Classical music can be found at Sinfo Radio (104.3FM). For pop and rock, tune in to 40 Principales (93.9FM) or Onda Cero (98FM).

TV

State-run TVE1 and La 2 broadcast a combination of pro-government news, good arts programs and films. Antena 3 and Tele 5 are commercial stations sending out woeful soaps and 'all tits and teeth' variety shows. Canal Plus is a pay channel mostly devoted to film and football. Telemadrid broadcasts some football matches.

Photography & Video

Most brands of film are widely available and processing is efficient and of a decent standard. A roll of film (36 exposures, 100 ISO) costs around €4.50 and can be processed for around €12. For slide (*diapositiva*) film, you're looking at around €5.50 plus €5.20 for processing.

You can find developers all over

the city, including El Corte Inglés (p62) and FNAC (p61). For repairs, Playmon (2, L9; ☎ 91 573 57 25, Calle de Jorge Juan 133) has a good reputation, but your best bet is to look in the telephone directory for a specialist dealing in your make of equipment.

Spain uses the PAL video system, which is not compatible with other standards unless converted.

Health

Immunisations

There are no vaccination require-ments for entry into Spain, although you may need to show proof of vaccination if you're com-ing from an area where yellow fever is endemic (Africa and South America).

Precautions

You should encounter no major health problems in Madrid. The water is potable, and health and hygiene standards are pretty good. The only problems you're likely to encounter are dehydration or sun-burn and/or initial gut problems if you're unused to large quantities of olive oil. Pharmacists are gener-ally quite sympathetic about dis-pensing most medicines without a prescription, although it's best to bring prescriptions for medication you are taking or may need.

Insurance & Medical Treatment

Travel insurance is advisable to cover any medical treatment you may need while in Madrid. Spain has reciprocal health agreements with other EU countries. Citizens of those countries need to get hold of an E111 form from their national health body. If you should require medical help you will need to present this, plus photocopies of

the form and your national health card.

Medical Services

Hospitals or *urgencias* (first-aid stations) with 24hr accident and emergency departments include:

Hospital General Gregorio Marañon
  Calle del Doctor Esquerdo (2, M9; ☎ 91 586 80 00; Ⓜ Sáinz de Baranda)
Centro de Salud
  Calle de la Navas de Tolosa 10 (3, E8; ☎ 91 521 00 25; Ⓜ Santo Domingo)
Hospital Clinico San Carlos
  Plaza del Cristo Rey (2, G2; ☎ 91 330 30 00; Ⓜ Moncloa)

Dental Services

If you chip a tooth or require emer-gency treatment, head to Clinica Dental Cisne (Calle de Magallanes 18; 4, H3; ☎ 91 446 32 21; 24hr emergency service).

Pharmacies

The following pharmacies are open 24hrs:

Farmacia del Globo
  Plaza de Antón Martín 46 (3, J11; ☎ 91 369 20 00)
Real Farmacia de la Reina
  Calle Mayor 59 (3, G7; ☎ 91 548 00 14)
Farmacia Velázquez
  Calle de Velázquez 70 (4, K10; ☎ 91 575 60 28)

Toilets

Public toilets are not common in Madrid. If you get caught short while sightseeing, you can pop into a bar or café, although some places might like you to buy a drink first.

Safety Concerns

Generally speaking, Madrid is very safe, although it's wise to keep a lookout for pickpockets on the metro and at major tourist attrac-tions. Keep only a limited amount of cash on your person, and the bulk of your money in replaceable forms, such as travellers cheques or plastic; use your hotel's safe. Money or valuables that you need to take out with you should be securely concealed in a money belt. If you're carrying a bag, wear it across your body, not hanging from your shoulder.

Never leave anything in your car and don't get a hire car that has marking identifying it as such. Foreign number plates make you even more vulnerable.

Avoid anyone playing the old 'ball under the three cups' game, especially near Real Madrid's Estadio Santiago Bernabéu.

Lost Property

For the main lost property office (*Negociado de Objetos Perdidos*) call ☎ 91 588 43 46; things found on metro trains and in taxis are generally handed in here. For items lost on Renfe trains call ☎ 91 902 24 02 02. For the EMT bus network call ☎ 91 406 88 43. If you've lost something at the airport call ☎ 91 393 60 00.

Keeping Copies

Make photocopies of important documents, keep some with you – separate from the originals – and leave a copy at home. You can also store details of documents in Lonely Planet's free online Travel Vault; it's password-protected and it's accessible worldwide. See [e] www.ekno.lonelyplanet.com.

Emergency Numbers

Ambulance	☎ 061
Fire	☎ 080
Municipal Police	☎ 092
National Police	☎ 091
Rape Crisis	☎ 91 574 01 10
(open Mon-Fri 10am-2pm & 4-7pm)	

Women Travellers

Despite Spain's chronic problem with domestic violence towards women, female visitors to Madrid will get the feeling that women's rights are respected. Lone women walking around late at night should encounter little troublesome attention, although the Lavapiés neighbourhood is best avoided in these circumstances.

Tampons and the contraceptive pill are widely available in Madrid at pharmacies – the RU-486 pill is another matter.

Gay & Lesbian Travellers

Madrid is very much a 'live and let live' city, and the gay and lesbian scene is out, loud and proud. Centred in the Chueca neighbourhood, but certainly not ghetto-ised, gay life here does not warrant furtive secrecy or segregation. In fact, it's fairly standard to see straight people in gay bars and clubs and gay people anywhere and everywhere. In Chueca though, you'll find bars, clubs, restaurants, shops and hotels that specifically cater to gay and lesbian customers.

Information & Organisations

The Colectivo de Gais y Lesbianas de Madrid (Cogam; 3, D10; ☎ 91 522 45 17; Calle de Fuencarral 37) has an information office and social centre and an information line (☎ 91 523 00 70). Fundación Triángulo (4, G5; ☎ 91 593 05 40; [e] www.fundaciontriangulo.es; Calle de Eloy Gonzalo 25) is another source of information on gay issues. Free publications worth picking up from the Chueca area include *Shangay*, *Shangay Express*, and *Mapa Gaya de Madrid*, which you can find at the Berkana bookshop (p61).

Senior Travellers

Madrid should present no major problems for senior travellers, although infernal summer heat may take its toll when combined with strenuous sightseeing timetables. See also Discounts (p115).

Disabled Travellers

There are wheelchair-adapted taxis, buses and metro stations. The streets however, have not been designed with impaired mobility in mind. Many older museums don't have wheelchair access, although the 'big three' museums have been kitted out. Look for the ♿ listed with individual reviews.

For deaf travellers, there are few concessions made in public infrastructure. There are some specially textured pavements at intersections for blind travellers, and some pedestrian crossing lights with sounded alternatives to the flashing green and red.

Information & Organisations

The Ayuntamiento de Madrid (see Useful Sites, p118) publishes a *Guia de Accesibilidad* that contains information on disabled access to everything from the city's cinemas to its public service buildings. It's designed more for disabled residents than visitors though. The Organización Nacional de Ciegos Españoles (ONCE; 4, J10; ☎ 91 577 37 56; Calle de José Ortega y Gasset 18) is the Spanish association for the blind.

Language

It's well worth the effort to try a few phrases in Spanish during your stay in Madrid, as English is not as widely spoken as many travellers may think. For an in-depth guide to the language, get a copy of Lonely Planet's *Spanish phrasebook*.

Basics

Hello	¡Hola!
Goodbye	¡Adiós!
Yes	Sí
No	No
Please	Por favor
Thank you	Gracias
You're welcome	De nada
OK/fine	Vale
Excuse me	Perdón/ Perdone
Sorry/Excuse me	Losiento/ Discúlpeme
Do you speak English?	¿Habla inglés?
I don't understand	No Entiendo
How much is it?	¿Cuánto cuesta/vale?
Where are the toilets?	¿Dónde están los servicios?
I'm a vegetarian	Soy vegetariano/a
Help!	¡Socorro!/ ¡Auxilio!

Days & Numbers

Monday	lunes
Tuesday	martes
Wednesday	miércoles
Thursday	jueves
Friday	viernes
Saturday	sábado
Sunday	domingo
0	cero
1	uno, una
2	dos
3	tres
4	cuatro
5	cinco
6	seis
7	siete
8	ocho
9	nueve
10	diez
100	cien/ciento
1000	mil

Conversion Table

Clothing Sizes
Measurements are approximate only; try before you buy.

Women's Clothing

Aust/NZ	8	10	12	14	16	18
Europe	36	38	40	42	44	46
Japan	5	7	9	11	13	15
UK	8	10	12	14	16	18
USA	6	8	10	12	14	16

Women's Shoes

Aust/NZ	5	6	7	8	9	10
Europe	35	36	37	38	39	40
France only	35	36	38	39	40	42
Japan	22	23	24	25	26	27
UK	3½	4½	5½	6½	7½	8½
USA	5	6	7	8	9	10

Men's Clothing

Aust/NZ	92	96	100	104	108	112
Europe	46	48	50	52	54	56
Japan	S		M	M		L
UK	35	36	37	38	39	40
USA	35	36	37	38	39	40

Men's Shirts (Collar Sizes)

Aust/NZ	38	39	40	41	42	43
Europe	38	39	40	41	42	43
Japan	38	39	40	41	42	43
UK	15	15½	16	16½	17	17½
USA	15	15½	16	16½	17	17½

Men's Shoes

Aust/NZ	7	8	9	10	11	12
Europe	41	42	43	44½	46	47
Japan	26	27	27.5	28	29	30
UK	7	8	9	10	11	12
USA	7½	8½	9½	10½	11½	12½

Weights & Measures

Weight
1kg = 2.2lb
1lb = 0.45kg
1g = 0.04oz
1oz = 28g

Volume
1 litre = 0.26 US gallons
1 US gallon = 3.8 litres
1 litre = 0.22 imperial gallons
1 imperial gallon = 4.55 litres

Length & Distance
1 inch = 2.54cm
1cm = 0.39 inches
1m = 3.3ft = 1.1yds
1ft = 0.3m
1km = 0.62 miles
1 mile = 1.6km

lonely planet

Lonely Planet is the world's most successful independent travel information company with offices in Australia, the USA, UK and France. With a reputation for comprehensive, reliable travel information, Lonely Planet is a print and electronic publishing leader, with over 650 titles and 22 series catering for travellers' individual needs.

At Lonely Planet we believe that travellers can make a positive contribution to the countries they visit – if they respect their host communities and spend their money wisely. Since 1986 a percentage of the income from books has been donated to aid and human rights projects.

www.lonelyplanet.com

For news, views and free subscriptions to print and email newsletters, and a full list of LP titles, click on Lonely Planet's award-winning website.

On the Town

A romantic escape to Paris or a mad shopping dash through New York City, the locals' secret bars or a city's top attractions – whether you have 24hrs to kill or months to explore, Lonely Planet's On the Town products will give you the low-down.

Condensed guides are ideal pocket guides for when time is tight. Their quick-view maps, full-colour layout and opinionated reviews help short-term visitors target the top sights and discover the very best eating, shopping and entertainment options a city has to offer.

For more indepth coverage, **City guides** offer insights into a city's character and cultural background as well as providing extensive coverage of where to eat, stay and play. **CitySync**, a digital guide for your handheld unit, allows you to reference stacks of opinionated, well-researched travel information. Portable and durable **City Maps** are perfect for locating those back-street bars or hard-to-find local haunts.

'Ideal for a generation of fast movers.'

– Gourmet Traveller on Condensed guides

Condensed Guides

- Amsterdam
- Athens
- Bangkok
- Barcelona
- Beijing (Sept 2003)
- Boston
- Brussels (March 2004)
- Chicago
- Dublin
- Florence (May 2003)
- Frankfurt
- Hong Kong
- Las Vegas (May 2003)
- London
- Los Angeles
- New Orleans
- New York City
- Paris
- Prague
- Rome
- San Francisco
- Singapore
- Sydney
- Tokyo
- Venice
- Washington, DC

index

See also separate indexes for Places to Eat (p. 126), Places to Stay (p. 127), Shops (p. 127) and Sights with map references (p. 128).

PLACES TO EAT

PLACES TO STAY

SHOPS

sights – quick index